SCINAN LEGACY

C. 1 - 9

By

KATHY BLACKLEDGE PICKEL

Oblique Creative, LLC

WELCOME

TO

A special gift awaits you!

Please go to **scinanlegacy.com/free-prequel**
for your *free download* of
SCINAN LEGACY – THE OPENING
An exclusive prequel story to *C. 1 - 9*

This story is presented
with respect and *kynd* intentions
for highly sensitive individuals
who would find comfort in
reading a story that maintains
the consecutive order
of its chapters and page numbers
throughout its book series.

It is also mindfully written
for anyone who may benefit from content
that has expanded descriptions
of characters' emotions
and motivations for their actions,
as well as those
who experience languages
as melodies.

You are not alone.

For Damon,
Yellow.

Kathy Blackledge Pickel
Oblique Creative, LLC
P.O. Box 10475, Knoxville, TN 37939
www.obliquecreative.com

For more information about this story, as well as
upcoming events and other works, please visit:
www.scinanlegacy.com

First hardcover edition: November 2,2021
First ebook edition: November 2, 2021

This is a work of fiction.
Some characters, places, and events are drawn from various mythologies
and cultures. Other characters, incidents, events, and dialogues were
formed within the author's imagination or are depicted from the author's
life in a fictitious manner. Any similarities to real people, living or dead,
are inspired by the author's close family and friends and are intended
with love and sincere admiration.

Hardcover edition: ISBN 978-1-7368600-0-7
Ebook edition: ISBN 978-1-7368600-1-4

Published in the United States of America

Contents

In a time of legend and magic, in a realm beyond
our true knowing, our story begins...

CHAPTER I

THE PRIZE IS LOST

There were flashes of light and a high shrieking roar as the wind tore particle from being. The walls, ground, and sky were trembling with the undeniable ending force of something that should never have been unleashed. Stone buckled unnaturally and was tossed about like crumpled paper, weightless. All matter was bending as the tempest formed in the open-air forum of The Great Hall.

The arrival of the horrific shrill piercing the air was the first call to attention, compelling onlookers to run to the balconies of their private quarters. The majestic view of the sprawling courtyard was interrupted by a horizon of devastation. All were in shock and confused by the spectacle they were witnessing... All but two.

Frija and Amicus looked to one another and knew the moment had come. Wodan's obsession had overtaken him. Frija, Queen of Aesingard, loved her husband Wodan dearly, but his quest for possessing all knowledge had taken him on a dangerous path by which she could not abide. Wodan had declared, as Ruler of the Nine Worlds, that by knowing all he could end the war that divided his realm. He spoke not of the motives that haunted him. Frija knew the consequences would be too much for anyone, even the mighty King of Aesingard. Wodan had already given one eye to his quest in exchange for vast knowledge at the Well of Wisdom, but it wasn't enough, not for his need. Frija had seen the acquired power only warp him inside with a craving he could not fulfill.

Frija and Amicus knew that Wodan, along with his brothers, Wiljo and Wæ, had formed a triad and were summoning that-which-should-not-be-woken from the outer realm's depths of death's dark knowing, Oblivion. The unspoken laws were being broken and all nature was retaliating. This conjuring would reveal the spirit of the dead, The Essence of Oblivion. She was the guardian of knowledge, from the past to the future and preserved its force inside her. Wodan would command her to give knowledge to him, and Frija feared he would soon have his prize— but at what cost this time?

She had to stop him, to save him as well as the worlds they protected. Amicus, her trusted companion, a Soul, bound to her in this realm as her guardian, confidant, and advisor for a time stretching over the Aesirs' eons, was by her side as they hurried to the forum.

The Great Hall was full of catastrophic motion, as its contents were lifted and smashed by the swirling mania. Wodan and his accomplices stood unharmed and steadfast at its epicenter. All three were dark and baleful figures. Wiljo and Wæ were seamless images of darkness, clad in black armament, with ebon beards and hair, casting the illusion of being fully cloaked. Only their dark eyes gave any hint of expression. Wodan was rooted to a fixed point, adorned in his heavy battle armor and crowning helmet. The intertwining symbols of the Nine Worlds, emblazoned across his armor, were animated by reflections of lightning that danced across them. In that moment, Wodan appeared all powerful, lethal and ready to strike. His brothers stood apart from him. Each was flanked by tall jagged dark stone pillars, all to make a Binding Circle. Frija could not hear their chants over the wind but could see the twisted tangles of angry red webbing, conjured by Wodan and his brothers, climbing higher and higher into the darkening sky and knew they were creating an unnatural breach between realms. Wodan had a wild look about him; his distorted expression was unknown to her. Her heart panicked and sank at the same time.

She wondered if she was too late. Had she lost the one she knew and loved to his growing addiction? Was *her* Wodan already gone forever?

Wind surged around the triad with such speed Frija could not pass through to reach Wodan without being swept up and crushed by its force and the shredded debris it suspended. Undaunted, Frija stood close and braved the winds as she held tight to a toppled column beside her. Her hair whipped around her in a frenzy of dark flames, stinging her face. Her cloak pulled against her, like wings in frantic flight wanting to escape certain harm. Amicus hovered over Frija in an attempt to protect her, but to no avail. The winds coursed directly through him. Amicus was barely touched by their force.

Directly above, in the center of the whirlwind, an opening was forming. The blood-red webbing had flawed the sky. The fabric of space was punctured, clawing at itself, screaming as it was ripped apart. The webbed binding retracted as the crude opening began to change. The tear turned itself inside out, creating a funnel that slowly descended into Wodan's circle and was anchored within its boundaries by their binding web. The funnel was made from a substance unrecognizable to Frija. Dark and murky, its consistency was fluid-like and thick, churning slowly. The movement within this vortex was labored and dull in contrast to the raging fury that divided Frija from Wodan.

An echo of light began to show through the funnel in all directions. It was The Essence emerging from her darkness. She radiated a blue light that was dimmed by the substance that contained her. Her body was not defined by mere arms and legs. She appeared as an undulating form stretching out in every direction, ever changing shape, draped in her own light, moving in tandem with the current of the vortex.

As she became fully present, her voice projected with a shattering force and asked, "WHY HAVE YOU TORN ME FROM MY ETERNAL SLEEP? WHAT DO YOU WANT OF ME?"

Wodan stood his ground with a stance worthy of all his might and replied, "I ask you to bestow me with ALL knowledge— What Has Been, What Is, and What Will Be!"

"And why should I give you that which you wish to possess?" The Essence retorted.

"As Ruler of the Nine Worlds, the knowing of all things would give me ultimate wisdom to rule justly and find an end to the war within my realm," said Wodan.

The spirit took little time to give her answer. "This would upset the balance within the universe! You have enough power and wisdom to rule with fairness. This would corrupt not only you but the order of life itself. I refuse."

"I asked only as a courtesy. I will not allow you to return to Oblivion until you comply," Wodan stated, ready for her refusal.

The Essence was aghast. She could see his true intentions now. They were not driven by honor or peace but had turned into a toxic and tormented craze. Her knowledge of Wodan was not of this. This was new.

She tested the boundary of her enclosure by trying to extend her reach beyond the binding, only to meet restraint. She tried to move back into the darkness she had emerged from, but it was sealed from her. She tried in every direction to find some leverage to move but could not. Her rage overtook her. She blindly thrashed and spouted curses, all to no useful end, until she tired. She could find no way out, no way to change her circumstances. Pain was visibly overtaking her. The binding's hold was causing the vortex to change and harden around her. Soon she would be trapped in crushing agony, to exist in that state for as long as Wodan pleased. She would be turned into a novelty standing in the middle of The Great Hall to be leered at by passersby, frozen in excruciating paralysis. There was only one way out, she thought, to give Wodan what he wanted.

The Essence conceded. A low hum began to grow louder and could be heard amongst the torrential winds still swirling around the circle. It was the sound not unlike creation's beginning. The ground and sky shook more violently. She began to glow brighter, and Wodan prepared himself to receive the prize he wanted most. With a nod to his brothers, the intensity of the binding's hold was decreased and the vortex began to soften. Instantly, the pain she was experiencing reduced, and she could move more freely.

She began turning in on herself like petals of a flower folding closed at night's fall, and the slow movement of the vortex was suspended momentarily. Soon she began to unfold and was bringing forward an orb, clear, bright, and radiant. Its purpose was to emanate the steady flow of knowledge that reaches throughout the universe, unseen, creating present thoughts and circumstance, and providing all that was needed for future's potential. The past was drawn back into it to be stored so as not to be lost, but to live on as memory. The orb created the perfect balance of flow and containment for all that existed: history, the now, and weaving of the future, all working in synchronization with life. Legend held that when all was finally known throughout the universe, existence would end, and by its nature, it should. That is why the orb was tucked safely away unseen and unaffected, protected in The Essence's cradle of Oblivion.

Overlooking the scene, there was no way Frija could reach Wodan to stop this transfer; but Amicus, being a Soul, had no solid form and could pass through the tornadic winds. He stood by Frija, watching as her face took on the characteristics of the devastation around her. His duty and love for her demanded he do something to help, but he was unsure how to stop it. He watched, hoping an opportunity would present itself. Then Amicus saw The Essence relinquishing the orb. If he was going to act, he had to do it now! He came up with only one possible solution, and with that thought, he turned to Frija. His thoughts and feelings connected with hers, as they had since she was a child. In that moment, she knew. One last simple knowing was shared, conveying all they had meant to each other, what he had to do now, and a single word, without saying it— *Goodbye.*

Amicus' intention was to intercept the orb and return it to The Essence before it was in Wodan's hands, and to disrupt the triad's will. This, in turn, would have relinquished their hold on the vortex, released The Essence to return to Oblivion, and reset the natural order. Amicus knew Wodan would see his actions as betrayal, and he would be banished from his beloved Frija when all had settled; or so he thought. No one could have foreseen what actually took place. The orb was never meant to exist outside The Essence. Its home was protective and in perfect balance. Outside of her, the atmosphere of Aesingard was too heavy, and the orb began to crack. The Essence screamed at the unthinkable horror. With striking speed, Amicus was through the whirling barrier and appeared between Wodan and The Essence. But instead of intercepting the orb, he took on its direct blast as the portion outside The Essence collapsed. Knowledge in its raw form penetrated Amicus! He was in line to absorb it all. He began to glow as The Essence did. Wodan stumbled back in shock. Wiljo and Wæ tried and failed to reach for Amicus, their grasps singeing as they went straight through him. The force growing inside Amicus caused a reactionary burst of energy that sent Wodan and his brothers flying backwards. The burst passed through the swirling winds, lessening the intensity but still knocking Frija to the ground as well. Only Amicus stood in front of The Essence now, locked to her. Her constant scream had almost drowned out every other noise. She was visibly beginning to weaken as Amicus shone more brightly, too brightly, beyond glowing to burning as if he himself had become a Sun. He had no control over what was happening inside him. Reaction after reaction was building internally. There was no way he could contain this power. His only thought was for the safety of Frija. His smallest movement was all the unstable forces inside him needed. Another pulse of pure energy radiated from him, more forceful than before, shattering the crystal columns, breaking the binding circle, and freeing The Essence to vanish into the vortex's dark depths. With its crushing blow, it dissolved the whirling barrier between Wodan and Frija. The vortex recoiled as Oblivion was once again sealed and restored. In that instance, Amicus was flying upward, using the explosive momentum to take him high above Aesingard, removing the potential harm. He continued to ascend. What was inside him was more than he could contain, not just in a physical sense, but in his thoughts and feelings. To know and feel everything at once by any being was never meant to be. Therefore, it could not continue to be.

From the ground, Frija, along with other stunned witnesses, looked to the sky at the rocketing glow, getting smaller and smaller but burning brightly. Suddenly the light flared again and became two. One part went spiraling off in one direction while the other changed its trajectory and was repelled in another. Both lights faded in the distance as they moved ever upward into silence. This night would later be known throughout the Nine Worlds as *The Night of the Twin Stars*.

THE NINE WORLDS
OF
WODAN'S REALM

FYRFOLDE
The Fyrs

AESINGARD
The Aesir

VANGARD
The Vane

LÉOHETWIN
The Léohets

SWEDUETWIN
The Swedus

MIDANGARD
The Midangardians

HEÍTANGRUND
The Heítaned

GICELFOLDE
The Gicels

THE ENDE
The Ende Dwellers

*Renderings of the world symbols are taken directly from the "Scinan Tablet" engravings.
Date of origin predates Earth's 8000 BCE.*

*°° All artifact images shown are representations from a private collection,
and were released with consent under terms that maintain the owner's anonymity. °°*

かん

CHAPTER 2
SEARCHING THROUGH THE AFTERMATH

L ife on the Nine Worlds continued as usual, at least in appearance. The same could be said universally. Though the natural flow of knowledge had been disrupted, nothing changed— and that was exactly the problem. In relative terms, little time had passed, and the effects were virtually undetectable. All that existed continued to exist. All that was in motion, continued in motion. Current daily life went about as it had up to *The Night of the Twin Stars*. The Nine Worlds' War had played itself out to its welcomed demise, with nothing gained and Wodan's rule still intact. History survived in those who had lived it and were taught it. Plants continued to grow, and seasons continued to cycle. Years went by, and room was made for new life to be born, just as it had always been. The only change was there were no changes, no new thoughts, nor new approaches. All advancement had halted.

As time moved forward, bright minds began to notice the absence of ideas and could find no cause or point of reference for knowledge's loss. They were the few who feared for the future and dared not speak of it publicly. Only those who took part in that fateful night on Aesingard witnessed the origin of this perpetual lack of creativity and invention. The wounded Essence's loss left its scar across the universe and her pain was felt throughout the outer realm on her return to Oblivion. The Essence's allies of the Nine Worlds' Ende rallied their support in the wake of her echo from the King's breach of trust. Queen Frija stood in opposition to Wodan with her conviction that knowledge must be restored, while Wodan continued to be driven to possess it. Amidst their different motives, The Essence, Frija and Wodan shared a single thought; the hope that the knowledge of the universe had not been lost, rather it had been removed and altered. As to how and where it existed, or how to restore it if it was ever found, no one knew for certain.

Frija and Wodan, damaged and isolated by their personal anguish, carried forward in separate recovery efforts. Frija moved through her days of searching shrouded in ever deepening grief. Her losses compounded to a staggering weight. Before the war, she and Wodan had lost their son, Baldar, to an unnatural death; she was next to suffer the loss of her husband to fixation, and then to lose her dearest friend who had sacrificed himself to save them all. Facing the repercussions of Amicus' tragedy, Frija's grief extended to encompass the futures of every worlds' existence stuck in never-ending sameness. Unlike his wife's compassion, Wodan could not see past his own losses to consider the future's fate. His mind was tainted by obsession, and it had turned him bitter and reclusive. The circumstances of Baldar's death had long before unhinged him, leaving him incapable of any sympathy or understanding of his wife's most recent mourning. Wodan was consumed by his anger and his perception had contorted into his own simple truth; Amicus had robbed him of what he desired and he blamed Frija for it all.

With the thought of carrying on without those she loved, and the looming circumstances of a dead future, Frija feared emptiness might overtake her. Amicus had always been there for her. During her greatest need, he had been her constant support; helping her move forward when she didn't think she could continue living without Baldar and the unresolved whereabouts of her child's soul. The unknown cause and bizarre nature of his death haunted her by day and in her dreams. Amicus had worked tirelessly with her to uncover the truth, but their efforts were to no end. She drove herself forward, compelled to find answers. Though the Queen had retained the allegiance of many throughout the Nine Worlds to aid her in her search, she never felt more alone.

Frija's memories of happier times were her only comfort. Baldar had been her shining light, golden and beaming. His bright happy face and sweet nature had brought her to revisit all the wonders of life through his innocent eyes. She could only recall the smallest moments of her memories of him, for the joy she found in them was still too easily eclipsed by the pain of his loss. Since Baldar's demise, Frija had carried with her one of his favorite toys. It was a small carved figure of a fleógan that fit in the palm of her hand. The toy's initial scaly surface had been rubbed smooth from years of her fingers tracing the undulating curves of its dragon-like shape. Though the carving stayed with her constantly, she rarely looked at it.

At her worst moments, she would make herself recall when she felt the safest— when she was with Amicus during her childhood. Frija remembered how she had decided to refer to him as a "he." Souls that have always existed without a living shell have no means to take on specific traits. They are neither male nor female, Aesir or otherwise. Only when they have been within a living form can they identify themselves as such a person, animal, etc. As a little girl, Frija could not grasp this fact of Amicus' existence, so she decided for him. He would delight her as a child by changing shape to meet her whims. He spent most of their early years together as various types of animals. With whatever shape she requested, she always saw him as a "him," and Amicus didn't mind. As she grew older, she preferred he be seen as a person, or as best he could, a shimmering mist in the form of a person, cloaked, with features not clearly defined.

Left without his guidance, she tried to imagine what Amicus would have her do, where she might begin to try to restore knowledge's balance and amend what she could for both Baldar and him. The Queen could only speculate. What had happened to knowledge; where had Amicus and Baldar gone; what had become of their souls; were these occurrences somehow linked? She felt sure not all was lost. It couldn't be. The fact that everything else still existed was proof. She clung to the hope that if it was within her power, she could restore what was taken.

Frija spent her days pouring over ancient prophecies, seeking the advice of her realm's counselors, intuitives, and The Wise. She was looking for any sign, any glimmer of possibility, or any probable answer to rectify these catastrophes. But for all of the seers within her counsel, the effect on their intuition was the same. Certain gifts of sight concerning the comings and goings of daily life remained with them, but when questioned about advancements, future changes or how to restore ingenuity; it was obscured by what they all would describe as a void. Anxiety was building amongst the elder seers, for they could only speculate at the ramifications of this enduring sameness and what would happen when it was generally known. Their advice to the Queen was unanimous; keep the worlds' populations unaware to avoid panic, and they assured her they would continue to search for a solution. But her faith in them wavered because she soon discovered they too were unknowingly altered. When asked as to when or why this void in their sight had occurred, their responses were identical. Their minds would not allow it. The question would be diverted involuntarily. All could remember *The Night of the Twin Stars* and could speculate as to its reason and meaning, but none were able to equate it to this blind spot in their abilities, recognize it as the cause for this lack of knowledge, or even realize that it was the last new spectacle they had seen. This frightened Frija and made her realize how alone in her quest she truly was. She knew she must protect the true cause of *The Night of the Twin Stars* if she were to have any hope of stopping Wodan. She was running out of time. The loss of advancement was not a secret that could be kept. People would eventually become aware. To speed her ongoing search, she commissioned more seekers to explore the Nine Worlds, listen for news of Amicus, and chronicle any sign of the smallest change within the order to which they had all become accustomed. No news had surfaced, not yet, but she could not deny the gut feeling she carried with her daily that something was about to change.

Wodan's own investigation was much along the lines of Frija's, with the exception that he enlisted spies to relay any findings brought to her. His favorites for this pursuit were his two pet ravens, Hyge and Myne. They were well named, considering the task at hand. Hyge meaning "thought" and Myne for "memory." Wodan's ravens served as his private window into the Nine Worlds. Hyge and Myne were linked to Wodan through his excised eye that rested at the bottom of the Well of Wisdom. His ravens could provide him with a captured view, from where they looked on from unassuming perches at Wodan's oblivious targets of interest.

The King had two other willing spies in his brothers, Wiljo and Wæ. They were more than eager and had enlisted themselves to try to discover Frija's secrets, but Wodan found their efforts less than discrete. Wiljo and Wæ were no match to the advantages he had in using Hyge and Myne.

Neither Frija nor Wodan had any intention of sharing their findings concerning the recovery of knowledge with one another. The divide between them had widened greatly since that ill-fated night. Frija no longer tried to restore her Wodan. Though she quietly continued to hope someday he would return to her as she had known him and that he would realize what he had done, she no longer had the strength to try to save him from himself. Instead, all her thoughts and energy were focused on finding answers. It was all she could do, it was all that was left of her.

As Frija and Wodan's seekers looked throughout the worlds, small events were aligning that could change every future. But before these would happen, the players had to be set into motion, and so they were, on the central world of Midangard.

CHAPTER 3

TAKING FLIGHT

S
ummer was at its end in the northern regions of Midangard. The surrounding territories of the city of Lerakrey readied themselves for winter's fall. Trading for necessary supplies had concluded with the festivities surrounding the Harvest's End, and most preparations for the long winter ahead were now in place. Anticipation was building amongst the people, far and near, as they awaited Winter's Nátt and the Wild Hunt that followed.

Winter's Nátt was a time for the worlds of the realm to come together in celebration of their unity through their connection to the living entity that allowed their passage between worlds, the Eormensyl. As the Sun dawned into winter, it was tradition to give thanks as the Eormensyl began its transition into a winter's slumber; with its promise of renewing the strength of its portal branches and continuing to unite the Nine Worlds. The heart of the Eormensyl resided in its ports at Lerakrey and was the reason the city hosted the Winter's Nátt festival each year. The themes of renewal and unity resonated through the four day celebration, and were why the Order of the Tjetajat chose Winter's Nátt as the time for the induction of its new members.

It had been over fifty Midangardian years since all the worlds of the realm were welcome at Winter's Nátt. At the start of the Nine Worlds' War, the realm was divided. Only the worlds that had stayed under King Wodan's rule or declared their neutrality continued to attend. This festival marked just over twenty years, by Midangard's time, since the war had ended. It had taken those twenty years to restore alliances within the realm's worlds and reunite all nine for the festival. Vendors and attendees from each world journeyed to Lerakrey in hopes of reestablishing lost connections and building trade. It was also, for most, the last opportunity to travel to the city before the oppression of a Midangardian winter. Preparations for the celebration were in full force, but for those whose winter toils were complete, the ending season offered a rare moment of rest and freedom.

Dagen Ságaher lay in the tall yellow grass of his grandparents' farmland. The last of summer was warm, yet a chilling hint of what was to come clung to the breeze. He had finished all his duties for his last season on this land his family called home. Soon he would be starting a new life in a new place, but he didn't want to think about that now. He didn't want to think at all. He was avoiding thoughts of the inevitable for as long as possible.

Exhausted and hungry, Dagen searched through his side satchel and pulled out a small round loaf of bread that was from the Harvest's End feast of the week prior. As he took a bite, the initial outer crunch of its golden crust and soft salty center reminded him of so many previous summers' endings. The loaf was still fresh, and he savored each bite. Dagen ate around the edges, carefully leaving the bread's embossed pattern of a sunstar intact. It was customary to do so, as one ate it, and to reflect on the importance of the Sun to the year's harvest. As he lay there, he held the small disc of bread at arm's length to cover the Sun shining in the sky. He closed one eye and then the other, to see how the disc changed position with his sight. He remembered doing this as a child. Memories of growing up on this land drifted in and out of his thoughts. He noticed how dark his arm was from its summer exposure, as it stretched out before him, holding the small sunstar.

"Another last. I'll be lucky to see the Sun where I'll be going." Dagen said to himself.

He finished the bread and felt the weight of him relax into the ground. There, he let himself be still. Dagen lazily looked up at the sky and watched clouds change their shapes and disappear. With heavy lids, he closed his eyes, not sleepy, but completely aware of everything around him. A bright yellow-orange illuminated his closed eyes. As he let this color draw him in, he began to breathe deeply. The color began to change. As his heartbeat slowed to half his normal pulse, his breath slowed as well. Everything around him slowed to half its time.

The bright hot yellow-orange changed to a soft yellow. As his vision came into focus, he could see it was no longer a color, but the yellow grass surrounding him. Dagen saw himself lying in the grass, so still below. Details became razor-sharp. Every blade was defined. Every fold in his clothes looked crisp as if starched and new, though they were well-worn to the point of threadbare in places. He even noticed the tiny beads of sweat, left by his labors, that appeared as prismed droplets, refracting the Sun's rays, outlining his narrow, impish nose and shining through the damp ringlets of dark hair plastered to his forehead. The sound of his heartbeat and breath faded as he floated above his body. He felt perfectly normal and calm as he looked down at himself. He had experienced similar sensations in the past, but never to this extent. This time he was unbound and aware this was his chance to fly. His sight drew away from his form as he soared upward. A short distance away, he could see the thatched roof of his grandparents' barn, and a little farther, the roofs of his parents' and relatives' houses.

This is home— for now, thought Dagen. *But not for much longer.*

He flew without a care, without a worry or thought that this was strange, leaving his body behind. He went over treetops of the Asbjorn Forest, over lakes and the Zoël River, nearing Lerakrey. The multi-colors of the terrain engulfed him, as they melded and flared with vibrance throughout the changing landscapes. He watched as the Sun shifted in the sky, making forms below cast elongated shadows. Dagen was in awe but completely at ease; he felt a part of everything around him.

He saw a hawk flying nearby and went closer to investigate. His first moment of surprise was when the hawk seemed to notice him as well. He accepted this encounter. There was no alarm, no question of how this was happening, just complete serenity. The hawk glided back and forth from him, and he followed in turn. Dagen felt an unexplainable kinship to this majestic bird of prey. They soared together, letting the wind carry them along. He felt he could have stayed like this forever but knew too well it was time to return. An instinctual pull was drawing him back. The hawk responded to this change within Dagen and gave him a knowing look as he withdrew.

He flew back over the river, over the forest's edge, back to his family's land, and once again, to see himself lying in the field of grass. A look of complete contentment was on his face. The yellow grass once again blurred into yellow light, and slowly, he found himself blinking at the late day Sun. He tried to move but his body felt weighted. Eventually, he sat up, gaining his composure, fully aware of what had just taken place— he had left his body for awhile.

Only now was Dagen's mind flooded with questions. How had he been able to accomplish this feat; how had he recognized all the landmarks from so far above? He had never viewed the countryside from a point of reference so high and especially never from directly overhead. How had the hawk seen him and why did he feel so connected to it; what had he just done? Whatever it was, Dagen knew better than to mention it. The consequences at their worst could be detrimental and at their least would be dismissed as the fancies of a daydreamer. His experience was too personal, too intimate to share. He felt perfectly right in his heart and mind about what he had experienced. But he knew if he spoke of it with conviction, he would have been told either something was wrong with him, or that he was wrong for it. His flight was best to be kept as his secret adventure, and he wondered how soon he would get a chance to try it again.

Dagen heard a familiar voice, calling his name from a distance, which snapped him back into his present circumstances. Thoughts of dread, riding in on cold winds, returned to him. This winter would bring many changes. He was never fond of change, and he hated to think of what was coming. He tried to focus on the more pleasant thoughts of the near future. Tomorrow he would travel with Brieg and Rûni, his friends since childhood, from their village of Carcadoc to the city of Lerakrey for the Winter's Nátt celebration. They had made this trip together three times before. Though they knew they had days of debauchery and antics ahead of them, the weight of this journey was heavy in the hearts of all three. These memories made would be added to the treasure-trove of their friendship's history, saved for their recollection after they settled into the responsibilities of their new lives. Soon, circumstance would take them in very different directions. This Winter's Nátt would be their last time together.

Dagen thought of his friends as he walked back home. The Sun was sinking on the horizon, and he stopped for a moment to admire the array of brilliant colors casting over the sky when he noticed a hawk drifting into view. It flew in his direction, circled above him for a moment, but was chased away by two black birds and disappeared into the approaching night.

By the time he reached home, darkness was settling and Dagen had to set aside his curiosity. The day's last faint light offset the telling signs of a common occurrence at the Ságaher home— tonight's meal would have several relatives in attendance. Dagen walked into the large main room of his parents' home and found that his grandparents, his aunts, uncles, cousins, and sister were all present. The voices and commotion created a familiar symphony of sounds and clatter. Talks of final preparations for the season's end and local news crisscrossed the massive wooden table. His family had started their evening meal without him, as usual. As they continued, everyone found Dagen to be unusually quiet. He had always been full of excitement and nervous energy before his trips, but instead of chattering about Lerakrey, he was silent. His sister, Llylit, sat across from him with a questioning look on her face, waiting for Dagen's facial expression to tell her what she wanted to know. This was how Dagen and Llylit conversed during most large family gatherings. Not only did they not have to compete with the noise, it served to keep them from breaking into an inevitable argument. More times than not, when they spoke to each other, they would find themselves on opposing sides of any topic. They enjoyed sparring, both relentless in refusing to give up or give in. Dagen and Llylit were two sides to the same coin, similar in features and tenaciousness, but opposites when it came to their opinions. She was a few years younger than him and his fiercest opponent with the aim of her words as well as her arrows. But, Llylit was also one of his most loyal allies. They were protective of each other where anyone else was concerned. Conveying thoughts with their expressions was their best choice when wanting to show concern for one another. Dagen glanced up from his plate to find his sister, still and staring at him, amongst the commotion.

What happened to you? Llylit asked, with furrowed eyebrows.

Dagen looked back at her with a blank face, *Nothing.*

You're lying, Llylit narrowed her eyes.

I don't want to talk about it. Will you let it go? Dagen sighed and slightly shook his head.

Fine! I was just trying to help... Stubborn! Llylit huffed.

Their mother, Meta, was keen to their ways and caught most of their conversation. She silently stood to the side of the table and took note with concern.

Dagen had turned his attention back to pushing food around on his plate when he received a quick jab in his side. His cousin, Ard, had put an elbow into his ribs.

"Third time's a charm! Eh, Dagen?" Ard chortled.

Llylit shot Ard a look that could kill. Ard was known for his smug, antagonizing nature, and he had just touched on the one subject that was understood by all at the table not to be discussed. Everyone went silent. Dagen's cousin, Hertrof, and his wife, Charmese, who were sitting closest to Llylit, discretely gave each other side glances as they bowed their heads, and did their best to avoid looking at Dagen and the rest of the family.

"So they say," Dagen delivered flatly, as he continued to stare at his plate.

Dagen's parents looked at each other as well— his mother with pains of concern, and his father trying to look reassuring.

Calmly, with his ever-steady manner and voice that could carry but was not usually raised, Dagen's father, Ezmund, interjected, "There will be no further talk of this matter. Am I understood?"

Llylit scanned the room for any others who might have issue. If anyone else wanted to elaborate on this statement, they would have to take it up with her. No answer was needed. It was understood, and soon the cacophony of voices resumed. Ard chuckled to himself until Llylit found his foot under the table and came down as hard as she could with the heel of her boot.

As if nothing had occurred, Llylit asked, "Pass the potatoes?"

Ard was visibly hurting, but he continued to snicker under his breath. Llylit glared back to let him know she wouldn't hesitate to stomp on him again.

Dagen could not pretend to eat anymore. He excused himself to ready his horse's tackle and retired to pack all he would need for his early morning start. Meta considered going to talk to her son but thought the matters Dagen was mulling over could be better served by a good night's sleep.

However, unable to rest, Dagen climbed up to the top of the thatched roof of his home, as he had done so many times before, and gazed up at the stars and the faint outline of the forest beyond. This was his place of refuge, where he could usually find some peace. He could see the distant lanterns of his relatives' wagons as they made their way to their nearby homes. From some of their chimneys, there were shadows of smoke coming from the newly lit hearth fires. Dagen realized he had not made the effort to say goodbye to his relatives, and neither had they. His mind shifted now to the more pleasant thought of his unexpected flight. As he lay there on the roof, trying to recapture the magic of the day, gentle winds blew over him, wafting the scent of distant burning leaves. He loved that smell. Comfort engulfed him, and he fell into a deep and restful sleep.

The next morning he awoke to the sound of birds excited by the approaching Sun. The sky had a hint of the bright, coral dawn coming to chase away the fading indigo of the witching hour. He was damp from frost that had tried to form on him as it had to every surface around him. The scene was coated in a silvery blanket and glistened with the touches of the sunrise. He got up chilled, which jogged his senses and reminded him what was in store for today. Dagen gathered a few belongings, and saddled his horse. Soon, he would be meeting his friends in the village square. He knew his somber mood would not last long once he was in the presence of Brieg and Rûni. Brieg's jovial nature was contagious, and with Rûni's cynical humor, they would soon be cracking jokes, and every other line would be an innuendo or part of a reawakened inside joke. Songs would be sung, laughter would ensue, and their cares would momentarily be forgotten. Dagen was eager to greet them and went to say goodbye to his parents. His mother and father came outside to see him off. He could see they still carried looks of concern, though their faces were shrouded in fog as their breath met the chill of the morning air.

Meta started, and her voice caught as she said, "Are you sure you have everything you need to get started? Here are a few more sunstar loaves to see you off. I saved them back especially for you. I know they're a favorite."

She handed him a small package, wrapped in a light cloth and bound with string, patting his hand as he took it from her. Meta's eyes were holding back tears, so she looked away from Dagen and toward the rising Sun. Ezmund put his arm around his wife and reached to grip his son's shoulder.

"Once you send us word that you are settled, we'll bring the rest of your belongings to you," said Ezmund.

Dagen nodded. He couldn't say anything. He hugged each of his parents, mounted his horse, and turned to go.

"Dagen!" his mother yelled and hurried to him as he stopped, "Please know, the other times… they weren't your fault," she said and paused before adding, "and if this doesn't work out for you, you can always come home."

But he, as well as his parents, knew that would not be the case. No matter how it fell together, home would never be the same for Dagen. If he returned unsuccessful, he could not tolerate living under the constant shadow of his family's disappointment. But if the arrangements his parents had made for him carried through this time, Dagen's "home" would be far away, and he would return to them a visitor.

His father joined them, "It's for the best. It's for your future. We love you, son. You know that?"

"I love you too. I'll get word to you as soon as I can," Dagen said, with his eyes watering while desperately feeling the need to go on.

There were no more goodbyes as he rode away from them. Dagen had no desire to turn back for one last look as the path topped the last hill displaying a view of his family's land. His parents, on the other hand, stayed rooted where they were until there was no longer any sign of Dagen in sight.

A small sense of relief came to Dagen as he once again found himself alone. He rode under the shade of the changing leaves. Feeling secure in his privacy, he had an idea that he wanted to attempt. It was a perfect opportunity to see what he could achieve if he were to pursue another transcendent flight. Dagen was reminded of how he had felt as a child when about to receive a new toy— almost giddy from the thought of what was in store. As he rode, he held his arms out, tilted his head back, and closed his eyes. Once again, he concentrated on the color he saw behind his eyelids. This time, it was indistinguishable; a color he was unable to name no matter how hard he tried. To add to his frustration, the color kept changing each time he rode through a sunny patch of path. He listened to his heart's excited beat and deliberately slowed his breath. Soon, his heart began to slow as well. He felt the gentle sway of his mare, Sunniva, as she walked along the familiar and well-traveled path. Sunniva, too, could have walked to Carcadoc with her eyes closed– she knew the way so well. Dagen attempted to relax as he had the day before, allowing himself to step outside his body, but the constant jostling in the saddle made it impossible for him to reach that same state.

"Oh well, it was worth a try," he said as he patted Sunniva and reclaimed the reins.

Sunniva turned her head for a brief look at him, snorted with the dignity and reserve that all horses possess, and thought that Dagen was most absurd.

When Dagen arrived at the square, his friends were waiting. Brieg, as usual, greeted him with a hearty hello and a slap on the back, flashed his laughing smile, and did a quick survey of their surroundings as if to see what trouble they should get into first. His mischief was usually harmless, other than the exception of the broken hearts he left in his wake. Brieg Ingólf was always the center of attention and preferred it that way. His bright red hair, tall stature, boisterous manner, and comfortable wealth all made him stand out in a crowd. And he was more than happy to share the good fortune he attracted with his friends, Rûni and Dagen.

Brieg was the son of Lygus Ingólf, a Dryhten to King Wodan. Dryhten Ingólf was the military officer in charge of the King's forces stationed at Kestel Midlen in Lerakrey and oversaw the enforcement of the King's law throughout Lerakrey and the surrounding regions. Carcadoc was included in this territory and was the beloved home of Brieg's mother. It had been her choice, and her husband's gift, to raise Brieg in Carcadoc instead of Lerakrey. She had hoped to instill in her son the values of a more conventional life. Brieg had embraced his simpler upbringing and preferred the company of his local friends to that of the nobles' progeny, much to his mother's delight and his father's dismay. But even with his present company, Brieg was allowed the privileges and exerted the confidence that came with his father's station and title. The time was past due for Brieg to join Wodan's forces and follow in his father's footsteps. At the close of Winter's Nátt, he would be stationed in Lerakrey as a guard at the Ports of Eormensyl for his initial post, followed by more extensive military training while his assigned unit participated in the Wild Hunt.

Rûni greeted Dagen with a nod and commented, "About time you showed up. I didn't know how much longer I could put up with Brieg on my own."

Rûni was in a sore mood and doing his best to conceal his pain through his usual sardonic tone, but the edge in his voice was unmistakable. Rûni's departure from his father had not gone well. For weeks, Rûni had anticipated a conflict, but now there was some comfort in the fact it was finally settled. Brieg and Dagen knew soon Rûni would put it aside and start enjoying their company.

Arlo Grûniag, or Rûni, was the son of a Smith. His mother had been a member of the Tjetajat, one of many orders of seers that respected the old magics and bound themselves to nature. Rûni's mother was known throughout Carcadoc for her kyndness and council. His father was a man of facts, not unkynd but stern. His mother and father had been an unlikely couple from the start, but they had begun in matrimony as a loving pair. Soon, their differences became sources of contention, and by the time of Rûni's arrival, their home was full of turmoil. The first of many ongoing quarrels was from his mother's insistence that her family name, Arlo, be at the beginning of Rûni's. This was the tradition of her matriarchal line and common amongst members of the Tjetajat. She accepted that her husband's name for his family line and profession would be last, as was his tradition. Rûni's father was not as accepting. Rûni found himself taking up this same argument at a young age, after his mother's death from prolonged illness. When he thought of his mother, he remembered her filling his imagination with stories of amazing creatures and far-off lands. His childhood by-name, Rûni, meaning "secret lore", was given to him, as well, by his mother because of his love for old tales and his unending search for evidential proof to the mysteries of legend. His father was not receptive to this either. Rûni insisted on going by his by-name and continuing to have Arlo as his first, in honor and remembrance of his mother. This drove an irreparable wedge between the father and son. And with Rûni's decision to leave and join the Order of the Tjetajat to be a historian instead of becoming a smith, there was little left between them. Rûni's last words to his father, as he left to meet his friends in the square, were that he would no longer carry Smith as his last name.

Of the three friends, Rûni was the most shy, reserved and sarcastic. He was, by every aspect, more cautious than Dagen or Brieg. Rûni was their nagging voice of reason and guarded himself with disdain where matters of the heart were concerned.

He was gangly and had an unassuming face. Rûni would have been content to remain obscure in Brieg's imposing shadow, but unfortunately, that had never been possible for him. Between his own striking white-blonde hair and his reoccurring role of dutifully resolving Brieg's calamities, he drew more attention to himself than pleased him.

Dagen was the binding force between these two opposing natures. He was trustworthy, understanding and accepting, with a natural propensity for listening— with most people. Above all things, Dagen was loyal. More often than not, his nature was useful in smoothing over the flaring tempers of Brieg and Rûni. He had the ability to put anyone at ease. When he was not being the peace keeper of his friends, he was the instigator of many of their misadventures. These usually started with Dagen stating, "Wouldn't it be funny if...?" Brieg would find the idea irresistible and follow through full force, while Rûni looked on and lectured them— occasionally joining in, but still lecturing. With Dagen's dark features and solid Midangardian build, the contrasts amongst the three made these friends a noticeable trio. But if there were any question that they would go unseen, Brieg made sure everyone was aware of their presence.

After greeting each other, they watered their horses in the square's fountain (which was not illegal but considered bad manners). The three were ready to set off on what they referred to as their most exciting adventure yet.

THE NINE WORLDS' WAR

THE DIVISIONS WITHIN THE REALM

 AESINGARD

King Wodan's Forces

 VANGARD

The Ing Fré & Bereness Fréa's Allies

 SWEDUETWIN

 LÉOHETWIN

 FYRFOLDE

 GICELFOLDE

 MIDANGARD

Neutral Worlds

 HEÍTANGRUND

 THE ENDE

*Spanning over thirty Midangardian years, the Nine Worlds' War
was the longest running conflict of King Wodan's reign.*

CHAPTER 4

A MATTER OF PERCEPTION

D ormant and undetected by most, the void from knowledge's loss was woven like an invisible thread throughout the undertones of daily life. For those who were aware, the thought of a future without change, without advancements, and being stuck in utter sameness, was a future without hope. Whispers rippled within these groups, fearing a future of mind numbing boredom and sloth, one of greed and cruelty fueled by raging crowds spouting doomsday prophecies— unless progress was restored. Even those who were unaware that knowledge was altered, were experiencing frustration and anger for being unable to resolve perpetual problems. Innovative minds began succumbing to depression and madness. There was another factor that was even more frightening, the generation born after the loss, were oblivious to what they were without. They were learning, but it was only of history. Those mindful of the situation, in all worlds, were terrified to think that when this secret was finally revealed to this generation and the following ones, it would be met with utter complacency and a total lack of concern. When every worlds' last generation predating the void had died out, the mission for knowledge's restoration would die along with it.

The Elders of the Tjetajat were no different in their concerns than anyone who had discovered that the movement of progress had halted. They too were aware of the dire implications and were desperately searching for solutions through ancient signs, legends, and prophecies. The Tjetajat Elders were close advisors to Queen Frija and kept their information internalized out of fear and to prevent panic throughout their own world. Yet the Elders knew a day would come when this could no longer be kept secret. The reason remained unseeable. Theories were without visions or evidence to support any confirmation. But unlike the others who harbored this secret, the Tjetajat Elders carried a secret of their own; their hope in one individual. Her name was Ellor Kitaj.

It had been five Midangardian years since *The Night of the Twin Stars* when Kitaj arrived, with some question, amongst some of the most powerful seers in all the Nine Worlds. She had the honor of being born on the last night of a Winter's Nátt celebration; a date that brought with it its own prophetic expectation. It was said any child born of that day would be gifted with special sight. Kitaj bore three signs indicating she would have great vision; she came from the strong matriarchal line of Ellor seers, there was the auspicious timing of her birth, and she had the distinguishing feature of one blue eye and one green. The nature of her conception was unusual in itself. Kitaj was the product of the brief return of her father's soul to her mother, after his death in the battle that marked the end of the Nine Worlds War. Beyond these traits and circumstances, she was thought to be extraordinarily special by the Tjetajat Elders and grew up under scrutiny within their protective circle. They knew, without doubt, Kitaj was somehow tied to this loss of knowledge; for when they looked at her, all they could sense was the void.

Kitaj grew to believe, from the sideways glances, and conversations that would stop as she entered a room, that everyone was keeping something from her. No one, not even her own mother, Ellor Corynth, a newly appointed member to the Tjetajat's Central Council, would tell her the reason behind this secrecy. Even Kitaj's "great vision" failed to give her any clue to her own mystery. She knew her mother, as well as other members of the Order, were anxious for her to reach her full potential. From Kitaj's perspective, all she thought she would be was a disappointment to them. Even with the Elders' tutelage and training, she could tell she was not achieving the level of sight everyone expected from her. Her abilities were fairly ordinary in comparison to other members of the Order. Kitaj had the distinct impression that these expectations involved her in ways she could not understand yet, or was not ready to face. She would be of official age to join the Tjetajat this Winter's Nátt, with the start of her twentieth Midangardian year. She hoped, that maybe through her initiation, she'd fulfill whatever it was they wanted of her.

Expectations and perceptions of Kitaj were two entirely different matters. Though secret hopes weighed heavily on her, opinions about her varied greatly since she seemed to stand at arm's length from most emotional attachments. This impression was partially caused by their own reaction, whether conscious or not, to the void that constantly surrounded her. Little did they know how Kitaj struggled when she was near people. It was almost unbearable for her at times. Their emotions came across to her with amplified intensity, bombarding her with their unwelcomed magnified projections. She had discovered, at a young age, different ways to filter out these external onslaughts of feelings and to lessen the pain she'd experience. One defense was to avoid holding someone's gaze. Emotions radiated from their eyes with such force and veracity, they could overpower her. When guarded, she could be perceived as being aloof, cold and even snobbish. When she felt brave, she would try to reach out to people, through humor or by sharing her opinion. It was usually met with uncomfortable silence or a quick change of the subject. Kitaj's ideas rarely matched convention. Some saw her as fake or mocking because she would mimic the patterns of people's voices. This was just her attempting to be heard, understood, and like them. Her work was painstaking and meticulous, saddling her with the label of a stickler. But this too was another focused attempt at trying not to blunder, to be accepted, and be "normal." Kitaj felt awkward within her own skin which made her even more unsure of herself. She was timid and anxious in most settings. She tried to blend into her surroundings but she always seemed to find herself obstructing someone's way. Most saw her as awkward and clumsy, which in truth, she often was. Kitaj was not fast with her reflexes; she was lanky and uncoordinated. Her nose bore the brunt of her clumsiness and had been broken more times than she cared to remember. It complemented the sharp angles of her face and was framed by her long brown hair. Her hair was a defining trait in itself, for it grew in unpredictable directions of waves and curls, adding to her persona of being unusual. Some of the Elders saw her as sweet, helpful and quiet, and thought her oddities were just her awkward phase of growing up. But all who knew Kitaj could agree, whether she was thought of as sweet, shy, snobbish, or lacking in graces, she was most definitely an odd girl.

In this swirl of misconceptions, Kitaj grew up withdrawn and frustrated. She was surrounded by seers who could not see her for who she was. Kitaj found some comfort in the few relationships she had. There was Tanadra, who had always treated her more as a person than a child. Tanadra, the Binder of Notions, was one of the most respected Elders of the Tjetajat. She had the ability to combine the visions and knowings of other seers into a broader picture and bring meaning to their fragments of sight. Tanadra had made herself available to Kitaj from the moment of her birth. She did this not only for the good of the Elders' quest to restore knowledge, but also to serve as Kitaj's mentor. Their relationship was one of trust, and respect for each other. Kitaj was more at ease whenever Tanadra was around her. Tanadra accepted Kitaj for how she was, even if she could not truly understand who she was.

Kitaj was also close to her mother, Corynth, but their relationship had its limitations. Kitaj found she couldn't convey to her mother what she was experiencing, and in moments of anguish, the understanding she craved from her was not there. Her mother tried to reach Kitaj but could not find her within the ever present void. Corynth had her own defenses that did not help their relationship. Part of her heart closed off after the loss of her husband. Kitaj knew her mother loved her, but duty and expectations always seemed to loom over their relationship. Corynth kept her daughter safe by instilling her own values as a realist to life's harshness, but this did not stop Kitaj from being a dreamer with a vivid imagination.

Kitaj's childhood could have been a very lonely time but she spent her free moments creating imaginary playmates. She would dream up adventures for herself, and the friends she longed to have, that took her to faraway lands where she encountered fabled creatures and recovered hidden treasures. Within her mind, there were no limits to where she could go or what she could do.

These childhood imaginings helped segue Kitaj into her first true friendship with a being, in all due respect, baring qualities of the surreal. Aergo was a rare creature of fading legends. Only a few of his kynd remained as only a few still remembered his kynd. He too was perceived as something he wasn't. Most often by his own choice, but still, it was a misconception. This commonality helped draw Kitaj and Aergo together. As it can be for those who are misunderstood, they bonded easily once they had found each other. Those like Aergo were thought to be bad omens for anyone who crossed their paths. A bad omen, he was not, but Aergo was a devious prankster and skilled mimic, easily bored, and delighted in causing trouble. These were the reasons for the compromised position in which Kitaj happened to find him. She had rescued Aergo from certain harm; and for her kyndness, he devoted himself to her. Such was the nature of his kynd when shown true compassion. For the first time in her life, Kitaj had the comfort of knowing, no matter what, she had someone who understood her and theirs was a friendship that would last a lifetime. Aergo's care and concern for Kitaj were constants of his character, just as were his features: his eyes— a luminous orange, and a coat the color of pitch with a perfectly round patch of white on his chest, that remained through each of the various forms he would take. Most often Aergo could be seen with Kitaj as a cat or dog, and on occasion, a horse, unbridled and barebacked, walking next to her. Aergo had a regal quality about him, which made Kitaj feel honored to be in his company. Those who knew of Aergo's kynd found he and Kitaj an odd match for friends, and their presence together was even more unsettling.

"We disturb people, don't we, Aergo?" Kitaj said as they walked along together through the woods, following the stream that led to their favorite place.

Aergo looked back to her with an oblique smile and a nod of his head. They were headed to the cleared patch of grazing land that was long since forgotten, with grass that was high and small shrubs and trees that were beginning to reclaim it for the forest. At one end, it a had a stream fed pond surrounded by rocks, that had been placed there by its previous tender. The rocks were now covered by moss and weeds sporadically jutted out between them. This pasture was surrounded by woods and the forest ridge, giving them the feeling of seclusion from the rest of the world, as if it was their own private sanctuary. To Kitaj and Aergo, this ground carried a sense of magic. They had discovered the abandoned pasture years before. It was nestled at the foot of the forest ridge, next to the city's edge, and not far from Kitaj's home. The convenience of its location allowed them to sneak away without raising suspicions of their whereabouts.

On this day, they reached their sanctuary in record time. It had been a day of pressures Kitaj was glad to be rid of; preparations for the final details were in motion for the Tjetajat's initiation rites that would take place at Winter's Nátt. Kitaj had taken part in helping with the initiations since she was a small child but the added weight of her own induction and lectures of "great things are expected of you" from her mother's wisdom rang in her ears! She knew that her mother, Ellor Corynth, feared Kitaj would somehow disappoint and embarrass her as well as reflect badly on her position within the Council. Kitaj knew much depended on her, even if she did not know exactly what that entailed. For this moment, she could put aside a life preoccupied with duties and enjoy her time with Aergo, and the rare pleasure of play.

Kitaj walked happily on the rocks across the stream. She had taken off her boots to feel the coolness of the grass underfoot. This always calmed her. She took time to feel the Sun on her shoulders and listen to the sounds of the stream and rustle of the leaves as the wind blew through the forest. It was as if nature were whispering to her a song, in a language she could not understand. The patting sound of Aergo's canine paws on the fallen leaves only added to nature's cadence. She could breathe here and felt she could truly be herself. Aergo sensed her relax and knew they could begin their game.

With a sudden transformation and an abrupt push from his head, he nudged her off the path and into the stream.

She caught her balance and kicked the water, splashing his face. The water made his black fur and mane shine only brighter. She tried to jump on his back, but he spun around and knocked her off. He faced her down. If she moved, he mirrored her. Within this sense of freedom, Kitaj was no longer awkward, much less self-conscious, and spontaneously changed her moves to see if Aergo would follow suit. He spun if she spun, he ran when she ran, he knew her so well he could guess her next move and follow.

She laughed at his interpretations of her actions since he had two more legs than she did to consider. Aergo loved to make her laugh and he felt privileged to be her sworn friend. They ran, danced, and hid from each other in the tree line near the pond. Kitaj's laughter carried on the wind and added to the music of nature around them. So engrossed in the joy of their play, they had no idea that they were being watched.

Dagen, Brieg and Rûni rode along the path at the top of the forest ridge. The mood had lightened, and their anticipation was growing the closer they came to Lerakrey.

"It will be hard to top last year," said Dagen.

"We were lucky we didn't get arrested. Too bad you don't remember it all, Brieg," added Rûni.

The view of the woodlands below was spectacular. But in all its majesty, it was no match to the bird's eye view from Dagen's flight; he thought with disappointment, but it would have to do for now. Dagen decided he could enjoy it for what it was, along with the help of a handy gadget he had purchased two years prior at Winter's Nátt— a Heítaned-crafted vastnear. It was a compact, metallic device that fit over one ear and closely to the eyes, and made far away images of interest appear closer. They started to descend into the tree line from the top of the ridge. The trees had thinned in some areas, and they could continue to see the mountains in the distance, the approaching sprawling city of Lerakrey, as well as some of the valley's terrain below. It was at one of these spots where Dagen noticed an isolated pasture surrounded by forest. As he looked through the vastnear, he saw two figures. One appeared to be a girl, and the other; he had trouble distinguishing from the nearby shadows. The form became clearer to him and revealed itself as a horse. They were jumping, running and twirling in an unchoreographed dance. The lightest bit of laughter drifted on the mountain winds.

"You were a sight for sore eyes when we found you up in that tree. How your hair happened to be dyed green, I guess we'll never know..." Dagen stopped in mid-conversation to watch the performance below.

Dagen was struck by what he saw. He thought it was one of the most beautiful, freeing sights he had ever seen, even in comparison to his recent flight.

"Of course, I remember. I was wooing a woodland sprite! The fair Paltheas! The green hair was worth it," Brieg carried on talking without missing Dagen in the conversation, and he and Rûni rode ahead without him.

"Too bad she wasn't really a woodland sprite," said Rûni.

"Well, she wasn't a woodland fairy. Why do you think I was up a tree?" replied Brieg.

"She was just a woman who lived in the Asbjorn Forest, Brieg. You know what I meant!" Rûni came back at him.

"Poor Rûni, in all these years, haven't I taught you anything? It's not a matter of what is real and what is not, it's how you tell the story that counts! You're so literal! For your sake, I hope someday you do find your real sprite, or monster, or whatever creature you are looking for, and that the two of you will be very happy together," Brieg added, laughing at Rûni.

The girl and horse had disappeared into the forest's edge nearest him. For a moment Dagen thought they had left.

Kitaj had to catch her breath; she was tired and still dizzy from spinning. She stepped out of the woodland shade to watch the sunshine twinkle on the pond's surface. It was moving in waves though she knew the surface was still. Her vision had not yet corrected itself.

From the ridge, Dagen looked down on the scene with quiet amusement. He laughed to himself as the girl stumbled out into the light.

Kitaj turned back to look for Aergo but could not distinguish him from the dark forest's edge. She did hear him; he was almost giggling. She lifted her head in Dagen's direction to face the Sun, closed her eyes and held her arms wide to bask in its fading heat. Still unsteady, Kitaj backed up to right herself and accidentally stepped onto a rock at the pond's edge. The rock beneath her wobbled. Unable to regain any sense of balance, she fell backwards into the murky water!

Both Dagen and Aergo laughed to themselves at the sight of Kitaj falling into the pond, but their musings changed to sudden and sincere concern. The thick sludge below the water's surface had swallowed her! Within an instant, Kitaj had been sucked completely under. She wasn't surfacing! Kitaj's breath had been knocked from her by the shock of the frigid pond and she had little air left in her lungs. The cold, stagnant sludge was forcing its way up her nose and trying to overtake her throat. The muck kept her from surfacing as if its purpose was to overtake her. Kitaj's arms and legs felt pinned by it's increasing weight.

Time slowed as Dagen held his breath and hoped, *One more moment. Come on, you have to...*

Aergo was stunned by Kitaj's disappearance. There was no sign of her! He felt as if the air had been knocked from his lungs as well. He knew he had to move but every nerve in his body was working against him.

What felt like a slow descent only took moments. Kitaj's back landed against the solid, slimy surface of the pond. Finding ground beneath her, she tried to dig her feet into the sediment. Her hands dug down as well to find some type of leverage. She was able to push her head upwards and found herself sitting in the knee deep mud. Coughing and gagging, she regained her breath but her voice and senses were stunned into silence by the cold muck and water that covered her.

Dagen let out an audible sigh of relief when he saw her head rise above the murky water. He was just beginning to feel all was well again when his feelings suddenly turned to panic!

Through the bright sunlight and the mud in her eyes, she could only see the silhouette of a huge form approaching her. Its growing shadow engulfed her.

༄

Dagen saw a large dark creature emerge from the forest's edge that was headed straight for her! Dagen dug his heels into his horse, much harder than he intended, and the two of them went racing down the side of the mountain. He could not keep his eye on what was happening below because of the trees flashing by. He just knew he had to help her if he could. Brieg and Rûni heard the commotion behind them and saw Dagen racing down toward the clearing and followed suit.

When he reached the pasture, Dagen abruptly stopped.

He saw the girl, still sitting in the muddy pond. She was laughing and her horse was near her, shaking its head. Brieg and Rûni soon reached Dagen and saw the object of his attention. Dagen didn't move. He was completely confused. He wasn't sure now what he thought he had seen. She was obviously well, and Dagen genuinely considered leaving at that point. He had the strangest and distinct feeling if he went any closer, the world as he knew it would turn on its end. But Brieg, being Brieg, was not about to pass up a chance to meet a girl, even one that was covered head to toe in mud. Brieg and Rûni proceeded to approach the compromised young lady and Dagen decided he better catch up with his friends or he'd be leaving her to Brieg's charms.

CHAPTER 5
CHANCE ENCOUNTERS

She sat laughing in the dark, greenish-gray muck, half blinded. Kitaj had tried groping at her neckline for a piece of fabric to wipe her eyes clear, but to no avail. Every bit of her was coated in mud. Aergo stood over her, waiting and relieved to see she was unharmed. Losing sight of her momentarily when she fell caused him to briefly, and accidentally, take his most defensive form. He found he had become overly protective of her, mainly in trying to protect her from her own accidental nature. Aergo knew now she had not been hurt; therefore he was able to relax into a less aggressive state and appreciate the humor of her predicament, but it wasn't to last.

Aergo heard them first, the approach of three men from the forest's edge, and went on alert. He weighed his options. His horse form was much faster than his common counterpart and swifter than his goblin form. Knowing he could best remove her from harm if he stayed as he was, Aergo managed to keep his form intact, but was ready to shift in case he needed to defend her while she was in a comical yet, vulnerable position. Kitaj sensed Aergo's distress and three men at the forest's edge. She stopped laughing and tried to clear her eyes so she could see who was approaching.

Brieg reached her first and said in a laughing and friendly manner, "What do we have here? I didn't realize mermaids swam this far upstream."

Embarrassed and exasperated by Brieg's comment, Rûni muttered, "Not again," and added aloud, "Pardon him, Miss. He can't help himself. It's a compulsion he has," as he joined Brieg's side.

Dagen approached them cautiously. Nervous energy was building inside him. He found he could not speak and could hardly move.

Kitaj said nothing. Her perception was befuddled. She was trying to regain enough sight to assess the situation. These three were coming into focus though their faces were dimmed in shadow. The Sun was at their backs and Aergo stood between them and her, partially blocking her view.

"Excuse me, but you look like you could use some help. Could I offer you some assistance?" said Brieg.

Kitaj thought about his offer carefully. She did not know these young men and wasn't sure if allowing them nearer was advisable.

"I believe my friend saw you fall, and we wanted to make sure you were unharmed," Brieg added.

Dagen knew Brieg was stretching the truth a bit, but he had assumed correctly the reasons for Dagen's hasty departure down the mountain. He was sure Brieg's statement of "we wanted to make sure you were unharmed" was just part of his intentions for approaching her.

Kitaj still said nothing. There was a strange current building in the air around her and she was uncertain what to make of it. Her eyes had now adjusted and she saw the brilliant smile of the red-haired gentleman speaking to her from horseback. She looked next to him and saw a blonde-haired young man. The Sun behind him illuminated his light hair and made it appear as a halo. He had a withdrawn way about him; one she knew very well for herself. From her first impression, she could tell these young men were a few years older than her, and they looked like travelers. She looked past them to the third. Her gaze became involuntarily targeted on this last individual. His gentle face had a wary expression, which soon changed into a look of blank shock when his dark eyes made a jolting connection with hers.

Before Kitaj could stop herself, she said, "Hello."

It was all she could get out, as if this was the last breath she would take. Her greeting's intention was completely directed at Dagen. Still visibly shocked, he said hello back.

In her mind, Kitaj knew she had never met him, and with only a hello between them, she had this overwhelming thought, *What are you doing here? You weren't supposed to show up yet!*

She was engulfed by the unexplainable recognition, as the power from his stare bore through her— straight to the depths of her soul. She couldn't stop him! She couldn't shield this prying energy! Kitaj was locked to him with her returning gaze. His stunned expression confirmed his response was a mirror of hers. The power originating from Kitaj had pierced him to his core. Her heart was racing. She couldn't look away. Dagen was aware enough to be thankful he was sitting on his horse. Had he been standing, he was sure his knees would have no longer supported him, buckled, and reduced him to a heap on the ground— unable to move. Kitaj was appreciating the fact her hands and knees were buried in sludge; otherwise, they all would have seen how badly she was shaking.

Most of their exchange was lost on Brieg and Rûni. They only saw the girl's eyes were on Dagen and that their surroundings had become very quiet and still. Brieg and Rûni were not attuned enough to feel the current of energy flooding the air around them. This current was causing the hairs to stand on end on Dagen's and Kitaj's arms and the backs of their necks. Aergo felt it as well, as a ridge of fur spiked down his spine. Brieg waved off the silence, assuming this young woman was intimidated by their presence and thought he'd attempt to assist her from the circumstances of her mishap one more time.

"Excuse me, dear lady. Can I help you out of the mud?" Brieg offered again.

With still no response, Brieg, as well as Rûni, couldn't help but wonder from her delay if she spoke their language. Maybe she had harmed herself and the injury was just beginning to surface. Had she hit her head, could she hear them?

She sat unaware that her weight was resting heavily on her left arm since her fall. The shifting sludge gave way, causing her wrist to falter. The pain of its sudden turning sprang up her arm, alerting her senses to her position. Concerns for her well-being began to translate in Kitaj's thoughts, though their connection stayed intact. She tried to correct herself.

"Yes, yes, I'm fine," Kitaj said, to answer one of Brieg's earlier questions, "I can get up. Thank you."

Aergo made his presence known even more to the three men by taking a defiant stance that blocked their access to her.

Kitaj struggled to free herself from the mud and stood unsteadily. Aergo side-stepped closer to the edge of the pond, and leaned his head in so Kitaj could grab his mane to steady herself and pull up onto his back. All the while Aergo's unblinking focus was on the three men, just as a precaution. Aergo's unease was not so much with the three, but came from what continued to transpire between Kitaj and the dark haired one. Kitaj threw herself ungracefully across Aergo's back and before she was completely astride, Aergo took off. Kitaj's eyes caught again on the third young man as their connections were released. Dagen sat still and dumbfounded, as he watched her and her horse disappear on the other side of the forest's edge.

"Well, that was interesting," Rûni commented on the scene.

"Never pass up an opportunity, as I always say," Brieg said heartily but with a hint of disappointment.

"And you never do," Rûni scoffed.

"Did you notice, she had one blue eye and one green?" Dagen said absentmindedly.

"No, not that I saw. How could you tell with mud all over her?" replied Brieg.

"Because Dagen was looking at her face. We know you were much more interested in the 'all over her' part," said Rûni.

Brieg laughed, "Ah, you know me well, my friend! We might as well head on. No point in trying to catch any more mermaids here today."

Rûni scoffed and shook his head at Brieg's ridiculous reply. Dagen seemed lost in the moment as he followed after his friends.

They started back up the mountain to the trail they had left. It was the clearest way they knew to reach Lerakrey. The path started its slow descent toward the city limits. Brieg carried on with his tales, Rûni chimed in here and there, but Dagen was in deep thought. He replayed the events that had just taken place over and over in his mind, trying to wrap logic around this strange encounter. As he recovered his thoughts, he pictured when he first saw this woman and horse playing below. He pondered how he felt when he saw her fall in the pond; his amusement from her comedy of errors, the urgency he felt when he thought she was in danger of drowning and his shock from the sight of some large incomprehensible creature coming towards her. Had he only imagined seeing it? That part of their meeting had almost been lost to him because it was completely pushed aside the moment he looked at her— how he had seen into her, with the deepest sense of recognition for who she was. Dagen was certain he knew her— somehow from before they had met. He knew she had experienced the same with him in that one instance. This unshakable fact left him puzzled, for her identity remained unknown.

As Dagen questioned their connection, his responses and reactions, he had a sudden and unsettling realization that he blurted out abruptly, "I didn't even ask her name!"

Brieg, being well versed in the matters of attraction, assumed he knew what Dagen was thinking. He stopped in mid-sentence of his current topic, turned around in his saddle and shot a knowing smile in Rûni's and Dagen's direction. Rûni responded with a blank expression to detour Brieg's interest.

"I didn't tell her mine! What's wrong with me?" Dagen continued, unaware his friends were now watching him over their shoulders as their horses moved forward.

A feeling of panic started from his stomach and moved up into his throat. How was he going to find her again? He sincerely considered turning back to see if he could pick up her trail and yet the thought of finding her caused him to freeze once more.

"If it's meant to be, you'll find her again," consoled Brieg.

"You don't really believe that, do you?" retorted Rûni.

"With all my heart," Brieg delivered flatly.

"Let it go, Dagen! It's not like you could do anything about it. Remember, your obligations..." Rûni insisted.

Rûni was right; Dagen wasn't thinking. Of course, there could be nothing made of it, not without dishonoring himself and his family, and possibly causing their downfall into ruin. His life was mapped out. It was done. He only had a few more days left of the illusion that his life was his own. Dagen withdrew into himself with these thoughts— but his mind kept drifting back to her eyes.

ঔ

What are you doing here? You weren't supposed to show up yet!
cycled through Kitaj's mind as she clung tightly to Aergo's back.

He raced cross the forest, desperately trying to put as much
distance as possible between her and that... incident. Matching
Aergo's speed, Kitaj's heart was racing. Unsettling feelings
fluttered inside her, like a moth desperate to escape a spider's
snare. She wasn't ready! She didn't want this! It wasn't time!
It took only a moment for those words to resonate an undeniable
truth; enabling Kitaj to release her panic and allow a resolving
calm to come forward in its place. She could not comprehend
the words' meaning, yet it did not matter. With this acceptance,
came a confidence in certainty— she would see this young
man again. It was not her concern how they knew the depths
of who each other was, yet nothing of his name or his past.
It did not matter that she was taken aback by their unanticipated
meeting, and completely unprepared and blind to what could
possibly follow. Kitaj knew exactly what she needed to know.
She was done.

Aergo sped on until he reached the stables at the edge of
the Tjetajat settlement. He did not slow his gait until he was
deep inside the security of the stable and skidded to a stop at
the very end. Other than a few horses, the stable offered the
privacy Aergo was seeking. He was shaken, angry, and barely
contained. Kitaj hurriedly thought of possible ways to calm him
down. It didn't help that Aergo was now covered in mud. She
knew too well how much he hated an untidy appearance. The
mud had caked and dried from the speed of Aergo's flight. It
cracked over her skin, matted in Aergo's mane and fur, adhering
her clothes to him. As Kitaj jumped off his back, Aergo let out
a screeching neigh from the hairs that were plucked as she
dismounted. She grabbed a grooming brush in an attempt to rid
him of the clots, and had only brushed three strokes when Aergo

put an end to her aid. He stomped his hooves indignantly and violently shook his head. Kitaj stepped back to give him space. She had never seen him this unnerved. Aergo changed into his smallest form, a black rabbit, to rid himself of the largest dirt clods, then transformed into his dog form to shake vigorously so he could remove even more of the dried residue, and concluded by returning to his cat form to feverishly lick his paws to clean his face and groom himself. His wide orange eyes never left her.

Kitaj responded calmly and reassuringly to her distressed friend, so calming that she even surprised herself, "Aergo, it's all right now. I know you were worried for me but I'm fine. See? I know you felt the strangeness of that energy building around us. I don't know what that was, but it was the most amazing experience that I have ever had. There was a connection, and this overwhelming recognition. Something has changed— something changed inside me. For the first time in my life, something feels undeniably right."

When Aergo found his hygiene sufficient, he changed into his largest form, as the goblin, so he would be able to talk to Kitaj. He sat stooped over to prevent his four twisted horns from getting caught in the rafters. He seemed preoccupied with attending to his appearance by running his claws through his shaggy fur to remove any tangles. This was his way of calming himself, but this time it did little to soothe him.

Without acknowledging anything Kitaj had said, Aergo spouted back at her through his long sharp teeth, "That brush was going to rip my hair out and it was taking too long! You need to go clean yourself up... and stop staring at me! I wish you could see yourself, you look more savage than I do and it's not at all becoming on you! Go! And when you get back, explain to me exactly what happened back there between you and... that... that boy! I've got to get some food! All of this turning is wearing me out!"

He changed back to his cat form, turned away from her and started cleaning himself again. Kitaj knew Aergo's temperament could be difficult when he was scared or tired, but this anger of his was directed straight at her! He had never been cross with her before. What had she done? It wasn't as if she had any control over what had transpired. How could she make Aergo understand what had occurred when Kitaj could not explain it for herself? Why was he furious? This hurt her and tears welled up in her eyes, but she was determined not to let Aergo's temper get the better of her. She felt a new found peace within her— solely from meeting this total stranger whom she was somehow inexplicably connected. Her best friend's anger was confusing her, and clouding her thoughts. If Aergo had not been upset, she might have actually enjoyed what she was experiencing. Kitaj tried to speak, but stopped herself. She was overwhelmed with too many emotions at once and the only words she could find were inadequate and senseless. She turned on her heels and marched off toward her home to clean up.

We will resolve this later, she thought. *For the moment, some distance between us could do us both good,* but she already knew; the dynamic of their relationship had been slightly, but permanently, altered.

As Kitaj walked home, her movement became more labored and slowed by the extra weight of her mud-encrusted clothes. She encountered stares, remarks, and some laughter as she made her way up the street. This was not new to her. Her clumsiness had left her in similar conditions that had drawn unwanted attention. Before this day, Kitaj would have timidly made her way home; darting behind every possible object to conceal herself and averted her eyes from their mocking stares. This time, she did not cower. Instead, Kitaj questioned the jeers of her unsolicited audience and their compulsion to humiliate her further. To her own surprise, she stared back at her taunters with such intensity, it made them stop and back away. She wondered if she was mistaking her senses, because she was reading embarrassment radiating from her mockers for their behavior. Kitaj questioned herself, she was deeply curious about her onlookers' change of heart, and again, uncharacteristically calm.

What is happening to me? she wondered.

She looked down at her arms and hands, and noticed the details of her skin in the thin cracked layer of dried mossy-green mud. She wondered if this was what a fleógan might look like at the time of outgrowing its skin; when the dragon-like creature would spread its wings to crack the surface, and shed the restrictive layer away for a fresh new beginning directly underneath.

Kitaj concluded, *This is my new beginning.*

Dagen was still lost in his thoughts when he, Brieg, and Rûni arrived at their lodging, The Idle Sickles. It was an adequate establishment with modest small rooms, soft beds, and most importantly to Brieg, a tavern at its entrance. It was conveniently located in the heart of the city, and smelled of open mead and glow wine, sawdust, iron and feathers. They had stayed there on their previous travels and were well remembered by the staff. Brieg always tipped extravagantly to ensure good service for their stay, as well as gain recognition that would serve him well in the future.

Brieg threw open the doors with his usual bravado and announced to the barkeep, "Good day to you, fine sir! A round of mead for my companions and myself! We are but weary travelers and in need of quenching our thirsts."

Brieg's roaming eyes surveyed the dim room as he spoke. The barkeep looked up in acknowledgment, and with a nod began preparing their drinks while Rûni found seating for three at one end of a long wooden table. Brieg followed and Dagen absentmindedly sat down with them.

"Dagen, are you with us yet?" asked Brieg. "We're here! Time to join in. Why should Rûni and I have all the fun?"

Rûni looked at Brieg wearily and rolled his eyes. He wondered how long their friendship would have lasted, or if it would ever have existed, had Dagen not been the common factor between them. The fact remained; it had always been the three of them. Rûni thought before long he'd be missing these moments of eye rolling on Brieg's account.

A barmaid with curly ash hair brought their drinks. She had a smirk on her face as she spoke, "Well, if it isn't my favorite customer, Brieg Ingólf ! It's been a while."

"Ismadalia, you never looked lovelier! I was hoping to find you here. The year has been good to you," said Brieg as he put his arm around her waist, and sat her on his knee.

"Many things have changed since I saw you last. I'm a vowed woman now, so you should address me as such," said Ismadalia, as she smiled and bit her lip.

"How disappointing for me. I mean, how wonderful for you—married. Who's the lucky man?" asked Brieg as he politely released his arm and let her stand.

Ismadalia smoothed out her skirt as she answered, "No one I think you would know. His name is Heolstor Rand; he serves under your father. Since we are in peaceful times, he currently guards Lerakrey's Ports of Eormensyl, in charge of transports to and from the Halls of Aesingard. I should also inform you that you are speaking to the owner of this establishment."

"Well, you have moved up in our world since I saw you last," said Brieg, also realizing he'd have the pleasure of meeting her husband soon enough.

"My husband and I thought it would be a sound security in case anything detrimental were to happen. That should bring you up to date. You missed out, Brieg, but I really don't have to tell you that. Do I?" said Ismadalia, as she patted his face and paused, "I see you and your friends have returned for the festival."

Rûni and Dagen nodded and gestured hello to her.

"Yes, and with this visit, it is very important that I show my dear friends a time to remember; one that will live on beyond our days!" stated Brieg.

"That shouldn't be hard to accomplish where you're concerned," Ismadalia replied.

Ismadalia waved over two unfamiliar barmaids, Cloette and Bainanne. Their resemblance was telling that they were her sisters. They came over and stood beside Dagen and Rûni. Rûni immediately looked uncomfortable; Dagen simply smiled at their friendly new faces.

"Aren't you a shy one," said Bainanne to Rûni.

"This one's adorable," said Cloette to her sisters in reference to Dagen.

"He gets that often. Answer me this; what exactly is it about him that makes him so... appealing?" Brieg asked.

Dagen's ears began to turn red. Women of all ages seemed to find Dagen easy to approach. He rarely was the one to speak first. Usually, the conversations were in request of helpful assistance of one type or another. Dagen was glad people thought of him as trustworthy, but he had not given much thought to any reason for it. He was aware that these simple occurrences did cause Brieg to envy him, which Dagen found laughable and ridiculous.

The three sisters looked at Dagen, then each other and said in unison, "It's the nose."

"His nose?" questioned Brieg. "Really!" he exclaimed at now knowing the source of his envy.

"Yes, that slight flip to the end makes him come across as playful and... safe," said Cloette.

Dagen gulped. His face now matched his ears. He wasn't sure if he should be flattered or insulted.

"Safe! I had no idea a nose could say so much. I could be safe," Brieg added.

"You're anything but safe," ended Ismadalia.

Happy to change the subject from himself, Dagen asked, "By chance, would you happen to know of a young lady in Lerakrey that has one blue and one green eye?"

Rûni looked at Dagen as if he had suddenly sprouted horns. Brieg laughed while the three sisters shook their heads.

"No, not that I have seen, but we don't get many young ladies in here. If she turns up, we'll let you know," said Ismadalia kyndly.

Dagen knew it wasn't likely, but worth asking. He did wonder what would he'd have done had they known of her. The more he thought about seeing her again, the more complicated everything became. Dagen's mind was not with his companions that evening, but he did his best to follow through as he usually did with Brieg's antics.

⸎

Kitaj returned to what she would have considered to be her usual self before she reached home. The expected responses to her arrival reset her mood. Her notions told her that both her mother and Tanadra would be there; and from experience, she knew they would not see her coming. She was used to their surprise at her sudden appearances— something

Aergo appreciated to no end. He too was an enigma, as he was undetectable to their sight. Aergo reveled in Kitaj and he being "the unsettling pair" that could stealthily go about their way amongst the Tjetajat, some of the greatest seers in all the Nine Worlds. But, Aergo was not with her and his enjoyment was absent and truly missed. Kitaj prepared herself for her mother's disappointed expression in response to seeing her current appearance. She knew too well that Corynth's reaction would be punctuated with an unspoken *Not again!* reflected in her exacerbated huff. Kitaj also knew to expect Tanadra's greeting as one of kyndness and concern. When Kitaj walked into her home's entry, covered head to toe in crumbling green clay, Tanadra and Corynth's reactions unfolded just as Kitaj had predicted, but she could not foresee what would come next. A deep jolting shock took hold of Corynth and Tanadra when Kitaj's eyes met theirs. Both women looked at her with awe as they backed away. Tanadra and Corynth turned to one another to confirm they were both having the same experience in Kitaj's presence.

"What is it?" Kitaj asked in alarm, as she looked back and forth at them, "WHAT ARE YOU SEEING?"

Corynth and Tanadra didn't answer. They just stood rigid, staring back at her. They had never revealed to Kitaj their perception of the void she carried with her. It was not something Kitaj actively sensed around herself, it was just how she had always been. For the first time in Kitaj's life, Tanadra and Corynth were sensing something from her, a foreign energy coming from Kitaj's gaze, projecting through the void that continued to surround her.

"It's time. She needs to know!" Tanadra whispered to Corynth, as her eyes stayed on Kitaj with a look of disbelief.

Corynth regained her composure as if nothing were out of the ordinary and said dismissively to her daughter, "Kitaj, why don't you go clean up?"

With her mother's statement, Kitaj reached her breaking point, "WHAT IS WRONG WITH EVERYONE TODAY? I KNOW YOU'VE BEEN DELIBERATELY BLOCKING SOMETHING FROM ME! YES, I DO THINK THE TIME IS PAST DUE FOR YOU TO TELL WHAT IS HAPPENING AND HOW IT INVOLVES ME! WELL? DON'T YOU HAVE ANYTHING TO SAY TO ME?" Kitaj said raising her voice and shaking from its force!

Tanadra looked at Kitaj with sympathy as her mother closed off from her and turned away. Kitaj had never spoken in this manner. She wanted to scream, but instead, she set her jaw, swallowed her frustration and left the room. Kitaj held her emotions in check, but could feel her passive nature was cracking as another part of her emerged.

It wasn't until she was scrubbing her skin pink that the tears came flooding down her cheeks. In her exhausted and overwhelmed state, Kitaj tugged her comb impatiently through the matted mess that was her hair. Muddy clumps remained tangled throughout the wind whipped mass, even after her attempt at removing them with soap and water. Kitaj sensed Tanadra's presence as she neared the door to her room; Tanadra had come to console her.

"Come in," said Kitaj, before Tanadra could ask to see her.

Tanadra entered, carrying a small tray containing a bowl of root stew, a loelplum, and a cup of glow wine that she sat on the table near the door. She gently took the comb from Kitaj's unsteady hand and began to slowly work through each entwined cluster. Kitaj sat still for her while continuing to face the window. Tanadra managed to undo all but a few of the large tangled knots at the ends of her hair. She resorted to using the small trimming shears Kitaj kept in the drawer of her bedroom table to remove the knots and restore her hair to an even edge.

Tanadra kept her voice in soothing tones as she finished, "Your young life has not been an easy one. You are correct. There have been secrets kept from you— about yourself, and I believe you have every right to know what we know. If it were my choice alone, I would tell you what I know as the truth, but it is not my decision to make. It is a small consolation, but you will have your answers, at least to the questions we can answer, very soon. Trust in that while you are waiting."

Kitaj said nothing, as she held back her tears and her breath while refusing to look up at her. Tanadra patted her shoulders and leaned down to give Kitaj a kiss on the crown of her head, picked up the trimmings, and quietly left her room.

After the last soiled remnants of the day's events were washed away, Kitaj crawled into her bed and lay there as the tears silently continued to slowly soak her pillow. Unmoving, she watched as the shadows grew longer across her wall and floor. Soon, only a faint light was cast through her window, allowing her to only see the outline of objects within her room. She numbly looked out at them. A familiar thud and weight graced her covers near the bend of her knees, and soft pads made their way to the top of her bed. Aergo had returned. Kitaj was lulled by his soothing purr as he placed his chin on her ear and kneaded the skin at the nape of her neck. He soon settled in her hair and continued purring into her ear, as he had done most nights since their meeting. Her words were few, but she hoped they were all that was needed to acknowledge that their relationship was changing and to reassure him of her affection and loyalty.

"You aren't going to lose me, no matter what comes," Kitaj said without moving, trying her best not to disrupt their shared comforting position.

Aergo stopped his purr, caught by her words, then began gain. Kitaj drifted into sleep as Aergo watched over her.

Brieg woke the next morning with his head pounding. The Sun was shining brightly into his room and it made his eyes hurt. Rûni was perched in a chair whittling a stick and whistling.

"Good morning, bright one! Feeling a little worse for wear today? Hmm... You certainly look it, and frankly smell like it," said Rûni, a little louder and cheerier than warranted.

"Thanks, and good morning to you too." Brieg managed, "So apparently, we made a time of it last night," he said as he acknowledged his condition.

"You certainly did, and as usual, I enjoyed watching you make a complete fool out of yourself. I see from your expression, you are wondering where all the dirt came from. Shall I tell you?" said Rûni smiling.

"Please go on, it will help jog my memory," said Brieg, as he winced, realizing how sore he was from his night's escapades.

Rûni began, "After a few generous rounds of glow wine and songs, which you encouraged the rest of the tavern's tenants to partake in, we set out with Ismadalia, Cloette and Bainanne..."

"With who?" asked Brieg, rubbing his head.

"Ismadalia's sisters," Rûni delivered flatly.

"Oh, that's right. She came along as a chaperone, or they did, or however you want to look at it," mumbled Brieg.

"It all started with you taking our little troop to the market where the vendors were setting up for opening day of the festival. Dagen made some comment about wondering how far you could toss a large mangelwurzel and it went from there. You decided to rent a cart and buy up all the rotten and bruised vegetables. We went out into the edge of the forest and made a catapult out of a sampling. We spent a good part of the evening just seeing how many we could launch at a time and how far they would go," said Rûni.

"It's coming back to me," said Brieg.

"When we ran out of vegetables, you suggested that we should launch the sisters. This did not go over well. By that point, you were referring to them as She, Her and That One. They didn't like that much either, so they decided to leave and we walked them back here, where Ismadalia slammed the door in your face. You owe her an apology; that was one debt last night I couldn't smooth over for you. Luckily, she didn't have us thrown out of her inn, mainly because you always pay well. From there, you comforted your wounded ego in the tavern with more mead and glow wine and we were off again to the streets. We saw a horse that had ribbons woven into its mane, and the conversation turned to animals looking like people, and likewise, the reverse. Dagen thought it would be amusing if animals wore clothes as we do, and you decided it was your duty that animals should have them! You started taking clothes that had been set out to dry and boots off doorsteps and wrestled them onto unsuspecting livestock. I tried to stop you, but you know how that goes. I took your coin purse and started leaving what I thought was a fair exchange at each of the houses, and tried to make sure all the gates were closed so the animals didn't get out, but there were a few that got away. Surprisingly, we did not wake anyone, and again, we were lucky not to get caught, arrested, or worse! WHEN ARE YOU GOING TO GROW UP?" stated Rûni.

"Where's Dagen?" Brieg asked blankly.

"He's off to the festival grounds. He left before daybreak. I think he was too anxious to sleep, he said he'd catch up with us there. Brieg, I believe he's struggling with what he's enlisted in," said Rûni.

He paused, and threw Brieg his much lighter coin purse. Brieg clumsily grabbed for it and was unable to acquire the pouch before it bounced off his face.

"Now that you're up, I'm going to check in with the Order to make sure there's nothing else I need to do before the initiation at the week's end. Clean yourself up and I'll meet you at the market stand from last night. You still have to return the cart. I've made sure it's in a returnable condition and it's waiting for you outside the tavern entrance," added Rûni.

Rûni left the room whistling again and intentionally slammed the door behind him, which made Brieg's head throb. Brieg stood up and squinted into the morning light shining through his window, just in time to catch a glimpse of his handy work from the night before. A pig, wearing pants and a bonnet, was crossing the street with hurried steps. It appeared to have somewhere important it needed to be.

ॐ

Dagen had watched solemnly as a violet glow began on the horizon, brightening the silhouettes of buzzing bodies through the ambient morning fog. The view was one of organized chaos as vendors readied their wares for the first day of the festival. Once the Sun's light had risen to greet the crisp morning, he could see the make-shift market sprouting from the fields on the outskirts of Lerakrey. The smells of smoked meats, dried fruit, spices, and livestock made a pungent aroma that hung in the brisk air. Colorful carts and tents were adorned with attractive banners, reflecting the cultural artistry native to each world. Every banner advertised the promise of last chance purchases for a seasonal surplus. Vendors filled their spaces with an abundance of late summer vegetables, exotic produce, cheeses and bread, barrels of drink, tanned skins, weapons, tools, or adornments. The carts and tents lined the edges of a grassy circle, which would serve as the stage for the Winter's Nátt celebrations, games and ceremonies.

Dagen soaked in the atmosphere, cherishing it; for very soon, sunrises would be far and few for him to see. He looked across the market, half wanting and half not, to find the banner that would be claiming him. His heart skipped when he saw it— a vertical display of black, embellished with a honeycomb design and three ornate luminous bees. Reality struck him in that moment; in a matter of days, he would be leaving to start his new life on the dark world of Sweduetwin.

Kitaj awoke to find Aergo still nestled in her hair. She hated to stir him, but knew she was expected to help with receiving induction candidates at the Tjetajat Council. She had worked with settling inductees in past years, but had never become comfortable with her role as greeter. She was repeatedly put in this position at her mother's insistence. Corynth believed the practical experience would help Kitaj in her interaction with others. Kitaj managed, but found her duties to be very stressful, at times painful, and always depleting. Though she would be going through the induction process herself, she was still expected to fulfill her duties.

Kitaj dressed in a plain linen tunic, traditionally signifying initiates, and threw on her lined cloak. The cloak's clasp; the Tjetajat symbol of three intertwining loops representing the past, present, and future, rested heavily against Kitaj's shoulder.

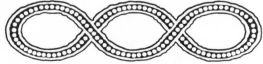

Tjetajat cloak clasp

She grabbed the fruit off of her otherwise untouched tray, and left her home before she could have another encounter with her mother. Aergo accompanied her as Kitaj navigated through an unusually dense and bustling morning crowd on her way to the Order's headquarters. She filtered out as much of the commotion as she could and scooped Aergo up in her arms to carry him, ensuring he would not being trodden on.

They arrived at the main receiving hall where she began setting up to greet new arrivals. With preparations in place, Kitaj settled into her chair as Aergo settled into her lap. With clammy palms, she anticipated the first inductee. She had not had a moment to consider the events of the previous day and wished for time, but her thoughts would have to wait. Kitaj's stomach rumbled loudly from not eating for almost a full day and demanded her attention. The plump loelplum she held in her eager hand seemed to beckon her to eat it. As she raised it to her mouth, she suddenly stiffened. The fruit fell from her hand and bounced across the floor. A notion had caught her off guard, alerting her that one of the young men who tried to help her the day before was about to walk through the door. Aergo sensed Kitaj's tension and involuntarily dug his claws into her legs as she stood up. Kitaj winced, as Aergo jumped down from her lap. She scrabbled to grab the rolling fruit and reposition herself into some state of composure for a proper greeting. Aergo's back was arched, his ears flattened, and his fur stood on end, as he hissed at Rûni's arrival and began to growl loudly as Rûni moved toward Kitaj.

It became clear to her that Rûni had no idea who she was. Kitaj looked exceptionally different from their first meeting, and she could sense Rûni possessed no developed abilities of special sight. Kitaj remained flustered and did her best to hide her enhanced awkwardness.

Rûni introduced himself, "My name is Arlo Grûniag," with no pause in leaving off his father's family name. He shyly added, "Rûni, if you would, please."

He hardly looked up at her. Kitaj's mind was racing as to what to do next; should she tell him who she was now or wait to know more about him— and his friend? Kitaj opted to learn more before admitting to their previous meeting. Aergo jumped up on the desk near them and continued his low modulating feline growl.

"Arlo Grûniag. Yes, I have your name. Welcome. We are pleased you have decided to join us. I'm Ellor Kitaj," her voice cracking as her throat tightened.

Any calm or confidence she had gained through yesterday's encounter was nowhere to be found. She noticed how hot and sweaty her palms had become as she swatted at Aergo to be quiet.

"My mother was a member, Arlo Yashel, from Carcadoc. That's where I'm from," Rûni mumbled.

Aergo was growling so loudly that Kitaj was having difficulty hearing Rûni's quiet voice. Because of Aergo's incessant noise and refusal to budge, the mutually nervous Kitaj and Rûni found the situation unbearably comical and each started to giggling uncontrollably.

"Your cat doesn't seem to like me very much," Rûni added.

"Don't mind him, he thinks he's being helpful," said Kitaj, stifling her laughter.

They had difficulty regaining their composure, but managed to in time for Kitaj to announce that she sensed her mother, Ellor Corynth, would be joining them momentarily to greet him. Aergo stopped growling as Corynth glided into the room, with her usual poise and grace. Rûni could tell she was ranked as a member of the Central Council by the appearance of her Tjetajat talisman etched in her skin below her collar bones. The center loop was filled with a solid, bright red.

Corynth interjected, "Arlo Yashel, I knew her well during our initiate training together here in Lerakrey. That was so many years ago," she said with a note of nostalgia. "Your mother was a lovely person and is a well-missed friend. How fortunate that you and my daughter should be taking your rites together. It is a pleasure to meet you, Rûni. I see you are interested in being a historian."

Rûni had not experienced being read since his mother's passing. It was a familiar and warm feeling to him, and it gave him a sense of comfort and reassurance in Kitaj and Corynth's presence.

Turning her attention toward Kitaj, "Dearest, will you escort Rûni to our library? I believe he is most anxious to see it," Corynth said coolly, hiding any trace of disturbance between her and her daughter.

Corynth was artful in camouflaging her agitation and aloofness towards Kitaj, while consciously avoiding looking directly at her. Yet, Kitaj was able to see through the depths of some of her mother's defenses; enough to know the discussion that she so desperately needed to have with her would not be taking place until after the initiation ceremonies.

Kitaj politely, and gladly, dismissed herself from Corynth and lead Rûni to the library, pointing out various other possible areas of interest along their way. Aergo slunk behind them, trying to look casual in his purpose.

When they arrived at the library, Rûni came alive. His mother had repeatedly described this space to him in as much detail as she possibly could, at his ever beckoning insistence. Yashel had done well to paint the picture of the library for him, but its vastness and tactile lushness left Rûni giddy.

"It's more than I could have hoped for! I grew up with this room always in my mind," Rûni said, elated.

"I'm so glad you're pleased. Would you like me to give you some time to yourself here?" asked Kitaj, feeling very happy for him, as the intensity of his joy magnified.

She could only envy what it must be like for Rûni, to finally be settling into the place where he had always felt he belonged.

Not waiting for his obvious answer, Kitaj walked between the aisles of archives to go toward the library's entrance. A stream of light coming through a high window illuminated her face as she passed through it. Rûni looked up at her from a massive row of books and scrolls to see her green and blue eyes. She had been discovered, and Kitaj blushed at his recognition.

"You're the girl from the pond," he said, before thinking through his response.

Aergo started to growl again softly from under a nearby table. Kitaj stepped farther away from the light and began fidgeting with a loose thread she found at the hem of her sleeve.

"Guilty. I apologize for my abrupt departure yesterday... and for not telling you straight away that I recognized you," Kitaj said, still looking down and twisting at the thread.

"You don't need to apologize. I imagine that was very... um... um... unsettling for you," said Rûni, looking at his feet, feeling equally awkward.

Kitaj understood Rûni's shyness; and because of it, she immediately appreciated his demeanor and liked him. She was surprised to find Rûni so instantly likable, and realized the noticeable change within herself; she was letting go of some of her defenses. Aergo began to growl loudly again. Kitaj gave Aergo a quick look to convey that he absolutely needed to stop. Aergo began quietly washing his face with his paws, as if he had no idea as to what she might be referring. Rûni began to relax a little as well. Both he and Kitaj let little nervous laughs escape them.

"So, you like the library?" Kitaj asked in an attempt to move past the subject of their initial meeting.

"YES, yes, I do!" said Rûni.

After a generous pause, Kitaj asked, "Now— would you like me to give you a little time alone to look around?" giving him and herself an out.

"That would be appreciated," Rûni's voice wavered.

"I'll come back for you in a while," said Kitaj, honestly wanting an exit and a few moments to compose herself.

Rûni nodded to her in thanks and started breathing again once she and her cat had left. He continued looking through the rows of archives, half believing he was finally here. He was truly home! He took in all the glorious details of his favorite place in existence and could see his future unfolding within this room. He would be building his new life here, a life with new possibilities and new experiences, with new people surrounding him— and without Dagen and Brieg.

A sobering pang of confliction began to form in Rûni's mind. With consideration to Dagen's circumstances of his looming departure and obligations, Rûni wondered if it would be kynder not to tell his friend he had found "their lady of mystery." The discovery of Kitaj had surprised Rûni in more than one way. She was gentle natured, welcoming, plus equally and endearingly awkward. In complete contrast to his usually skeptical self, Rûni found her very engaging. He discerned, if Kitaj were to ask him presently about his friends, he truly wasn't sure what he would tell her. He resolved his thoughts by logically concluding there was no reason for Kitaj to become briefly entangled with Dagen, or with Brieg, for that matter. His friends would both soon be off and involved in their new lives, and away from him. He would remain here where he belonged— which by chance, just happened to be near Kitaj.

Kitaj returned, with a better behaved Aergo beside her. She was more composed and hoped she could maintain it through Rûni's remaining visit.

"Did you enjoy your tour?" she asked politely.

"Yes, very much. I would like to come back before the end of the week. Maybe you could show me more of the Order and could tell me what to expect with the induction services?" Rûni asked.

"I think that might be possible. Do you have set plans with your friends for the festival? Kitaj asked, introducing the topic.

He was not sure what her intentions were in asking him and he honestly didn't want to know. Rûni remembered a lesson well learned from his mother, which was never lie to a seer. Being vague and avoiding the subject was the best he could do to conceal his intentions. The fact he honestly had no idea what Brieg and Dagen would be getting into next was working to his advantage for once.

"We'll see each other over the next few days. There should be plenty of opportunities for me to return. Would tomorrow morning be possible for you? Rûni said, trying to keep the conversation directed back to him seeing Kitaj again.

"I will be helping with other initiates, but I can try to arrange time for you. If you tell me where you and your friends are staying, I can get word to you," once again, Kitaj tactfully tried to get more information from him, still surprised by her own assertiveness.

Rûni was relieved to know Kitaj's sight could not reveal the specifics of their lodging arrangements. He did steer the conversation away from the subject in fear of Kitaj asking him directly.

"Don't worry about going through the trouble, I will come by around the same time tomorrow morning and see when you'll be available. I really must let you get back to your duties. It was my pleasure meeting you, Kitaj. Thank you for the tour and I look forward to seeing you tomorrow," he said, as he skirted all vital pieces of information and exited in haste.

"Let me walk you out," Kitaj attempted but failed.

"That's not necessary. I can find my way. Thank you again and goodbye. Until tomorrow," Rûni added in his haste to leave.

Aergo was at Kitaj's feet, purring loudly and throwing his body against her shins as he weaved around and between her boots. He was intentionally making it impossible for her to try to follow Rûni, without the risk of tripping and falling flat on her face. Kitaj could only clumsily wave to Rûni in his hurry to disappear around a corner.

Rûni took a winding path through Lerakrey to reach the city's edge and the festival grounds. As he walked, he considered his decision to keep Kitaj's identity and whereabouts secret from Dagen. Rûni had never kept a secret from his friend in all the years they had known each other. He reassured himself that this was the right decision, and was in Dagen's best interest. Though he was convincing himself of his own logic, his decision was not completely effective at keeping the nagging feeling of betrayal at bay. His friends were easily found; Brieg's height and bright red hair stood out above most of the crowd and shown like a beacon in the mid-morning Sun. They were waiting, as expected, at the Midangardian produce stand where they had made purchases the night before. Brieg was still without full capacity of his faculties and Dagen stood with a quiet, pained look of resignation about him.

"How was your visit to the Order?" asked Dagen.

"Fine, fine. Where do you want to go first?" Rûni said fidgeting.

Dagen and Brieg looked to each other with surprise. "Fine" was not the response they had expected from Rûni. They knew how much being a part of the Tjetajat meant to him.

"Did you get to see the library?" Brieg asked.

"Yes, it was everything I had hoped," Rûni added.

There was a prolonged pause. Dagen and Brieg expected Rûni to elaborate about the library. They had heard so much about it over the years and were stunned by Rûni's lack of detail, now that he had actually seen it. Brieg shrugged his shoulders.

"I haven't had a chance to see what's here, and I should get some food. Dagen, you've been here since first light. Any suggestions?" asked Rûni.

All Dagen could think was he wanted to avoid the one particular banner for as long as he possibly could. In his own best interest, Dagen played to Rûni's finicky palate.

"Let's start with the familiar, I think it will be more to your liking," he suggested.

The three made their way through the already bustling crowd. They knew to keep their purse strings tight and close to their skins as they were casually bumped into by possible pick-pockets.

The festival grounds were divided into plots, designated for each world's displays. Each world's section was a glimpse into their way of life, their strengths, their beliefs, and what their people valued most.

It was easy enough to find familiar food and drink in the Midangard section. Neither Dagen, Brieg, and to no surprise, Rûni, were up for any culinary adventures that morning. Dagen found nothing to his liking and pulled another sunstar loaf from his satchel. It was palatable and helped to ease his nervous stomach, but he could only force himself to nibble around the edges. Rûni could not help but feel more pangs of guilt as he looked at his miserable friend, and questioned again if his news of Kitaj would lighten his friends' spirits for a few days or only add to his burden. Rûni resolved himself to stay quiet and keep to his original, logical and self-convinced "correct" course of action.

Dagen just needs a distraction. Brieg will be feeling his usual boisterous self shortly and we can surely get Dagen in a better frame of mind, thought Rûni.

Two imposing men in detail armor caught Brieg, Rûni and Dagen's attention as they worked their way through the crowd towards them. The guards' facial expressions were as serious as the long spears they carried with their authority.

"These must be for me," Brieg said, without surprise but with sincere disappointment.

"What have you done now? I only left you alone for a short while. What could you have possibly gotten into on the way to meet us?" asked Rûni, half jokingly.

"They're royal guardsmen," said Dagen, without inflection.

"A message from Father," added Brieg, in a similar flat tone.

"Brieg Ingólf," said the first guardsman.

"That would be me," Brieg answered with a comical bow.

"You are to come with us," said the second guardsman.

"But I was just starting to enjoy myself. Look around you, kynd sirs!" Brieg made a sweeping motion with his arms. "You should take a moment and partake in the festival! It seems the two of you could use some levity."

Neither guardsmen responded. They just stared blankly back at Brieg.

"Fine. I'll go with you, peaceably," Brieg said, and turning to his friends and exclaimed with sarcastic seriousness, "Dagen, Rûni, I leave the festival in your good hands. Enjoy. I will find you as soon as I am able," he said, looking back at the guards. "Preferably by tonight's celebration."

The guardsmen stood aside in the customary manner for escorting dignitaries. Brieg's noble lineage was on show.

"After you, gentlemen," said Brieg.

The guardsmen did not move and said nothing. They had been ordered not to let Brieg out of their sight until he was delivered to his father. Brieg could have too easily slipped away if he were to follow behind them.

"Have it your way— after me!" Brieg concluded.

Brieg started walking away with the two guards on his heels. He decided he could not leave his friends so solemnly. He impulsively turned and blew kisses and waved feverishly to Dagen and Rûni while bouncing in front of the guards. As Brieg expected, the guardsmen did not respond to his ridiculous behavior, not even a smile, as they dutifully edged him along through the crowd.

Alone with Dagen for the day, Rûni wondered how he was going to keep up the pretense of normality. At least with Brieg around, there had been easy distractions. Now, Rûni was left to his own devises to maintain his concealment of meeting Kitaj, and his more secretive intent, which turned his own stomach for bordering on diabolical. Rûni was not built for deception. That was Brieg's territory. With Dagen self-absorbed by thoughts of his future and wishing to avoid what was to take place, Rûni hoped Dagen's mindset would work to his advantage. Moving forward seemed the obvious choice to Rûni.

"Dagen," said Rûni, momentarily pulling Dagen into the present.

"Hmm, what?" answered Dagen.

"We must follow our orders, Brieg would not want us to mope about. On to Heítangrund?" asked Rûni.

"Understood," Dagen replied, though with little thought, and trudged along behind his friend through the bustling crowd.

On reaching the Heítaned's section, Dagen began emerging from his inner distractions, yet he kept a mindful eye for the young woman he sought. The mastery of the Heítaned's specialized tools, gadgets, and mechanized aides always brightened his spirits. He was fascinated by the Heítaned's expertise with design and function. In every corner of their display, there were contraptions of all sorts. Dagen found the Heítaned people to be just as intriguing. He admired their soaring intellect and thought it matched well with their towering stature. They were the giants that walked amongst them. The Heítaned were a mostly quiet and calm people, or at least appeared so, for they communicated with one another through their thoughts. In appearance, they could be mistaken as frail, but in fact, they were extremely strong. They had pale blue-grey skin and large black eyes set wide below their exaggerated foreheads. Their large craniums balanced delicately on small jaws with thin mouths.

The Heítaned were the origin for most of the ingenuity to be found within King Wodan's realm. They were well recognized throughout their neighboring worlds for excelling at calculations, sciences, and defining solutions through their practical, exacting manner. The Heítaned ensured their intellect would carry forward in each generation by selectively creating their young from the uniting of multiple parents' mental strengths, and having a chosen prime parent to guide their collective offspring. It was only within their latest generation that unrest within their people had surfaced. Boredom and frustration ran rampant in the young. Signs of the younglings' discontent were surfacing with more incidents of troubled behavior and violence. Their brilliant minds were eager to make their own discoveries, find their own solutions, and were baffled that none could be found.

Dagen spanned the venue with eagerness. He momentarily set aside his troubles and basked in the awe and artistry of the Heítaned's inventions. He wished his mind could create such wonders. Whatever the task, there was a Heítaned creation to make the work more precise, yield the most benefit, and save time.

Dagen would have been happy to spend his entire visits to Winter's Nátt in the one venue, but he knew neither Rûni nor Brieg would have that much patience for his curiosity. Dagen perused as many stands as Rûni could tolerate and settled on making a purchase of a celestial sight navigator, or what was commonly called a sky sight. The ingenious tool was compact and extremely versatile. The inner workings and fluid lines of the metalwork were captivating in itself, but Dagen was also intrigued that it could easily be converted to locate any world in the night sky from any vantage point within the King's realm.

"It'll allow me to find Midangard, no matter where the Swedus might send me," stated Dagen to Rûni.

Rûni understood his sentiment and curbed his growing impatience as Dagen completed his purchase. Not so could be said for the young Heítaned woman who sold him the sky sight. She made no attempt at hiding her extreme lack of enthusiasm. Her heavy sighs and disdainful looks peppered the entire transaction.

Rûni eagerly dragged Dagen to the next venue, until he discovered it to be Fyrfolde's. He had always felt intimidated by the Fyrs. They were not as tall as him, but the Fyrs were very stocky and strongly built, and their skin had the appearance of a natural armor. To Rûni, they seemed to be forged from the same molten material as their famed weapons. No metal was stronger. Next to them, Rûni felt overly frail and perceived the Fyrs saw him only as a weakling.

Dagen thought Rûni's concerns were over-exaggerated. The Fyrs, like the Heítaned, had little care for social niceties. They were straight forward, hardworking craftsman that believed in the quality of their creations. Simply showing respect was all that was needed to gain their trust and respect in return. Where the approach became difficult was when customs were unknown, resulting in accidental insults. Rûni was aware his chances of being guilty of such a misstep were fairly high. He hoped once he became a historian for the Tjetajat he would be able to conduct himself in a more diplomatic manner. Until then, his solution was to stay close to Dagen and follow his lead, all the while wishing Brieg were with them, as they maneuvered through the Fyrfolde exhibits.

Rûni did not expect their visit in the Fyrfolde venue would be long, since Dagen and he both had little need for weaponry, farming tools or metal wares. Dagen did admire the Fyrs' skill and artful craft. He especially enjoyed seeing the designs that were influenced by Heítaned ingenuity. The person Dagen knew who would have truly appreciated the Fyrfolde pavilion was his sister, Llylit. He thought it unfortunate that she'd never taken an interest in attending Winter's Nátt. Rûni tried to hurry Dagen through, but Dagen found his own patience to be uncharacteristically worn. His looming concerns were wearing on him and his mood was short for Rûni's insistence.

"We came to see the festival. If you're in such a hurry, don't let me stop you! Otherwise, could you let me look?" Dagen stated firmly.

"Sorry," said Rûni, "I just get the feeling we aren't very welcome here."

"That again. Look around you, closely. Is anyone here even looking at us? No, they're not. Compose yourself. We are all here in friendship— Fyrfolde and Midangard have always been allies. There's no history to show otherwise! Remember?" Dagen added, noting how the harsh tone of his response was unlike him.

"Again, sorry. I know it's my own doing," said Rûni, feeling more guilt for Dagen's mindset.

Dagen tried to clear his thoughts and focus on his surroundings. He noticed a nearby fletcher, and once again thought how much his sister would have enjoyed being here. The Fyr fletcher had numerous options of arrows available. Dagen's eye was caught by one in particular. The arrow's head and fletching both were formed in a spiral design that had to be a collaboration of Heítaned and Fyr designs.

"I'm not sure how this will fly, but if anyone can make it, Llylit could. At least it's something to remember her annoying brother by," said Dagen.

Seeing Dagen struggling, Rûni solemnly added, "I'll make sure it's deliver to her."

After buying the arrow, he and Rûni proceeded to the next venue, The Ende. It was an encounter that neither Dagen nor Rûni had ever felt adventurous enough to explore. The Ende Dwellers allowed participants a glimpse of what was to come in the after life. Dagen and Rûni still agreed. The current unknowns to their futures was enough mystery for them and they decided to continue to the next section, Aesingard's.

The King's venue was mainly a showing of his private forces. The Aesir had never displayed other aspects of their culture at the festival. It was thought that the King wished to only show his authority. Dagen and Rûni stopped to watch the various demonstrations conducted by the King's guard. Dagen and Rûni both found it difficult to imagine Brieg in their ranks; but in a few days, these would be his circumstances.

They had made their way halfway through the festival grounds and found themselves venturing into territories unknown as they entered the Vangard venue. Since it had been fifty Midangardian years since the opposition's participation, neither Dagen, Rûni, nor many of the festival's attendants had ever experienced the Vane's, Gicels' or Léohet's cultures.

Though crowded, the pace of the Vane pavilion was slower, calmer, and to Rûni and Dagen's surprise, most welcoming. Long cultivated rumors of the Vane's elitist attitudes appeared to be unfounded. Rûni and Dagen, along with everyone else visiting the Vane pavilion, were greeted with the utmost hospitality. Hosts moved about the crowd, distributing free refreshments and welcoming everyone to their venue. The atmosphere was lighter than the other worlds' sections Rûni and Dagen had visited. They were known to be advocates of beauty, health, desires, and sublime artistry. The Vane's interests were lush and it explained their deep fondness for exotic Swedu and Léohet cultures. References to etwin-kynd art, music, and culinary pleasures accentuated their own expressions of sensuous quality and taste. The Vane display incorporated natural elements, with lush foliage and water features. The scent from aromatic blooms floated through the air. The full grown trees had been transported from Vangard and stationed throughout the venue at the special request of the reigning Vane— the Ing Fré and his sister, Bereness Fréa. Artists, poets, and musicians were scattered about under the trees' vast shade.

Dagen and Rûni wandered about the winding Vane paths, exploring the culinary delights, apothecaries, and make-shift studios. In spite of the light and joyous atmosphere, Dagen's spirits began to drop again from no sight of "her." Rûni recognized Dagen's low and suggested they continue onward.

They stood in awe at the entrance to Gicelfolde section, for the entire pavilion appeared to shimmer. Crystals of every conceivable color had been extracted from the world's frozen underbelly, and lay exposed and glistening in the late summer Sun. There were stones ranging from the size of a pea, polished and faceted for adornment, to large monolithic chunks, plucked from the ground's own veins. All were available at a negotiable price. As well as the mining of precious stones, Gicelfolde was also known for luxurious furs. Being the coldest of the Nine Worlds, the Gicelfolde animals had the thickest coats for braving the elements of their hostile, and frigid home. Anyone would prize having Gicelfolde fur to warm them through the winters of their own world. Pelts of white to gray, or beige to russet were available as raw, or already fashioned coats and cloaks. The ready-made wares were cut in an array of sizes, to fit the smallest folde-kynd to the largest of the Heítaned.

The Gicels were never known to wear their furs at Winter's Nátt. The Midangardian weather was too hot for them. Even with the air carrying the onset of winter, their venue's stands were arranged with intentional shaded areas to help keep the Gicel vendors cool. The Gicels had brought with them huge slabs of ice. They used the ice to back their shade and provide a small cooling comfort from their home world. Though the ice would last but a few days, it was the Gicels' best defense against their misery from Lerakrey's late summer heat. The colder setting of the Gicel pavilion served a secondary purpose in promoting the sales of their furs to the unacclimatized customers.

Dagen and Rûni noticed the air turning colder as they entered Gicelfolde section, and even they inadvertently found themselves looking over the inviting furs, exactly how the fur tradesmen had intended. One Gicel fur trader jumped at the opportunity to barter with the young men. The Gicels' bartering skills were almost as infamous as their jewels and furs. It was part of the show. He introduced himself as Pyos Prenot and spoke clear Midangardian. Dagen felt embarrassed that they could not return the courtesy; for neither he, nor Rûni, spoke a word of Gicelian.

Pyos had a round face, that matched his solid, round, muscular form. His complexion was that of a permanent wind burn. His large hairy arms hung from his broad hairy shoulders and gave balance to his strong shape. He was of average Gicel height; with his head barely topping at Dagen's shoulder. Pyos wore a colorful summery patterned undershirt of Léohet design. His shirt appeared strikingly out of place in the wintry atmosphere of Gicelfolde's pavilion, but it seemed to match his gregarious nature. Pyos greeted Dagen and Rûni with a wide grin spread across his face and was genuinely happy to be speaking to the two young Midangardians.

Pyos began his spiel on the advantages to his tanned hides; heavy fur for warmth and water tight from rain. Impressed and persuaded as he was with Pyos's pitch, Dagen wasn't keen for such an expensive purchase so early in his visit.

Rûni nudged Dagen to draw his attention to a young Fyr that was approaching. The Fyr was carrying armfuls of beautifully crafted daggers and swords. Each weapon looked to be of the highest quality and was adorned with intricate Fyr designs and encrusted with Gicel jewels. Pyos excused himself to deal with the young Fyr.

Rûni was fascinated by the contrasts and similarities between the two folde-kynd. Their height, shape, and strength looked matched, but that was where their similarities ended. It was apparent their shared ancestors had adapted to equally harsh but opposed climates, causing distinct trait differences to occur between the two. The climate of the Midangard late summer was very cool for the Fyrs. With the added cold of the Gicelfolde venue, the young Fyr wore heavy Gicel furs to enter. His bald head and wrists were all that was exposed, but showed the notable differences between the people of his world and that of his cold climate relations. The Fyr's skin was much thicker and tougher than the Gicel's. It was the perfect protection against their world's intense heat but was no match for the cold. The Fyr's stern face could not hide he was shivering under his heavy furs.

The Gicelfolde and Fyrfolde languages were much the same, but with noticeable differences in inflections and accents. Pyos's sentences seemed more chopped by harsher sounds, while the young Fyr's language had a more even flow and timing.

Rûni found the most outstanding aspect of the two folde-kynds' exchange was concerning the weaponry carried by the young Fyr. Gicels and Fyrs had not collaborated on weapon design since the onset of the war. To find a shared piece of their craftsmanship was a rarity. Most pieces had been melted down as a symbolic gesture of the break in alliance. Their separate loyalties to the King and the Vane had unwantedly divided them. The fact they had begun working together again was a healing sign from the years of being pitted against each other. These new pieces of weaponry would be a testament to the restored partnership between their worlds.

Other Gicel vendors came over to examine the results from the labors of their restored union. Emotions were triggered as a crowd formed around them. Not all wounds had healed, and one particular Gicel could not contain his reaction. Dagen just happened to be standing close enough to become the recipient of the man's grievances.

He grabbed Dagen by the collar of his coat and began fervently speaking to him in strongly Gicel accented Midangardian, "Posh, khose Aesir and Vane, khey must look down on us loike pawns! So high and ancient! You know kheir not as old as khey say— sure by kheir years are in terms of forever days, but khem days are short to yours and mine. Khey khink khemselves gods. Posh! ev not gods— but khey do loive long — longer than we. Khe War— all between khem— but No! Khey had to pull we in— divide us! Not right! Not our reason to foight! We were foine before khem. The Heítaned very khink mostest. Khey do no choose soides. Khey stay neutral. But we— we were made to— My khinks Koing Wodan started oit, cause he khinked the Vane koilled khe Prince! Don't try to stop me, my says what my khinks! And khat ois what my khinks! Sa! Mya own son and brokhers koilled oin khat war for our Koing— but do he care— No! My say! He only feels hois own pain– not ours. My know khis cause my feel khat same pain— but our Koing not care! Selfoish! Very all are selfoish — selfoish." the Gicel trailed off, sinking deeper into the depths of his sorrow while still holding onto Dagen's collar.

Rûni and Dagen helped the distraught Gicel back into the care of his friends, leaving Dagen with a sense of selfishness. He had been so consumed in his own disappointments, he had not considered what was going on around him.

"Poor man. There are too many stories like his," said Rûni.

People from all of the worlds were here together. Most every family had a story of loss because of the war. Dagen's family had been fortunate in that they had all lived through it. He did not know the personal pain of losing someone in battle.

Now, these people, from each war-scarred world, were trying to move forward together through the damage they had caused to each other. This festival was a symbolic start.

After Dagen and Rûni's encounter at the Gicel pavilion, they took a moment to compose themselves. Though moved by the awareness of the underlying importance of this year's festival, Dagen's experience with the distraught Gicel had not swayed his feelings for wanting to avoid the Swedu pavilion for as long as possible. For that purpose, he and Rûni began to backtrack their way through their previously visited sections. The other purpose for turning back was the venue following Sweduetwin's was the last, Léohetwin's. Both Dagen and Rûni knew with certainty Brieg would never forgive them if they went to the Léohet pavilion without him.

Each, for his own reasons, anxiously awaited for Brieg's return from his father's summons. Rûni needed Brieg's distracting presence. He didn't know how much longer he could manage the pretense of knowing nothing of Kitaj, and he continued to wrestle internally with his decision. Rûni's guilt was ever growing, while he continued working toward convincing himself he was doing what was best. Dagen remained shaken by the Gicel's words. His new understanding had been an awakening for him. The festival looked different to him now. Winter's Nátt was no longer only about his last adventure with his friends, or him being caught up in his own wishes or disappointments. Dagen recognized the scars around him and worlds' struggling to move beyond the divisions in their past. Though Brieg would never admit to knowing, Dagen realized Brieg felt the weight of these scars more than he or Rûni ever could.

By the afternoon, the combined elements of stress and lack of rest they had both experienced over the last full day took their toll on Dagen and Rûni. Their minds were strained and exhausted. Together, they agreed to opt for a shaded patch under the trees lining the festival grounds. The spot they chose was located behind the quietest of the venues, The Ende section. Dagen and Rûni welcomed the opportunity not to speak and settled into a tranquil late day slumber.

Kitaj could not help being distracted for the rest of her day at the Tjetajat Council. She kept watching the time dial, anticipating the moment she could leave her post. She had made a direct connection to someone who could lead her to… the nameless enigma she only knew to refer to as Rûni's friend.

She had finished her duties. She watched the door, projecting to detect if there were any more induction candidates arriving. With no indication of anyone else coming, she became more anxious for the moment she could leave. Her eyes darted back and forth from the doorway to the dial. Aergo watched her carefully and shook his head back and forth to indicate he thought she was a lost cause. Kitaj felt like she was at a starting line of a race, waiting for the signaling horn to sprint. As soon as the shadow barely touched the head-mark of the dial, she sprang to the door and on to the street with great haste. Aergo shifted to his dog form and stayed on her heels, as she weaved in and out of the congested walkways. People from all worlds had descended on Lerakrey. Kitaj did not stop to pause until she reached the hill overlooking the festival grounds.

Spread across the field below, was the largest turnout for Winter's Nátt that Kitaj had ever witnessed, and she recognized it as a promising sign of recovery from the Nine World's War. There were twice as many venues, tents and stands to match the oversized crowd.

Normally, the thought of being in such a large crowd would have completely repulsed Kitaj. There would be overwhelming amounts of emotional input for her to take on. The idea of what she was walking into still gave her reason to hesitate, but she had her focus on a set purpose.

"He must be down there somewhere!" she said to herself.

That thought alone gave her the courage that she could deflect the onslaught of emotional projections she'd most certainly encounter by being amid the rowdy crowd. Kitaj's determination helped her find the calm within her that she had gained from their clandestine happenstance. Whatever was between them had brought forth something inside her— as if it were a distant memory reemerging, and yet bringing forward an aspect of her that felt altogether new. Kitaj recognized a wholeness about her that stood apart from anything— or anyone else. This nameless person she was seeking seemed to amplify this reckoning within her, and she craved more; more of the feeling of being solely complete unto herself, and for more of the energy that passed between them. She wanted to bask in it, drink it in and grow. Kitaj took a deep breath, and with her strange new confidence, stepped into the crowd filing into the festival.

When she reached the entrance, the aromas of various foods mingled through the air, reminding Kitaj she had eaten very little during the last few days. Her stomach began to growl loudly. Aergo cocked his head sideways and stared at her through one of her larger rumbles. Kitaj tried to hide her embarrassment and hoped that no one else had noticed. She was anxious to begin her search, but her hunger could not be ignored. Food was her answer. She chose to start with a new adventure. She followed the path to her right, heeding the beckoning call of the lush smells coming from the Léohetwin pavilion. It was a simple decision when compared to the familiar, rustic venue of Midangard. The warmth of Léohet's exotic, spicy and floral fragrances drew her in. The savory perfume was matched in invitation by the brilliant colored tribal designs of Léohetwin's banners and offset by the intoxicating rhythm of background drumming. Kitaj's thoughts transported her to the famed Léohet shores; she could almost feel the warm sea breezes, rushing tides, and the sensation of sand slipping between her toes as she basked in the ever present summer Sun. She had always hoped that someday she would experience Léohetwin first hand. It's beauty, she was told, had been incomparable, and was understandably a favored world to the Vane. Though scarred by the war's first great battle, the Léohet culture had survived and its majestic terrain was restoring. Her thoughts dared to go further and she could see herself on Léohetwin, and the person she sought by her side. Kitaj's stomach growled again, as mouth-watering aromas wafted through the air, calling her back from her romantic notion, or from what she wondered was just another wishful thought. With recent events, the distinction between her daydreams and sightful notions had become decidedly blurred.

Aergo flattened his ears to another groan of her stomach and gave Kitaj a look that something must immediately be done to stop that infernal noise. He sniffed the air and was able to locate what he considered to be her best choice for food options amongst the mulling of smells. Aergo nudged the back of Kitaj's knees with his nose to signal her to follow. They worked their way through the crowd to a beckoning food stand near the middle of the pavilion. Roasting on spits were rows of small Bantanese hens, an array of sea crawlers and lizards, with bright colored chunks of various Léohet fruits and vegetables between them. Kitaj knew little of the Léohetwin language but attempted a few words to inquire about purchasing a meal. The older gentleman serving her behind the stand was a native Léohet. Kitaj saw, not only from his thoughts but from his appearance, that he spent his life happily living on the coast. He wore a short beige Gicel fur that covered most of his beautifully designed tribal shirt. His wavy light brown and grey hair was Sun streaked with blonde, and his olive skin was tanned even darker from years of exposure to their Sun. The white shells he wore pierced through his tragus ear points were highlighted against his dark complexion. He winked at Kitaj with his secondary eyelid that vertically crossed the large blue of his eye and white iris, and laughed in a playful and relaxed manner in response to Kitaj's attempt to speak his language. The vendor commended Kitaj on her effort as he spoke perfect Midangardian, that was slightly accented by the rolling ease of his Léohet tongue. She purchased a mixed portion and eagerly began eating as her eyes continued to scan the crowd for Rûni's friend. Kitaj could tell the Léohet vendor was watching to see if she was enjoying her meal. She smiled and nodded as she chewed and swallowed. To Kitaj's response, the man clapped his hands in joy above his head and smiled broadly. Aergo nudged Kitaj's side. She knew exactly why Aergo wanted her attention. He *had* found the best food in the pavilion for her; the least she could do would be to share it with him. To show her gratitude, Kitaj held out a large sea crawler for Aergo, which he graciously snatched from her fingers and swallowed in two bites. Kitaj rubbed Aergo under the chin, and returned to searching the crowd as they walked forward.

The music and savory, sweet air of the Léohet pavilion slowly faded as Kitaj and Aergo neared the Sweduetwin section. White reflective tents covered the entire area to block their venue from Midangard's end of summer Sun; for prolonged daylight exposure was intolerable for the Swedus. Kitaj marveled at how these twin worlds that shared a binding moon, and originally the same inhabitants, differed so greatly from one another. The tents' entrances were rolled back to feature samples and goods they had for sale. Day-glow bright banners, backed with black, were displayed high above, lining the aisleways between the tents, and advertising each vendor's purpose.

Kitaj's eyes caught on a banner depicting three ornate illuminated bees against a honeycomb design— and she felt involuntarily drawn to it. Aergo noticed the shift within her, and was immediately on edge as he followed her. Kitaj had a sinking feeling in the pit of her stomach that caught her as she walked toward the tent's entrance. Despite her foreboding feeling, Kitaj was compelled to enter.

Once inside, she saw barrels of mead lining the tent walls, and potential customers ogling over samples. There were tables covered with jars of honey, dried herbs, and pots brimming with night blooming flowers. Her eyes drifted through the displays of the tent until they locked on a large honeycomb. It was encased in glass and mica and on display near the back of the tent. Luminous bees were busying themselves between the comb's glass casing. Their ever moving light cast a glow in the otherwise shadowed area of the tent and gave Kitaj a clear view of the three Swedu men that were standing by its edge. Their manner and appearance were in complete contrast to her encounter with the Léohetwin vendor. By nature, the Swedus were not as welcoming at first meeting and did not trust as easily as their etwin-kynd relatives, the Léohets. The Swedus' reserved behavior stemmed from a history of being taunted and unfounded fears toward them. This ridicule was due to their physical traits as night dwellers. Their pale veined skin and white eyes often made others wary of their kynd.

Adding to the three men's intimidating appearance, each man wore the traditional Swedu black garments; two wore sleeveless clothes, while the third was shirtless. Their attire reflected their attempt to combat the Midangard temperatures that were uncomfortably warm for the Swedus' thin skin. Their choice of attire inadvertently accentuated their structures, making evident that the Swedus were slightly more muscular in build than their longer and leaner related Léohets.

The shirtless male's appearance distinguished him further from his two companions. Swedu etwin-kynd were characteristically thought of as having dark or black hair, but this young man's was almost colorless with only a hint of glossy silver. He also had permanent inking under his skin that spanned across his chest and back. His body art was of an intricate and distinct tribal design. The design showed similarities to the art of Léohet tribes, but Swedu art had an unmistakable aggressive edge and weight to its lines and imagery. The ink itself was of phosphorus make, with heightened colors that glowed with a life of its own under the dim light of the tent. Kitaj watched as the young man spoke solemnly to the eldest of the three. She could read his intentions were sincere in the words he spoke to his elder, though she could not read their meaning.

Kitaj's attention diverted to the elder Swedu. He had remained silent while the young man spoke, but an eruption approached, boiling up inside him. Kitaj could feel Aergo shuttering beside her, trying to hold his form within the tension filled atmosphere. She held tight to Aergo's neck and instinctively sought protection behind a table before the elder Swedu reacted by turning around and throwing a jar of dried herbs and a potted flower at the young Swedu's head. The young man ducked, unrattled as if he had anticipated this reaction. The jar and plant smashed to the ground. Customers from other worlds who could not translate the onslaught of vulgarities the Swedu elder launched at the younger could still decipher the unmistakable unrest of the elder Swedu. Again, the young man stood very still and accepted the verbal assault with dignity and by no means tried to defend himself.

In that moment, another young Swedu, wearing a protective mica visor over his eyes, entered the tent. His arms were loaded down with different foods from the Léohet pavilion. He was obviously bringing meals to his companions. At first sight of the elder's upset, he maintained his steady pace and gently turned and walked back out of the tent. Kitaj and Aergo exchanged a look of agreement, concluding this must be a family business argument.

Kitaj could not get a fixed read from the Swedu relatives. All she could tell was that the relayed emotions from the elder were a reaction to unexpected and unpleasant news. Kitaj sensed there was another party involved, waiting outside the tent, who was doing her best to be as small and unseen as possible. The young woman had done well to conceal herself and her feelings until the elder's eruption. Anxiety for those she loved radiated from her. Kitaj felt a gravitating connection to this unseen person as well as the need to find her, and slipped out of the tent with Aergo close at her side. Kitaj discovered the young woman behind the tent, nervously biting her nails. The foreboding feeling that had gripped Kitaj earlier returned at the sight of this stranger. Kitaj's notion was not of a present danger but of some looming future event. She could not help herself noticing how the young woman's striking appearance differed from her Swedu relatives. She also wore the traditional black, distinguishing her as Swedu, but beyond that, her features told another story. The woman's hair was very long, wavy, and a surprising shade of medium brown. She wore it up in a messy twist that was held back by a Léohet heirloom hair comb made from shell. The comb itself struck Kitaj as a puzzling mystery. Its unusual design and shape seemed somehow out of place for its applied use. With the young woman's hair swept away from her face and neck, Kitaj could see only a hint of veins was visible through her complexion of pale gold. She also noticed the woman's worried eyes were an unprecedented icy green surrounding her white irises. A bright colored totem inking of combined Swedu and Léohet design covered the inside of her left arm and extended down to her wrist. Kitaj discerned from her unique characteristics that one of the young woman's parents, most likely her mother, must be Léohetwin. Kitaj sensed the etwin woman's prime source of concern growing within her; it was for the one she was protecting closest to her heart. When the young woman caught sight of Kitaj and Aergo, she became immediately defensive.

Kitaj tried to reassure her, "I'm sorry to startle you. I was only concerned. I hope tempers will be soothed and in your favor again soon."

The young etwin woman noticed the Tjetajat cloak clasp on Kitaj's shoulder and immediately understood how this person unknown to her could possibly have some knowledge of her situation. Her expression began to soften.

"Thank you for your kyndness. It will all be well in time," the young woman replied.

"Can I assist you in any way?" Kitaj asked.

"I don't believe so, but it is generous of you to offer," the young woman stated, "I should probably go join them now."

Kitaj nodded to her as she and Aergo backed away and watched her apprehensively enter the tent.

There were no more outbursts; just an overwhelming feeling of combined disappointment and worry exuding from the elder Swedu, matched with the anxiety from the others. Kitaj felt she needed to remove herself from their presence. Their feelings were thick in the atmosphere and were overwhelming her and she needed to compose herself.

The Gicel venue they were approaching carried its own emotional weight. She wondered what she would feel, visiting the Gicel section for the first time, knowing it was the world on which the father she had never met had died. She could not help but ponder how his last waking visions of Gicelfolde were of war-torn snow and ice, and nothing like the bejeweled surroundings in crystal that lay ahead of her. She found herself desperately needing to find a place to sit. But before she could reach one, Kitaj broke down. The intensity of the scene at the Swedu tent and the onslaught of the public's and her private emotions had overtaken her. Aergo escorted her off the main path around the worlds' sections to a secluded spot behind one of the last white Swedu tents. Kitaj thought she was prepared to deflect whatever came through to her but found herself to be proven wrong. Aergo looked at her to ask if she was soon to recover.

"Yes, I'll be fine. Just wasn't ready," she managed to say.

Kitaj took a few deep breaths and focused her thoughts back to her original happier intent for the evening. Those thoughts, she knew, could carry her through.

She hoped for Aergo's understanding, "I truly could use your help. You can recognize Rûni and his friends. Would you consider us going in opposite directions, so we might cover more ground to find them?"

Aergo looked up at her with a lowered head and leaned all his full weight against her leg.

"I didn't think so," she said.

Kitaj regained her composure, along with a new sense of annoyance she felt towards her best friend. She raised the hood of her cloak, with the excuse of blocking the chill of the Gicel section, but Aergo knew her main purpose was to conceal any remaining traces of distress that could be found on her face. Together, they rushed through the Gicel pavilion onto the Vangard's.

"There you are! I have been looking everywhere for you!"

Dagen and Rûni were abruptly awakened by the booming voice of Brieg. He had returned triumphant, or so he exclaimed, from his father's summons. The Sun hung low at the edge of the forest valley, indicating Dagen and Rûni's nap had claimed the remaining afternoon and into early evening.

"The opening processional will be starting soon, we have to find a good view! I don't want to miss anymore. This is too *important*!" Brieg said, as he encouraged his friends to stand and follow him.

Dagen was caught by Brieg's use of the word "important." His emphasis carried extra weight and intensity. Dagen recalled his recent epiphany to the festival's circumstances and thought again of Brieg's position. Brieg was a master of redirection when it came to his feelings. But, with that one word Brieg had slipped. It made Dagen wonder what might have transpired during Brieg's meeting with his father.

⚘

Kitaj and Aergo had made their way to the middle of the Vane's displays. Amongst the beautiful garden-like areas of the Vangard pavilion, Kitaj's appreciation for its majesty was waning as her frustration continued to grow; there was still no sight of the person she sought. She could feel a low humming vibration; much like what she felt building in the air when they met. She knew the vibration must be alerting her that he was near, but she had no possible way of knowing in which direction he could be. The emotions projecting from the people surrounding her did nothing to help hone her perception of his location.

While horns blared to signify the processional for the Winter's Nátt opening ceremony would soon commence, Kitaj hoped she would be able to spot him along the inner borders of the festival grounds. Spectators and vendors alike left their pavilions for the official showing. She and Aergo hurried to find a good view before the crowd gathered around the grassy center of the festival grounds.

The crowd thickened. Aergo maneuvered their way through the sea of people by pushing them aside and growling as he went, until he and Kitaj reached the front of the Vangard section. They were fortunate to have claimed standing room near the raised seating set aside for the honored Vane. The unobstructed view gave Kitaj the opportunity to search the crowd fronts of most of the worlds' venues. She held to hope as she watched the Dryhtens from each world assemble and stand at attention in front of the world section they represented.

As drums beat in a slow rhythm, the Dryhtens step forward from each side until they neared the ground's center. They formed two lines on the grassy plain, creating a direct path that extended from the field's entrance to its farthest end, where the Aesingard section was centrally located.

Brieg rushed his groggy friends into The Ende venue in hopes of finding a space near its front, but as they neared the prime locations Brieg had scouted earlier, they saw they were already filled. The drums continued to beat as the Dryhtens positioned themselves to receive the royalty of the Nine Worlds. Frustrated, Brieg searched the crowd to see any possible opening that could give them a better view. The general consensus must have been that it was more appealing being in close proximity to the eerie Ende Dwellers and their followers than it was to stand with their backs to the Swedus; for Brieg saw a few locations left where the crowd was thin and the views were clear from the Sweduetwin area. He urged Dagen and Rûni to follow him. They hurried behind the Aesingard and Vangard sections, but when they began to pass behind the Gicelfolde's, Dagen stopped.

"Swedu? Brieg, you know it's too soon for me to go there," stated Dagen.

"It's the best location left to watch. Come on!" pleaded Brieg.

"I don't think I can," said Dagen.

"You couldn't be recognized! Stop stalling, we're going to miss the beginning!" yelled Brieg.

"Go on without me," Dagen yelled back.

Brieg shook his head and said, " Meet us at the Vangard's afterwards!" and stalked off.

Rûni looked confused as to what he should do. Dagen waved to him to go on. Rûni hesitated but decided to follow Brieg. He had been with Dagen all day; it was only fair, he thought with some relief. Dagen went in the opposite direction. If he was supposed to meet them at the Vangard pavilion afterwards, he might as well go there to watch the opening ceremony. He found a planter box at the back of the crowd that served as a stand for him to look over everyone's heads, and have a full view of the ceremony. Dagen wondered if it was possible that the girl with the green and blue eyes could be anywhere near.

As he wishfully searched the anxious crowd, a member of the crowd caught his attention at the front of the Vangard section, and he wondered, *What must that dog be thinking of this spectacle?*

ﻋﻠ

Kitaj continued to search the crowd across from her for familiar faces. Her knowing of his presence was stronger than ever, as was the oppressing layer of muddled emotions surrounding her.

Her anticipation and anxiety were consuming her to the point of desperation as her mind questioned, *Would I even see him if he were right under my nose?*

Kitaj jumped from the sudden sound of horns joining the drums to announce the arrival of the Nine Worlds' ruling powers. The light was beginning to fade and the torches around the edges began to shine prominently. The first to arrive were the Vane. Beautiful men and women, dressed in gossamer fabrics, glided into view and made their way down the aisle. Some sprinkled fragrant flowers and herbs, accentuating the path for their nobles' grand entrance. Some waved their arms in a graceful fashion or spun together with hands placed about each other's waists. Their movements were poised and fluid. Musicians followed, playing stringed instruments to accompany the already present horns and drums in the background. The procession momentarily stopped in its place.

ﻋﻠ

Brieg watched as his father stepped out of line and turned to face the crowd. Lygus Ingólf stood at the top of the festival entrance, in front of the Midangard section. It was his duty, as the Lerakrey Dryhten, to announce the entrance of the ultra-beings: the Vane, the Ende Dwellers, and the Aesir.

The Vane and the Aesir were the influential powers guiding the Nine Worlds; they were very similar in appearance and shared the same extreme longevity. Their own home worlds, Vangard and Aesingard, ran course in the same cycle around the Sun, though at complete opposites of season. It was these two forces that had initiated the war and severed the alliances of other worlds. In the end, the Vane conceded to the Aesir but maintained their status. The world powers carried forward as uneasy allies. The sight of Vangard nobles sitting next to the King and Queen of Aesingard was a hopeful gesture to solidify any remaining doubts about their post-war alliance.

Lygus Ingólf's voice carried with the booming qualities of a fierce commander and hinted of his aristocracy, as he presented the Vane's leaders, "Ing Fré, and Bereness Fréa, of Vangard."

The music changed to a formal processional, fittingly characteristic of the Vane's appetite for artistic expression and refinement. Two opulent chariots appeared at the entrance carrying The Ing and Bereness. The chariots were pulled by two large, imposing lynxes. Vane guards flanked either side of them while an entourage of servers, artists, poets, and handlers followed in fashion. The music soared, as the brother and sister nobles entered of the festival grounds. The crowd gasped at the Vane's display of opulence. The Ing and his sister were images of symmetry by natural design and arguably two of the most elegant beings within the Nine Worlds. They were accentuated by numerous Gicel crystals adorning their headdresses and clothes that shone brightly in the fading after light. They proceeded in time to the music across the open grounds to their stands at the Vangard pavilion. The two nobles disembarked at their arrival and their entourage followed. Once all were settled into their exclusive stands, their music concluded.

Next, Dryhten Ingólf announced, " The Ende."

His statement was all the formal ceremony that was required. Ende Dwellers did not go by names, and could not be distinguished one from another. Each appeared shrouded in cloaks that covered their features completely. Occasionally, a glimpse could be caught of one of their thin knobby hands. It was unknown, even to King Wodan, if there was a defined leader amongst them, or if the Ende Dwellers rotated the responsibility. Even The Ende's own world symbol was not of their making or concern. Their official emblem was a royally commissioned Heítaned design, illustrating the Eormensyl's Sacred Passages to The Ende's gate and the outer realm. Five Ende Dwellers crossed the field. Dryhten Ingólf felt there should be some ceremony to their arrival and had arranged for drums to play as they crossed. The End Dwellers paid no attention to their entrance music. All crossed at their own pace to reach their section on the other side of the Aesingard venue where they were greeted by three small groups of devoted followers. Characteristically, the Ende Dwellers showed no acknowledgment of their admirers' presence.

Last, he announced, "Wodan, King of Aesingard, Ruler of the Nine Worlds, Keeper of the Sacred Passages of Eormensyl, and Frija, Queen of Aesingard, Sovereign of Unity, and Matron of the Nine Worlds."

The crowd erupted as horns blared the traditional processional music of Aesingard. King Wodan and Queen Frija entered, side by side, on horseback. The King's grey and white steed, Slepsil, possessed twice the speed of other horses and was straining for his lead against the slow pace of the processional. The Queen's black mare showed no signs of agitation and walked with ease in front of the noisy crowd. Their arrival was presented with fewer flourishes than the Vane but was displayed as a show of the King's strength and veracity. The Aesir royals were accompanied by guards carrying banners bearing the emblems of each world in the kingdom, and Wodan intentionally wore the breast plate from his ceremonial armor, depicting the Nine Worlds stationed around their Sun, united by the branch portals of the Eormensyl. The King had purposely arranged this show of alliance to illustrate his intentions for the Winter's Nátt gathering. His soul reason for insisting all Nine Worlds attend the festival was to publicly acknowledge the renewed unification between worlds. This opportunity took many years to arrive for the Aesir and Vane. But to the other worlds of the realm, the time differences in the counting of years brought unity much sooner; leaving those worlds with much fresher scars.

The King and Queen rode down the field until they reached their private box at the head of the Aesingard pavilion, where they dismounted and took their places as the center attraction. Dryhten Ingólf drew the attention of the crowd to quiet themselves and remain standing.

King Wodan and Queen Frija politely acknowledged the Ing and Bereness to their left and the Ende Dwellers to their right before the King began to speak.

"We gather today as one realm, united in our diversity and strengths; displaying the best of each of our worlds in a celebration of our vast cultures. We come to honor our shared Sun and express our gratitude for the realm's unification through the Eormensyl. As the Eormensyl moves into its slumbering state with Midangard's approaching winter, we renew our promise that it will awaken in the New Year to the warmth of summer, and find its realm flourishing and whole. As a gesture of renewal, to strengthen the bonds between our worlds, I wish to restore the old ways of the Wild Hunt. It pleases me to announce this Hunt will be open to all our worlds, and that its hunting grounds shall no longer be exclusive to Midangard. The Hunt will return to its glory and be conducted on all our worlds simultaneously. The selected game will be announced at the closing of Winter's Nátt," announced the King.

The crowd rumbled with excitement and speculation. Small eruptions sprung up within some of the different sections. It had been over fifty Midangardian years since the old ways of the Hunt had been observed. The King showed restraint as he waited for the crowd to settle so he could conclude his speech. Lygus Ingólf recognized the agitated crowd needed to calm and signaled for silence. It was missed by most of the enthralled group, causing him to resort to signaling the horns to blow to regain their attention. The crowd again settled for the King to conclude his speech. King Wodan knew there was no reason to prolong; his audience's anticipation for the opening was at its peak.

"I declare this Winter's Nátt celebration to officially begin!" proclaimed King Wodan.

The King's statement was met with an uproar in every direction. As the crowd was cheering, a Midangardian band assembled in the grassy center of the festival grounds. Without announcement, they began to play music on pipes, drums, and strings. The melody was a joyful jig that matched the enthusiasm spreading throughout the crowd.

Royal servers began weaving throughout the audience, distributing cups of mead and glow wine, compliments of the Aesir and the Vane's combined efforts. The gesture was well received by a very appreciative crowd.

Running out onto the field were more Midangardian performers. They were in matching dress of the forest's colors and carrying long bright yellow scarves. They encircled the band and danced around them, weaving in and out in a joyous reel. Their yellow scarves trailed behind them, jerking, and arching in an interlaced pattern to mimic the rays of their Sun. The music's tempo quickened, as the men and women locked arms around each other's waists and spun, waving their scarves as a ring of fire. The dancing couples broke apart and ran out from the center, as a child, representing the Eormensyl, began to run half way around the Sun in the opposite direction. Her costume looked similar to a tree trunk with branches spanning in eight directions. The center of her trunk held a large illuminated opalescent stone, representing the Heart of Eormensyl, its life's essence. Smaller stones of the same were inlaid along the branches, characterizing the Eormensyl's inner portal paths. When the child reached one-quarter of the distance around the Sun, the dancers ran backwards toward their starting spots as a tighter center group encircling the band. Reaching their original placement, they quickly recoiled the scarves to give the appearance of shortening the Sun's rays until they disappeared. The dancers turned their backs to the crowd and pulled strings connected to the rolls of their collars, unfurling grey capes down each one's back, depicting the blanketing of the Sun by the grey winter clouds. The melody converted from a lively round into a soft lullaby. The crowd responded with stillness. The Eormensyl child's light grew dimmer as she slowed, yawning and stretching her arms above her head as she reached the halfway mark around the Sun. A woman, representing Winter's Nátt, dressed in a black flowing cloak studded with glittering white gems, walked onto the field. She picked up the Eormensyl child and carried her in her arms the remaining half around the winter's Sun as the lullaby ended to close the performance. It was an anticipated moment synonymous with Midangard's Winter's Nátt and the crowd erupted. The celebration was formally underway.

The Midangardian group dispensed from the grassy middle as the Léohetwin performers entered the grounds from their pavilion. They were dressed in bright colored tribal prints with bands of white shells around their wrists, heads, and ankles that jingled as they moved. The bright white and colors were offset by each performer's dark golden to olive complexion, still highly visible in the waning light of sunset. The Léohets were lead onto the field by members playing metal drums that gave out a tinny sound. Other musicians blew into large horns carved from towering palms and enormous shells. Their sound was deep and rang out like the calls from the depths of Mer.

They took a similar formation as the Midangardian performers, with the musicians set center as the dancers encircled them. The music continued as the Léohets told their story through their movements. Each, with the swaying of arms and stepping in unison, was conveying the beauty of their world, as they sang in chorus in their native language. Their movements told the story of their oceans, clear water, white sands, lush palms and soothing breezes. They concluded by circling the center with alternating bows, turning from one side and stepping with curved arms and backs, creating the illusion of rolling waves. The wave movement masked the Léohet performers that were moving to the farthest end of the field. With the assistance of Heítaned calculations, the Léohet show's transition coincided perfectly with the oncoming darkness and made room for the Swedu performance to join them.

Sweduetwin participants, covered by dark cloaks, were barely noticed as they placed themselves in a circular formation to match their Léohet twin kynd. A new tune emerged from the apparent void on the field. It was an exuberant accompaniment to the soothing rhythm of Léohet performance. Though more aggressive in sound, with heavier drums and lower horns, it blended beautifully with the Léohetwins' music and served to show the unity of the Swedu with their sister world. The Swedu performers discarded their cloaks to reveal their forms covered in day-glow designs of paint and permanent inkings. Their glow was so bright, it illuminated the Léohet performers. The Winter's Nátt audience was enthralled by the spectacle and their own cheers momentarily overtook the music from the field.

The Swedus movements were a match to their musical accompaniment. Their powerful gestures and dynamic stomping were in contrast to the soothing Léohet staging. But like the combined musical arrangements, their expressive implementations complimented one another.

Kitaj recognized one of the brilliantly inked performers as the young man with silver hair she had seen earlier in the beekeepers' tent. The young Swedu positioned himself closely to the Léohets and was met by one of their male performers in a mid position between the two circles. It was only when the silver-haired Swedu removed a dark cloth covering his left hand, did Kitaj realize he had carried something to the Léohet performer across from him. The drop of the cloth revealed a large bright red glowing orb that radiated an entrancing aura of sanguine around both etwin-kynd. The silver-haired Swedu presented the orb to the Léohet performer, who held it high above his head with one hand. Members of the crowd who understood the meaning of the orb cheered wildly, but Kitaj, as well as many others, were uncertain what the orb signified. This performance had not been conducted within the lifetimes of most of the audience. Kitaj held her breath as the Léohet performer slowly raised his fist to meet the orb. With one swift strike, he sent the orb sailing. The silver-haired Swedu ran to a position on the outer edge of his circle. The orb's path naturally curved around the Swedu formation and was met by another member, who threw the orb to the far edge of their circle. The orb was speedily sent around the Swedus' circle and met back with the Léohet who had initiated it. Next, he sent the orb flying to a member of his own formation in the opposite direction. The red orb was sent around both performing circles in the pattern of infinite design. Kitaj now understood, this display was to illustrate the binding of these two worlds to each other by the path of their shared moon, the Mahyna Ula. Another ovation of approval was sent up by the spectators.

As their joined exhibition concluded, the Léohet performers departed the field, giving the Swedus center stage. The Swedus' music deepened with heavy tribal drums beating and rattling at the heartbeats of a mesmerized crowd. The Ula orb disappeared with the appearance of several multicolored glowing spheres. Their colors constantly shifted, alluding to movement within them. The Swedu performers threw the spheres high into the air and caught them on their backs and bounced them to another performer to catch. The spheres' light trailed from person to person as they bounced in every direction. The intensity built from the increasing tempo and swiftness of the Swedu's movements. Their glowing, patterned forms spun, jumped, and stomped until the music's peak, then a sudden darkness and silence.

Dagen had a bird's eye view from his perch and watched as the entire audience leapt with amazement at the Swedu's conclusion, even King Wodan appeared moved. Yet Dagen was aware the stunning performance was unfortunately lost on him. His mind remained too preoccupied to fully appreciate what was directly in front of him.

The night torches were lit and revealed an empty field with a large group assembled near its entrance. The Heítaned, Gicels and Fyrs had combined their talents for the final presentation. The Heítaned had placed oversized drums on either side of the entrance, that towered over the of tallest of their kynd. They had also placed a large free standing metal box, laid out in a horizontal fashion, directly in the entry way. Most of the onlookers were unfamiliar with this elongated ancient instrument and were puzzled at its purpose. The box's sides were covered in metal panels and the top appeared to be composed of separate plated bars. An older Heítaned gentleman stood behind the metallic instrument and was accompanied by two others atop ladders posing with mallets ready to strike each massive drum.

The Gicels positioned themselves on either side the Heítaned by setting six tall monolithic slabs of brightly colored crystals in front of the mammoth drums. There was one Gicel to each crystal monolith. Each slab was back-lit by strategically placed lanterns, causing the crystals to emit a contradictory icy heat.

Four Fyrs stood on far ends of either side, awaiting their part. They had backed the Gicel and the Heítaned's display with several rows of large metal canisters. At first glance, these canons appeared to be some type of weaponry rather than a source of entertainment. Fyrfolde's natural resources of molten metals, ignitable powders and accelerants had been combined with the Heítaned's' ingenuity, and the crowd was about to be treated to an aerial light display rivaling those of a bygone era.

Their presentation began with a low metallic tonal hum. As it began to grow, the Gicelian crystals burned brighter. The Heítaned gentleman stood at the metal board with his long fingers spread above the individual bars. Each finger's movement changed the instrument's tone and created a richer hum. The crystal slabs reacted to the tones and projected their own high pitched sounds, similar to that of chimes. Each slab produced its own array of sounds as they responded to the various metallic tones activating the crystals' cores. The production was not of a musical tune but as a series of notes reverberating through the constant low hum.

Kitaj began to feel very odd; the hum was seeping into her. She felt it throughout her skin, moving into bones and to the depths of her core. The sensation was unsettling and she felt she might be ill, lose consciousness, or that her physical being might possibly disintegrate. The hum was affecting Aergo's hearing and his canine ears began to hurt, but he could sense the effects were more extreme for Kitaj. She reached down to Aergo and grabbed a large amount of hair on his back with too much force. Aergo yelped, but Kitaj was unaware of her own strength and did not release her grip. She could not think; she could not move. She was confined in torture.

The tone changed to a higher pitch and Kitaj's pain and panic lifted in an the instant. Her bones still carried the deep ache, but the feeling of being hollowed from the inside out had left her. She looked to Aergo, who looked back to her with no understanding of what had just occurred. She began to laugh out of relief from her release. Aergo furrowed his brow with concern for her. Considering she had never encountered a crowd of such vast size, in addition to her response at entering the Gicel pavilion, and her reaction to the Heítaned's' resonating hum, Aergo feared Kitaj's senses were overrun. He concluded he should remove her from the grounds as soon as they could possibly make way. Aergo continued to stare at Kitaj as she fought to contain her laughter.

The presentation continued with a deeper layering of notes. As the Fyrs moved behind the drums to man the canisters, large thundering booms echoed through the night air with the Heítaned lowering their mallets to the massive, taut surface of their drums. With each strike, the Fyrs lit the nested canisters and launched them from their individual catapults. The Heítaned team had configured each launch to a specific trajectory, creating a synchronized bombardment of colorful crackling sparks exploding over the night sky.

The crowd ducked and shrieked at the sudden bursts and blanket of shining embers, while the Midangardian, Swedu, and Léohet performers returned to the field to improvise a combined performance with the Heítaned, Gicels and Fyrs. The combinations of sounds and beats flowed into a rhythm of its own, creating intoxicating measures that beckoned the audience to join in. People began to spill onto the field, and melding in with the performances in a mass celebration. Some took up instruments and props or joined in dances. A few climbed on top the Heítaned drums and bounced about. Others ran on the field in aimless joviality. In the midst of the celebration's frenzy, King Wodan quietly exited his stand, followed by his brothers and guards, while Queen Frija joined the Ing and Bereness to enjoy the delight of witnessing their worlds celebrating as one realm again.

Brieg badly wished to join the thick of the mob, but Rûni nudged him ever closer to the Vangard section. Brieg bounced onward when he spotted Dagen high above the swirling crowd. Upon reaching him, Brieg grabbed Dagen's legs and hoisted him onto his shoulders. Dagen protested his position but Brieg ignored him. Rûni saw Brieg's stunt in the heavy crowd as a recipe for disaster and urged his friend to put Dagen down. Brieg conceded and released Dagen. As they moved forward, Dagen found himself near the edge of the field on a patch of ground that noticeably felt warmer to him. As he moved through it, he felt small surging zaps meet his fingertips, causing him to flinch. Little did he know, he had just walked through the spot where Kitaj had been standing. He spun around to see what could have created the surge but could find nothing of the cause. He knew he had felt something similar the day before, and it gave him hope. She had to be near!

Aergo nudged Kitaj's side to guide her through the crowd. His concerns for her grew with her unsteady manner. She continued to giggle uncontrollably and walked as if she were inebriated. He was uncertain as to what had initially altered her, but could see the rhythm of the celebration was overtaking her. Kitaj danced along as they moved through the boisterous crowd. Without warning, she broke away from him and ran toward the ground's entrance. She halted at the Heítaned drums. Aergo stood dumbfounded as Kitaj was lifted by the two Heítaned to the top of one of the large drums. She joined in jumping along with the other celebrators. Aergo dashed through the sea of merrymakers to reach her. Each bounce sent her higher into the air. Kitaj's hood fell back, sending her untamed curls flailing around her. Aergo waited for her below. A perplexing mix of feelings coursed through him as he watched Kitaj. He was concerned because of her uncharacteristic behavior, and watchful for her safety, but seeping into his worry was an increasing amount of pride. He had never seen her in such a state of release. With each bound, she threw her arms out wider. The crowd below began to notice the high bounds of the people atop the tall drums. Each ascension was accompanied by excited yells of genuine concern. Kitaj no longer cared. She felt unabashedly alive.

ۚۚ

Brieg joined in the nearby yelling before knowing the reason for the uproar. Out of the corner of his eye, the flying girl with wild hair drew his attention. He bumped Dagen in the back to point out the joyful scene and impending accident. The moment was too reckless to end well, but too enthralling to stop watching. Dagen turned around to see what Brieg wanted him to witness. Rûni turned as well to see what the commotion was and immediately recognized Kitaj as she flew up into the air. Rûni caught his breath. Dagen watched as she and the others on the drum soared higher with each bound. Something inside Dagen caught. He knew before it happened; the girl missed the drum on the return landing and disappeared on the opposite side. Screams were heard from the direction of her fall as people scattered. Dagen found himself running toward the accident. Rûni was on his heels and Brieg was following behind trying to push his way through the crowd. When Dagen reached the tall drum, there was no sign of the girl. The witnesses stood dumbfounded and confused.

"Something caught her and carried her off, I say!" said a stunned bystander.

"It was dark, I couldn't see, but it was big and had orange glowing eyes!" said another eyewitness.

"How much have you had to drink? You're seeing things!" said another.

"I am not!" said the bystander indignantly, as he hiccuped. "If it's not true, then where's the girl?" he added.

"Where is she?" Dagen demanded, and turned to Brieg. "That had to be her— the way she moved was the same as when I saw her in the glen."

Brieg tried to reassure his distraught friend, "You can't know that for sure," but realized his statement was the exact wrong thing to say and tried to correct himself, "But, if it was her, she obviously didn't hit the ground."

Dagen thought back to what he believed he saw coming after her when she fell in the pond, which in the end appeared to be nothing more than her horse. Now, she had disappeared, caught by something large and dark. Dagen's thoughts spiraled. He didn't know if he should think some creature had been following her and now she was its captive or if there was some reasonable explanation for what had occurred.

"What did it look like? Did anyone else see it? Does anyone know who she is?" Dagen pleaded with the dispensing crowd.

The celebration was over. No one cared what had happened; it was time to leave. Dagen looked at the trampled ground to see if he could find any signs or tracks. Nothing was conclusive. There were too many overlapping footprints to make out any distinguishing marks. Dagen grabbed the bystander who stated he saw "orange glowing eyes." The man's attention was focused on finding somewhere to lay down and sleep off his intoxicated state.

"Which way did it go?" Dagen asked, as he shook the man.

The eyewitness clumsily pointed in a direction, and Dagen took off into the darkness. Rûni and Brieg called after him and tried to follow, but lost him as well.

⚓

Brieg and Rûni searched for Dagen and the missing woman for most of the night without luck. When they could barely see their hands in front of their faces in the pitch darkness of the woods, they decided their attempt was futile and abandoned their search to return to the Idle Sickles. Rûni was unable to sleep, and not from Brieg's snoring that could be heard through the inn's walls. He too, was concerned for Kitaj's safety and concluded his best course of action was to go to the Order at first light and make sure she had returned unharmed. Rûni also deduced that her mother and other seers of the Tjetajat would know exactly where she was if she had yet to return. His plan felt right to him and was enough to give him some reassurance. His concern that Dagen had found Kitaj weighed just as heavily on him. Multitudes of scenarios raced through his mind, leaving him wishing he had inherited his mother's gift, so he might know these answers for himself.

Before dawn's arrival, Rûni sneaked out of the inn. He noticed on leaving, there was no sign that Dagen had returned. His need for answers compelled him directly to the Order's gates. The gates were still locked. Rûni sat impatiently waiting for anyone to let him inside. His wait was short, for Corynth came out to meet him in the dark of morning.

"You are concerned for Kitaj. How kynd of you, Rûni. I saw her this morning before coming to the Order. She was still asleep. Apparently, she is over tired from last night's festivities," offered Corynth as she opened the gate for Rûni to enter.

It was no surprise to Rûni that Kitaj's mother read his concern for her daughter, but one of her words struck him as very out of place. Corynth had said the word "apparently."

Was she guessing at what Kitaj had done the night before? Rûni dismissed his thought, *It was one word. It meant nothing.* He was exhausted and over thinking the entire matter.

"Do come in dear, she will arrive later, I am sure. Until then you can help me," Corynth said with a smile. She stopped and held her hand up for Rûni to wait while she read him more deeply, "As for the matter of your friend and his interest in Kitaj, considering his circumstances, I have to say I agree with your decision not to tell him. But Rûni, I must warn you. These matters have a way of surfacing. Tread carefully," Corynth warned, and paused again, "I see you are uncertain if she might share in this interest. If I may advise you, it might be best if you did not give Kitaj opportunity to access this information until after the initiation rites, when there will be nothing to be done of it," Corynth said kyndly.

Rûni's face turned bright red with his embarrassment and shame. Kitaj's mother knew he was deceiving his best friend and his reasons why, and yet, she agreed with him. Rûni's embarrassment faded to a sense of relief and appreciation that Corynth understood him.

"There, there now," said Corynth, as she patted Rûni's arm, "Try not to worry."

"Pardon me for my lack of knowing, but even with me out of Kitaj's sight until our initiation, won't she be able to read about this from you?" asked Rûni."

"Don't concern yourself on that. Your mother did not get the chance to teach you, but we have our ways of keeping our secrets close. You, my dear, are an open book. Since you will be initiated soon, I see no harm in a few private lessons to help you along. I can make sure Kitaj is stationed at the farthest distance from our work so she won't even be aware you are on the grounds," said Corynth.

"You would do that for me?" asked Rûni, and replied, "Thank you."

"Yes, but it truly is in everyone's best interest. There is no reason why we can't begin now," said Corynth, as she ushered Rûni inside.

CHAPTER 6
VEILED TRUTHS

Frija and Wodan had played their official roles for the opening ceremony as tradition dictated. They kept up the pretense of a unified king and queen when public appearances were required. The importance of appearing unified to the leaders and representatives of the other worlds was crucial for mending relations among the healing realm. Mending the kingdom was a slow process for everyone. Tensions still ran high between rival worlds, but efforts were being made to restore faith in one another.

Such efforts could not be said for the marriage of the King and Queen. Wodan and Frija were rarely in the same room. Privately, few words were passed between one another, and always with a strained cordiality. Most communications passing between the King and Queen were dispensed through the hands of messengers. The details of their messages were clipped and short, Fortunately for both, they were only required to be present for the opening and closing ceremonies of Winter's Nátt. An entire Midangardian week in close quarters with the Vane at Kestel Midlen, and being under the watchful care of their host, Dryhten Ingólf, would be straining for both members of the royal couple to keep up pretenses. Discretely, as they had done for many years on Aesir, Wodan would continue to have Frija followed to gain information, and Frija would continue to find ways to slip past the King's spies— or so she thought. Her foremost concern was with her loyal supporters, who put themselves at great risk to help her. On Midangard, her allies lie within the Tjetajat. Wodan was wise not to break the established chain of communication that Frija had with their Central Council. The more allies she had, the more likely he could intercept her news and triumph in their shared quest.

After departing the opening ceremony, Wodan had retired to his private quarters at Midlen. His evening's plans were the same as they had been for most of his wakeful nights— pace through until morning, steadfast for any new intelligence that might arrive within a given moment. Wodan couldn't sleep— not since his waking of The Essence. His fatigued mind made the King as easily provoked as he was distracted, and infamous for his sudden outbursts. His obsession and the absence of joy in his life only fed into his bitterness, anger, weariness, and paranoia. His brothers, Wiljo and Wæ, saw their advantage in Wodan's state of mind and had maneuvered more and more power to be allocated to them in governing the Nine Worlds. As King, Wodan still maintained final say, but beyond restoring relations between the worlds, he showed little interest in the matters of his realm.

As the Sun crept up over the mountain ridge, Wodan stood on his balcony, overlooking the scene of Winter's Nátt in the valley of Lerakrey. It was the start of its second day. Music and chatter lifted into the air as a mess of noise to Wodan's ears. A small laugh rang out over the top of the garbled sounds. Wodan's eye darted with precision to the obnoxious source. Directly below him, he saw a father carrying his small son on his shoulders. The child squealed with delight as the father unexpectedly spun in one direction or the other. Next to them was a woman Wodan could only assume was the mother, who would send her arms flying up protectively to steady her husband and prevent her child from falling. They looked to be on their way to the festival and were sickeningly happy.

That laugh rang in Wodan's head, assaulting parts of his mind he did not want to revisit. Visions of a by-gone time crept out of the dark recesses of his memories. Blurred moments flashed back at him. A laugh he had equated to the sweetest of music that used to lift his heart over any obstacle, drifted forward in his thoughts and left him shattered. Blonde curls bouncing in the Sun, entangled in the dark tresses of his beloved Frija, were tortuously beyond his reach. The pure and radiant light that emanated from his little boy, had vanished without a trace and left Wodan a hollow shell to be filled with his own bile. Remembering the closeness of the three of them, his family, happy faces together within a mass hug; the memory alone ripped him into pieces. He thought they had forever. It should have been forever, but it was taken away without any warning or reason. Wodan's loss of all he loved and the unanswered questions that ate through him like acid every moment, poisoned any beauty in a memory he might recall of his son, Baldar.

He looked again at the unknowing family below him. The diseased vessel that was his heart overflowed with great disdain and jealousy at the sight of them.

"The answers are out there somewhere! It will return to me!" Wodan said quietly through clenched teeth the phrases he often muttered to himself.

ৎ

Dagen staggered back to the inn. He had searched the entire night and began to question if anything he saw had been real or just his wishful thinking that he had seen her. Dagen found Brieg sitting in the tavern, starting his day with a morning meal. The sausages, bread, and cheese on his plate did nothing to entice Dagen's appetite.

"Look what the cat drug in. You look awful," said Brieg.

"And good morning to you too," managed Dagen.

"No luck, I take it?" asked Brieg.

Dagen shook his head to confirm, "What am I doing, Brieg?"

"Chasing your last hope for a different life," said Brieg flatly.

"You're right. This is insanity," said Dagen.

"I didn't say that. Remember this is me you are talking to, not Rûni," said Brieg.

"Sorry, it's so easy to get the two of you confused," added Dagen with a small tired laugh.

"This girl means something to you, and the odds are against you. You have three more days to find her. I wouldn't give up," stated Brieg.

"If that was her last night, what happened to her? Was she taken? No one could answer what they saw. How do I have any hope of finding her, much less knowing if she is all right?"

Rûni returned to overhear Dagen's plight. The anguish in Dagen's voice pained Rûni. He could not let his friend go on wondering about Kitaj.

Rûni took a deep breath, walked up behind Dagen and admitted, "I went back to the Order this morning to hopefully get some insight on what we witnessed last night, and spoke to a member of the Central Council. I hope this will put your mind at ease; she was able to tell me the girl we saw fall from the drum did not come to any harm."

Dagen jumped up and grabbed his friend by the shoulders, "Thank you Rûni! This is wonderful news! Who is she? Where is she now?"

Rûni backed away from Dagen slightly, "I am sorry, that I can't tell you. It is not for me to say. That was not part of the Council member's deduction."

Dagen's demeanor immediately sank. He consoled himself with the little information Rûni could provide.

Rûni tried to cover his tracks further, "It would be inadvisable to say for sure that was who you sought, but at least we all know that particular girl did not come to harm last night."

"Thank you for trying, Rûni. You're a good friend," Dagen added sincerely.

"It's a small consolation," said Rûni as he turned away.

Brieg thought Rûni was acting strange, even for Rûni, but decided to look past it to lightening Dagen's somber mood.

"See, there is some good news in it. Maybe that was her, and if it was, she's close. Don't give up Dagen, remember you have three days left," said Brieg brightly.

"Don't encourage him!" retorted Rûni.

"What exactly is your problem with this?" asked Brieg pointedly at Rûni.

"I just don't want to see Dagen hurt!" stated Rûni, backing even farther away from his friends.

"All right, both of you, stop it! I appreciate the concern," looking to Rûni, "and the encouragement," looking back to Brieg, "We came here to enjoy this time together, I suggest we start doing that. Enough on the subject, please!" stated Dagen.

Kitaj woke slowly and painfully. Foggy thoughts of the night before danced around in her head. In her groggy mind, she wondered if she had dreamt most of what had happened. The pain in her joints and overwhelming feeling of exhaustion told her otherwise. Aergo lay curled up on her pillow. At her waking, he yawned and stretched out his front and back legs, extending his feline claws into her hair. Kitaj turned her head to look at him. His expression was flat.

"Don't look at me like that. It's too early," Kitaj mumbled and rolled over to hide her face from the light trickling through her window.

There was a knock at the chamber door. The sudden noise startled and confused the Queen as she awoke from another of her nightmares. She thought it was too early for any formal engagement or it was later in the Midangardian day than she realized. The Sun's placement at the end of a Midangard summer was easily misleading.

Queen Frija gathered herself and replied, "Enter."

Unannounced, Bereness Fréa let herself in.

"Good morning, Bereness, what do I owe this unexpected visit?" said Queen Frija.

"I come to you this morning as your friend. May I ask of my Queen to disregard our formalities?" asked the Bereness.

"It would be a most welcomed change, my dear Wela!" Frija said with a smile.

"Sága," replied the Bereness, addressing the Queen by the name she had known her as in their childhood. "I have missed you!" she stated, as she hugged Frija.

"These have been long and difficult years. I am pleased we can again speak freely," stated Frija, returning the hug.

"With all that has transpired, please know, Sága, I never saw you as my enemy. The discord between your husband and my brother was just that. It's a travesty that our worlds should have been divided and forced against each other. I cannot fathom the pain you and Wodan must still suffer. I grieve for both of you at the loss of your Baldar, but it should have never merited our war," said the Bereness.

"I have always appreciated your honesty, Wela. You are one of my oldest friends and need to know I did not suspect you or your brother to have harmed my son, and I don't to this day," Queen Frija replied.

"I heard of your other loss, of Amicus, but regret I know little of the circumstances. Reports of his... inexistence... were unclear," said Bereness Fréa.

"His loss was yet another unnatural act, defying anything we know. I cannot begin to explain it you," said the Queen.

"I so enjoyed him when we were children, and through the years of our visits. I know how dear he was to you," said the Bereness.

"Thank you. Few understand," stated the Queen quietly.

"If I may be so bold to say, few understand how you can stay with that madman of a husband you have," flared the Bereness.

With the Bereness's words, Frija saw no reason to maintain appearances with her, "We rarely speak. We just appear together when needed. We no longer understand each other."

"I am sorry, I know you truly loved him," added the Bereness.

"If only..." Frija trailed off.

The Bereness continued, "My dear Sága, you have lost so much. I realize what I am about to say can not diminish your grief, but please know you have many sympathizers throughout the worlds. Your people love you and will continue to support you through whatever the King's madness might bring."

"I may need your help someday soon, Wela," said the Queen, as her eyes rimmed with tears.

Bereness Fréa held tight to the Queen's hands, while she fervently said, "I'm here for you. You can trust in that."

༄

Dagen led the way from the inn to the festival grounds in great haste, while Rûni and Brieg struggled to keep up. Dagen had decided he would no longer mention the young woman he sought— at least not anywhere near his friends. Their help was not helping. The sooner he could change their focus to the entertainment of the festival, the better off he would be.

The second day of Winter's Nátt was in full force at early day's light. Dagen, Brieg and Rûni could not believe how much more densely packed the festival was compared to the day before. Looking down from the hill above the grounds, it appeared that every possible space between the vendors' carts and tents had been overtaken by performers of all kynds. There were musicians playing for passers-by. Children from all worlds gathered around puppet shows, jugglers, and magicians. Tellers of stories and fortunes were scattered about in each pavilion. These new additions to the pavilions were the cast of performers from the previous night's opening ceremonies. Their special talents were now melded into the presentations of their worlds. The crowd weaved their way through the maze created within each world's display and were overtaken with a sense of wonder, slowing at certain points, and causing clogged and uneven flows. The overall mood of the crowd came across as jovial, but Dagen and his friends were wary that tempers could easily turn with newly re-formed alliances if movement became too restricted. The field games were to begin at midday which they hoped would solve part of the overflow congestion. The three continued into the festival grounds with a keen awareness of the conditions they were entering.

"I say we start in the other direction this time, with Léohet. The best remedies to put our minds at ease can be found there, or so I've been told. Seems to me, we could all use our share of that this morning," stated Brieg, as he shot a stern look in Rûni's direction.

Dagen and Rûni were reassured they had made the right decision in postponing the Léohetwin pavilion until Brieg could join them. They would not have been able to contain their impressions from him and would have dampened Brieg's wide-eyed wonder. It was a marvel, the colors alone that popped in every direction. The atmosphere was one of underlying celebration. Brieg's grin covered the entirety of his face.

"I have found my people!" he announced loudly, as Brieg was known to do.

The food, the music, the Léohets' welcoming nature, and ease transported all three to a world without worries. The Léohets had done well in creating an atmosphere that reflected their home. The three were happily focusing on the splendid attractions, while nearby an attractive Léohet was focusing on Brieg. He noticed her as well and hastily left his friends' side.

"That didn't take long," said Rûni.

"What did you expect?" asked Dagen.

"Are you hungry?" asked Rûni.

"Come on, we'll find him later," said Dagen.

Dagen and Rûni were once again without Brieg. At least this time, they had a general idea where to find him. They meandered through the pavilion, taking in all the sites. The dancers and musicians with metal drums were parading down the pavilion's pathway. Many of the bystanders joined in the joyous trek, adding their voices, blowing shell horns and waving their hands to the early morning sunshine. Rûni even smiled at watching them pass, though his sensibilities told him it was too early in the morning for a parade.

Amazing aromas from roasting fires were filling the air, compelling Rûni and Dagen to seek them out. As they searched for the sources, Dagen noticed an unusual looking tent near the back of the venue. It was striped with bright colors of every imaginable shade and covered with large symbols painted in white on all sides. He wondered what the symbols meant. They were so large; he was curious if they meant an exuberant welcome, or as caution to keep out. It had to be the first, Dagen deduced, for they were in the Léohetwin section, where hospitality was their way of life. Dagen asked a nearby Léohet boy about the tent.

"Tells your life," said the boy in newly learned Midangardian.

Dagen had not previously given much thought to seers, especially those on other worlds. His exposure had been limited to what he knew about the Tjetajat through Rûni, only whispers concerning Ende Dwellers, and childhood tales of the Wise traveling to the homes of newborns throughout the worlds. But now, the possibilities intrigued him about seers in every world. Dagen turned his attention back to his young helper. He wished he knew how to say "thank you" in the boy's language, but thanked him as best he could, and gave the child a coin for his courtesy. The boy gratefully accepted it and disappeared into the crowd.

Dagen spotted a food vendor turning some type of sausage and adding them to a grain mixture that he served in large shell bowls. The smell alone was mouth-watering.

"It looks and smells appetizing, but do you have any idea what it is made from?" questioned Rûni.

"No, Rûni, and I don't care. Just try it and see what you think," encouraged Dagen.

Dagen tried to communicate with the vendor to buy a bowlful. He was successful, but came away with more than he anticipated. The adjoining stand's vendor insisted Dagen take a baked pie, some sort of green fruit and bright drink that had flowers floating in it.

"What did they give you?" Rûni asked as Dagen walked back towards him with his arms full.

"I have no idea. They were so happy, I couldn't say no," answered Dagen, "They're watching. Here, have some," as he handed over the drink and green fruit to Rûni.

Rûni took one sip, then drained his cup. He took one bite of the spiky green fruit and devoured it in front of Dagen.

"You could have saved some for me," stated Dagen.

"Can I try some of your bowl?" Rûni asked.

"Get your own," Dagen said protectively of his remaining food.

"How about the pie?" asked Rûni.

"Only if you behave," jabbed Dagen.

Meanwhile, the Léohet food vendors looked on in pleasure to see the Midangardians filling their stomachs.

えし

With her second attempt at waking, Kitaj was successful. Though she was far from refreshed and vibrant from her extended sleep, she was at the very least coherent. She drug herself into a seated position and rubbed her hands over her face. The Sun was higher in the morning sky and she resolved to begin her day. Aergo was nowhere to be seen.

"He must have given up on me waking anytime soon and went hunting for his morning meal. Looks like I'm on my own," she said aloud as a means to coax herself to get up.

The thought resonated through her groggy mind that she was not under anyone's eye to scrutinize her decisions. This was a rare opportunity she could not pass. Impulsively, she decided to dismiss her morning duties, pull herself together, throw on her clothes and race down to the festival grounds.

えし

Rûni was about to walk back to the stands to order more food and drink, when Brieg appeared. His happy disposition had been replaced by a darkened, stern expression.

"We have to go," said Brieg.

"But we just arrived, and I'm still hungry," said Rûni with disappointment, "There's so much more to see!"

"Later, we need to go. Trust me," said Brieg.

"What have you done now? And hand over your coin purse," said Rûni.

Dagen was saying nothing. He was too involved with shoveling his remaining food in his mouth. Dagen knew well enough when Brieg said it was time to go, it was best to be ready to leave in moments.

"Are you going to tell me what's happened?" asked Rûni.

"No," stated Brieg firmly.

"Fine!" huffed Rûni, but he knew Brieg was serious and tried to turn to a lighter subject, "Where to next?"

"Sweduetwin," said Brieg.

Kitaj could imagine Aergo's voice in her head, warning her as she went on her way, *After what happened to you last night, you're going back down into that barrage of mess? It's even more crowded today. How do you plan to manage? You haven't even recovered from last night!* Kitaj thought, *With or without Aergo's approval, I'm still going.*

She was tired of over-thinking the situation, but her impulsiveness was no match against the multitude of people currently on the grounds, and their emotions hit her like a towering wave as she reached the entrance gate. Her mind immediately muddled, and her sense of direction left her.

One useful line of thought managed to surface for her, *Because the Tjetajat cannot read me, it does not necessarily mean that all seers can't.*

Kitaj believed the possibility was worth exploring. She continued to think maybe a power beyond what was known to her could provide the answers she sought. Holding to that hope, Kitaj harnessed all her mental defenses to shield herself as she made her way to the Ende.

ﻋﻟﻪ

"You can't be serious!" said Dagen, as he choked on his mouthful of food.

"I am. I know you weren't up for going last night, but how about trying. We need to move, and soon," Brieg said as he scanned the crowd.

"You're going to have to go soon anyway. It won't hurt to at least walk through the pavilion," said Rûni. "Otherwise, we will have to walk all the way around to get to Gicelfolde again."

"Fine by me," Dagen replied.

"You're being ridiculous," said Rûni.

Brieg thought Rûni had overstepped with his last statement and chimed in, "Dagen, do as you wish. We'll make our way through Swedu. You can to get to Gicel however you want and we'll meet up with you there. Rûni, leave him alone. He has two more days before he has to go there. End the subject now," Brieg growled.

"Pulling rank already? Maybe military life will suit you after all," retorted Rûni.

"While you go live your life out with your nose stuck in dusty manuscripts," added Brieg.

"Go on, I'll meet up with you at Gicel as planned," stated Dagen, consciously omitting exactly how he would make his way there.

Dagen waited until his friends were out of his line of vision before he moved from the spot where they spoke. Tensions were running unusually high for all three of them.

Dagen's idea was now fully formed, *If the Tjetajat cannot be of help to me, maybe another seer can.*

He retraced his steps to the Léohet seer's tent. The brightly decorated exterior was no match for the spectacle Dagen saw inside. The interior was draped on all sides and across the floor in lush fabrics of rich reds and deep purples that shimmered gold in the folds of the light. Each panel was embossed with tribal symbols. Whether each panel consisted of a verse unto itself or was arranged to tell an entire story; Dagen could not tell. Several pillows lay scattered at the edges of the tent, ready to make a small audience comfortable. A sweet thick fragrant smoke permeated the air and curled around Dagen's thoughts. Though the atmosphere was welcoming, the overall effect had darker tones than what Dagen had experienced in the Léohetwin section. Other than himself, the tent appeared to be empty.

Dagen stepped forward to take a closer look when he felt something move under his foot. Unknown to him, under the layers of scarves and drapes in the center of the tent was the Léohetwin seer, and he accidentally stepped on some part of her. She did not let out a sound, she simply rose from the tent floor in a motion of uncoiling herself and stood directly in front of him. Dagen looked at the unnamed woman's veiled face. All he could see of her was her violet eyes with white centers, and a small bit of tanned skin across her forehead that was marked with more tribal designs. The small points of her ears' tragi were sticking out through her veils. As he looked closer, it appeared that it was not paint, nor inking across her forehead, but actual embroidered thread sewn into her skin.

She raised her hands and said, "Welcome. Please remove your shoes and come sit."

As Dagen took off his boots, he noticed the Léohet seer had similar embroidered marks in the palms of her hands. She turned and glided to the back of the tent, trailing her layers of fabric behind her and exposing the tent floor that was covered in white sand.

"You have come for answers. Let me first tell you I am not a seer, but a reader. I read the symbols. It is up to you to reveal what you want me to read about you."

Dagen was unsure how helpful a reading would be to him, but he decided since he was already inside her tent, it would be rude to not accept her offer, and he hoped his staying would somehow make up for stepping on her.

"Please, sit in the center," she directed.

Dagen obliged, but felt very self-conscious, sitting barefoot, as she moved around him. She methodically smoothed out his footprints, while encircling him in marks she drew in the sand from a cane she had retrieved from beneath her gowns. Next, she retrieved a large pail containing sea water and sprinkled him and the sand.

"Do you carry something that is precious to you?" she asked.

Dagen took his satchel off his shoulder and began to rummage through its contents. He was unsure what he might have with him that could be useful.

The reader immediately held up her hand and announced, "No coins! They have passed through too many hands, they are only useful as payment."

"What about this?" asked Dagen, as he removed and unwrapped one of his mother's sunstar loafs.

"Yes, that will do nicely," said the veiled reader, with crinkled smiling eyes.

     ﻋﻠﻢ

Kitaj navigated her way from the Midangardian section, through the Heitaned and Fyrfolde pavilions, to arrive at The Ende. There were very few people about in their venue at the time of her arrival. Ende Dwellers were not very welcoming by nature and saw no reason to make any special efforts during the festival.

Of the people there, Kitaj saw members from the three groups of the Ende Dwellers' disregarded following. These were people of Wodan's realm who admired the Ende Dwellers as their closest connection to the outer realm. Each group had their own philosophies as to the purpose and power of the Ende Dwellers. Their convictions were patterned in reference to what they believed the true world symbol of The Ende should be; an outlined circle inked into their palms, another with a solid black circle on the last segment of their left middle finger, and those who simply cloaked themselves to honor the Ende Dwellers.

Kitaj walked forward to speak to the Ende Dweller nearest her. She could tell little of his or her features. Each one was fully cloaked and their faces could not be seen. The only part of them that was visible was their bony hands protruding from the cuffs of their heavy cloaks. She was undaunted by their off-putting manner and proceeded to ask for help.

"Excuse me—" Kitaj said to Ende Dweller closest to her, "I was wondering if..."

Tjetajat, you seek answers you cannot see.

Kitaj was taken aback. She had not anticipated the volume of the Ende Dweller's voice inside her head.

We are merely Gate Keepers. Step inside to see. We only provide you with a glimpse of who you truly are and where you are on your life's journey. If your soul were to pass today, you can see what would become of it. We do not control the outcome. That is entirely based on your choices. You will not remember the experience itself. You will only be left with the feeling of satisfaction for who your are, or are becoming; that is unless you discover you wish to make different choices for your outcome, said the Ende Dweller.

Kitaj hesitated; she was unsure if this was the type of help she was seeking, and asked, "But, don't you see the results?"

Yes, replied the Ende Dweller's voice through her mind.

"Then why not tell me?" Kitaj asked.

That is for you to discover— if you dare.

ℓ

The Léohet reader took the sunstar loaf and laid it out on the sand. She took the cloth it was wrapped in and added it to a small dark pouch. The reader placed the pouch in Dagen's hands and placed her hands on either side of his. She began singing in a language Dagen assumed was ancient etwin-kynd. He noticed the strangeness of her palms against the back of his hands, the unsettling feeling of their embroidered symbols against his skin. As the reader finished her ceremonial chant, she removed her hands from his and asked Dagen to open the pouch. He did as he was told.

"Place the cloth on the sand next to the bread, then stand."

Dagen followed her instructions. He was unsure where this reading was leading and his uneasiness made him eager for a conclusion.

"Now, turn the pouch upside down to empty it and let the signs fall where they may," she added.

The contents scattered across the sand onto the symbols the reader had marked throughout it. The signs consisted of various sea shells, dried flowers, bright colored stones, what appeared to be a small fleógan tooth from it's distinctive serrated, slanted shape, and a small skull that was most likely from a mouse.

"Step out of the circle without disturbing your footprints."

Dagen did his best not to disturb his prints or any of the signs, but a small jagged black stone had caught at the hem of his pant leg and fell in between his footprints.

ℓ

Kitaj asked within her own mind, *What is the payment?*

The Ende Dweller answered, *Your payment is at your outcome. It will reveal itself on your face. Either a smile or one of your tears will do. You will know which to give when your glimpse has completed.*

The Ende Dwellers statement piqued Kitaj's curiosity. She wondered what the significance of the required payment was to people who did not show their own faces.

Do you see anything unusual about me? she asked.

There is nothing for me to see, answered the Ende Dweller.

"There is nothing for me to read," answered the Léohet reader with a perplexed look in her eyes. Dagen watched as her eye widened in an unmistakable expression of fear.

"You need to go!" the reader exclaimed, and threw the remaining sea water in his face.

"What's the meaning of this! What did I do... or not do?" Dagen retorted.

"You need to go!" the reader demanded.

You need to go inside, stated the Ende Dweller, and signaled Kitaj to enter.

She walked past two other Ende Dwellers, who appeared to ignore her, and into a dark opening. Inside, a bright white light began to grow around her. It was the last sight Kitaj remembered seeing before her glimpse was over.

The Léohet reader abruptly ushered Dagen out of her tent and threw his boots after him. He was more confused than ever. The reader's curtness was uncharacteristic for her culture. The Léohets prided themselves on their kyndness. The reader was in no way what Dagen had anticipated. Soaking wet, he staggered out into the busy pavilion. People questioned and laughed at his wet, barefooted appearance, but Dagen barely noticed. He felt disoriented, and was unsure which direction he should go.

Find Brieg and Rûni! was his one clear thought that helped him as he staggered forward.

He sat down to allow his head to clear and he realized he was sitting amongst several white tents. The black banner with the three bees hung directly in front of him.

ه

Kitaj emerged from her experience feeling quietly introspective and grounded. She walked up to the Ende Dweller and smiled, as a tear rolled slowly down her face. She could not and would not have wanted to explain the sensation she was experiencing, but it could have been described as having several strong emotions all at once. The Ende Dweller gently extended one bony finger to her face and captured a tear on its fingertip, then traced the corners of her mouth to experience her delicate somber smile.

Your experience was unique, said the Ende Dweller.

Whether her voice was inside or outside her head, Kitaj could not tell for sure. It was of no importance.

I can't remember, she said softly.

Correct, said the Ende Dweller.

But I feel... I see myself more clearly. I am part of something beyond me; something vast, but I'm infinitesimal. "Do you know?" asked Kitaj.

The Ende Dweller said nothing and turned away.

ه

Kitaj left the Ende venue and wandered aimlessly through the Aesingard pavilion. The clanging of swords and spectacles of force did not shake her from her entranced state. She was lost in a deeper sense of knowing, yet the details of her glimpse into her soul remained a mystery. The experience, along with the late summer Sun shining down on her, left Kitaj feeling flush. She absentmindedly removed her cloak and decided to settle in a beautiful and quiet spot in the courtyard setting of the Vane's pavilion. Kitaj was preoccupied by her thoughts as she carelessly folded her cloak to cushion the stone bench she had chosen next to a soothing water feature.

Kitaj was unsure how long she had been sitting and staring into the rippling water when a young woman approached her. The woman's voice slowly pulled Kitaj back into the present.

"Please excuse my interruption of your thoughts, but may I have your permission to capture your likeness?"

"I'm sorry... what?" Kitaj said, trying to extract the meaning of what the person in front of her had just said.

Kitaj looked up into the Sun, blinking. It shadowed the face of a Vane artisan. Immediately, Kitaj's eyes caught the artist's attention.

The artist pleaded, "You must sit for me, please."

"I really don't have time," replied Kitaj.

"It looks to me that you have all the time of the worlds. You've been as still as one of my statues," the artist added.

"More the reason why I must go," said Kitaj.

"I beg you. You don't have to move. It will be a short and painless process," encouraged the artist.

Kitaj felt very awkward at the thought of someone studying her features, but decided to allow it. The artist pulled different colored chalk sticks from her pocket, and began to move them across her tablet's surface.

"There, how's that?" asked the artist, as she turned the tablet to show Kitaj her own eyes.

"Do I honestly look like that?" Kitaj asked, as a means to compliment the artist's work improving on how Kitaj saw herself.

"You did when you were spellbound by your thoughts," replied the artist with a smile. "The depth and the colors; it is rare to find someone with two such distinct eyes. But beyond that, there is something intriguing behind them. There is something trying to come forward," she paused, "I believe you have an interesting life in front of you," the artist concluded.

Kitaj reached forward and lightly touched the drawing. It appeared to her that a tear was trying to form in her green eye. She traced the small wisps of wavy tresses the artist had drawn to frame her brow.

"I usually sell my work, but you've inspired me, may I keep your sketch?" asked the artist.

"Ah, of course?" replied Kitaj, unsure exactly how to respond.

"Thank you," replied the Vane artist as she reached down and squeezed Kitaj's hand, and departed by saying, "I will leave you now to your thoughts."

After the artist left her, Kitaj glanced back into the rippling fountains and thought, *Water— there's something important concerning water.*

Dagen thought, *Of all places, I end up here.*

The destination he had been trying to avoid was within a few steps of him. He let out a large disgruntled sigh, put on his boots, and walked at a fast pace through the heart of the Swedu venue while doing his best not to draw attention to his soggy self. He was relieved when he finally reached the Gicelfolde pavilion.

He felt fortunate to find Rûni and Brieg immediately. From their location, they had newly arrived.

"What happened to you?" asked Brieg, commenting on Dagen's drenched appearance.

Dagen, still reeling from his recent encounter, was in no mood for questions, "Why did you have to leave Léohet's?"

Dagen and Brieg stood their ground, staring at each other with set jaws, waiting for the other to answer, while Rûni's anxiety grew.

Dagen spoke next, directly to Brieg, "So this is what we've come to— keeping secrets from one another."

Rûni's face turned bright red. Little did his friends know, he was to be included in that statement. He felt his guilt was written across his face.

"You're right. What's happening to us?" answered Brieg. "Time to lighten the mood!" Brieg said in his characteristically light and mischievous manner. "What should we get into next?"

Rûni interjected meekly, "If you were wanting to take part in any of the contests, it's probably time to sign in for them."

Registration for the Winter's Nátt contests was located at the farthest end of the field in front of the Aesingard venue. Brieg, Rûni, and Dagen, along with other hopeful participants, crossed the post fence barrier around the field's edge and walked across a clear strip of open ground to the registration area. Members of the King's guard supervised as different events were set up throughout the field. Stationary contests were positioned along the edge, while the large strip through the center was left available for the events involving distance. Several people were gathered around a large posted banner at the registration area to see the order of events for the day. To accommodate the numerous choices and volume of the crowd, several events were being held at the same time and allowing a set number of participants for each event. This was unlike the years before when the festival was smaller, and all events had been set at staggered times with no limit to the number competing. The mood around the posted events was agitated by this change, but the crowd dissipated to secure their spots. The day's games were usually solo tests of strength, skill, agility, aim, and stamina. The choices were overwhelming. Brieg could not tell what over half the of contest options were by their titles.

"Most of these must be games they played before the war," thought Brieg out loud. "Whatever they are, it should be exciting to see something new."

"But they're not new. You just said so yourself. They are the same games that were offered before the war," said an exacerbated Heítaned young man from behind Brieg.

"My mistake," replied Brieg.

He did not want to add any friction. There seemed to be enough of that rumbling through the crowd, as well as his friends. Brieg managed to sign up for two of his favorite solo events and a third that was completely unknown to him. He was also able to talk Rûni into joining him and Dagen for the last team event of the day.

"It's part of the adventure," he said for Rûni's benefit while smiling widely.

Rûni reluctantly replied, "If you say so."

علم

Kitaj had spent more time than she had planned at the festival that morning. Though the day had given her some insight about herself, she had yet to gain any information concerning Rûni's friend. She had thought she might have sensed him earlier when she was near the fountains, but again, the volume of people was muddling her perceptions. After her encounter with the artist, Kitaj knew she needed to return to the Order. The time was nearing noon, and she wanted to leave before the crowd thickened to a standstill to watch the games. Kitaj was certain she was in store for tongue lashings and more questions than she cared to answer on her return, from both her mother and Aergo. The sooner she could get their worry and frustration settled, the better for her. Kitaj had decided to brave the nearest route to the entrance and proceed through the Gicel venue. The crowd had already started to form around the edges of the field, and more were pouring in. She found she had to move toward to the center of the Gicel pavilion to escape the densest part of the crowd. With the thinned out pathways through the venue, the sunlight directly above was free to bounce off the high pillars of crystal and walls of ice, catching the gemstones that lay out on exhibit, and causing multiple beams of colors to cascade throughout the entire display. The sight alone took her breath away. When Kitaj remembered to breathe, the crispness of the Gicel's air reawakened her. She *knew* she would need to return here to help her find some resolve with the circumstances of her father's death.

Kitaj hurried through to reach the Swedu venue. She hoped her path would allow the opportunity to find the young woman she had met there the day before, and see if her concerns had sorted in her favor. Kitaj reached the beekeepers' tent and looked inside. The young woman was there, with her family, and the young Swedu man with silver hair. The silver haired man saw Kitaj first. She smiled and pointed to the young woman who's back was to her. The silver-haired Swedu walked over to the young woman and drew her attention to Kitaj who was standing at the tent opening. The young woman was first puzzled by Kitaj's appearance, but placed her as the person who tried to help her the day before. She approached Kitaj and stepped outside the tent to talk to her.

"I just wanted to check with you, to see how you were," said Kitaj.

"Thank you for your concern; it is better today, " said the young woman.

Kitaj was able to read her to some extent and said, "I'm glad to see it's so. Please take care of you— both of you."

"May I ask your name?" inquired the young woman.

"Kitaj."

"I'm Isla. Kitaj, you're very kynd."

"As are you. I'm sorry I must go," Kitaj added.

"I hope we meet again," said Isla.

"I believe we will," said Kitaj.

As she left the beekeepers' tent, Kitaj's foot found a loose rock, causing her ankle to give. A nearby tent wall caught her fall and she slid down its side to sit flat on the ground. Kitaj was surprised to receive a small zap from the damp ground where she landed. The ground itself seemed to carry a low buzzing charge. Her fingers stung from the small shock. Kitaj wondered what she may have landed in to cause this. Cautiously, she lifted her fingers to her nose, prepared for a repulsive smell, but instead smelled something entirely different. Her best guess as to what she had landed in was sea water, and she smiled.

ﻌﻠﻌ

Once Brieg was registered, Dagen and Rûni followed him as he located the stations for the different games he had entered. Brieg's excitement was building as he waited for his first event. He was bouncing about and constantly fidgeting with anticipation.

A warning horn blew, alerting participants that the contests were about to begin. Brieg flapped his arms in front and behind him to loosen his shoulders in preparation for Groshdas, which was a type of wrestling that originated on Fyrfolde.

The rules of the game were for two opponents to face each other; putting their left forearm directly below the their opponent's collar bone and their right fist next to their opposition's left shoulder. When the signal horn blew, each was to try to push the other backwards across a drawn line to win their match. Loss of contact meant immediate disqualification. The victor would move to the next round of matches until one person remained as the winner. The rounds were usually short-lived, but occasionally competitors were too well matched causing a draw to be decided by a judge and allowing the two participants to move to the next round to face new opponents.

Brieg had always thought of Groshdas as a simple game of force and leverage. He had never been affected by taunts. During previous games, he had some opponents that would try to slip in a punch when the judge wasn't looking, but he had learned he could easily dig his thumb of his fisted hand into a sensitive spot deep in the shoulder socket to get their attention if necessary.

A total of sixteen pairs would start the first match. Brieg's first pairing was with a burly Midangardian that looked about ten years older than him. They met each other with respectful nods and got into position. The signal horn sounded and the match was on. Dagen and Rûni cheered Brieg on from the sidelines. It was a well-mannered match that was over in moments with Brieg as the winner. His Midangardian opponent nodded to him again in acknowledgment of the win and left the playing field. Brieg, and the other fourteen winners of the first round stood back and watched as the match between a Gicel and Fyr continued. Judges were closing in to see if they needed to call a draw. The Fyr lost his temper and kicked the Gicel's leg out from under him. Their match was stopped with the Fyr being ejected.

He was heard to say, "It was worth it!" as he was escorted away by two of the King's guards.

The judges did a quick drawing to determine the next sets between the remaining sixteen opponents. For his second match, Brieg was paired with a wiry Léohet. Brieg was unsure about his strength compared to his new opponent but felt sure it would be another clean contest. His Léohet opponent smiled back and blinked with his second eyelids as he and Brieg got into position. The Léohet was not intentionally trying to startle Brieg, but his blink caught him off guard and gave the Léohet a small advantage at the beginning. Brieg recovered his ground before being pushed over the line behind him and managed to make his opponent cross his line first.

There were now eight people left going into the third match. Brieg was paired with the Gicel who had advanced through his first opponent's disqualification. Brieg had to crouch lower to get into position with the Gicel. When the signal horn sounded, Brieg was surprised at the Gicel's determination not to budge. This must have been his strategy for his other matches; let his opponent keep pushing until he tired, then push them over the line. There was no rule against that, so Brieg adopted his opponent's tactic. They both stood there leaning into each other, without either budging. Time was called with a draw between the two. Instead of four participants going into the next round, there were six. Brieg was matched next with the Heítaned boy who had stood behind him at the posting of the games.

"We meet again so soon, Midan," sneered the boy.

Brieg just nodded to him as the Heítaned boy leaned down to get into position for their match. Brieg found this opponent perplexing. It was not unheard of, but rare for Heítaned to compete. The Heítaned culture found no merit in contests. This young man was not only competing but aggressive and meant to cause trouble. The Heítaned boy's attitude was oddly uncharacteristic to the ways of his culture and Brieg prepared himself for what might follow the signal horn. Dagen and Rûni could tell something was off with this match and hoped Brieg could handle himself.

The signal horn blew, and the Heîtaned boy let out a loud yell as he shoved Brieg backwards and hard into the ground. The boy managed not to lose contact so the win counted until, in celebration, the boy grabbed Brieg and lifted him over his head then slammed him back into the ground. The judges and guards ran over to Brieg and the boy. Four guardsmen escorted the Heîtaned boy off the field, while two judges helped Brieg up. Dagen and Rûni ran out to meet him and each put one of Brieg's arms over their shoulder to help him off the field.

"I'll be fine," Brieg said, with effort. "Just some bruises. That boy was strong!" he managed.

"We know, we saw. But are you sure you're all right?" Rûni asked cautiously.

"Yes, just let me sit and I'll be good as new," stated Brieg, who was obviously in pain.

Dagen and Rûni got Brieg settled in front of the Vane pavilion. Dagen checked Brieg's ribs for any breaks and luckily found none. Seeing Brieg was not seriously injured, Rûni turned to go find something cooling for Brieg to drink and found he did not need to take two steps.

"We saw what happened," said a lovely Vane woman, accompanied by three other ladies, as she offered drinks to Brieg, Rûni, and Dagen.

Next, four very strong Vane men carrying a palanquin arrived to assist Brieg. Without another word, two of the men helped Brieg into it. One of the Vane ladies climbed in with Brieg to assist him with his drink, while Dagen and Rûni were ushered along on either side of the palanquin. Both Dagen and Rûni were dumbfounded at the degree of care Brieg was receiving from the Vane, and Brieg, though in pain, was loving every moment of the attention.

They carried Brieg to a draped tent within the Vangard section that was tucked quietly away from the noisy crowd. He was gently moved to an awaiting oversized, overstuffed, reclined lounge to rest and regain his strength. Brieg, Rûni, and Dagen continued to thank everyone involved with Brieg's care. A Vane gentleman, dressed in white, came in to check Brieg over and agreed he had sustained deep bruising but no breaks. The physician explained that the Vane were aware no other worlds' pavilions were readily prepared to treat injuries from the games or other maladies that might befall the crowd and saw a need to provide the extra service for Winter's Nátt. He gave Brieg a powder of herbs to help with the pain and excused himself to attend to other injuries. Brieg lost track of how many times he had said thank you to his hosts, who he found beyond kynd and generous.

Brieg remained under the Vane's care, with Rûni and Dagen, through the early afternoon. He had missed his second event and agreed to bow out of his remaining two, but decided he felt well enough to at least watch from the sidelines. He went to stand and found the herb powder to have dulled the pain but had not removed it completely.

"Walking will help," said Brieg, though neither he nor his friends fully believed his words.

As they were leaving the tent, they saw the Vane physician that had treated Brieg rushing over to another tent to assist. The three heard a man yelling from within.

"I THOUGHT I'D BE INSPIRED! I CAN'T MAKE IT HAPPEN! LET ME GO!" the voice continued to cry from inside the tent.

A different Vane physician met the other before reaching the tent. She looked very concerned and was shaking her head side to side as she spoke.

Brieg, Dagen and Rûni were close enough to overhear her say to Brieg's physician, "This is the fourth incident today."

"There were nine yesterday." Brieg's physician added.

Dagen, Brieg, and Rûni watched as the other physician shook her head again before both entered the tent that held the yelling man. A fleeting thought of curiosity crossed each of their minds but was soon redirected by the gaming spectacle on the field.

Kitaj arrived at the Order with a smile still on her face. She was first accosted by her mother; wondering where she had been, what she had been doing, and why she thought it was permissible to ignore her duties.

"Sorry, I'll stay 'til I finish," was Kitaj's only reply, as she walked past her mother and down the hall, without her smile faltering.

Aergo was waiting for her, curled up on a stack of robes she was meant to ready for the induction ceremony. He looked at her to ask the same questions, but altered his expression in response to the smile she wore. Kitaj could tell easily from his widened eyes what he was thinking.

"Yes, I am happy and no, I did not find him, not exactly," she continued to grin.

Aergo flattened his ears and began his low feline growl. Kitaj went over to him and rubbed his head.

"You fuss too much," she said, as Aergo continued growling.

She gently moved him off the stack, carefully detaching the material of the top robe from his extended claws and scratched him under his chin. Adding to Aergo's agitation, Kitaj began humming over his growls as she started sorting the robes.

Brieg, Dagen, and Rûni stood near the field barrier in the Vangard section, watching the competitions taking place.

This was not the day Brieg had planned, but he was determined to make the best of what was left to him. Brieg had his friends; he was not severely hurt, he had seen many wonders throughout their stay, and he could convince himself he would enjoy watching instead of doing— at least for the rest of the day. He asked the people around him about the event he had missed and decided it was best he had not participated. It had been a Gicel game called Qinutsuitok, where participants would see how long they could stay seated in large vessels of ice and water.

Brieg longingly looked on as the Obstacle Course was about to begin. This Winter's Nátt had more tasks; eight in total, and stretched the entire length of the field. Each world, with the exception of The Ende, had set up stations across the course. Only five participants would be competing in this event. These five were the lucky few to have their names drawn for the competition. The crowd sent up cries of disappointment when they realized the competition was only one round. It had been shortened to a drawing of five participants to allow for the complexity and length of the course. After the ensuing boos, everyone settled in to enjoy watching the game, even if it was too short.

High climbing barricades were set at the front of the course to prevent the participants from seeing what was ahead. Traditionally, the surrounding crowd would yell out what they saw as the tasks, or more to the truth for fun, would yell out falsehoods about what was on the course. Bystanders would compete with one another by seeing who could yell the loudest and come up with the most absurd idea for a task. The actual tasks were just as ridiculous. Judges stood close by at each station to direct the participants, for some had several parts and what was expected of them to do with the props was not always obvious.

The horn blared to announce the start, prompting the competitors to scale their blinder barricades. They found on the other side that the first task was from the host world, Midangard. Participants had to stand on a plank that rested on a log and balance a mug of mead on their heads while they shot an arrow into a target. All five fell and had to start over again. The crowd laughed loudly at their efforts. Accuracy could help in winning, but it was more important to attempt the full task of each station and reach the finish line in the shortest amount of time.

The second task was from the Heítaned, who had decided to participate for the good of world relations. The task consisted of five small tables set across the field, each had a Heítaned toddlers' puzzle to assemble. An example of what the puzzle should look like when finished sat next to a disassembled one. The Heítaned tried to make the task as easy as possible for, as they saw them, their less clever otherworlders— the puzzle only contained four parts, but together they formed a sphere. The contestants hardly tried before discarding the pieces and moving on to the next task.

The third was from Fyrfolde, and participants had to carry small cauldrons of molten metal from one location to the other. They were allowed to use protective aprons and gloves, though the Fyr participant required no gloves or apron, and simply picked his up under his arm and carried it from one side to the other. The other competitors found the small cauldrons to be surprisingly heavy and were struggling in lifting them carefully so not to spill any of the molten metal. One participant accidentally dropped some on his foot and was immediately rushed to the care of the Vangard pavilion.

The four remaining competitors went into the fourth task as the crowd feverishly cheered them on. The King's guard showed little interest in their task, and had assembled sparring dummies for the competitors to battle with the weapon of their choice. The participants took advantage of their options in weaponry and improvised comical ends to their straw stuffed foes. One of the dummies heads went rolling across the field and had to be retrieved by a judge.

The fifth task was from Vangard. Contestants had to paint quick portraits of their judges as they stood in ridiculous poses.

The sixth task consisted of each participant chopping through a block of Gicel ice to retrieve a noticeably large gem. Judges instructed the participants if they released the gemstones, they could keep them. One of the remaining four chipped at the ice, stopped, and picked up the block to carry it off. The judge would not allow it. The decision was met with hardy boos and laughs from the crowd.

The seventh event was from Swedu. Competitors put on mica visors, that considerably darkened their vision, and had to juggle three glowing spheres while balancing on yet a larger sphere. These were the same type of spheres used in the performance of the opening ceremony. The Swedu had decided to include the spheres in the contest because they were the most requested item to purchase at their pavilion and hoped to continue their popularity. Otherworlders loved playing with them and if something so small could help soften opinions of the Swedu, they were willing to make the spheres available to whomever wanted them.

The eighth task, from Léohet, ended the course with more humor. The competitors had to adorn themselves in flowers and shell necklaces and try to follow Léohet dancers in traditional dance moves, pick up large sea crawlers, and carry them over the finish line. The sea crawlers were very slippery and not very cooperative. Two participants dropped theirs and went chasing after them across the field, while one was unfortunate to have the animal's pincers latch on to his earlobe. The onlookers roared, as the first participant crossed the finish line, and continued to cheer as the other three soon followed.

The field had to be cleared for the last event of the day. The crowd was unsure if they should give up their spots for viewing the field or if they should stay. The decision was left to the individual; no announcement had been made as to how soon the last event would take place.

Dagen looked around at all the faces, again hoping he might find the person he sought within the sea of people, and again, he saw no sign of her. He noticed a clearing of the people from in front of the Aesingard section as the King's guard assembled at the head of it.

"The King must be joining us for this event," said Brieg, noticing the guard as well.

On the field, large carts of mud were carried across and dumped into its center. A very long rope was being extended from one end of the grounds to the other and was laid to one side of the muddy center. Once the rope's middle was determined, a bright red flag was tied to indicate it.

Brieg tried to encourage Rûni and Dagen to join in the Worlds' Tugging Trial without him since their names were already registered, but both declined and stayed to watch with Brieg. Participants started assembling on the field, as judges directed which side to go to in attempts to keep the teams equal. Some taunts started to fly from one group to the other and a few interjected with vulgar slurs. Those participants were identified and given the choice of ejection or to trade teams for the competition; therefore making them pull with the people they had harassed. Participants were rearranged and redirected as the judges monitored how each team was shaping up. When the groups on either side of the rope looked fairly matched, the warning horn blew. The crowd congregated around the field once more to witness the Tugging Trial. The rope was covered with hands prepared to pull, but they stood anxiously waiting. A sudden short processional sounded from the Aesingard stands as everyone expected the King's arrival for the event. Instead, the Queen and the Vangard Bereness appeared while King

Wodan and Ing Fré walked out onto the field. The Ing and King Wodan curtly bowed to one another, then to both teams, and took their places as the heads for each side. Participants looked from one to the another in shock. The man who stood directly behind the King had an unmistakable expression of terror across his face.

"When I said he was joining the event, I didn't expect this!" announced Brieg.

One judge stood at the red flag, awaiting the King's signal. At his nod, the judge blew the final horn and the competition began. The people on either end of the rope had wrapped it around them and dug their legs into the ground, serving as anchors. The sides were matched well and little movement could be seen from the red flag. It would be a matter of footing and which side tired first. Onlookers cheered as the sides struggled against each other. The Ing kept smiling at Wodan. The thought of the King covered in mud could not please him more. The ground beneath the participants was slowly turning to mud itself as the competitors dug in deeper with their heels. As the trial continued, people began to move through the crowd to get refreshments and return. Eventually, the Ing's side held a stronger footing and began to pull back. There was nothing more the King's side could do to prevent the front several members of their crew from being drug into the mud as the red flag crossed over to the Ing's side. The crowd applauded and roared to see their King fall into the muck. The Ing walked over to help King Wodan up. Wodan kept his temper in check but intentionally patted Ing Fré on the back and shoulder with his mud-encrusted hand. It was an action the Ing had anticipated and took it with good humor for the crowd.

The tired participants slowly cleared the field as the rope was removed and mud shoveled back onto the carts. The once lush, grassy field was now torn apart. The majority of the crowd fringing its edges moved back into the heart of the pavilions as evening fell.

The Midangardian band reassembled on the muddy arena and began to play, and slowly a small group began to form around them.

Brieg, Rûni, and Dagen all agreed that the day had been full enough for them. They were more tired than not and decided to return to the inn for a decent night's rest.

CHAPTER 7
ENKINDLED PATHS

Wodan had returned to his quarters at Kestel Midlen after his performance in the Tugging Trial for yet another night of pacing on his balcony. The King was closed off in his private wing and unaware that he was not alone. After being observed for an extended time, his watcher stepped out of the shadows.

Your actions have not gone unnoticed, said the voice coming out from the darkness in Wodan's own mind.

Wodan's initial start was replaced with resolve as he replied aloud, "Somehow I don't believe you are referring to my muddy crowd-pleasing fall from grace. Your visit has been expected, and far past due, Ende Dweller. I am glad my actions finally merited our meeting. A formal announcement would have been appreciated, but then again— that's not in your nature."

From our understanding, your devastating acts were not formally announced either. Why should we extend you any courtesy?

"Come to read me my crimes?" asked Wodan, keeping his back to the Ende Dweller as he walked to a table at the other end of the balcony and poured himself a cup of glow wine.

You know well what they are, replied the Ende Dweller.

"Remind me," said Wodan. "My mind lags from that tired memory I've carried for over a hundred Aesingardian years. Not that the years are relevant. My life has stretched out so long, it means nothing to me anymore.

Yet, it is still a fresh cut to us and in Oblivion! Apparently, I must remind you that not one Ende year has passed since your treason against the Eormensyl and the Essence! the Ende Dwellers voice rang inwardly.

Wodan dropped his cup to press his palms against his temples. On impact with the stone floor, the cup shattered; as did the Ende Dwellers voice inside Wodan's head, sending shards of judgment scattering and piercing different parts of his mind. Wodan regained himself and turned to confront the Ende Dweller. He walked through the broken bits and splatter to face the gaping hole of the Ende Dweller's hood.

"I'm listening," Wodan said, through clenched teeth.

You started a war, dividing your own realm, to gain the knowledge you sought. This realm remains yours, to do with as you see fit, and we have no say nor care in your actions regarding it. It is only when your decisions affect The Ende and the outer realm do we involve ourselves in your matters. When the results of your war did not appease you, you resorted to more extreme measures; measures that fall outside of your jurisdiction, and the reason why I speak to you now. Your rerouting of the Eormensyl tore a breach between this realm and the outer reaches of Oblivion. You were the Eormensyl's Keeper in Trust, and you have desecrated your oath! Your abduction, unsanctioned awakening, attempt to imprison, and assault of the Essence are all crimes most heinous within the outer realm! Your actions have resulted in an abomination of the natural order, and STILL, you remain unmoved by what the loss of progressive knowledge will eventually mean to every sentient being within every realm connected by this universe! stated the Ende Dweller.

Wodan started, "If you know so much about what happened…"

The Night of the Twin Stars, so it is called, interjected the Ende Dweller.

"...then tell me WHY I resorted to such extreme actions!" shouted Wodan.

You are driven to obsession to possess the knowledge of the circumstances surrounding your son's untimely death and the whereabouts of his soul.

"And for this, I would go to any extreme! We found him dead, with no sign of cause or reason! Not only was he murdered by someone's hand, his soul had vanished! It did not pass over as Aesir souls do! As Keeper of the Sacred Passages of Eormensyl, I should have known! There is no account of Baldar's soul ever reaching the Eormensyl's passage to Ende's Gate," strained Wodan.

You are correct, Baldar's soul did not arrive at Ende's Gate to Oblivion as it should have, and we still have no information as to why this would occur, the Ende Dweller stated without feeling.

"You know what I seek! If I were to possess all knowledge, I would most certainly possess the knowledge of the cause of Baldar's death and how to find his soul, as well as the means to restore it, to make its Ende's journey. I am not disillusioned! I know I cannot return my son to me. I only want to give his soul it's proper passage. "

Yes, but you admit you seek to possess knowledge and not to restore it! said the Ende Dweller. *You have not learned, Wodan. You have gained nothing from this quest; you have only lost. It was a waste of lives and resources to have your war. Don't you think the Vane would have told you if they knew of Baldar's death than to risk the worlds they covet?*

"I since have realized that," said Wodan, "and am trying to mend my realm."

But it is too late, I'm afraid. You have shown no sign of trying to rectify your crimes, said the Ende Dweller.

"Were you waiting for me to repent?" asked Wodan sardonically.

Other than the kyndness you have shown your own realm by ending the war, you have done nothing to mend what you have broken, nor do you see the need to do so. You need to restore what you have destroyed, said the Ende Dweller.

"Or what? Are you here to punish me?" Wodan laughed.

That is not our place. I can only stress that your time is running out. Your punishment will be that you, as well as every living being, will have to live with the results from your actions. These consequences reach farther than even your vast comprehension can imagine, stated the Ende Dweller.

"This is my warning," said Wodan, with disdain.

If you wish. We have been advised by the Beyond Dwellers to revoke your access to any gates of the Eormensyl that span into the outer realm. Contact with Oblivion, and any of the outer reaches, has been banned. You are limited to the confines of the inner realms within this universe. You can still redeem yourself, Wodan. I will say again, restore what you have destroyed, and you may yet be able to put a proper close to the death of Baldar. I cannot offer any hope beyond that. It is your choice for your fate, the Ende Dweller said before disappearing into the passage of shadows.

As morning rose, one of Wodan's many informants arrived at his Majesty's quarters with word of the Queen, only to find closed doors and Wiljo and Wæ hovering like vultures in the corridor. The King's brothers assured the informant they would tell his Majesty and intercepted the message on the King's behalf.

"We have received word that the Queen will be visiting the Tjetajat Central Council today in her official capacity. This is an unscheduled meeting and could easily be an attempt to conceal the true purpose of her visit," said Wæ, to the King.

"Her beloved seers! What good have they ever been? They provided nothing useful in all these years of our search. And what good were they before; the Tjetajat, the Wise, or any of the others of notions throughout our worlds? A complete waste! Nothing! They saw or said nothing about the approach of..." Wodan paused, "of Baldar's..." His voice trailed off as the words drained from him. "Yet, Frija goes running off to her precious Tjetajat. Why does she not feel betrayed? How can she find any worth in them?"

"If it pleases you brother, we would be most glad to follow her Majesty and..." began Wiljo.

"Yes, yes," said the King, waving Wiljo off, with this familiar exercise in futility. Wodan added a hollowly scripted, "Go and let me know if anything significant comes of it."

"You are gracious and kynd in your trust, brother," said Wæ, as he and Wiljo extended bows.

Wodan responded with a final resigned wave. As his brothers exited the room, Wodan's ravens returned from their morning hunt and perched on the balcony's edge, tearing at their prize, a rabbit that was their unfortunate prey.

Wodan stroked their heads as they devoured their meal. He admired their fierceness and their unwavering loyalty.

"You, my pets, are about the only two left around me that I can trust," said Wodan as he raised their bloodied beaks to look at him.

Wodan watched as Hyge and Myne finished the rabbit, then walked across his room to a shelf that held an alabaster stone jar. The jar's stone surface, though smooth and solid, appeared as waves of white swirling and rolling over one another in their perpetual tide. Wodan had brought the jar with him from Aesingard, for he carried it with him wherever he traveled. Wodan opened the jar and poured a small amount of water from it into the palm of his hand. He rubbed his hands together and returned to his raven. As he stroked the top of their heads, visions and emotions of what the birds had seen rushed by Wodan's sight as if they were his own memories of experiences and feelings.

"Nothing to report from this day past, I see. No sign of your discovery, but don't fret. You were on the trail of something significant a few days ago— and I know you feel it's very close. If it had not been for that meddlesome hawk, you might have found it... whatever it was. I have faith in you both. You'll find it again. Now rest."

Kitaj awoke to find her forehead pressed against the tabletop. She had fallen asleep in her chair after finishing her tasks for the Order. Aergo was happily asleep in her lap. She rubbed her face and tried to regain her thoughts. She was still caught up in her night's dream. She had finally met the young man she sought and they were simply having a conversation. Kitaj recalled the experience she had the day before in the Swedu pavilion and was reassured by the thought that at some point they would meet again. If she could help it along she would.

Be it one way or another, it will happen, she told herself.

Her mother came into the room in a huff and asked, "Did you finish the..?"

Before Corynth could complete her question, Kitaj replied, "Yes, it's all ready."

"You need to hurry, you.." Corynth started.

"...have to meet with all of the suppliers to make sure they deliver to the camp today," Kitaj droned. "Yes, Mother, I know. I'm leaving now."

"Well, good. And don't forget..." Corynth added.

"...that you love me. No? Wait, that the milk supplier knows to deliver to our camp twice a week instead of once until summer."

"What has gotten into you lately?" her mother asked.

"Just me," Kitaj replied with the most truthful answer she could give.

Her mother shook her head at her daughter's nonsense and urged her to leave immediately. Corynth kept her mind sharply focused on the camp's preparations to avoid disclosing that Rûni was to arrive shortly for his lesson.

Kitaj picked up the sleeping Aergo, and held him to her shoulder as she started for the door, but paused to ask her mother one question.

"Have you seen Rûni lately?" she asked.

Corynth was afraid her concealment was slipping and replied, "Not since yesterday. You weren't here." Corynth added.

To her mother's answer, Kitaj asked, "Do you expect to see him today?"

Corynth turned away from her daughter, too busy to stop and answered, "Possibly. Now, you need to hurry on."

Kitaj thought something was amiss in her mother's answers but had little time to question her further.

⁂

Brieg woke to find he was feeling much better than he could have expected. The powder the Vane physician had given him the day before had a miraculous effect and the large black bruise that had spanned his side was barely visible. He rose to his feet with only a slight stiffness to his shoulder and he hoped that this last full day of the festival he and his friends had together would be a much better day.

Dagen awoke feeling much more himself. A full night's sleep was just what he needed. The realization surprised him that he had been functioning without sleep for two days. He met Brieg downstairs in the tavern and found Rûni had left word with Ismadalia that he had returned to the Order and would meet them at the games registration.

After a morning meal, Brieg and Dagen walked to the festival grounds and enjoyed the crisp, bright morning. Dagen apologized to Brieg for his behavior the day before when they had met in the Gicel section and told him about his experience with the Léohet reader. Brieg didn't know whether to laugh or be concerned.

"That is strange," was Brieg's first thought to say, but added, "You keep surprising me with the states you keep showing up in. Whenever I find you lately, you're a mess."

"And every time I'm with you lately, you're trying to get out of a mess," laughed Dagen.

"True, but hasn't it always been that way?" laughed Brieg. "Don't think twice on yesterday. I should have told you what was happening. It was those same two guards my father sent to fetch me. They were looking for me again. I'd had enough and did not want to discuss my problems. I'll be under my father's watch soon enough. Today we are going enjoy ourselves," Brieg said with determination.

"I understand about not wanting to discuss problems anymore. You're right, today is ours," returned Dagen.

As Dagen and Brieg reached the hill looking down at the festival, they noticed a large structure was being constructed outside the entrance. Two Heítaned appeared to be overseeing the project, as folde and etwin-kynd, Midangardians, Vane, and the Aesir King's guard carried out the duties of erecting the structure.

"Do you have any idea what they're building?" asked Dagen, marveling at the height.

"None what so ever. If I had to guess I would say some sort of Heítaned/Fyr light display for the festival's closing tomorrow night. I guess we'll find out soon enough," said Brieg.

Registration for the day's games opened early that morning in the same location as the day before, at the end of the field in front of the Aesir section.

Reassuring Dagen he had recovered, Brieg's intentions were to sign up for three events. While standing in line, he overheard that the structure outside the festival entrance was a Léohet game that had not been part of the festival since pre-war times. It was a large ramp for a three manned sled. As word spread, everyone around Brieg wanted to get their names on the list for the sport the Léohet called Holu. Brieg managed to get his, Dagen and Rûni's names on the list as a team. He knew Dagen would agree, but Rûni would take coaxing. It was the last large event of the day before the eating and drinking contests, for which Brieg also signed up.

Brieg was excited to tell Dagen about Holu, and they both agreed not to mention it to Rûni until time was closer, or Rûni would fret about it throughout the day. Neither Dagen nor Brieg wanted to put him, or themselves, through the anguish. Rûni found them soon after the decision had been made, and both of his friends stayed true to their agreement, even when Rûni asked what was being built outside the festival.

"I think it's a surprise," said Brieg.

Dagen had to turn away before he started to laugh.

"Brieg, when's your first event?" asked Dagen, in an attempt to change the subject.

"Soon, I better get ready," said Brieg.

"Is he all right?" asked Rûni, questioning Brieg's giddy mood.

"He's fine. Brieg's just happy to be feeling better and enjoying the day," said Dagen with a smirk.

"I'm glad to see you both are feeling better today," said Rûni, still wondering about the complete change of temperament in his friends from the day before.

Brieg's first event was another he had participated in the years prior. A section of the field in front the Fyrfolde pavilion had been roped off and reinforced to contain the contest rounds of Avemnati Riding.

Avemnaties were large, lumpy, lizard-like bird creatures with thick leathery skin, long necks, and appeared to be bald. Their feathers were few and similar to course bristles, which stuck out of the tops of their lumps. Though they were strong animals that did not care much for being ridden, there was little danger to riding one. Their beaks were naturally rounded and their claws had been trimmed back to a less lethal length. The animals themselves seem to take pleasure in throwing people off them and followed the launching of their riders with a distinct call that sounded like a deep chuckle.

The Fyr avemnati trainers had fit four animals with saddles, and the winners were whomever could stay on the longest and which animal could lose their riders the quickest. The winning rider won a Fyr crafted dagger and the animal that won received a large bowl of spicy Fyrfolde peppers, called pippops. Brieg had discovered two years before that if he wrapped his legs around the avemnati's neck, he could stay on longer. The protective avemnati trainers did not find Brieg's solution harmful to them and allowed it. Dagen and Rûni always found Brieg's rides to be one of the highlights of their trips. When Brieg's turn came, he climbed aboard his avemnati, named Augu. On the judge's signal, the trainers let go of their animals and the avemnaties began to spin in circles, doing their best to remove their riders. Dagen and Rûni laughed so hard, their sides hurt. Brieg had managed to stay on, while the other three animals chuckled at their riders on the ground. Augu's trainer caught him, helped the dizzy Brieg out of the saddle, and steadied him on his feet. Brieg had advanced to challenge the other round winners and stood to the side to watch as other contestants rode the avemnaties. Brieg, Dagen, and Rûni laughed to the point they started snorting. After four more rounds, Brieg was the only rider to stay on, and an avemnati named Lacerta had won the pippops. Brieg was presented with the dagger, and quietly lifted a pippop from the winner's bowl, and sneaked it to Augu.

After Brieg's win, Dagen, Brieg, and Rûni decided to ignore convention, and get to the venues they wished to see by crossing the busy field of games. Crossing the field also allowed Dagen to easily stay away from the Swedu venue, which he was determined to avoid until the next day. It was nearing noon and all three were starving. The best food and drink they had found was in Vangard and Léohetwin. They followed their noses and stomachs to the origins of amazing aromas in both welcoming pavilions and settled in a colorful and sunny spot in the Léohetwin venue to savor their culinary finds. Rûni had decided to no longer ask about the contents of what they were eating and enjoy his meal— as well as the atmosphere and his friends.

They had almost finished eating when Rûni noticed the activity in the middle of the festival field. They were closing off the main strip that ran from the entrance to the Aesingard pavilion. Workers from all worlds were preparing the ground with an oil, or some other slick substance.

"What are they doing?" Rûni questioned.

Brieg looked to Dagen, and together they decided it was time to include Rûni in what the three of them would be doing that afternoon.

"I guess they are preparing for the Holu," said Brieg casually.

"What's the Holu?" asked Rûni.

"Interesting that you should ask..." started Brieg.

"Oh no, what have you done?" asked Rûni.

Dagen thought it was best to be direct with Rûni before speculation got the better of him, and said, "It's a three manned sled. It's simple. You go down a ramp in a sled."

"Where's the ramp?" asked Rûni, before it dawned on him. "That monstrous contraption outside the entrance! You can't be serious!" he exclaimed.

"Do I look serious?" Brieg plainly asked Dagen.

"Yes, you look serious. Do I look serious?" Dagen asked just as blankly.

"Yes Dagen, I believe you look very serious. There you have it, we're serious." Brieg managed without smirking.

"But, it's so high! No, I'm not doing it! You can't make me!" said Rûni.

"All right, we'll find someone to ride with us and have a memory to last a lifetime. Oh... isn't that why we came here, Dagen?" asked Brieg, still keeping his face blank.

"You're correct, Brieg. That is why we came here. But not to worry, Rûni. We'll find someone else to ride with us," stated Dagen.

"We should probably get in line," said Brieg. "You can come stand with us, if you want, Rûni."

"Do either of you think I don't know what you're doing? There's no way I'm going!" stated Rûni.

Once they were in line with the other participants for the Holu contest, Rûni looked up at the high tower that held the long ramp. The steps to the top loomed over him and he exclaimed, "There's no way I'm going up those steps!"

Rûni was adamant. Brieg and Dagen remained calm and agreed he did not have to go up the steps.

Once they were climbing the steps, Rûni looked up to see their end and retorted, "I'm just keeping you company, but I'm not riding that sled with the two of you!"

Rûni was unwavering. Dagen and Brieg again kept calm and reaffirmed Rûni did not have to ride in the sled with them to the bottom.

When they reached the top of the stand and Brieg gave the judge the name of his team, Rûni still insisted he was not going. The judge, who apparently had this conversation before, did not show the same restraint as Dagen and Brieg and made it extremely clear to Rûni there was only one way down.

"Unless you push him off the stand," Brieg playfully suggested to the judge, who appeared to have had that conversation before as well.

"You three, now! Get in!" said the judge, without humor.

"Yes sir," they answered and climbed into the hollowed out tree that felt like the only thing left between them, the sky and ground.

Dagen agreed, from this vantage point, it did seem much higher. Brieg excitedly took the front and Rûni huddled in behind him. Dagen jumped into the back and before he could settle himself, they were off. Dagen and Brieg watched as the sky dropped before their eyes. It was over in a blink. They had landed a little past the midpoint of the festival field and were facing the Aesingard venue. Judges ran out to mark where they had landed and handed Brieg a note displaying their distance. Rûni had not made a sound, he was tucked into a ball, clinging to Brieg's back. The judges urged them to clear the field for they were running three sleds and had to remove theirs before they could send another one down. An elated Dagen and Brieg exited the sled, but had to uncoil Rûni and lift him out.

"I hate you," Rûni said as he tried to walk on his shaking legs.

"Yes, but wasn't that amazing?" asked Dagen, mostly directed to Brieg than to Rûni.

"I loved it!" Brieg said, grinning his largest grin.

Rûni did not smile or say anything. He just glared.

The three waited on the side near the Vangard section, watching the sleds shoot down the field's center.

Rûni mumbled, "Is that what we looked like? We actually just did that!"

"Yes Rûni, we did!" said Brieg and patted Rûni on the back.

When the contest had concluded, their distance was neither the longest nor the shortest. They had managed to come closer to the winning distance than not. Brieg concluded that it was Rûni's ducking that caused their sled to travel so far because the three members of the winning team had all huddled into the belly of the sled. Hearing those words from Brieg secretly helped Rûni feel better.

The Holu had drawn so much attention, that the ramp remained open after the contest. The line to ride was wrapped around the outer rim of the festival grounds.

"Do you want to go again?" asked Brieg eagerly.

Rûni respectfully bowed out, but Dagen was willing. Rûni remained where they had been watching, while Dagen and Brieg went for another round.

Kitaj had finally completed her duties. Preparation for the next day's induction ceremony and supplies for the Order's camp were guaranteed through winter. She had not discussed the day before with Aergo in depth, he knew there was no longer a point in trying to hold her back from whatever she wanted to do.

"I'm going back to the festival. I want to explore the Gicel venue. You can come with me if you want," said Kitaj.

Aergo converted into his dog form quietly and followed along. For someone whose life revolved around change, it was difficult for Aergo to watch Kitaj changing in front of him. He hated change, outside of himself, but he had to respect what Kitaj was experiencing.

He thought as he followed along, *This is a dangerous time, I could lose her, and that's the last thing I want. As her friend, I should support her judgment. She knows what she's doing; no matter how reckless, ill-minded, ridiculous or potentially dangerous her ideas might be. Who am I kidding? She doesn't know what she's doing. I better stay close.*

Both she and Aergo could not miss the enormous ramp standing in front of the festival entrance. They both watched in wonder as people in sleds rapidly descended, continued through the entrance, and across the field. Exciting as it was, Kitaj knew she was one to watch instead of ride— much to Aergo's relief.

They came through the entrance as the ramp was being prepared for another sled, and started in the direction of the Léohet pavilion. Kitaj stepped into the evening crowd with more confidence. Her exposure to the crowd was getting easier for her. Both she and Aergo could take solace in her advancing skill. She navigated through the Léohet and Swedu pavilions without incident. She smiled as she passed the spot where she had been zapped the day before and the beekeepers' tent. A feeling that all would be well warmed her as she entered the Gicel's section. The cold air reached out to embrace her without consequence. The venue was still beautiful, but the light was very different this time of day and did not make the ice and crystals gleam as it had the day before. Kitaj's thoughts went to her father, and she wondered if he would have found Gicelfolde to be beautiful, had he been there at a different point in time. Her thoughts were interrupted when a gregarious Gicel tradesman greeted her. His broad smile and happy disposition made her think of Léohet. The Léohet motif of his clothes reinforced her opinion. He was very likable— and she wanted to like him. Kitaj ashamedly wondered if she was capable.

"Ah, the cold here, it does not bother you," said Pyos. "But, it will be a cold winter."

He tried to sell her on the advantages to his tanned hides and furs, and told her about newly united metal works between

Gicel and Fyrfolde. Kitaj kept looking into his happy red face as he spoke. His words fell away as she found herself reading him. Pyos was so open to her, it was as simple as walking through a wide doorway. He was genuinely a happy person and enjoying his life, because he had to— for the family he had lost. When the King's forces invaded Gicel, they were determined to make it the last battle of the war. Few were spared. Pyos had lost everyone dear to him, including his wife and small children. His home was destroyed, and had he been with them, he would have certainly died as well. But, he had survived and been left with the task of burying everyone he loved and rebuilding his life. He still wished he had died with his family, but it was Gicel belief to carry on for all of those you lost and enjoy life for those from whom the chance of life was taken. Pyos felt deeply for his fellow Gicel whose emotions broke once he saw official signs of reunion with Fyrfolde. He had experienced similar times, but it was a dishonor to his family to stay in a sorrowful state of mind. The more you loved and lost the more you lived for them. This was his expression of grief, his atonement.

Pyos noticed Kitaj's expression change and asked, "Wha? What did I say? I made you sad. We aren't to be sad, we are all to be happy together— you and I, *all worlds' kynd* together again. We can all be *kynd* to each other. Is it not right?"

She wiped the tears rolling down her face and replied, "Yes, it is right. We should be. I'm sorry, thank you."

Kitaj was embarrassed to have vividly read him without his knowing. From everything she saw about him, she knew it was best not to bring his past forward, it was too personal. She was turning a red that matched his complexion, and she asked to excuse herself. Aergo stayed next to her as they walked back to the Swedu venue.

Kitaj's impression of Gicelfolde had changed with her better understanding their people. She noted the expansion of her thoughts, as her feelings and ideas evolved, taking on new forms and depths.

As she was leaving, she overheard a Gicel storyteller recounting a vividly frightening and cautionary tale of the Midangardian Bezerks. She stopped to listen. Kitaj could not help but think of the underlying purpose of the storyteller's choice, as she heard his tale and the gasps of his audience from many worlds.

She thought, *This is how we teach our young to be wary of the worlds' horrors, through the safety of children's stories.*

ᶜᶫ

The summer's Sun moved closer to its last setting for the season as Rûni patiently waited for Brieg and Dagen to slide into view. He knew patience was a better alternative than riding in the sled with them again. While he waited, he saw identical tables being set along the edge of the field for the eating contest. This year's selection looked very different from the previous years'. Instead of one food in mass quantities to finish, there were several. Most were unrecognizable to him. Being curious, Rûni went over to one of the judges to ask about the identically mounded tables. He was told, that in the spirit of community within the Winter's Nátt Festival, delicacies from all Nine Worlds were represented, and a winner would only be declared when the contents of the entire table were cleared. One of the judges handed Rûni a list of the table contents, which he saved for Brieg.

Dagen and Brieg's sled arrived in the middle of the field, with an unfamiliar passenger dressed in a reflective white cover, from Swedu, sitting behind Dagen. Rûni thought their ride must have been extra interesting. All three climbed out of the sled smiling and laughing. Dagen waved to the Swedu boy, as he walked back toward his pavilion. Brieg spotted Rûni and signaled Dagen to go in his direction as the sled they were in was carted away from the field.

"There's a story here, tell me about your ride," said Rûni, with enthusiasm and surprise directed toward Dagen.

"Thanks, Dagen! Thanks, Brieg!" the Swedu boy yelled,

"You're welcome, Nalo!" Dagen yelled back as Brieg waved.

"What?" said Brieg, "It was another great ride!"

"You know. Tell me about your passenger," asked Rûni.

Dagen replied, "There's not much to tell. He was alone in the line and we needed a third person. Nice boy. We all enjoyed the ride."

"Is that all?" asked Rûni.

"Yes, that's all," said Dagen.

Rûni could not help but think there had to be more to Dagen's encounter with their passenger, but moved on from his thoughts to say, "Um... Brieg, before I forget, you might want to take a look at this," as he handed Brieg the menu for the eating contest.

Brieg scanned over the list, nodding at each item, then frowned deeply and announced, "All right, I won't be doing that.

"Doing what?" asked Dagen.

Brieg handed him the list. Most of the items were palatable until he reached live Léohet eels and unhatched twin Fyrfolde avemnaties.

"Understood," replied Dagen.

Kitaj was curious to check on Isla as she passed the Swedu beekeepers but was concerned that looking in on her again might be taken as oddly intrusive. She decided to try and scan the feelings of the individuals inside the tent as she and Aergo walked by. Their overall feelings were much more at ease and accepting, with more anxiety than disappointment coming from the elder, and remnants of enjoyment from the Swedu boy.

Kitaj looked down at Aergo to tell him, "They're better. I think we should go on."

But before she could leave, Kitaj wanted to see if the place she had fallen still had any type of surge remaining. Aergo cocked his head as she ran over to the spot. The ground was dry and no charge or feeling was left. Disappointed, she reassured herself all would be well, and moved on through the Léohet section. Kitaj realized she had hardly seen the other side of the festival. She had rushed through when she went to see the Ende Dwellers.

"We have the entire other half of the festival to cover, and this is our last chance," she said to Aergo.

He put his head under her hand to let her know he was with her in her decision. She smiled back at him.

"You're awfully agreeable today," added Kitaj.

Aergo leaned into her leg and she bent down and hugged him around the neck. Aergo let out a long huff from his canine nose as he rested his chin on her shoulder.

ﻋﻠ

"It's our last night together, I'm determined we are going to have the most memorable of evenings! Before this night is over, I promise you, my friends, each of us will be bestowed with affection by all the Nine Worlds, as a proper launch to send us on our way!" announced Brieg.

"Are you serious? You plan to go around begging for sentiment for us? How humiliating!" said Rûni.

"I expected as much from you, but I would like to wager you will surprise yourself," added Brieg.

"This is ridiculous! Isn't it Dagen?" Rûni said, turning red.

"Sounds like Brieg," Dagen stated.

Brieg threw his arms around the shoulders of his friends as he began to explain, "We have a wonderfully sympathetic tale of the imminent departure of long time friends. It's perfect for tugging at heartstrings!"

"Even from Ende?" said Rûni.

"Even from Ende," said Brieg.

"I don't think that's possible," concluded Rûni.

"I'll accept your challenge, just to prove you wrong and enjoy your embarrassment," Brieg laughed.

They entered the festival grounds again, in their familiar route to avoid the Swedu pavilion, by starting at the Midangard section. It wasn't long before Brieg found a mead maid at a drink stand to approach. Dagen and Rûni couldn't hear over the noisy crowd around them what Brieg was saying to her, but from his gestures, it was clear he was talking about them. She was an intriguing young lady by most world's standards, with eyes that flashed with mischief when she looked at Rûni and Dagen. Brieg had her laughing as she signaled for Dagen and Rûni to come closer. The mead maid grabbed Rûni's collar and pulled him to her. He turned his head at the last second so she planted a kiss on his cheek. Rûni's face turned bright red under his white blonde bangs. The maid smiled at Dagen next. Brieg pushed him toward her. She leaned forward and closed her eyes. Dagen gave her a quick peck on the lips, like a kiss he might give to a family member.

"Your heart belongs to someone," she said with care.

Dagen didn't answer but returned a sad smile.

"Good luck to you," she added.

Brieg stepped up and the young lady entangled her fingers into Brieg's hair as they exchanged a much more passionate display. The customers around them began to cheer and yell. When they broke their embrace, Brieg stepped back, bowed to her, and kissed the back of her hand while he looked up at her with smiling eyes. The mead maid blushed at his gesture and playfully fanned herself with her free hand.

The next stop was the Heítaned. Not known for their public displays of affection, Brieg knew this would probably be the biggest challenge of his charms, next to persuading an Ende Dweller. A bored Heítaned girl sat slumped over the stand where Dagen had purchased his sky sight a few days before. Brieg was rubbish at guessing the age of Heítaned and comparing it to Midangardian years for reference, and decided this was his in.

"Excuse me Miss, but I was wondering if you could show me how to determine different worlds' year spans with your time-trackers," he asked.

She looked at Brieg as if he were something stuck to the bottom of her boot and spoke to him as she would a child, "The Sun is in the middle. Move Midangard around the Sun. See how the other worlds move around the Sun as well. Notice the number of times a certain world circles the Sun in one of Midangard's rotations and that will tell you the difference in years between worlds."

Brieg leaned in closer, as he manipulated the time-tracker, and hopefully her. The Heítaned girl continued to be unamused.

"There is also a reference at the bottom that tells you not only the number of days in a year but when the seasons occur for each world. Here's a simple example: Since Aesingard and Vangard are opposites within the same path around the Sun, their seasons are always opposite; one is in summer while the other is in winter. If you think about it, right now Aesingard is going into winter, which means...?" she sarcastically paused and Brieg just smiled and looked at her, "that Vangard is approaching summer," she paused again, "Are you truly that dense?" the young Heítaned asked.

"I am sorry, I got lost looking in the vast depths of your eyes," Brieg said as he moved closer.

The Heítaned girl rolled her eyes in response to Brieg's last statement, but it was a break from the monotony of her boredom and she decided to play along.

"So, I know twenty Midangardian years is equivalent to roughly 7 cet 374 of yours. How old does that make you?" Brieg asked.

"Old enough. I'm 6c344," she smiled, "*Roughly* 18 and one-quarter years by your standards."

"Old enough," Brieg's smile brightened.

"Yes," she added, knowing very well he was up to some type of mischief.

"You make your own decisions now, don't you?" Brieg chimed.

"Yes," she returned.

"Well my dear, you seem very bored. You already know all there is to know," Brieg said, oblivious to the weight of his own words. "What does a smart girl like you do for amusement? Let me guess; upset your prime parent? Is this your prime's stand?"

"You are full of questions," the Heítaned stated.

"I'm curious. You didn't answer. What do you do for fun?" Brieg asked.

"Upset my prime," she smiled and gracefully stood to her full height and towered over Brieg.

He looked up at her and she down on him with her sculpted face and enormous black eyes. She had a fragile and stretched frame to her appearance. Her pale grey skin had a faint iridescent quality that shimmered slightly in the fading light. Brieg caught glimpses of that same shimmer dispersed throughout the woven pattern in her sleek dark cropped hair. She was elegant without realizing her own presence. Physical attractiveness was not acknowledged in the culture of the Heítaned. Intelligence was the most desirable feature.

Brieg decided to appeal to her with effective logic, "If your prime were to see you display a social familiarity, say an act of affection, towards myself and my two friends, this, of course, would cause distress to said family member."

"I believe you are correct in your assumption, only being that I would encourage the affections of someone, pardon my terms, so beneath my intellect. It would defy understanding. And you are right; it would be senseless and irresponsible."

"And fun," Brieg added.

"There is that," she smiled again.

"I'm Brieg, and you are?"

"Xandri," she said as she leaned toward him.

"When would such a transaction be most beneficial to you?" Brieg asked delicately.

Rûni stood back in awe as he watched Brieg change Xandri's mind in a matter of moments. Dagen looked bemused.

"Now would be timely. I see my prime father returning," Xandri said as she reached up and placed her long index and middle fingers on either side of Brieg's face and closed her eyes. Had Brieg returned her gesture, they might be considered united. The encounter was brief and it left Brieg's temples tingling. Xandri looked up to see her prime's large forehead furrow as he walked in her direction. Her response was to tap both Rûni's and Dagen's temples.

"I hope that was as exhilarating for you as it was for me," Brieg said to Xandri.

"I'd leave now if I were you," Xandri added as her voiced dropped back to its monotone and bored pattern.

With their abrupt send off, Dagen, Brieg and Rûni departed. Brieg looked back to see Xandri's prime and thought it was best to put some distance between themselves and Heítaned, so they bypassed the Fyrfolde pavilion, the Ende's, and the Aesingard's venue to arrive at the Vangard's.

Kitaj and Aergo left the Léohet pavilion, and passed through the Midangard section. She, nor Aergo, saw anything that intrigued them in Midangard. It was all too familiar.

She and Aergo reach the Heítaneds' section. The various array of mechanized inventions was exciting and new to both of them. She received some puzzled looks from the Heítaned vendors at the sight of Aergo with her, and she reassured them they would not cause trouble.

"Do they know what you are, or are they concerned to have a dog near? I've never been able to tell," whispered Kitaj.

Aergo didn't know, but puzzled looks on Heítaned's faces were unheard of, and they made Aergo smile, causing his canine tongue to flop lazily out of his mouth.

Kitaj found herself drawn to the time trackers and timidly approached the young Heítaned woman at the stand.

"You're pledged to the Tjetajat," announced Xandri, commenting on Kitaj's clothing.

"Not officially, not until tomorrow," Kitaj replied awkwardly, surprised to be spoken to by the Heítaned girl in such a direct manner.

"The Great Seers," Xandri said, laughing sarcastically. "In the state our worlds are in, don't you think you're a bit— obsolete?"

Overhearing her, her already aggravated prime yelled, *Xandri!* within her mind, causing her to slightly wince.

"Excuse me," she added curtly, still squinting from the volume of her prime's voice in her head.

Kitaj looked at the young Heítaned warily and thought the girl was overly bitter and barely holding onto the facade of cordiality. Kitaj could not understand the meaning of her statement.

Why would the Tjetajat be considered obsolete?, she thought.

"Um, what about this one? I've not seen this design before," Kitaj said, hoping to change the subject and find out more about the intricate workings of the elaborate time tracker.

"That one? Like everything else," Xandri said with distinct boredom, "it's an old design, but we are including it this Winter's Nátt— since we are all back together again," she stated with more dripping sarcasm. "It celebrates the Eormensyl Arc, when the Nine Worlds' positions allow the Eormensyl to form a perfect arc to our shared Sun." Xandri ended dully.

"I have not heard of this. When is it to happen?" asked Kitaj.

"It will happen in 22 and 3 fourth segments of your years, add 3 days. This *phenomenon,*" Xandri said, as she rolled her large black eyes, "has occurred before, but far before King Wodan's time."

"Is it important?" Kitaj inquired.

"Records of the previous event make my prime think it so. I personally don't share his... what you would equate to... enthusiasm," she admitted but followed with the droning voice of her sales spiel. "With the Eormensyl's portal branches all fanned, it will be renewed and strengthened from our Sun's light, stronger than we have ever known it to be. Since the Eormensyl is so important to all our worlds, it's worth celebrating."

Kitaj admired the beautiful weaving design of the Eormensyl Arc time tracker. It was more intricate that the standard models and she wondered if she would be capable of reading it on her own. It's complexity intimidated her, where to Xandri, this was a child's plaything. The way it caught the light as it spun intrigued Kitaj and won her over. She rarely bought anything just for her and felt the urge to treat herself with an induction present.

"I'll take it," said Kitaj.

Xandri collapsed the time tracker and placed it in a small cloth pouch and drew the strings tight to close it.

"That will be 20 gem." said Xandri.

Kitaj emptied out her coin purse to come up with 5 coins that would equal the asking price. She was not one to barter. Xandri took her payment without another word, handed her the time tracker and turned away.

"Friendly girl," Kitaj said under her breath, as she and Aergo walked away from Xandri's stand.

ﷺ

At their new destination, Brieg's request was most welcomed amongst the Vane. Brieg stood in the middle of Vane's pavilion and politely asked for attention. Several heads turned in their direction.

He began in a humble but bounding voice, "My lifelong friends and I are departing tomorrow, to embark on separate lives, and must say goodbye to each other as well as who we know ourselves to be. It would be sincerely appreciated if any of you wished to bid us the kyndnesses of farewell."

A small circle of beautifully adorned and perfumed faces formed around them, and they shortly found themselves showered in hugs, kisses and well wishes for their journey. As to be expected, Brieg was loving the attention, while Rûni had a sense of suffocation, and Dagen kept his encounters polite and brief. The crowd began to grow around them, and Rûni began to panic. Suddenly the crowd parted and left the three standing in the center. Two Vane guards approached them and moved to either side as Ing Fré and Bereness Fréa approached. Brieg, Rûni, and Dagen were stunned but composed themselves to bow in their royal presence.

The Bereness spoke first, "News of you and your friends was brought to our attention. We want to extend our well wishes to you on your journey."

For once, Brieg was speechless in the presence of the fabled allure of Bereness Fréa. Dagen spoke up in his stead.

"We humbly thank you for your generosity and kyndness," Dagen said graciously.

"Where are your lives taking you?" Ing Fré inquired.

Dagen started, "To Sweduetwin for myself," as he nudged Rûni with his elbow.

"We love Swedu, don't we dear brother?" purred the Bereness.

"I am joining the Tjetajat and will be staying here," Rûni added with more enthusiasm than he intended.

"Very compelling, can you read me?" asked the Ing.

"I regret I have not developed that talent yet," Rûni stated nervously.

"We will look for you during the induction tomorrow," said the Bereness.

"And I will be joining the service of King Wodan, under my father Lygus Ingólf," said Brieg without pleasure.

"You're the local Dryhten's son, are you not?" asked Ing Fré.

Brieg was unsure where this question might lead him and prepared himself to follow through, "I am."

"And what are your thoughts on relations between worlds since the war?" asked the Ing.

Brieg rarely made any comment about the war. He was born into it and was only five years old at its end. His mother was able to isolate him in Carcadoc from many of its horrors, but Brieg had heard stories from his father's missions. It was enough for Brieg to know his views and his father's did not necessarily match.

Brieg stood straight and answered the Ing truthfully, "I am glad to see all worlds represented at this Winter's Nátt. It gives me hope for a better understanding of one another and reestablishing trust and unity between us all."

"I would have to agree. We have not been properly introduced. Your names, please?" requested Ing Fré.

Brieg, Rûni, and Dagen stated their names. Each was able to maintain a fairly calm exterior that masked their nervousness for being unprepared to meet the Vane royalty.

"We wish you well in your future journeys," said the Ing.

In the farewell custom of the Vane, Ing Fré and Bereness Fréa gave Dagen, Brieg, and Rûni each a kiss on each cheek and on their foreheads. The Bereness playfully ran one fingernail under Brieg's chin, causing him to become very self-conscious as a small shiver ran from his chin to his spine. The young men bowed and waited for the nobles to depart before they moved. Dagen and Rûni had never seen Brieg stunned to silence. All three were befuddled from their experience and all agreed to take pause before they continued.

The properties of the Vane's glow wine revived their senses, and Dagen, Rûni, and Brieg proceeded to the Gicelfolde pavilion. There, they were met with the rubbing of noses by a set of sweetly eager Gicel sisters.

From the Gicel venue, they went back to Aesingard's and found a Vane artist sketching scenes from the Aesir pavilion. She was compelled by their circumstances and willingly anointed each with the Vane's customary kisses, in return for allowing her to make quick sketches of them. Brieg decided since the Vane and the Aesir were so similar and she was in the Aesingard venue, the artist's participation could count for Aesingard. Dagen and Rûni agreed that they wanted this particular quest of theirs to conclude as soon as possible and seconded Brieg's decision for substitution for the Aesir. As Dagen obligingly sat for her, he felt he needed to distract himself from her keen study of his every feature. The process made him extremely uncomfortable. He looked around at the different sketches the artist had scattered about her— and a pair of rendered eyes locked with his.

The artist noticed the immediate change in Dagen's expression and asked, "Pardon me, but you just transformed—

just now, right in front of me! All of your features have shifted! May I ask what has happened?"

Dagen reached down and gently picked up a drawing that was laying amongst her other sketches, and asked in astonishment, "When did you draw this?"

"It was yesterday. Yes, the two colors of her eyes caught my attention as well. I remember her; she was intriguing. Those eyes and that wild hair— I had to draw her. She was reluctant, but I can be very persuasive when I'm inspired," said the artist, as she smiled at Brieg.

"What can you tell me about her? Did you get her name? Anything would be helpful!" said Dagen in a fevered pitch.

"Ah, you've met! You pine, I can see! I'm sorry, I don't have her name, nor know anything about her... other than she was..."

Rûni held his breath. If she were to say "Tjetajat," his pretense would crumble on the spot, along with Dagen's friendship.

"... Midangardian," concluded the Vane artist.

Rûni could not help letting out a silent sigh of relief behind Dagen's back, which did not go unnoticed by Brieg.

"She was here!" Dagen exclaimed to his friends. "She was here," as he slumped back into his depression.

Brieg looked at Dagen, and back to Rûni, "Well, at least you know you're close Dagen, I would hold tight to that. I believe fate is on your side, against whatever obstacles are in your way," he added by shooting another look in Rûni's direction. "We won't find her standing here, we have to keep moving."

The artist took pity on Dagen and added, "I had planned to keep the sketch, but I think you should have it."

Dagen thanked the artist for her kyndness, as he, Brieg and Rûni departed. Dagen's thoughts were lost in the sketch as they walked along. His only distraction from it was to frequently glance up and scan the crowd. Rûni was also more alert to the crowd around them and his actions seemed overly nervous to Brieg.

Dagen and Rûni barely noticed when they arrived at The Ende. Brieg's quest seemed to be lost to both of them but they carried through to humor their friend. There were only two Ende Dwellers to be found. One offered his (or her) hand raised to press palms with Dagen, Rûni, and Brieg which seemed like a benign gesture, but each soon found their body heat extracted and overcome with an internally icy core.

Brieg's answer to thawing themselves was a venture to the Fyrfolde section. There, they found more mead and plenty of small fire pits to warm themselves.

Brieg began to show signs of over warming as sweat began to roll off his drink induced crimson cheeks and nose. His speech began to slur and he needed Dagen and Rûni to help steady him as he walked. Brieg insisted venturing over to the Fyr powder stand that was next to the Heítaned time trackers they had visited earlier. Xandri spotted Brieg and his friends immediately. Brieg, in an attempt to get the attention of a lovely Fyr woman, turned around and accidentally hit the stand, knocking over a keg of ignition powder, and sending the powder airborne. When the powder reached the open flames of the torchlight at Xandri's stand, the air ignited in a colorful array of flash flames, accompanied by a loud boom and a crackling fizz. The explosion could be heard throughout the grounds. Everyone near ducked for protection.

Kitaj and Aergo had remained in the Heítaned pavilion. There had been too many items to explore and Aergo was enjoying himself too much by making the Heítaned elders uncomfortable. They were at the beginning of the venue, nearest the Midangard section when the fire started. Kitaj heard the explosion behind her and ducked from reflex. Aergo did not react in time to change and shield her, but grabbed one of her arms in his teeth, and drug her behind a Heítaned display table.

꙳

The fire was over in an instant without injury, and luckily, with little damage. Only a few tarps were singed. Once the shock of the accident had passed, the Fyr owner of the powder stand launched into a tirade aimed at Brieg. Though Brieg was not versed in Fyr, he could tell the words the stand owner was using were far from complimentary. Rûni stepped up into his familiar role as Brieg's damage control by placating the powder stand owner with the remaining coins from Brieg's almost empty purse. Dagen caught a glimpse of Xandri laughing, a rarity for a Heítaned. He also saw her prime standing behind her with an even more pronounced furrowing of his enlarged brow. Dagen helped Rûni in carting off Brieg from the scene before more calamity ensued.

Staggering with the weight of their intoxicated friend, they took the swiftest and most direct route away from Fyrfolde to the Léohetwin pavilion by crossing the field arena. They avoided the attention of the King's guardsmen by blending in with the confused and dispensing crowd.

꙳

Kitaj saw nothing of what had happened, and Aergo refused to let her peek out until the commotion died down. She had only heard and sensed the stampede of people as they fled through the Heítaned venue. Just for an instant, she thought she caught a moment of the familiar charge, but it was faint and fleeting. She tried to seek it out but could distinguish little from the residue of panic and confusion swirling around her. There was one calm spot directly in front of her. It was the Heítaned merchant who was still standing behind his display.

Kitaj and Aergo overheard him say, whether for their benefit or someone else's, "Explosions are common with Fyrs."

ᷱᷟ

After the commotion, Brieg seemed to have lost sight of his goal of collecting affections and was insisting on observing the upcoming Léohet and Swedu performances. It was rumored their combined display would be a highlight of the festival. Word had spread that the opening ceremony had only hinted at the talent and spectacle of their upcoming showcase. Dagen maneuvered seating for them to watch the sunset performance, and sat Brieg between him and Rûni to keep Brieg contained. They could not remember seeing Brieg in such a bad state. Dagen and Rûni were not aware how deeply the Ing Frey's question had affected Brieg and his condition stemmed from struggling with the terms of his own fate.

ᷱᷟ

Aergo released Kitaj once their surroundings regained order. She climbed out from under the table and thanked the Heítaned merchant for allowing her and her "dog" to find safety under his display. He blankly nodded to them as they went about their way. Aergo was unsure of heading in the direction of the explosion, but Kitaj argued that everything and everyone seemed to be fine, other than her bruised arm from his bite. When they reached the damaged sight, Xandri was still laughing.

Kitaj and Aergo moved deeper into the Fyrfolde section. The weapons and metal wares did not intrigue Kitaj, but her interest peaked when she spotted the avemnaties. Their trainers were still trying to calm them after the explosion. With their natural instinct to run and find shelter from the common occurrence of explosions on Fyrfolde, the animals had done all they could to break away. Their trainers held tight to them as they stroked their necks to ease them. Kitaj approached the trainers to see if they would allow her to get closer. Aergo could tell his presence would not be of help and would scare the animals further, so he remained back to give Kitaj the opportunity to see the avemnaties up close. One trainer thought his avemnati was calm enough to where it would allow Kitaj to pet it. Kitaj reached out her hand and felt the animal's rough skin and bristly feathers on its neck. She caught a glimpse from the animal's memory. It was clearly Rûni's red headed friend feeding the avemnati some type of pepper. Kitaj laughed lightly from her vision, while the trainer assumed she had been tickled by the avemnati's bristly feathers. She thanked the trainer and walked back to Aergo.

"I've seen enough. I'm ready to leave," Kitaj concluded.

Aergo was completely puzzled. He thought at the very least she would have wanted to see the Léohet and Swedu performances, but more importantly, Kitaj would have wanted to continue her search until the close of the festival. Kitaj smiled and began humming again as she turned around and slowly walked back toward the festival entrance.

♪

The Holu had stopped and the field had been cleared. Torches were lit and large horns bellowed, signaling that the Léohet performance would begin. The excited audience, packed around the edge of the field, jumped to its feet in hopes of somehow getting a better view. Drummers banged slowly on their metal drums as they walked across the field, escorting large carts that were decorated in flowers, sea shells, and large palms.

Bronzed performers emerged from the carts which halted in the middle of the field. The performers gracefully disembarked and placed themselves in staggered rows. The female dancer stood at the front of the row, dressed in their tribal tradition of bright colors and adorned with flowers. The dancers began to sway as the drums and horns grew louder and faster. Brieg was mesmerized by the movement and began to clumsily sway with them. He was causing no harm, so Dagen and Rûni thought nothing of him dancing in place. The performers began to bend and sway faster. They leapt into the air and sprang across the field as the music heightened.

In the next moment, Brieg lunged out onto the field and was stumbling throughout the performers. Dagen and Rûni tried to run out after him, but were stopped by members of the King's guard. They could only watch as Brieg was tackled and escorted off the field. Dagen and Rûni tried to keep watch of where Brieg was being taken. Two guardsmen were escorting him out the entrance. Dagen and Rûni ran after them. Rûni hoped he would not have to pay the guards to let Brieg go; there was very little money left between him and Dagen to make a substantial offer.

When Dagen and Rûni reached the entrance, they saw the guards toss Brieg to the ground and ordered him to stay out. Dagen and Rûni ran to him, reassured the guards they did not mean to cause trouble and helped Brieg back to his feet. From the guards' reactions, it was clear that all three were no longer welcomed back into the festival that night.

The King retreated into his chamber. He could not stand the noise from the festival performance below Kestel Midlen and shut the doors to his balcony. The sound of the music and the crowd was grating on his last nerve. He had to leave! The thought of a night's ride through the Asbjorn Forest on

Slepsil was an appealing option. He flung open his chamber door to find his brothers about to request entry.

"What is it?" Wodan stormed.

"Kynd brother, we wished to tell you our findings from the Queen's meeting with the Tjetajat Central Council," Wæ offered meekly as he and Wiljo scrambled to follow their brother's pace.

"Let me guess, you discovered nothing," said Wodan as he continued in haste.

"We regret we cannot deliver any word for your benefit," added Wiljo.

"Throughout the day, we know she—," started Wæ, but was abruptly cut short by the King.

"Then get out of my way!" yelled Wodan as he departed from them.

ﻌﻟﻌ

Small bonfires were set near the surrounding edges of the festival grounds. Many attendees were gathered around them, telling tales, singing songs, and settling in to reach the morning. Dagen and Rûni toted Brieg to one of the smaller bonfires where they were welcomed by happy strangers. People from various worlds started singing a song of The Wild Hunt. Brieg tried to join in while Rûni and Dagen tried to keep Brieg in check. Brieg resigned himself to sitting down while spouting sincere professions of endearment to his friends, and began to recant some of their many adventures of bygone times.

"Remember the time I raced you while riding backwards on my horse all the way from the center of Carcadoc to your home, Dagen?" slurred Brieg.

"Yes, I do," said Dagen.

"How old were we?" asked Brieg.

"About thirteen or fourteen," answered Dagen.

"Yes, that's right. About thirteen or fourteen. I did it on a dare, you know," said Brieg.

"I remember," Rûni paused. "So this is how the night is going to go," he said back to Dagen.

"Dags, Dagi, Rûni, remember, remind me the night we took apart that wagon and reassembled it on top of the pub's roof?" Brieg stumbled.

"Yes, Brieg," said Dagen.

"How old were we then?" asked Brieg.

"Seventeen."

"Yes, seventeen!" said Brieg shutting and opening his eyes slowly. "And Rûnini, how about the time we were daring our wits in Carcadoc mill?"

Rûni stiffened.

"And Rûni got his arm caught and we thought he was going to be crushed."

"Yes, I remember," said Rûni.

"And how old were we then?" About twenty?" asked Brieg.

"Try twelve," said Rûni.

"Oh! Dagen, what about— when we were shooting and your sister Llylit shot my arrow down before it reached its target."

"Yes, she has good aim," added Dagen.

"Good aim? She's amazing! I always liked your sister," said Brieg earnestly.

Dagen gave Brieg a leery and questioning look. Dagen had never been aware of Brieg showing any interest in his sister.

"No need for worry, friend," said Brieg, as he sloppily patted Dagen across his back, "Only admired her from afar— cross my heart!" Brieg gestured, fell over onto his side, and began to snore.

"We might be here for the night— from the looks of him," said Rûni.

Dagen added, "He's always made our lives interesting."

"True. Never a dull moment," said Rûni.

"He tries so hard to take care of us, to make sure we enjoy ourselves, but somehow it always ends up with us taking care of him," said Dagen.

"What's he going to do without us? I hate to think about it," said Rûni.

"I think he does too," said Dagen.

"I know," Rûni paused, and added, "We'll all have to adjust eventually."

"You have a head start on us, Rûni," Dagen said sincerely. "We're glad you're going to have the life you wanted."

Guilt pangs began washing over Rûni again. He turned his eyes away from Dagen to look up at the stars.

"Dagen, do you think you could be happy... on Swedu?

"I don't have much choice," said Dagen.

"I don't mean a choice about going, I meant do you think you could try to find some happiness in your circumstances?" Rûni clarified, realizing he was not asking for Dagen's sake but for his own.

"I guess in time, I'll have to resign myself to it and I'll try," said Dagen.

Rûni added, "You should try." I'm sure you'll find happiness somehow and at some point," hoping to make himself feel more assured.

"I can't help but think I'm leaving every chance I had of that here behind me," Dagen sighed, and continued as he rolled Brieg over to stifle his snore, "I just wish I could have seen her one more time, to know for sure, to know I didn't dream it."

"Her," said Rûni, fighting down his own internal reactions of a guilty conscience.

"Oh well, guess it wasn't in the stars," he paused. "Anyway, I'm really happy for you Rûni. It looks like everything you wanted is coming together. You deserve it," Dagen said as he patted Rûni on the shoulder, turned his eyes away from the studded night sky, and settled into sleep.

Rûni, on the other hand, could not sleep. He sat, watching over his two friends, knowing tomorrow they would never be the same.

Dagen woke up to the sound of thuds, as Rûni's heels pounded into the packed clay ground while he paced back and forth. The fires had burned out and he could see the outline of bodies laying listless and strewn about on the ground in their slumbering states. The air was thick and grey with fog, but Dagen could make out Rûni's form pacing near him. He was chewing his nails down to the quick and was as grey as the morning itself.

"Good, you're awake," Rûni said, in a manic manner, while still pacing. "I'm sorry, I thought I was doing the right thing—and I admit, I had some hopes myself," Rûni blurted out.

"What are you so worked up about?" asked Dagen.

"I should have told you, but I had my reasons. Please don't hate me. I don't want us to part like that," Rûni continued.

Dagen was not ready for the onslaught of Rûni's words, and it left him confused and disoriented. Meanwhile, Brieg lie unmoving.

"Rûni, calm down. What are you talking about?" Dagen asked while trying to get his bearings.

"Her," Rûni stopped. "Her name is Kitaj."

It took a moment to register with Dagen to what and whom Rûni was referring. He caught his breath as a stinging surge of energy coursed through his nerves.

"Kitaj," repeated Dagen.

"Ellor Kitaj, to be exact," said Rûni, looking at the ground.

Dagen paused. He rubbed his hands over his face to help wake himself and stood to face Rûni.

"How do you know this?" Dagen asked slowly.

"She is with the Tjetajat. She recognized me when I went to admissions," Rûni said without looking up at Dagen.

"You've known for four days," he paused, "and you let me walk around miserable— FOR FOUR DAYS!" Dagen exclaimed.

"You're leaving tomorrow. I thought it would be better that you didn't know under the circumstances of your arrangement," pleaded Rûni.

"And you decided this for me?" Dagen said, raising his voice and facing him.

"You weren't thinking clearly," said Rûni.

"*I* wasn't thinking clearly? When did you realize you'd be better at making decisions for me?" Dagen asked.

Rûni started to answer, but Dagen cut him off. He could not contain his frustration.

"Never mind!" he yelled.

"I'm sorry," said Rûni.

"Why are you telling me this now?" asked Dagen.

"I didn't want us to part with this between us," said Rûni.

"In other words, the guilt got to you," Dagen said bitterly. He began pacing again. His mind was reeling. "Where is she? I need to see her," he demanded.

"You can't. I mean, not until tonight!" Rûni blurted.

Dagen glared at him. He had never been this angry and disappointed with his friend.

"We are to be sequestered this morning until the induction ceremony tonight. Remember?" Rûni clarified.

"She is being inducted with you?" Dagen asked with some composure.

"Yes," said Rûni.

"I don't know what to think— you had no right to decide what was best for me!" said Dagen.

"I know," Rûni stated.

"Wait," Dagen paused and looked Rûni in the eye, "there's more to this than what you're telling me."

Events started coming together for Dagen to form a complete picture of Rûni's deception. The thought alone made his stomach turn.

"All this week, the mornings at the Council, because of her!"

"Dagen, I, I didn't..." stammered Rûni.

"No, I understand! You don't have to say another word," Dagen ended.

They stood with Dagen staring at Rûni with wishful disbelief and Rûni not able to look his friend straight on.

Brieg stirred and sat up, "What did I miss?"

"Nothing," they both said, but Dagen's reply had a biting edge.

"Rûni was just leaving," Dagen added, still staring at him.

Brieg yawned and rose to say, "The day is upon us."

He staggered over to stand next to Rûni and took him by the shoulders, "You can be a complete pain, but you're a dear friend. I will miss sparring with you. Good luck, I know you'll be happy."

Brieg hugged Rûni heartily, picking him up so that his feet did not touch the ground and said, "This is just in case we don't get to talk to you after your induction."

"It's unlikely," Rûni added weakly as the last of his air escaped him from Brieg's crushing hug.

As Brieg set him back on the ground, Rûni held his ribs and interjected, "You oaf! You could have crushed me! But that's just like you, not to think. Do me, yourself and everyone around you a favor Brieg, and think before you act! I worry about you. I wish you well."

Rûni turned to Dagen, "This is how we are going to leave each other?"

Dagen grabbed him by the arm and dragged him away as he spoke over his shoulder back to Brieg, "I'm going to walk with Rûni part of the way. I'll meet you back at the inn."

"Excellent idea! We'll be looking for you tonight, Rûni!" Brieg called out to them, flashing one of his winning smiles across his disheveled face.

ﻌﻟ

Kitaj arrived at the Order early the next morning. She and Aergo trudged through the dense fog to reach the gates. As they went inside, Corynth caught sight of Kitaj.

"I am sorry dear, Aergo can't be with you now. It wouldn't be fair to the other initiates. You know you have solitary contemplation to prepare for your induction this evening and you're required to be alone," said Corynth.

Kitaj knew what her mother said was true and tried to reassure Aergo, "It will be fine. You can stay close, just not with me. Find me tonight after the induction. It will be our secret," she whispered.

Aergo nuzzled his head against Kitaj's hand, flattened his ears, and growled as he passed Corynth before disappearing from the hall.

"And Kitaj, Eo-y, today you are twenty. I am glad to see the day is here for your induction," said Corynth with the most feeling Kitaj had heard from her mother in a long while.

Kitaj went to hug her, but her mother looked down and stepped away. To Corynth's response, Kitaj thanked her mother for her well wishes, bid her goodbye and went to her assigned room for contemplation. She would remain there until the induction with nothing to do but think and stare at four walls. It was to be a time of centering and reflection, but all Kitaj could think about was her near encounters with the one she sought and reaffirm her belief they would meet somehow and soon.

⟡

Dagen hurried with Rûni through the dense early fog in the nearly deserted streets. He had not relinquished the grip on his arm.

"We've been friends for years, I just don't know how you could do this to me. I guess I'll have the rest of my life on Swedu to figure out your actions," said Dagen.

He decided to let go of Rûni's arm and slowed his pace. Together, they walked in silence for part of the way.

Dagen spoke first, "Tell me about her."

"She's exactly how you'd think she would be," said Rûni.

"You already know this about her?" said Dagen with the bite back in his voice. "Are you getting your inner sight finally?"

"No," Rûni said sulking. "I just know *you.*"

Dagen stopped walking to say, "I don't want us to end in this way." He took a deep breath and asked, "Did you tell her anything about me?"

"Not much," Rûni mumbled.

"I see," Dagen stated in a resigned tone.

"She did ask about you, casually," Rûni added with some brightness to his delivery.

This gave Dagen an awkward feeling of hope— and he considered his hope was more than he should have.

"You'll see her tonight," Rûni said, with his own hope of redeeming himself to Dagen.

Dagen was still angry and disappointed, but an excitement was starting to grow within him at the prospect of finally seeing Kitaj that coming night.

They had arrived at the Council's gate. They both stood in front of it in a moment of awkward silence.

"I have to leave you here," finally stated Rûni.

"Don't tell her what we talked about, at least not before the induction," said Dagen.

"I had not thought to, but why?" asked Rûni.

"It will make her more nervous during the ceremony if she knew," said Dagen.

"And you know this? How?" puzzled Rûni.

"I just do. Promise me," Dagen said sternly.

"All right, I promise," consoled Rûni.

Dagen turned away from Rûni and threw his arms up in despair, "We shouldn't be ending like this!"

"It's my fault," said Rûni.

"I would have to agree with you there!" Dagen said with a slight laugh.

"If I don't get to say it later, please know I will always wish the best for you," said Rûni.

"As I do for you," said Dagen.

"Take care of yourself," Rûni added.

"Enough of this. I'll look for you tonight," Dagen said.

"Right, tonight," said Rûni as he threw himself into Dagen and patted him hard on the back, "I'm very sorry!"

"I know," Dagen added as he pulled away. "Tonight."

"Tonight," Rûni ended as he turned and walked through the gate, and disappeared into the fog.

Dagen walked across the street but found exhaustion overtaking him. His arms and legs felt as weighted as his heart and mind felt sick and inspired at the same time. He needed an opportunity to compose himself before he walked back to the inn. Dagen leaned against the stone wall of the building facing the Council Headquarters. He was barely able to make out the design of the iron gates through the dense grey fog.

Dagen reached into his satchel and retrieved the drawing of Kitaj. As his eyes followed the lines depicting her features, a compelling sense of loss awoke in him.

He tried to reconcile himself, *At least now I know her name and where she'll be.*

Dagen turned his attention back to the faint outline of the heavy gates that separated them.

His frustration grew as he thought, *She's right in front of me! Rûni is with her, and he'll be staying near her.*

He felt another wave of jumbled emotions engulf him as he rolled up the drawing and returned it to his satchel.

"We were so close," he said while closing his eyes and taking a few deep breaths. *I'll get to see her tonight— one last time.*

Without warning, a loud shrieking noise descended on him! Dagen had little time to react, other than to jump. A small black figure swept down from above and landed directly at his feet. He was startled by the black cat's appearance but was unnerved further by its behavior. It looked at him with ears flat, and hair on end. It hissed at Dagen, and with a low modulating growl, slowly slunk across the street and between the gate's bars of the Council Headquarters. The cat turned around and crouched down, while it continued to stare and growl at him. Dagen stood puzzled by the cat's behavior. It seemed to be guarding the gate against him, and projecting the clearest message it could relay for him to stay out. Dagen realized, with no hope of seeing Kitaj until tonight, the time had come for him to go and face his own responsibilities.

و

Dagen had done everything but prepare himself for this moment. He had found as many distractions as possible and had avoided the inevitable meeting until he knew he could no longer. At the inn, Dagen had rested and cleaned up as best he could to present himself to the Swedu family, the Malus, but the mirror did not lie. He looked haggard. Dark bluish circles lay just under the thin skin beneath his eyes. Had he any clue his emotional state was going to be doubly compromised, he would have put more care into preparing himself. There was no way he could have known of Rûni's deception. It didn't matter anymore. Dagen was out of time. He left the inn and walked alone back to the festival grounds, to face his fate.

As he approached the tent, he noticed again the banner with the three intricately painted luminous bees. He would be aligning himself with their symbol and these people. Dagen walked inside to find the Malu family very busy with customers. He watched for a moment and considered coming back later when the eldest member spotted him and waved him over.

"You must be Dagen," the Swedu elder said.

"Yes. Hello," Dagen said as he extended his hand.

The elder took Dagen's hand and shook it in the manner of Midangardian custom to welcome him. Dagen was surprised by the strength in his grip.

"We have been expecting you. I am Kama. There is much we need to discuss," he said.

There was a strain in Kama's voice that Dagen could not help but notice. Something was out of sorts.

Dagen offered, "I wanted to let you know I was here. I have some unfinished business that I must attend but will return after the ceremonies of tonight. I hope you find that acceptable."

"We are night people, as you should know. The dead of night is our day," replied a younger Swedu man with silver-blonde hair as he walked past.

"Qy!" Kama said, as he frowned at his helper and turned back to Dagen, "That is probably for the best. I will be freer to speak to you at length once we close tonight at the festival's end."

"Thank you..." Dagen said and was about to continue but Kama turned at that point and went back to his customers.

Qy eyed Dagen with some curiosity and little trust as Dagen exited the tent. Dagen was relieved to have his initial meeting behind him, but it was little comfort when he considered talking with Kama after the festival.

~ℓ~

Kitaj had been preparing for this moment all of her life. After tonight, she knew whatever her fate or these long lingering expectations of her, the answers would finally begin to reveal themselves. Her mother, Corynth, was performing part of the induction rites and she wanted to make her proud. All her anticipation was building to the point she felt her teeth chattering, her knees were hardly supporting her, and her hands had gone numb.

Remember to breathe, that will get you through, she thought.

Not only was the weight of her induction on her, but she could not help but wonder and hope that Rûni's unnamed friend would be there to see his induction as well. Kitaj was thankful for the darkness. The dim light could help conceal her physical signs of nerves. The thought of the King and Queen being present, along with spectators from the other worlds made her stomach turn. She looked around her in the holding tent area at the other candidates. It was a field of white robes, coated in the golden glow from the lanterns. The level of their anxiety was feeding into hers. There she finally found Rûni, excited and anxious. His sheet of white-blonde hair bounced back the faint light, reflecting the energy building within the tent. She so wanted to ask Rûni about his friend but thought better of it.

"Here we are," his voice said with a crack.

Rûni wanted to hurry on with the induction. He was overly nervous and was afraid he would accidentally let Kitaj in his mind. He consciously ran through the drills that Corynth had taught him for blocking. Rûni had to agree with Dagen; now was not the time to let Kitaj know what he knew.

"You will do fine, I'm sure," Kitaj said, trying to reassure him, and herself. "Before you know it, it will be over. Good wishes for tonight."

"You as well, as if you needed it," said Rûni.

"If you only knew how much," Kitaj added.

They made their way to the line that was forming at the front of the tent for the first stage of the induction rites known as The Passage. Each candidate had been given a small token at their induction briefing before going to the festival grounds. These small coins were stamped with the symbols of a form with radiating lines for the soul and a small red jewel to represent the heart. On the opposite side, the coins were embossed with the Tjetajat symbol of the past, present, and future; the same symbol used in the Order's cloak clasp and the permanently etched talisman that could be found on their members' skin. These coins were to be given as tokens of their loyalty to the Tjetajat. The candidates would proceed to the arched gateway that signified their passage and give their coin to the gatekeeper.

From outside the tent, she could hear the ceremonial drums and chants starting. Her palm was sweaty, making the coin very slippery in her grasp. She just wanted to transfer it safely to the gatekeeper. Fears of dropping it on the dark ground and frantically searching for it crossed her mind as they moved forward. Stepping out of the tent, the crowd let out raucous cheers, not that most were invested in the ceremony, but because they were in a very celebratory mood on this last night of the festival. She tried to close focus on the person in front of her as they moved forward and could see the arch approaching. She had seen this ceremony every year of her life, but to now be part of it was a very different experience. Kitaj reached the arch. To her pleasure, the gatekeeper this year was Tanadra. This part of the ceremony was usually performed by one of the previous year's inductees, but Tanadra, in spite of her standing as one of the Central Council, had requested the appointment for Kitaj's sake, and she greeted her with a proud smile.

"Eo-y! A new year of wishes for you this day!" Tanadra said to Kitaj, in acknowledgment of the date marking her birth.

Kitaj handed her the token without incident and smiled back at her mentor. She stepped through the arched gateway, and disappointedly did not feel any sense of miraculous difference, other than the relief to have the first stage behind her. She heard Rûni's sigh from a few steps behind her as he passed through.

The second stage of the rites was The Promise, where candidates were presented to the Central Council and offered themselves for service. It was a memorized pledge that Kitaj knew by heart, yet she was thankful she would not have to speak alone. She was doing her best to shield herself from the overwhelming input of the crowd. The candidates stood before the elevated platform of the Central Council, who were all dressed in their ceremonial red cloaks. Corynth stood expressionless, front and center— just as Kitaj had expected.

Corynth began, "Welcome Your Majesties, honored guests, representatives of our Nine Worlds, and induction candidates of the Tjetajat."

A boastful roar erupted from the crowd causing Kitaj to guard herself more closely. The rowdy crowd's enthusiasm was bombarding her.

"You come here today as inductees, chosen, not only on the birthright of long standing family bloodlines as members of the Order or your abilities as seers, but on the desire to continue to uphold the traditions, practices, and values we hold sacred," continued Corynth.

Kitaj knew this speech so well, she could recite it in its entirety. The words were drifting into the surrounding sounds until they became part of the background. She knew her focus should have been on her induction, but her anticipation of knowing the person she had been seeking was somewhere near made her realize what was most important to her.

She could feel it; he had already spotted her. Their shared energy started to surge. She was having difficulty focusing. The sound of her heartbeat took over, pounding in her ears, causing every other noise to fade to a distant murmur. She scanned the crowd for his welcoming face and found him standing next to his tall friend with the fiery hair. There he was, finally. His eyes met with hers and the scene around them was falling away. Kitaj knew with certainty what drew them to one another could only be explained as *right*. Both Dagen and Kitaj were lost to the moment, forgetting where they were and what was happening around them.

Brieg bumped Dagen's shoulder to get his attention. For how long he had tried, Dagen was not sure. Their connection was broken and Kitaj was snapped back into the moment. Panic hit her! What was she doing? Where were they in the ceremony? She was supposed to be reciting the oath and for a sickening moment, she could not remember what to say.

Breathe! she yelled in her head.

She took in a large gulp of the damp chilled night air and it shocked her as if she had plunged into an icy lake. Her eyes kept darting back to Dagen. She could see he knew she was struggling. Dagen's eyes held steady on her, in hopes of giving her support. The Promise Oath was almost finished and Kitaj had not heard half of it. She found her place and joined the others in their pledge. Kitaj was upset with herself.

Today of all days, and all moments! she thought.

She was hopeful that her mother and the Central Council had not noticed. She could perceive no additional concerns or disappointment from her mother's feelings or in the stone serious expression on her face.

"... and with this pledge I solemnly swear to uphold the codes of the Tjetajat and strive for a life of harmony in nature of being and what will be, to open myself to the life source and use my given gifts as a seer to work within the balance of existence. With this pledge, I give of myself humbly, and am reminded of the power of all, that I am but a small piece of the universe, and will serve as a conduit for harmony's sake. I accept this responsibility freely and honor those before me by carrying this sacred work forward. With these words, I give myself to the Tjetajat."

As Kitaj finished reciting her vow, she looked back to Dagen. She could see he was moved by the ceremony and his expression had shifted. She could sense him being proud of her, but it was shadowed by his own feelings of melancholy. Kitaj had perceived him correctly, Dagen took pride in her accomplishment but could only see this moment as the beginning of the end for them. In truth, both his and her circumstances were set to separate them. Kitaj, along with the other inductees, were to be sequestered for a year of training by the Elders, to master their talents; and Dagen was to be leaving the next day for Sweduetwin. Though Kitaj was unseeing to his situation, she was confident the barrier of her circumstances could not come between them. The absolution of their fates was strong within her and she knew, without a doubt, they would be together. Kitaj still was without details as to how this would come to be, just that it would. To Dagen's disadvantage, he did not carry with him the same assurance that Kitaj had of their inevitability and the thought of losing her so soon eclipsed him.

He turned his attention to Rûni, who was standing next to Kitaj. Though they had said their good-byes, and Rûni had disclosed the whereabouts and identity of Kitaj, Dagen still felt betrayed by him for not telling him sooner. Rûni's face was ecstatic from finishing his second stage of induction, but when he looked at his friend, his mood dropped. It was clear to him that Dagen had not forgiven him yet.

After the public rites, the initiates were to leave the Winter's Nátt celebration before the closing ceremonies, and be led to the burial grounds that spanned the outer edge of Lerakrey. Here, each initiate would spend the entire night on top of a barrow mound. These sanctified burial sites were part of the webbing of the Eormensyl's sacred passages that spanned between Wodan's realm and the outer realm, into Oblivion. Only by being close to these passages, would the Tjetajat initiates be open to receiving the full range of their gifts of sight.

As Kitaj and her fellow inductees were led to their night's stay, tensions were running high amongst some of the initiates. A following crowd was erupting around them. Cautionary tales of draugs; the unsettled lives that caused their corpses to seek revenge, were spouted by the surrounding entourage who intended to put the inductees on edge. Warnings of those who could not cope with what they had experienced and lost their minds rang out to feed the frenzy of taunts. Only when the Sun rose the next day, would they see who had survived.

Kitaj did not let this trouble her. It was rare that someone had an unhinging experience. Most often the circumstances were of frightening their own selves into a state. She could easily pick out the inductees who she doubted would withstand the entire night. There was no fear of the dead for her. Rûni, though nervous, was excited about the possibility of seeing some type of apparition or communicating with the beyond. He hoped maybe this would be his gift and was eager for what might happen.

To conceal his actual motive, Dagen suggested to Brieg, "Let's see where they're placing Rûni."

Brieg recognized the opportunity for mischief. He followed along with Dagen while grinning from ear to ear.

"He's always looking for proof. It would only be fitting to give him a proper send-off. He already looks like he's about to jump out of his skin. It wouldn't take much," said Brieg.

Dagen had no mind to pull tricks on Rûni, but following did allow him a way to see where they were taking Kitaj. He was not about to tell Brieg his true intentions. Dagen wasn't sure where this design was leading him, and was wearied at the thought of Brieg's special brand of encouragement on the subject.

CHAPTER 8
CONVERGENCE

Dagen and Brieg followed the initiates' procession to Lerakrey's burial grounds on the outer edge of the city and made sure they were not seen in their pursuit. Rûni would not have seen them even if they had stood near him. He was caught up in the moment and could not see beyond his next step.

When the procession came to a halt, Dagen and Brieg ducked behind a tree. They could overhear the initiates receiving instructions to the next phase of their induction. It was in that moment Dagen and Brieg realized they were intruding on a sacred moment in the ceremony. The initiates were divided into smaller groups and disbursed. Dagen watched closely to see which direction they were taking Kitaj. He was trying to figure out how to follow her without having to explain to Brieg what he was doing. Much to Dagen's relief, Brieg's attention was whisked away when he caught sight of a lovely red haired inductee.

"Ah, Rûni would be expecting us to pull something on him tonight, let's make him sweat it out a little. Plus, you know very well that red is my favorite color," said Brieg.

"Yes, and we've always wondered why," Dagen joked.

"Has something lightened your spirits?" asked Brieg.

"What makes you ask that?" Dagen returned.

"It's the first time you've seemed more yourself in days," said Brieg.

"Maybe I finally have a glimmer of hope about my future," said Dagen.

"Glad to hear it, but I guess this is where we part. I hate farewells— and if I'm going to see where that red beauty is going, it has to be now," said Brieg.

"I completely understand — a fitting end," said Dagen.

They exchanged nods of acknowledgment and a quick hardy hug between them before Dagen watched Brieg's form fade into darkness.

Dagen could see Rûni, Kitaj, and two other initiates being lead to three barrow mounds nearby. He watched from a distance as Rûni and the other two climbed ladders to the top of the barrow mounds. The tops of the mounds were blanketed with furs and skins for protection from the elements. Ladders were removed and placed on the ground to ensure each initiate stayed through the night, and they would be retrieved the coming dawn. Kitaj was the last remaining initiate and was lead away a fair distance from the others to the other side of the hill. Dagen followed her and the Order members to a single barrow mound placed by the forest's edge. Kitaj climbed to the top of it. A few more words were exchanged between her and the Order members before they retreated and concealed her ladder in the edge of the trees.

It was a calm night and the moon shone brightly. Clouds drifted in and out of its view. A constant hazy ring clung around the moon, indicating there would be rain in Lerakrey within the next day and a half. Noises were few. Kitaj began to settle in and gather herself after the ceremony's events.

Though she was relieved to have the ceremony behind her and was anxious to know what would be revealed to her the next day, her mind was elsewhere. Kitaj sat smiling, content and excited that she had finally seen "him," Rûni's friend, who still remained nameless to her. She knew she should be using her time to reflect on her gifts of sight and try to see into this sacred moment, but her thoughts were singularly of him. A small buzzing charge entwined with her thoughts of him. She was happily caught up in those thoughts when she heard movement below. Kitaj had been beyond distraction to not sense the source. She heard the tumbling of rocks under foot. Her thoughts and senses were indistinguishable as she soon discovered why. A hand reached up to the top of the mound and grabbed a handful of grass, then another. The hands and arms tensed and pulled until— he landed flat on his stomach in front of her!

The first words that went through Kitaj's mind were her thoughts from their initial encounter and she could not help but laugh as she said, "You know you're not supposed to be here—" and thought for her own amusement, *yet.*

"I had to see you, so here I am," Dagen said matter of factly while trying to catch his breath. "Who knows when or where I might find you again. If you do know, please tell me now and I'll leave. I don't wish any trouble on you," added Dagen earnestly.

Kitaj replied sincerely, "I can't see past now. I don't have the knowledge of when we can meet again. We won't be disturbed for a while. Please, just stay."

His presence felt perfectly placed and she appeared oddly calm, but Kitaj's mind was struggling in its elated and euphoric state. She couldn't think clearly and wasn't sure what to say next.

Dagen had not thought beyond reaching her. His natural ease of making conversation was momentarily lost to him. He felt befuddled in the comfort of her presence.

They both sat quietly in an awkward pause. The smallest of sounds seemed to magnify around them as the underlying power between them grew.

"I'm glad you came," Kitaj reluctantly blurted out.

"I'm glad I found you," replied Dagen.

"I knew we'd see each other again, I just didn't know when," added Kitaj.

"I'm relieved I recognized you, without the mud," said Dagen.

"So am I!" Kitaj laughed.

"We have not been properly introduced," Dagen said as he offered her a small seated bow. "My name is Dagen Ságaher."

"I'm Ellor Kitaj," she said as she smiled back at him.

"Very nice to finally talk to you," said Dagen.

"And you as well," added Kitaj.

Small nervous laughs escaped from both of them, followed by another awkward silence. Each found their strange familiarity both assuring and confounding.

Dagen started, "It was fortunate that you were standing next to Rûni at the ceremony. It made you easier to find."

Kitaj confessed, "That wasn't a coincidence, I hoped you would be there to see him. During the ceremony, I knew you were near, but my senses couldn't be exact because of the intensity of the crowd."

"We came to see him off. All three of us are headed in different directions now," Dagen stated.

"You're referring to your other friend that was with you," Kitaj added.

"Yes, that would be Brieg. We've been friends for most of our lives," said Dagen.

"You're fortunate to have them," said Kitaj.

"I'd have to agree," Dagen said, even taking into account Rûni's recent actions.

Dagen's statement made her think of Aergo. She was even more grateful that Aergo would be beside her going forward.

Dagen began to tell Kitaj about Brieg and Rûni, how they had been friends in spite all their differences and the nature of their trip, but intentionally changed the subject when he came close to talking about his own departure. He wished so strongly he could stop time and stay in their moment to avoid the inevitable. Knowing their time was limited, Dagen wanted to learn all he could about her.

"This was our third year to come to Winter's Nátt. Were you there for them?" he asked.

"Yes, I was. I've been to every Winter's Nátt since my birth. I was actually born during the closing ceremonies of Winter's Nátt twenty years ago. Tonight, I was exactly old enough for induction," said Kitaj.

" Well, this is a special night for you! Eo-y! Congratulations!" and Dagen gave her another small bow from his seated position.

Kitaj laughed and said, "You honestly have no idea!"

"I regret we didn't meet before now. To think you were here all along and I didn't find you," said Dagen.

"We weren't supposed to meet before. Actually, when we first saw each other was before we were meant to meet. That was my first thought when I saw you. Seeing each other tonight, our timing feels more—" Kitaj said factually before she could censor herself, "right." She was afraid she had disclosed too much too soon and diverted with, "Besides, you wouldn't have thought much of me a few years ago."

"I understand what you mean about our timing—" Dagen stated, for he too felt the weight of approaching something deeper than he was ready to face. "But I believe it's you who would not have cared much for me. I was young and stupid then, compared to now when I am so much more mature and wise," Dagen said jokingly, with his sincere delivery.

Kitaj enjoyed him making light of himself. She was enjoying everything about him. She studied his features, she realized this was the face of a person she had been unknowingly seeking. Kitaj was frustrated that she could read very little about him as far as facts of his history. She was correct that he was a few years older than her, but exactly how much, she was still unsure.

She desperately wanted to know more, but the essence of him remained fully open and undefinably recognizable to her. Kitaj saw they were of the same, yet peculiarly separate and complete in who they both were. The mystery of their connection taunted her, as if something she had forgotten.

They spoke of where they were from, their backgrounds and families. When Kitaj told Dagen that her mother was a member the Tjetajat Central Council, it was clear to Dagen the jeopardy and scandal that would be brought down on Kitaj if they were to be found together. The repercussions to Dagen could be painful, but nothing in comparison to the lasting disgrace it would bring her. Dagen realized he had only one course of action left to take, no matter how difficult or what fallout his choices might bring. The only struggle he carried with his decision was not including Kitaj on the full meaning of what he was about to do, and to his favor, Kitaj's insight gave her no warning.

Colorful lights exploded in the sky signifying the end of Winter's Nátt. The closing ceremonies had concluded, the celebration was ending, and pavilions would be closing down with people returning to their home worlds. It was the beginning.

"Kitaj, I should leave you now. There is too much at stake—complications. I don't want to cause any problems for you," Dagen struggled with the words he had just said, realizing how final they might sound to her. "Do you see any chance of how I could possibly see you again?" asked Dagen.

Kitaj did not falter, "Tomorrow all the inductees will be taken into the forest to train with the Elders for a year."

"Yes, I'm aware. Rûni told me." Dagen said, with some constriction in his chest.

"I don't know where to tell you to meet me. It is easy to get lost in the forest if you're not familiar with its paths, and I can't foresee me being able to go back to the glen where we first met or even as far as the edge of town. You did well to follow us here.

Could you try to follow again tomorrow morning so you can see where we are?" Kitaj paused to consider their options and suggested, "There is a cave we'll pass along the way. Once you see where it is, I can do my best to slip away and meet you there tomorrow night or the next," Kitaj said, surprised at herself for what she had decided.

"That could work. I'll watch for you tomorrow and follow the procession as far as the cave," Dagen said, not quite believing he was agreeing to this. "If for some reason I am detained, I'll find a way to get word to you. Hopefully, it won't come to that."

Dagen was not sure what life would bring between now and tomorrow, but there was no other option he could see but to try. They could only hope their plan would work in their favor. Drawn to each other by an underlying truth they were yet to understand, they could not stop themselves.

"Well, until tomorrow, Good night, and don't let the draugs bite," Dagen cringed at his choice for levity with his departure.

"Not to worry about draugs, these are old mounds and it's not the New Year. Little chance the dead will be walking about tonight," Kitaj returned, also questioning why she had continued the subject.

"Um, fine. Good night," said Dagen, aggravated at himself for leaving on those words.

He jumped down from the barrow mound without Kitaj saying another word. It was a strange parting, but Kitaj was still consoled with knowing that this would not be their last and that she would be seeing Dagen again soon. The energy between them faded back to the small buzz accompanying her thoughts.

Dagen walked back to the festival grounds. The air was thick with the warning of oncoming rain. He thought again about his options, and to what he knew to be true. There was only one choice.

He cut across the emptying grounds. All the fanfare was gone. The only excited chatter that remained was what

Dagen overheard about the upcoming Wild Hunt. The King was going to release nine designated fleógans, one on each world, as this year's prey.

He could have walked a straight path to the Swedu pavilion; it was unencumbered by its previous barricades. Dagen decided to pass what remained of the Gicel displays and purchased two oiled hide tarps from Pyos, who was grateful to have two fewer items to pack away at that late hour.

As he reached the remains of the Swedu venue, he saw the Malus disassembling their white reflective tent. The family busied themselves in the night air, unrestricted with the absence of the Sun's light.

"So, you're *that* Dagen," said a familiar face amongst the Malu family.

Dagen felt even more uncomfortable in his approach with Nalo's recognition of him. Nalo caught Qy's and Kama's attention. As Dagen stood in front of them, he knew whatever may come he had to follow through.

Kitaj watched as the moon moved slowly across the sky, still followed by its yellow halo as clouds thickened. The air smelled of approaching rain. She had sat quietly in the stillness and tried to regain any sibilance of concentration on her vows, on her gifts and connecting with nature around her to strengthen her sight, but found herself too excited by the night's events to focus on any thought other than Dagen.

Sounds shifted as she heard the rain's downfall crossing the field of darkness and random drops began to find her. There was faint thunder in the distance that interrupted the soft melody of the rain showering on the trees and grass nearest her. Kitaj heard the sound of something sliding down the hill behind her and she smiled as the air around her began to hum. Again, a hand was nearing the top of the barrow mound, when two tanned tarps flew up and landed next to her. Struggling upward on the damp rocks and grass of the mound, Dagen appeared, soaking wet.

"I was concerned about you being out in the rain," his voice was broken with chattering while steam rose from his head and shoulders, "so I brought you these."

"You're drenched and freezing!" Kitaj said as she motioned for him to sit near her. Dagen gladly sat beside her but was careful to keep his distance to avoid passing on his miserably wet condition. She pulled a tarp over their heads in time to shield them from the onslaught of the last late summer shower. They sat together on top of the grave saying nothing as the cold rain poured down upon them until Kitaj could not contain herself any longer and started giggling uncontrollably.

"What?" said Dagen, also finding the humor in their current circumstances.

"Oh, nothing. Um... thank you for thinking of me," she added.

"I just wanted to make sure you were in good surroundings," Dagen reiterated.

"Again, thank you," Kitaj said fighting back more giggles.

She was not about to tell him she was already prepared for the weather with the furs she had been provided. He didn't need to know the premise for his return visit was unnecessary. She was just pleased he had come back. Dagen's teeth were still chattering and Kitaj could feel the cold of his skin without even a touch. She tucked one of the furs around him in hopes he would warm soon.

"It doesn't look as if you'll be going anywhere now," she stated.

"You know?" Dagen asked, startled by her statement.

"I was referring to the rain. What did you think I meant?" she replied.

"It's of little consequence," Dagen said trying to convince himself more so than an attempt to convince her.

They sat again quietly together under the tarp. Kitaj and Dagen settled into the comfort around them, enjoying just listening and waiting.

Dagen decided to interject, "I don't know what it is about you. It's not that I think you can't take care of yourself..."

"Aergo would argue that point with you," she laughed.

"Who's Aergo?" Dagen asked.

"My friend," Kitaj said, intentionally not elaborating, but she knew she would have to explain Aergo soon enough.

"I had to know you were all right. That feeling has stayed with me— ever since I first saw you in the glen with your horse," Dagen said shyly.

"Exactly how long were you watching me? Kitaj said, feeling slightly self-conscious.

"I wasn't spying on you. It wasn't like that," he said, feeling slightly embarrassed and tried to explain, "We were on our way to Lerakrey when I saw you in the clearing," Dagen said, remembering the beauty of the scene and the fear that overtook him. "I was afraid for you. There was a moment where I thought you might have drowned," Dagen hesitated before continuing, he felt uncertain and somewhat foolish for what he was about to disclose, "Then, I thought I saw a large dark creature coming after you. The next thing I knew I was riding as fast as I could down the mountain."

"You would have done the same for anyone you thought was in danger," said Kitaj.

"I'd like to think so, but this was different. It was out of my control; another part of me took over and had to be sure of your well being. Now I know I reacted in haste. You were fine and it was just a trick of the shadows and the figure of your horse," Dagen concluded.

Kitaj smiled remembering the comical scene of their meeting and to think that it was inadvertently all her dear friend's doing. She enjoyed the thought of pointing this out to Aergo, to his dismay and frustration.

She knew she could trust Dagen and it was probably best he knew the circumstances surrounding her friend now rather than later, "To a degree, it was a trick on the eyes, but you're right. That was Aergo."

"What do you mean Aergo? Aergo's your horse, isn't he?" puzzled Dagen.

Kitaj began to explain, hoping Dagen would take her news well, "Aergo is not a horse; he's a pucca, or maybe where you come from they're called puki."

"I thought they were just legend!" Dagen said astonished.

"Most people do. There are very few left and they're rarely recognized. Aergo can take on the form of a rabbit, goat, dog, cat, and a horse so he can go about undetected. But if he senses danger, he takes the form of a large goblin.

"I'm familiar with the stories, but I've never heard of a pucca being a cat," said Dagen.

"I didn't know that either until I met Aergo. I guess people never noticed them in that form. Maybe that's because there are so many black cats with orange eyes," said Kitaj.

"Wait— that explains what happened the opening night of the festival!" Dagen exclaimed. "It was you on the Heïtaned drum! I saw you fall and disappear. A few people said you were carried off by something large and black. One said he saw its orange eyes. I didn't know what to think. Finally, it makes sense!" Dagen stated with a sense of relief.

"You knew that was me?" asked Kitaj.

"It was how you moved that made me think it was you. It was the same as when I saw you with your horse— I mean Aergo— who is not a horse at all. I searched for you that night..." Dagen trailed off.

Kitaj felt the blood rush to her face with embarrassment, and heartfully replied, "I'm sorry I made you worry!"

The conversation took on another air of awkwardness. Dagen was reminded that was the beginning of Rûni's deception. He was not ready to mention his involvement and redirected their exchange, "How did you and Aergo become friends?"

Kitaj welcomed the diversion, "As I am sure you have heard with the legend, puccas are notorious tricksters. True to form, Aergo had been pulling pranks on some of the local merchants. They were completely harmless but annoying— replacing mead with vinegar, filling fountains with soap so they bubble over, putting wagons on top of barns..." she explained.

"I did that once," admitted Dagen.

"The two of you should get along just fine," laughed Kitaj. "No one had seen Aergo, but the merchants were highly superstitious and suspected these acts were the work of a pucca. Rumors spiraled around the legend and more incidents occurred that Aergo had not committed. All was being blamed as the work of a pucca. Searches lead to nothing, because he hid well during the day in his smallest form as a rabbit. Clever as Aergo was, his vanity got the better of him and he stayed to enjoy the havoc of his mischief. He was not paying attention and found himself caught in a farmer's trap. I'm not sure which was worse for Aergo; the pain of his back leg clamped in irons or, according to him, the indignity of it all. He was truly stuck. Had he transformed into a larger form, he would have lost his leg. He weighed the risks of waiting to be released and considered that his best option. I just happened upon him when I was out wandering. He had been there for days. He was near starvation, thirsty and desperate. He started squealing to get my attention. I knew well what he was before I released him. His markings gave away his true nature. He could tell I meant him no harm and was ever grateful that I had saved him from such a bad end. Because I helped him in his dire hour, he's been with me ever since. Beyond that, we understand each other. He's my dearest friend. I don't know what I would do without him," she added, thinking of how her and Aergo's relationship had taken a turn since she had met Dagen.

"And your other friends?" asked Dagen.

"There's just Tanadra, my mentor. You would like her; she's very kynd," answered Kitaj.

"Pardon my asking, but how is it you've so few close to you?" asked Dagen.

"I don't fit well with people," she explained.

"You seem to be doing pretty well with me," he said with a smile.

Kitaj appreciated the darkness so Dagen would not see her blushing and added, "Of course, now there's you," as the air around them crackled.

"I'm honored to be considered one of the few," said Dagen.

"I do hope to get to know Rûni better and consider him a friend as well," she added.

Dagen's emotions darkened at the mention of Rûni. Under different circumstances, Kitaj's statement would have made him very happy. He didn't want to think about what Rûni had done; he wanted to keep his focus on Kitaj.

Dagen noticed he had unknowingly moved closer to her under the tarp. Steam was still coming off his clothes and their breath was visible as it rose and drifted out into the rain. He felt himself settling into the comfort of Kitaj's presence and he wanted to stay. She seemed to radiate a warming glow that drew him in. She was different than anyone he had ever met, but being beside her, he too shared the same recognition of which he could not understand. She was foreign, yet compellingly known to him. With this strange awareness, he too felt the innate but complete separateness within both of them. This intrinsic completeness within each was drawing them together.

"That day in the glen, for you to see Aergo in his goblin form, I must have truly scared him when I disappeared in the pond. I was unaware he had changed. He, like you, can be a little overly concerned," she said.

Dagen scoffed, "I'm not overly concerned."

"Of course you're not," said Kitaj.

"I'll admit it. Maybe a bit. But as I told you, I honestly have no control over that. And what's wrong with wanting to make sure you're well?" asked Dagen.

"I imagine Aergo would agree with you, but I've managed to stay in one piece this long. But accident prone, that I'll have to claim," Kitaj said pointing to her three-quarter profile in the dim light, where the telling signs from the brunt of her clumsiness were reflected in the crooked bridge of her nose.

"I hadn't noticed. But I did notice your eyes," said Dagen.

"Oh, the color difference. Yes, it's supposed to be a sign of a great seer. My mother had high hopes for me. That, along with the date of my birth, I was destined for greatness!" Kitaj jokingly said with humorous flourishing gestures.

"You're not the only one whose parents have your future planned and hopes hinging on you," Dagen said with a pang of guilt.

He briefly told Kitaj of Brieg's and Rûni's purpose with their farewell trip together while intentionally skirting his. He explained about Rûni disavowing his father and joining the Order to honor his mother's memory, along with Rûni's long time wish to be a historian, and Brieg's long eluded post under his father, the Lerakrey Dryhten. He went on to tell how Brieg's path had been set by his family's standing, his initial assignment at the Ports of Eormensyl and his required military training that would take place during this winter's Wild Hunt.

After divulging his friends' circumstances, Dagen conceded he needed to tell Kitaj about himself, "Which brings us to my situation..."

"You don't have to tell me if you don't want," Kitaj said with empathy.

Dagen appreciated her understanding words but wanted to continue. He felt assured she would understand his circumstances.

"No, I need to tell you as much as I need to put it behind me," said Dagen as he took a deep breath to begin. "My family is spread throughout Carcadoc. Basically, both sides of my family *are* Carcadoc. They were united by my parents' marriage. We are made up of craftsmen, ironworkers, millers, builders, and farmers. We had enough land for crops, timber, and cattle. We're not wealthy but rich in diversity of abilities. Our combined skills made my family almost self-sustaining during the war, in spite of trade being cut off to half the worlds. I am the oldest son and the oldest grandson from both sides. The families are looking for me to carry us forward into the next age. We understand we're in a time where re-establishing relations between other worlds is crucial to restoring the way things were before the war. My uncles were negotiating with a shipwright on Léohet. The alliance was thought to be mutually beneficial, and a good gesture for reestablishing relations between our world's so soon after the war, so I was arranged to marry the shipwright's daughter."

Kitaj sat up straight. She thought she should have seen this coming, but she had not.

"All was set for several years, until she met the son of a wealthy family from Vangard and the marriage was called off," said Dagen.

Kitaj exhaled and wondered where Dagen's story was headed. She waited uncomfortably, while the limits of her sight left her unknowing.

"My family was outraged. Negotiations went sour and the Léohet shipwright's supply of timber was cut off. Not all, but some of my family members blamed me for losing such a valuable alliance because I had not held her interest. I didn't love her, nor she me. We were just children when we met and I only saw her a few times, and never alone— like this."

Kitaj became awkwardly aware of how alone they were. Yet, the stillness around them could not divert how comfortable she was being near Dagen.

"The next thing I knew, another girl was being pushed into my presence. Her family had livestock, much more than my own and were supplying to four other worlds. My mother thought this would make a good match. I suppose my family wanted to make sure we knew each other well so the marriage would proceed, and they had this girl come to stay with different members of my family. I felt nothing for her, and it was obvious she felt nothing for me, but it did allow her the opportunity to develop an eye for my cousin. The feeling was mutual for him. I would help Hertrof, by letting him know when Charmese and I would be scheduled to see each other so he could pass messages through me. I carried messages back and forth for them over the winter, until we were found out. It was eventually decided amongst the families that the alliance would hold, after Charmese and Hertrof begged in the name of true love for one another. Her father convinced my family to allow their marriage and pass me aside. All was finally agreed and accepted, except for me. More members of my family saw me as unlucky, and considered I should be outcast."

Kitaj looked appalled. She braced herself for what was to follow.

Dagen continued, the toll of his burden was showing, "The next match I found out about started at the beginning of the summer. Negotiations were made without my prior knowledge. My parents informed me that I was to marry a girl from Sweduetwin."

Kitaj felt her nerves crackle as his last words met her ears. She tried to appear at ease, while the odd sensation cycled its course through her. Kitaj's sight was still of no help to her.

"Her father approached my family about supplying herbs that do not grow on Swedu. He is of the same mind of mending relations between worlds and wants to offer works that reflect his convictions. They needed me. Even though the worlds are restoring trust between opposing sides, the Swedu people are still prone to encounter misgivings by others solely because of their physical appearance. I was to come to Winter's Nátt to join them. The thought was I would live with her family through the winter and learn about their business, a marriage by summer, and represent them when establishing trade with other worlds. I've met him, he's a good man; he's trying to do what he can to take care of his family and help our worlds."

"What happens now?" Kitaj asked warily, though not feeling any ending in store for her and Dagen.

"Nothing," said Dagen.

"Nothing?" puzzled Kitaj. "Please explain."

"When I left you, I went to tell them that I could not follow through with his and my family's terms because I had met you," Dagen stated.

"You did WHAT?" exclaimed Kitaj.

Her head was spinning. Whatever was between she and Dagen was progressing too fast! He had destroyed his future, and his relationship with his family— over meeting her.

Kitaj's initial panic began to subside as she searched herself and thought, *Dagen's right. Whether or not we're prepared for what's to become of us, there is nothing else to be done. We have to accept what we both know is true.*

"I knew I had to do what was honorable and make my decision known first before I saw you again. It would be wrong to go forward with you while I was still committed to Isla," stated Dagen.

"Isla?" Kitaj questioned, as another crackling surge ran through her.

"Yes," said Dagen, with some trepidation, and awkwardly continued, guessing Kitaj already knew what he was about to say, "Her relatives, the Malu's, are beekeepers. They mainly trade in brewing mead, and make other items from honey and wax..."

"I know, I've met them— well, more accurately, I've seen them. I met only her," she added, as the banner of the illuminated bees came forward in her mind, carried on a whisper of foreboding.

Dagen proceeded, disregarding his own surprise and unaware of Kitaj's premonition, "I had every intention of waiting until tomorrow to see you, but on my way, it started to rain and I thought about you being out here in this freezing dampness. That urged me to hurry on with it and talk to Kama, Isla's father, so I could come back to you."

"What happened when you spoke to him?" Kitaj said, recalling to mind what she already knew of Isla's situation.

"When I arrived, Kama was very distressed. He had news of a surprising development for me that he had only discovered after arriving for the festival," said Dagen.

As Dagen spoke, Kitaj kept getting flashes of the older Swedu gentleman, the younger man with the silver hair and Isla, with the Léohetwin comb in her hair. Since she had already experienced part of their story first hand, she found herself able to piece together the details, even before Dagen explained.

"Unknown to Kama, his daughter became secretly vowed to his apprentice, Qy Tajey, just prior to the news of her engagement to me. Kama was also informed that Isla would be expecting her and Qy's first child soon. She had hidden her relationship well from her family. Kama confessed he believes she wanted to wait to tell him when there was nothing left for him to do but accept her choices."

"Yes, I knew she had been keeping the anticipation of her child secret from her family. I am glad Kama is beginning to accept his daughter and Qy's circumstances," Kitaj said, trying to hide her concern.

Knowing he should have been surprised but instead, was settling into a general acceptance of Kitaj already knowing so much about the Malus, Dagen continued, "Kama apologized to me for his family's turn of events and is concerned if there will be any retaliation from my family. I did my best to put him at ease."

"And this is where you told him your intentions had been not to go through with the arrangement," Kitaj added, seeing flashes of Dagen and Kama's conversation clearly in her mind.

"Yes. I made sure he knew I wished his family no disrespect and confessed I had come to tell him I could not proceed with our families' arrangement and marry his daughter. In some way, Kama was relieved knowing this was never meant to be, from either side. I also told him I would immediately get word to my family that I was the one to dissolve the contract, and only then did I find out that the engagement was already invalid. I believe my parents and sister will understand. I cannot speak for the rest of my family, in my eyes, this should not discount any trade agreement that was in place other than me representing them. Kama also told me he was very appreciative of my honesty. He said I had no reason to go through with telling him my plans, considering the outcome on his side, but I let him know that would go against everything I know to be right, had I not told him the truth. I admire his character and acceptance of the changes around him. We left on good terms. Kama wanted me to be sure to know he felt a debt of gratitude towards me and I would always be welcomed as a friend. Now, I just need to let my family know and hopefully all will go well with acceptance of the news," Dagen ended, with a huge sigh of relief.

Kitaj sat stunned from the ordeal of their conversation, and asked, "Are you always this impetuous?"

"I'm never impetuous. That's what Brieg's for," said Dagen, in all seriousness.

A huge weight had lifted from him by telling Kitaj. Dagen had laid his heart bare to her. He was done. What he would do from here, Dagen had no idea. His life had never been his own before.

They sat completely still. The rain had stopped and the moon still hung within a glowing haze of more showers to come, not that either had noticed. Kitaj realized they had been sitting next to one another with their heads turned. They had been facing each other for some time; so close that their noses were almost touching, but they still had not touched.

Kitaj quietly asked, "What are we going to do about this?"

"This, meaning us?" asked Dagen.

"Yes," answered Kitaj.

Dagen pondered his answer carefully before he responded, "I know I can't go back to Carcadoc, not now. I only know I will be seeing you tomorrow."

"It is tomorrow," said Kitaj, with a very happy smile.

"You're right, it is," Dagen laughed.

Neither could look away. The gravity of their words held each other's gaze.

Dagen turned the question to Kitaj, "So, what *are* we going to do about this?"

She paused and smiled, "That is a very good question."

"I thought so," said Dagen mischievously.

"Seems I've heard that somewhere before," Kitaj jokingly pondered while tapping her fingers on her chin.

Dagen reinitiated the line of conversation, "What about you? What does your future hold?"

Kitaj answered, "As far as I know..."

Dagen interrupted, "I thought you were a great seer?" trying to break the seriousness of the moment's tone.

"Very amusing. As I was saying, as far as I know, I am finishing my training and taking my place in the Order," she said with some uneasiness.

"You don't sound very certain," said Dagen.

"There has been secrecy hanging over me for as long as I can remember. Order members speak in whispers in my presence. All I can sense from them is an underlying fear and unknowing. For some reason, not one of them can read anything from me. It's as if I am not present, even when standing right in front of them, and this scares them," said Kitaj.

Dagen looked concerned and added, "Well, you're very much present with me."

"Thank you. You and Aergo are the only two who have ever told me that. I am so grateful you actually see me for me," she added.

"What about your mother, surely she can see you?" asked Dagen, trying to be helpful, but could see on Kitaj's face the answer was to the contrary.

"Today I am a full member of the Order and I expect I'll be told," Kitaj said, with determination.

"I hope you get your answers," Dagen replied.

"Don't worry. To my knowledge, I am not betrothed. I can marry who I choose. The name, Ellor, will be passed on through my daughters, and their daughters," she said, also trying to make light of their weighted topics.

Dagen smiled at her intentions and nudged her in a playful manner with his elbow. This first contact caused a small jolt to run through both of them, leaving each wringing their hands from the sting! They both looked at each other and laughed while shaking off their subsiding pain.

What's causing that, that energy around us? " asked Dagen.

"I wish I knew!" Kitaj added, just as puzzled as he was.

"Is it us?" Dagen questioned.

"Maybe," Kitaj stated with uncertainty.

Next, they heard a low loud growl; it was coming from Kitaj's stomach. She clutched at it and laughed even harder.

"That was almost as loud as Aergo!" she said, embarrassed.

"I thought it might be him coming to check on you," said Dagen, laughing with her.

"Don't be surprised if that happens later and your presence doesn't go over well with him," said Kitaj.

"I fully expect it," said Dagen, remembering him as her protector, in his horse form, and realizing Aergo had to be the cat he encountered at the Order's gates.

Kitaj's stomach growled again. It was demanding to be heard.

"I have something that might help," said Dagen.

He reached back into his satchel. Luckily, the contents had remained dry within their wrappings. He presented her with a few small sunstar loaves. Dagen watched as Kitaj traced her finger over the sunstar design on its surface and he thought the symbol fit her. It fit how he felt being near her; cast in a warming glow of a radiant light. Dagen took one of the loaves and began eating around the edges. Kitaj mirrored him. She was still in awe that he was actually beside her.

"Can you tell me about your seeing gifts?" he asked politely, not sure if his question was prying.

"Yes, I'm allowed. There really is not much to tell, my sight is merely average and spotty at best. Certainly not what everyone was expecting, but then again, maybe it will develop more fully during my training," said Kitaj.

"Such as?" asked Dagen.

Kitaj began, "Well, when I was little, I could see and talk to souls of those who have died and were on their way to passing over, like most children can."

"Like most children? That's not common to anything I know," said Dagen.

"I'm sorry. It is very common to children born of seers. I still have visitation from passed souls from time to time, especially when the veil is thinnest at the New Year and crossing back over to here from Oblivion is easiest for them. I do regret I have never seen my father."

"Your father?" Dagen asked.

"He died before I was born, actually before I came into being— in a way. It's complicated, I'll save that for another time," said Kitaj, knowing well there would be more talks like these ahead for the two of them.

Dagen, though curious, did not want to press Kitaj for information. He had not wished to detour her from his original question and felt relieved as she continued.

"Also, when I was small, I could move objects but I had little control and it mostly went away as I grew older. As I became more mature, I could tell when someone was going to have a child, as I did with Isla, and sometimes even before the mother-to-be knew. I could know if it would be a boy or girl, when it would be born, and details about the birth. The name could also be known to me before it was announced. Let's see, what else, hmm... I would get a sense to avoid a certain path because of a danger, though none was visible. I ignored it only once and my travel ended with trauma and trouble. Sometimes, I know when someone else is injured or in distress without being near them. What else? I can sense sometimes people I am about to encounter like I did with you tonight. Well, let me confess, not too clearly with your first arrival, but that was because I was thinking of you before you arrived and it was difficult to distinguish between the two. I saw parts of your conversation with Kama as you were telling me... am I leaving anything out? I think that's about it. Nothing unusual," Kitaj concluded.

"You call that not unusual? You're the most unusual person I've ever met," said Dagen.

"I am assuming you did not meet Rûni's mother," she said.

"No, she died before I met him. He told Brieg and me so much about her but never disclosed what her talents were, other than she could read his thoughts. I concluded that must have been too personal for him to share with us and we wanted to be respectful of her memory," said Dagen.

"I have nothing like my mother's abilities. She can read anyone, other than me, and of course Aergo," she said.

Dagen gave Kitaj a look expressing his confusion. She had not considered Dagen would be lost by the meaning of her last statement.

"On account of him being a pucca. No one can read puccas, I just know him very well and am familiar with his behaviors," stated Kitaj.

"My mother's distinguishing trait is her ability with the weather. She probably arranged these little rain showers just to make tonight more challenging," said Kitaj, fully imagining her mother was behind these conditions.

"Your mother controls the weather, like King Wodan?" asked Dagen.

"No, and she doesn't summon it in the same way as the King. I doubt they use the same method, but it could be possible. I do know it is a very old form of magic. It's more that she knows who or what to channel to ask for specific weather. She doesn't create it herself, that I know for sure. But she's never discussed with me the ritual or process. She holds her secrets close," Kitaj said, thinking her last words were understated.

"Until tonight, I had no idea what was possible," said Dagen.

"If you are going to be near me, I hope what you consider unusual will become more common place in time," said Kitaj.

"But that's just it, everything you have told me, though it's all new to me, doesn't seem strange. I'm not sure I have the right words for this, but it is fact, I mean the truth is... I don't know how to describe it.

The rain returned and they huddled closer together under the tarp.

"There is something else I forgot to mention earlier, I have traveled a few times. I have far from mastered it. I imagine that will encompass a large part of the winter season for me," said Kitaj.

"When you say traveled, what do you mean? asked Dagen.

"Traveled outside of myself, by leaving my body behind," Kitaj stated.

"I have done that as well!" exclaimed Dagen. "Just recently, it happened without trying. I went from laying in a field to flying from Carcadoc to Lerakrey. I flew with a hawk that seemed to see me!

Kitaj said as a matter of fact, "I'm sure it did. Most birds can perceive disembodied souls, no matter their circumstances for traveling. Within the Tjetajat, it is known that some can achieve the ability to become a bird to travel."

"I'm confused. Are you saying that you think I turned into a bird?" asked Dagen.

"Not necessarily. Did you see your reflection or a shadow of your form?" asked Kitaj.

"No, I only saw my body below me as I left and on my return," Dagen said with concern.

"In that case, it was probably just your soul traveling," she said so easily as if traveling was nothing out of the ordinary.

"Oh, is that all?" asked Dagen.

"Yes, that's all," said Kitaj.

Dagen laughed. This was how he could see his life, going forward. The extraordinary would remain amazing and special, not as rare moments, but part of his every day.

"Is there anything else I need to know about you? he asked.

"Of course, there's always more," she said playfully, but dropped into a more serious tone, "It's important I tell you that somewhere inside me I knew I'd meet you someday. I didn't know who you would be. I don't even understand it myself. But I can say for sure, you arrived sooner than expected, but..." Kitaj's voice trailed off.

"For me, I feel I knew you, before I even met you," Dagen added, with a small smile.

Dagen and Kitaj could not deny their feelings of connection with one another. Somehow, these two were reuniting through the shared knowing they were yet to understand. Theirs was a convergence where each self was complimented by the light of the other.

Kitaj smiled and turned her face back to him. Dagen leaned in and she followed. As they reached each other, a small charge ignited between them; the spark arced from each of their mouths, stinging both of them!

Instinctually, they both retracted by putting their hands to their own lips, and with a unison, "Ouch!"

Once the stings had sufficiently subsided, Dagen suggested that they try again. This time, their closeness was without painful incident. Their first kiss confirmed what they felt for each other, in only the way a shared kiss can when love is found. The rain had stopped, though neither was aware or cared, nor did they know of the glow they projected, hovering outside their tarp like a ghostly halo in the mist.

CHAPTER 9

REVELATIONS OF GELIC KYND

With the dawning of the new day's light, Kitaj awoke to find Dagen still with her on top of the barrow mound. She blinked several times, half believing she was awake and that he was actually next to her. But they were not alone. Aergo had found them and wedged himself between them. He had all four of his paws pressing against Dagen to create as much space as possible. Aergo had managed to maintain his posturing while he slept. Even with Aergo's awkward placement, Kitaj found she and Dagen cozily seated, propped against each other, perfectly placed in the luxury of waking in each other's arms.

Aergo stirred next, arching his back and stretching his length with his feline claws extended, where he happily sank them into Dagen's thigh. Dagen woke to the sharp pinch of needles, in part from Aergo's morning greeting, but mainly by the fact both of his legs had fallen asleep and the feeling was starting to return to them.

"Good morning," Kitaj said, still groggy from her happy restful slumber.

"Good morning," said Dagen, pleased to see the dawning light had not whisked away their night together, as if it were a dream.

His contentment remained in spite of the prickly stings from urging his waking legs to move. They would not budge.

Kitaj's bliss was abruptly shattered when reality crashed in on her consciousness. She sensed her mother and two Elders were coming.

"You have to go. Now!" she said as she panicked.

"I can't!" said Dagen.

Dagen tried but his legs were still unresponsive. He began to rub and hit them, trying to speed their recovery. She tried to help move him, but Dagen clumsily tumbled off the side of the barrow mound.

"They'll be here any moment! You have to go! said Kitaj in a yelling whisper. She turned to Aergo, "You have to help him!" seeing that Dagen was not able to hide himself.

Aergo yawned, stretched again, and looked at her to convey, *Why should I? This is your problem.*

"Aergo, please!" she pleaded.

Aergo rolled his eyes, shook his head, and lightly jumped from the barrow mound beside Dagen. He changed into his goblin form, tossed the dazed and shocked Dagen over his shoulder, gave Kitaj a devilish grin, and disappeared beyond the tree line. As they escaped from sight, Corynth and two other senior members of the Tjetajat topped the hill. None had sensed anything out of the ordinary to Kitaj's relief, but she was perplexed as to why they had not read Dagen. She crossed it off as fortune, for once, being in her favor.

"Good morning, Kitaj," Corynth said, with little expression.

"Mother," Kitaj returned, with equal flatness.

"We are meeting with the Central Council shortly and need you to come with us," stated Corynth.

Kitaj thought, *Finally, I'll know.*

She followed her mother and the two Council members deep into the forest. They came to a stop in an area especially thick with trees. Nothing else was visible— at first glance. But, as if looking through an open doorway placed in a wall that was identical to their surroundings, she could see a small portion of a structure that sat a short distance away from them.

As she aligned herself with the mystifying entryway, she saw the structure was a large domed hut. Kitaj had never seen this structure before, though she had been through this part of the forest many times. From the weathered condition of its thatch and bark covered exterior, it looked to have been part of the forest for many years, possibly before her or her mother's time.

Corynth stepped through the opening first, followed by Kitaj and the two Council members. As she went through, Kitaj saw two other Elders were standing on either side of the opening marked by a large incomplete circle of a white salt powder encompassing the ground around the hut. Once they had walked through the entrance of the circle, the two Elders sprinkled more powder, to complete the circle and seal them in. Kitaj did not know this magic but assumed correctly that they were now completely concealed within the confines of the invisible barrier.

When Kitaj entered the hut, she saw Tanadra's warm face amongst the other Central Council members. It was a welcoming site and a reassuring comfort considering the ominous mood that filled the space. Tanadra was standing at the end of the hut, next to a woman cloaked in grey. Though she did not know who this woman was, Kitaj sensed fairness and charity from her. The woman turned and lowered her hood. It was Queen Frija. Kitaj immediately bent her knees and lowered her head to her Queen.

"That's not necessary my dear, if anyone should be bowing, it might be me to you," Frija said kyndly to Kitaj.

The Queen's words struck Kitaj as strange. She was puzzled by their possible meaning. Kitaj was also puzzled but relieved to find the Queen to be warm and unintimidating.

Corynth put out her arms to welcome everyone to be seated on the stumps bordering the room that were covered with throws. Kitaj became aware, there was nowhere for her to sit. She was to remain standing in the center. She began to feel she was under examination.

The Head of the Tjetajat Central Council, Adrex Sorrel, began to address the Queen. "We come together, at this time to formally address our findings and our speculations concerning Ellor Kitaj. We believe we have discovered evidence..."

Evidence?! Kitaj thought, *Am I being tried?*

Her readings from most everyone in the room were not telling, especially from her mother. There were the exceptions of Tanadra and Queen Frija, who exuded reassurance in Kitaj's direction. Frija gave Kitaj a small smile and radiated a sense of calm which was most helpful.

"... to support your Majesty's quest. We hope you will forgive our delay in presenting Kitaj to you. I speak for the Tjetajat as a whole by saying we did not want to give your Majesty false hope," Head Council Adrex stated.

The Queen spoke, "I understand you wanted to be sure and I appreciate the discrete manner in which you have conducted yourselves."

"As we have recently shared with you..." Adrex began again.

With you?! No one has shared anything with me! thought Kitaj as the pent up frustration she had carried with her all her knowing life began to bubble to the surface.

"Ellor Kitaj was born with several signs marking her as a great seer. Her eye color, her unconventional conception, the timing of her birth..." Head Council Adrex continued.

These I did know, Kitaj contented herself with this thought though her anticipation rose as she awaited Adrex's next statement.

"...all gave us hope in our tireless quest. But beyond her traits and circumstances, the fact the Tjetajat could not read her made us believe she was connected to the Great Mystery that plagues us all," said Adrex.

Kitaj was well aware they could not read her but her connection to a "Great Mystery" was new information.

Now we're getting to the heart of it, she thought.

"In our minds' eyes, Kitaj is shrouded in the void, the same void we experience whenever we try to find answers to the questions you seek," said Adrex.

I carry a VOID around me? questioned Kitaj.

She wished someone would have explained to her what they suspected and perceived before this gathering. Instead, she was to be talked about, as if she were not in the room.

But why should I expect more from them? They've never sensed me. I read the same as an object to them, she considered and decided to hold her tongue to be sure to get the rest of their information.

"Recently, Tanadra and her mother, Corynth, reported experiencing an undefinable energy emitting from Kitaj through the void surrounding her. We do not know the reason or purpose why this sudden change has occurred— but it is most definitely a change. An actual change has occurred in the perpetuating sameness we have experienced for the last twenty-five Midangardian years," stated Adrex.

Kitaj thoughts raced, *Perpetuating sameness, what are they talking about? Life has always been this way,* for she had no reference of understanding.

"Currently, only Tanadra and Corynth have been witness to experiencing this emanation. We believe it is because they are the closest to her," Adrex added.

"Have either of you noticed any changes in yourselves since your exposure to this new energy?" Queen Frija directed to Tanadra and Corynth.

"Not that is known to say at this time, your Majesty," answered Tanadra.

"Come here my dear," Frija beckoned Kitaj nearer.

Queen Frija stood and gently held out her hands to Kitaj. She walked to the Queen and nervously put her hands in hers.

"Look at me, child," requested the Queen.

Frija was not sensitive to detecting the void, as the Tjetajat were, while she stood holding onto Kitaj's hands. Her experience was in complete contrast to theirs. When the Queen and Kitaj's eyes connected, Frija felt a depth of familiarity with Kitaj, that Kitaj could also sense. This made Frija smile and put Kitaj slightly more at ease, though her knees were still shaking.

"I think it's time you were let in on our secret," Queen Frija whispered to Kitaj.

Frija released her hands from Kitaj's and briefly place them on either side of Kitaj's face. Kitaj nodded to agree.

"Up until just a few Midangardian years prior to your birth, change was all around us. It was natural and part of everyday life. There were new inventions and thoughts. Problems were worked through and solved. There was progress as knowledge flowed through the universe. For reasons unknown to the people throughout the worlds, in one moment, life as we had known changed," Frija said, still having to guard the truth of the cause. "Knowledge was altered; the knowledge of the past remained to carry us to our present state, but innovation halted. Knowledge for continuing progress was lost. We have been trying to look into the future for any sign of change; only to encounter a void where future sight should be. All our efforts have been fruitless, until you."

Kitaj was having difficulty relating to the Queen's words. Life was going along better than she had ever known. Unity was restoring amongst the worlds. She didn't understand what this could possibly mean for existence going forward.

Surely, this could not be so, she thought.

"Everything you have thought, everything you know and have known is based on past knowledge. I imagine, you being so young, that this does not make sense to you," said the Queen.

Kitaj nodded again wearily, and added, "You believe somehow I am the key to solving this... Great Mystery?"

"Yes," said Frija, "Our hope is to discover how to restore the balance of knowledge."

"But, I don't know anything about this," Kitaj said as her voice shook.

"I wouldn't expect you would," added Frija, then asked Kitaj directly, "What do you think caused this change in you?"

Kitaj panicked! She did not want to tell them about Dagen, but she knew without a doubt, he was integral to her situation.

"I can see you are upset, dear. It's all right. Hearing this must be overwhelming to you. You will need some time to think about what we have told you. We can talk more of this later," Queen Frija said understandingly.

Kitaj was able to breathe again. She was grateful for the Queen's kyndness and that Frija had turned her attention away from her and back to the Council.

"I want you to keep her close and protected at all times," commanded the Queen.

"Yes, your Majesty," replied the Head of the Council, Tanadra and Corynth in unison.

Frija was careful to add, "But, we must let Kitaj's evolvement unfold as it is was meant to be. We have had no results on our own for finding a solution and I have hopes that some answers will be coming to us soon.

Exactly how they were going to watch her but stand aside to see where her changes lead left her baffled. Kitaj's mind was becoming muddled. She didn't feel she could take in any more, but Queen Frija was not finished with her yet.

"Kitaj, this is the utmost secret that you carry with you. If this information were to become public knowledge, we would see the destructive forces of chaos to complacency tear our worlds apart. Some, outside of the seers, are already beginning to realize the alteration of our reality and we are running out of time."

Kitaj wondered how was she supposed to let this power manifest naturally in her, while anxious that a timely discovery was crucial to the fate of the future.

"There is something else you must know. You have been kept a secret from me, not only out of hope but for your own protection. You may be aware of the stories of King Wodan and his quest for knowledge," said Frija.

"Yes, that he gave an eye to acquire knowing and that he is very wise because of it. The knowledge he gained helped him to end the Nine World's War," said Kitaj.

The Queen shielded her personal reaction to Kitaj's recollection of the stories from her childhood. These were the acceptable tales to be passed forward throughout the worlds.

Frija guarded her next words and emotions carefully, "There is truth in what you say, but you need to be aware King Wodan is also trying to solve where the knowledge of the future has gone. He wants it for himself and will stop at nothing to get it. We have to protect you from Wodan."

Kitaj turned pale. She questioned how this could actually be happening to her!

"The Tjetajat have been instrumental in my quest for restoring knowledge and I fully pardon and understand their delay in presenting you to me," Queen Frija said to Kitaj, but it was intended for the benefit of the Council.

The intensity of the truth was beginning to sink in. Kitaj did not know how much more she could literally stand to hear.

"Speak of this to no one, Kitaj. The consequences are too high," Queen Frija warned.

Kitaj was shaking again, from anxiety and weariness. The Queen was showing signs of strain as well.

Frija concluded with Kitaj, " I must leave you now before my absence is discovered."

"Safeguards remain intact, your Majesty, for concealing your attendance of this meeting," said Adrex.

"Thank you, Head Council, and I thank all of you for your continued help and loyalty," stated Queen Frija before departing.

"My Queen, may I have a moment to speak with you?" asked Tanadra.

The Queen nodded in agreement to her request. Tanadra gave Kitaj another reassuring smile as she departed with the Queen and disappeared from sight once they exited the entrance to the hut.

Kitaj looked toward her mother. There was a sadness in Corynth's eyes Kitaj had always felt but had never seen before.

"Mother, please can we speak?" asked Kitaj.

Corynth walked past her daughter as she departed and quietly said, "Soon."

Kitaj was escorted by three members of the Council out of the hut and to the edge of the protective circle. The Elders she had seen when she arrived were still standing in place where the entry through the barrier had been. One used his foot to rub away part of the powdered line, dissipating it into the dirt and reopening the entry to the barrier. Kitaj and the three Council members stepped through the entry. As she stepped over the broken line, her view of the forest appeared exactly as it had when emerged from the hut, but when she looked behind her, the domed hut was gone.

Kitaj's escorts stayed close and silent as they walked with her to the Tjetajat's wooded sanctuary, where she and the other inductees were to spend the next year honing their skills of sight. She knew her way through the forest and did not need any guidance. The presence of her guardians was becoming increasingly off-putting, stifling, and overbearing with each step of their path. Kitaj understood this was part of the Queen's orders but wondered exactly how much protection would be required in the days, and possibly years ahead.

She was relieved to be deposited on the doorstep of a cabin that would be her own. By some will of fate, or more likely, an arrangement by her mother or Tanadra, she managed to have her living quarters to herself. Whatever the reason, she was sincerely grateful. She would do best to have her own space, especially considering her new found circumstances. The information she had learned about herself was astonishing. It explained so much, but she was left with even more questions. Kitaj was also relieved to find Aergo curled up on her pillow, waiting for her, but her feelings immediately turned to serious concern.

"What have you done with Dagen?" she asked Aergo.

Aergo gave her his best cat expression to convey, *Well! How rude, not even a hello or thank you!* as he got up and headed for the door.

He turned, with his nose and tail still in the air, and urged Kitaj to follow as he crossed her at the doorway. Directly behind the cabin was a patch of thick evergreens that gave Aergo ample room to transform and where they could speak privately. Kitaj was again grateful; the convenience of a small patch of solitude so close to her quarters was ideal. Had they needed to travel a further distance from the cabin, she was sure someone would have stepped out of the shadows to escort her— for her own protection.

"Is that the first thing you have to say to me? Don't you trust me?" said Aergo, as he smiled his sinister grin, just to upset her.

"Aergo!" Kitaj said, as she swatted at his massive form.

"Don't go getting yourself all worked up! I returned your Dagen safely to the forest's edge near the festival, that is.... after we had a little discussion about you."

"What did you do?" Kitaj asked accusingly.

"Oh, nothing," Aergo replied, picking his teeth with his claws.

Kitaj crossed her arms and set her jaw. Aergo knew he was pushing his limits with her and should put her at ease.

"I really was quite impressed with him. I think I might even be able to like him... someday. He obviously cares about you, to risk his whole future and his family's reputation like that— and to have just met you. I can admire his conviction. And the answer is yes! Of course, I was listening in on your conversation. I wasn't pleased about it, but the more I heard, the more I knew you were contented, more so than I have ever known you to be. So calm down and give me some time to get used to this!"

But, there was not time. Kitaj told Aergo what she had learned from the Central Council and the Queen, and how she must be part of this "restoration effort." She explained to Aergo how she believed Dagen played a role in her own transformation. It was only after meeting him and the strange connection that passed between them that she, using the term that referred to her new ability, started "omitting energy through the void."

"Do you see it or feel it? Tanadra and my mother do, and you know me better than I know myself... most of the time," said Kitaj.

"Hmm, I wonder if it has anything to do with your eye color, or I should say colors?" added Aergo.

"Maybe," she said with uncertainty.

"Look deep into my eyes and let's see what happens," Aergo said as he put one large clawed paw on her shoulder. "Yes, there is something there," Aergo said, pondering his next words. "But honestly, I've never felt any sort of void around you."

"I never sensed any void either, I only knew they couldn't read me!" said Kitaj, exacerbated. "Aergo, I have to tell Dagen what I know."

Aergo spoke sincerely, "I can see you do. This energy coming from you; it's not nearly as strong at the moment, but it is the same as I felt between the two of you. It was as obvious last night as it was with your meeting. This power, whatever it might be, was so present when you met, it honestly scared me. Because of my fear, I behaved so badly this last week. I don't know what it is, or what it will do to you."

Kitaj smiled at Aergo, "So, you will help me?"

"Of course I will. Do I have a choice?" he said, as he hugged her.

"You really don't," she said muffled with her face against him. "I'll admit I'm scared too," Kitaj added.

From their comforting hug, Aergo looked down at her so she could see his face. His solemn expression conveyed his assurance.

"You will never be alone through whatever might come. You'll always have your secret weapon— me!" he declared.

"You and your pucca powers," Kitaj added with a small laugh, trying to make light of her circumstances.

"We need to devise a plan," said Aergo.

"The Queen has the Council protecting me, so we are going to have to find a way around watchful eyes and without seeming to disappear for an unknown reason or extended period of time," said Kitaj.

"Tanadra and Corynth both know I can defend you, as should the Council. We could convince them that I have control of the situation," Aergo added confidently.

"I know they appreciate you for your loyalty and care for me, but I believe the Queen wants people she knows and trusts to be involved as well."

"That just leaves nights," stated Aergo.

"Can you arrange for Dagen to meet me tonight? asked Kitaj.

"I can go to him at the Idle Sickles. If you're concerned about how he will respond to your news, I don't think there's need to worry. He plans to stay near. Dagen told me he had enough coin to support himself for a few weeks and that he'd look for work to stay close, in hopes of seeing you."

Kitaj lit up from Aergo's words, "I had wished as much."

"What did you think he would do? The boy's smitten," Aergo smiled a bit more deviously again with his statement. "I can appreciate that he makes you happy. That's all that matters to me. And, I made it very clear to Dagen, if he ever hurts you— well, I used a few large rocks to demonstrate."

"You didn't scare him badly, I hope?" asked Kitaj.

"Just enough," grinned Aergo.

"You know I love you," she said to Aergo.

"I know," he paused, " I will take a message from you to Dagen as soon as you write it. But where will you meet?"

"We spoke of meeting tonight at the cave near our glen, but as you know, he was unable to follow me and doesn't know how to get there. I need you to show him the way."

"The cave, I missed that part of your little chat. That must have been early in your conversation, was it not? I was off being ill at the sight of you at that point," Aergo added, "But I'm fine now. Good choice, very secluded— and romantic."

"Oh, stop it!" Kitaj was turning red. "We have information to discuss."

"Yes, there's that too," stated Aergo.

Kitaj turned a deeper red and Aergo smiled to see she could find some happiness within the moment, in spite of the extremes. Aergo hated to interrupt her mood but knew he had to touch on the seriousness of her and Dagen's safety.

"Kitaj, I advise you to not use your names in your correspondence, on the off chance it were to make its way into the hands of the King. Take the Queen's warning to heart.

Wodan may possess wisdom, but is not known for his fairness or understanding," said Aergo.

"Very good idea," Kitaj said with consideration.

"I will get Dagen to the cave, one way or another, by this evening," Aergo said with a streak of mischief, "then take you to him once it is very late. It's terribly handy for you that I can see so well in the dark," he said adding levity.

"Thank you Aergo, I couldn't do this without you," said Kitaj as she kissed him on the nose.

Aergo turned back into his cat form, which was much more suitable for reentering the small space of Kitaj's room. He and Kitaj returned from behind the evergreens and proceeded to go inside. As if one were cued, an Elder Council member stepped into view as Kitaj and her cat went back into the cabin. She waved to acknowledge his presence and he receded into the shade.

Once inside, Kitaj explored the contents of a drawer in her small table. She found a piece of slate, small parchment scrolls, a few charcoal sticks, some thin red ribbons, a sleek quill and a small pot of dark, ash brown ink. These were standard supplies for each cabin, so inductees could send letters to relations and friends over the next year. She picked up the slate, along with a scroll, quill, and ink, and thought of what to say. Kitaj knew to keep her message short with little detail.

I need to see you tonight.
Follow, and I will meet you
as soon as I am able.

"That will do. No names, dates or locations... just to be sure," Kitaj said to reassure herself as well as Aergo.

She rolled the scroll as tight and small as possible and tied a thread from her sleeve around it. The red ribbon was too obvious as to where the note could have originated.

"Do you want it tied around your neck or to carry it in your mouth?" she asked.

The light color of the parchment showed brightly against his black fur, which left Aergo unsettled. He opted for the less conspicuous choice of carrying the scroll in his mouth like prey.

She picked him up and held him close to whisper in his ear, "I will see you tonight. And again, Aergo, thank you."

Kitaj nuzzled his face, set him down, and he was off. She stretched out on her small cot and surveyed her room. The ceiling was lined with beams coated in soft green moss, and a small fireplace was in one corner. In front of it was an oval shaped woven rug. Across from her cot were the table and two wooden chairs. On top of her table was a basket filled with various fruits, preserves, different breads, some dried salted meat and cheese, and a clay pitcher holding water and a matching cup. These were also standard supplies for each inductee's cabin. She did not have an appetite but nibbled on a few items. Her body was feeling shocked and she knew she needed to keep up her strength. Kitaj decided she would take the basket with her tonight. The thought of seeing Dagen again soon recharged her mind, but her body would not abide and succumbed to a wave of exhaustion. It was midmorning; the light and forest sounds streamed into her room from her high window but did not stir her. She knew she would not be disturbed until later. It was expected that most of the inductees would sleep at this time, after their night on the barrow mound. They would all be roused and gathered for supper and receive their assignments. With that reassurance, Kitaj fell deep and fast asleep.

۶

The color of the room had changed when she awoke. "It must be close to sunset," she thought. She got up and poured some water from the pitcher into her hand and splashed her face. It took her a while to get her bearings when all the information she had learned came flooding back to her. She jumped when she heard a knock at her door.

"Kitaj, it's Tanadra. May I come in?"

"Um, yes, please," she said, alarmed not be aware of Tanadra's presence, and tried to regain her senses.

Tanadra let herself inside as Kitaj composed herself further by straightening her clothes that had twisted around her during her sleep and ran her fingers through her bushy hair.

"Oh good, you've rested. You poor dear, that was a great deal for you to take in this morning. I did not agree with how they presented this news to you— without any warning! But, I am one voice," said Tanadra.

Tanadra's statement was telling; it let Kitaj know her mother had agreed with the Council. Had she expected anything less?

"I have something for you," said Tanadra, as she placed the palm of her hand just below Kitaj's collar bones, marking the Tjetajat talisman into her skin.

Kitaj traced the raised curves of the newly placed design. Her fingertip lightly followed over the three entwined loops.

"You weren't able to be at the final stage of your induction; I wanted to present it to you myself. You are officially Tjetajat," Tanadra said, smiling sweetly back at her.

Now that Kitaj was one of them, she wondered if they would include her in their findings and concerns. She also questioned if what she had been told was the entire truth.

"I'm glad it was you to present it to me," Kitaj added.

"I thought you might wish to talk about what you have learned," said Tanadra, with sincere concern.

"Thank you Tanadra, you have always been so kynd to me," said Kitaj, but she could not conceal the edge that crept into her voice as she continued, "Since secrets are no longer being kept from me, I'd like to hear your interpretation of the events.

"I understand that you must be angry," said Tanadra.

"I'm not sure what I am, honestly. Please, tell me what you know," Kitaj replied.

Tanadra told Kitaj everything she could and her thoughts about the situation. It only reconfirmed what was said in the meeting with Queen Frija and not as illuminating as Kitaj had hoped.

"Do you still see or sense this foreign energy coming through me? asked Kitaj, determined to get more insight to what Tanadra was experiencing.

"Yes dear, it seems to have grown stronger. It is only omitting from behind your eyes and is penetrating the void we still sense around you," said Tanadra.

"I appreciate you telling me. Will you let me know first if you detect any change in it?" asked Kitaj.

Tanadra answered sincerely, "I will do my best. My dear one, little did we know..." Tanadra replied as she started to leave Kitaj's quarters.

"Can I ask you a few more questions before you go? How does this energy emitting from me make you feel?" Kitaj thought she could already detect Tanadra's answer, but wanted to hear it in her own words.

"It is hard to describe. I believe it closely feels like standing in a direct light, as if light's energy is filling me, brightening me. It seems to have a purpose— an intention scinan," said Tanadra.

"Scinan? asked Kitaj.

"Yes, it's a word found in the magic of the outer realm. It's the closest I can think to describe what occurs when it reaches me through you. It's shine illuminates. I feel it to my core and it gently intertwines itself into every aspect of my being when I am in its presence," said Tanadra.

"And you said being in its presence hasn't changed you?" asked Kitaj.

Tanadra replied, "Why do you ask?"

Kitaj didn't answer, though she was thinking, *Because it's changing me.*

Dagen asked, "How soon will you be bringing her here?" as he paced around the interior of the cave.

""It will be late. We have to make it appear she has retired for the evening to throw off her watchdogs," said Aergo.

"They have dogs watching her?" asked Dagen, alarmed.

"No. Not dogs, people," Aergo said, surprised at Dagen's literal take on his words.

"Thank you again for bringing me here to meet her," said Dagen.

"I'm doing this for her, not you," Aergo clarified. "She's happy when she is with you, she needs that."

"I won't take that for granted," said Dagen.

"You best not," stated Aergo. "I'll be going now, we'll return as soon as we can."

"Right, watchdogs," Dagen said awkwardly, as Aergo left the cave shaking his head.

Kitaj sat next to Rûni at the group supper for the inductees. Rûni was beaming with excitement and pride. He finally had his talisman mark displayed on his skin and was officially a member of the Tjetajat. He was where he had dreamt of being for so long. Corynth walked by to go to the head of the large slab table and stopped to pat both Rûni and Kitaj's shoulders.

"I am so glad you are both here," said Corynth, as she smiled.

This was Kitaj's first contact with her mother since their morning's meeting and Corynth's sincerity in the joy of having her daughter's membership complete fell flat in Kitaj's heart. Kitaj wondered how she could stand there, displaying herself as the proud mother, but Kitaj thought again that Corynth always knew how to handle herself in public.

Rûni could not wait to tell Kitaj about his night on the barrow mound. For an uneventful dark night, he had much to tell about it. Kitaj tried to share in his happiness but was having difficulty being distracted by her own thoughts.

"I know you're pleased to have the induction behind you. Congratulations on your membership to the Tjetajat," Kitaj said, hoping to move him on to another topic.

"And how was your night?" Rûni asked eagerly.

Kitaj wished now she had let him continue. She was in no position or mindset to discuss anything that had occurred.

She settled with replying, "Oh, much the same as yours. It rained, but that was not a problem," she smiled at the thought, "It was a wonderful night. I wouldn't trade it for anything."

She realized at some point, she would have to confide in Rûni about Dagen, at least as much as she was allowed. Kitaj was concerned when that time came how Rûni might respond. Not well was her guess.

꙲

The Sun had set and the moon finally appeared through the dense trees. Kitaj paced the length of her dark room, waiting for Aergo. She had packed everything she thought they could use and blown out her candles to make it appear she was going to sleep. Fidgeting, she tried to sit on her cot to pass the time. Her basket of supplies sat beside her as a comfort. It felt as if time were slowing down to spite her anticipation. It was very late in the night when Aergo finally appeared. He jumped up on the windowsill to signal her to open it for their exit. Kitaj stood on her cot to lift herself through the opening and scrambled through it as quietly as she could while carrying the basket. Aergo had already changed into his goblin form and placed Kitaj on his back. He knew Kitaj was bound to stumble over rocks, roots or herself in the darkened forest. His ability to see without light gave them an advantage. Aergo waited until they were a safe distance from the sanctuary to speak to her.

"I had to make sure your watchdogs were asleep or detained before we tried to leave. This was more complicated than I expected," said Aergo, as he carried her swiftly through the woods.

"Dogs?" asked Kitaj, "I only sensed people."

"Not literally dogs. Yes, people— what is it with you two?" Aergo said as he shook his head in disbelief, and continued, "They have more than one watching you at a time. There is one that makes himself known and two others that remain unseen."

"I'm aware of them. I honestly didn't expect to be this heavily watched," said Kitaj.

"We won't be able to stay long," said Aergo.

"I truly couldn't do this without you," said Kitaj.

"You've never been more right," Aergo said with a laugh.

She could hear the stream rushing before she could see it through the trees. The moon was bright and showed their way. As they came upon the stream by the cave, Kitaj was amazed how these familiar grounds were magically transformed by the moon's light. Aergo jumped the stream in a bound. A small orange glow flickered from inside the cave.

Aergo wanted to be certain of Kitaj's safety so he put her down and proceeded into the cave far enough to see Dagen anxiously waiting. Dagen found it odd, that in such a short time, he now found himself relieved by the sight of the massive four horned goblin.

Aergo stepped aside to let Kitaj pass. She sat the basket down and wanted to run to Dagen, but wasn't sure if that was what she should do. Dagen met her half way. They stood staring at each other. Aergo moved to a discrete distance outside the cave. He stayed close enough to keep Kitaj secure, and he supposed that included Dagen as well, but far enough to give them some privacy.

"Hello," Dagen managed.

"Hello," Kitaj said, raising her chin to him and smiling.

Dagen noticed the Tjetajat symbol etched into her skin just below her collar bones. He felt drawn to the image. He was compelled to trace it with the edge of his finger, but found before reaching her that a small energy charge was extending between them. Her skin responded by tingling in the path of the gentle current that followed his fingertip just above her skin. He bent to kiss her, and ZAP! Again, their lips were stinging from an arcing charge.

"We really have to stop doing that," Kitaj laughed, while she held her hand to her mouth.

They cautiously put their arms around each other and attempted their kiss again. Fortunately, their second try was without incident.

As Aergo stood outside the cave, he saw a pale glow framed by the darkness, shining out to accompany the candle's light coming from inside. He had seen the same glow the night before, hovering over the barrow mound in the rain. Whatever this energy was between them, it grew stronger when Dagen and Kitaj were near each other. Aergo thought it worrisome, but he also knew it was not his place to interfere and should leave them be.

"I have some disturbing news," Kitaj said to Dagen, knowing there was no good way to broach the conversation.

Concern crossed Dagen's face as he suggested for them to sit. He had already prepared a blanket to cushion them against the cave's hard ground and walls. They sat folded into each other, supporting one another in a shared awareness that what Kitaj was about to say would bring repercussions for both of them.

She decided to start at the beginning; that would be the beginning she had been told earlier that morning. She explained how her prophetic traits and the anomaly of an impenetrable void that engulfed her were the reasons for the Tjetajat to keep her under watch since birth. Recent developments, along with her induction, presented the time they could share this information with her. She began to shake at the thought of disclosing the details to Dagen. He recognized her anxiety and brought Kitaj closer to him in his arms.

"Ever since I met you, I've been changing," she paused and took a deep breath to continue. "Apparently since we met, an unfamiliar energy is emitting from me, through the void that surrounds me. So far, it has only been detected by my mentor, Tanadra, and my mother. Dagen, I can't feel it happening, not like the energy that sparks between us. But I know without a doubt, from knowing you I am not as I was. I've discovered a part of me that I did not know existed— and I don't know what it means yet."

"Well, it's nice to know I have an effect on you," said Dagen, trying to conceal his own nervousness with humor.

"Now, for the frightening part," said Kitaj as she turned to face him.

"What you just told me wasn't the frightening part?" asked Dagen.

"I'm afraid not, and I'm sorry to have to tell you, but you need to know," Kitaj said.

"Go on," said Dagen.

"The Queen is interested in my.... abilities; what is happening to me somehow ties with an accident that happened before our lives' time that caused progress to stop and knowledge to be altered. You and I are not aware of this because we've always lived this way of learning only history and not creating anything new," stated Kitaj.

This caught Dagen off guard. Kitaj went on to tell Dagen she had been presented to the Queen because she was to play some part in the Queen's quest for restoring knowledge's order and that it not only affected her but him as well.

"They think you're the key? Dagen asked, astonished.

"They think I may be part of finding the solution, but honestly— I think you're the key," Kitaj said with worry, "because you're the cause of my changes. I'm fairly sure you can't be read either. You weren't detected when they came to get me at the barrow mound."

Dagen took a breath and sat up straight, shocked and trying to process what Kitaj had shared with him.

"Do you sense any void around me?" asked Dagen.

"Not at all," answered Kitaj.

"When you asked to see me tonight, I had no idea... I don't detect any void from you either nor any strange energy coming from you... just what builds around us," he paused. "I believe you. It's just a part of you... as I guess a part of me and this connection between us." Dagen stated, "Somehow I've always known you or knew I was going to know you. I truly can't explain it."

"Neither can I, but I knew I'd find you again, without any reservations. It just happened too soon. Don't ask me how I... I still don't understand," said Kitaj.

They both paused and tried to let the facts of what they knew to be true bring more clarity to their situation. No revelations of their connection came.

Kitaj continued, "There's more. Queen Frija and the Central Council are keeping me under watchful protection. It would seem King Wodan has his own agenda for restoring knowledge. His searches have led to nothing. If he were to find out; there's no telling what he would do to try to extract information— or at least that was the impression I was given. The Queen does not want to impede the natural progress of this *change* in me. I know it grows stronger when I am near you; I want to be near you, as much as I can. But, I don't want you getting involved."

"It would appear that I already am," said Dagen.

"Other than Aergo, no one else knows about you and me. I think until you and I have a better understanding of what is happening... we don't need to tell anyone about us," Kitaj blushed, "I mean what we're experiencing," she added.

"I don't like hiding and leaving you to face the Queen and Council alone," said Dagen.

"Please trust me to wait, we need time to see how all of this develops before we present what we know," said Kitaj.

"I'm not comfortable with your plan," said Dagen.

"I have trustworthy allies, but we'll have to be careful that the King does not discover us," said Kitaj, "and no one suspects..." said Kitaj, but was interrupted.

"Rûni," said Dagen with trepidation in his voice.

"What about Rûni?" asked Kitaj.

"He knew how badly I wanted to see you but didn't tell me he had found you," said Dagen.

"Why didn't you mention this last night? asked Kitaj. "And why didn't I know this..." she questioned herself aloud.

"I honestly didn't want to talk about it," said Dagen, "He said it was for my own protection, but he gave in and told me the morning of the Induction."

"I didn't read any of this from him when I saw him during the ceremony," said Kitaj.

"You didn't see him before then, I mean after you two first met? " asked Dagen.

"No, the next time I saw him was the night of the Induction," said Kitaj, "That was yesterday. It seems like a lifetime ago."

Dagen was puzzled by trying to piece together the facts he knew, "Something's off. Rûni spent each morning at the Order since we arrived in Lerakrey, and you only saw him that first and last day."

"I believe I know what happened— my mother! She must have tutored him in blocking his thoughts. I would have had some impression otherwise," said Kitaj.

"I think Rûni had other motives; he cares for you," Dagen said with concern.

"I know," she paused to give her next words special care, "He's one of the few people that I've instantly liked when I met him. I can see why you're friends. I don't want to hurt him, but I can't see a way around disappointing him."

"Kitaj, he's never expressed an interest in anyone before you. I don't want him hurt either. We left each other on better terms but I wouldn't say they were resolved. I don't think he's going to take this well when he finds out I'm not on Swedu and am here with you. I hope he'll be able to accept us," Dagen said sincerely.

"I hope we can resolve all of this soon," Kitaj added with deep concern.

Dagen tried to sound encouraging, "It will all work out somehow," and added with a jesting tone, "that is once we discover the cause and meaning for this new found energy and have restored the natural balance of knowledge to the universe."

"When you put it that way, we should have this solved within a week or so," Kitaj added, in a matched jesting tone but then returned to the gravity of their situation, "Dagen, I didn't want this for you. I'm so sorry."

"There's no need to be sorry. I think you'd have to agree, our circumstances were inevitable. Hopefully, soon we'll find the meaning to what's happening to us," he added.

"Speaking of trying to find meaning— I have something else I need to tell you. It concerns Isla. I thought of telling you last night when I realized how you knew her, but I wish I knew more... to tell you what it is. There's something looming in her future. I can't see it, I only know it. It's in shadow," said Kitaj.

"Does it have anything to do with us and what we're facing?" asked Dagen.

"I don't think it does. It seems separate. I don't know how help her." Kitaj stated.

"Maybe we'll discover that too." said Dagen.

"I hope so," she added.

Kitaj started feeling ill and shaky. The room began to move when she blinked. She started to rummage through the basket for something but nothing looked or smelled appealing. A wave of nausea hit her.

"Are you all right?" Dagen asked with concern.

"I will be, I just need something to eat," she said as a cold sweat broke out on her forehead.

"I have these," said Dagen as he handed her his last two sunstar loaves. He grabbed the pitcher in the basket, "Let me go get you some water," he said as he started to leave the cave for the stream.

"That's not necessary, this will be fine," Kitaj said, as she began to nibble on one of the sunstar loaves.

Dagen sat next to her wondering if there was anything else he could do to help. Her skin had turned pale and clammy. He sat nervously fiddling with the handle on the pitcher, watching her closely. He was relieved to see the sunstar loaf was helping her to a quick recovery.

"Better, thank you. I think what I found out today got the most of me," Kitaj said weakly and embarrassed.

"And counting tonight, you've had little sleep in two days. You've received extreme and altering news. Your reaction is completely understandable. Honestly, I'd be concerned if your composure stayed intact after what you've learned," said Dagen.

"You seem to be doing fine," said Kitaj.

"Don't worry, it will sink in for me later," Dagen said, trying to make her feel less embarrassed.

"What worries me the most is Wodan," said Kitaj.

"That's a legitimate worry," Dagen couldn't deny, "I thought the reason why you didn't put our names on your note from Aergo was because you were concerned about the Tjetajat finding out about us seeing one another. Now I know there are bigger concerns."

"That was Aergo's idea. He wanted to keep us safe. He's warming up to you," said Kitaj.

"I like him too, I'll win him over yet," said Dagen.

"In given time," said Kitaj.

Dagen held the last sunstar loaf in his palm and gazed at the pattern, "You know you are like this to me."

"A baked good?" said Kitaj, as playful banter.

"No, now look who's making jokes," Dagen said smiling, as he traced the sunstar pattern, "You're warm and brighten everything around you and within me," while he drew the symbol in the loose dirt of the cave floor between them.

Kitaj snuggled in closer and put her head against his chest to hear his heartbeat, and confessed, "I see you the same way, you're my shining constant, the brightest point within and without all the madness around us."

She rubbed her finger in the center circle of the pattern he had drawn to represent filling it in. Kitaj had changed the symbol he made for her into one for him.

A thought occurred to her. She sat up to face Dagen and said with pause, "I wonder... This may seem very strange, but just follow me." Kitaj stated cautiously.

She held her hand up, with fingers spread, and reached forward with her fingertips. Dagen extended his hand to hers in the same manner. The ends of the fingers were close but not touching and they watched as a glow grew and arced from one finger to the others.

"How are we doing this?" questioned Dagen in astonishment.

Kitaj just shook her head and suggested, "I have an idea, let's try thinking of the same thing and see if it changes."

"What should we think of?" asked Dagen.

"How about when we first met?" said Kitaj.

As soon as she spoke the words, the glow erupted! Sparks flew and ricocheted around the room, shattering the pitcher next to them. Jagged pieces of pottery showered them both.

"That was a little dangerous!" said Dagen.

"All right, let's try something calmer— a still pond?" Kitaj laughed.

The glow continued to arc back and forth from Kitaj's fingers to Dagen's. It maintained a slow and steady pulse.

Kitaj interjected, "That's better, how do you feel?"

Dagen replied with a smile, "Fine. I just feel the warmth."

"Are you ready to try something with more risk?" asked Kitaj.

"If we are ever going to solve this, I think we are going to have to take some risks," said Dagen.

"Let's concentrate on this loss— the alteration of knowledge. Try to stay open to anything that might come from it," said Kitaj.

Dagen took a deep, uneasy breath. Kitaj closed her eyes, while Dagen sat watching her. The energy retracted, then burst into the air between them covering them in a dome of light. Kitaj opened her eyes to see it. She reached up with her other hand to touch it, causing ripples in the cascading light.

Their concentration broke and the light faded. Only the glow between their hands remained.

"What do you think it means?" asked Dagen.

"I can't say for sure, but I think we are on the right path. Did you see anything?" asked Kitaj.

"Other than the light around us, no. And of course, there was the sound that was coming from it," said Dagen.

"What sound? I didn't hear anything," said Kitaj.

"You couldn't hear it? It was a low sound that resonated through the light. It was very full and soothing," said Dagen. "Did you see something?" he asked.

"I believe I saw the outline of two shapes. They weren't very clear. I don't know what they were. The first one was an odd shape, curved and narrow at one end. It reminded me of a feather. It seems vaguely familiar, but I can't place where I know it from. The other was round, and I think it had some sort of spiral shape in the center," said Kitaj.

Dagen asked her, "Are you tired from this?"

"Actually, no. Not at all," she replied. "What about you? How are you feeling?'

"I think I am trying too hard and over thinking what we're doing," said Dagen.

"You did very well for our first try," assured Kitaj. "We can try again when you wish."

Dagen took another deep breath and stated, "I'm ready."

As they faced each other with their next attempt, they interlaced their clasped hands and held their index fingers against each other's in a pointing motion. The glow intensified as it streamed from the end of their extended fingers. As they moved their joined hands above them, the light trailed across the air. The glow remained intact and suspended. Kitaj and Dagen smiled to see the line of light that floated above them.

"Your turn to follow me," Dagen asked of Kitaj, as she let his hand lead hers by drawing a large circle, set aglow, floating between them.

He reached up with his other hand and touched its edge. With a sweeping motion from his free hand, he made the suspended circle spin in place and had Kitaj's hand follow his to complete a drawing of Kitaj's sunstar symbol. It stood as a glowing open frame between them. Dagen was delighted to see Kitaj's smile as the light of her sunstar shown around her. It was a fitting portrait of her in his eyes. Kitaj blushed from Dagen's intense focus on her. She reached up with her other hand and rubbed the inside edge of the glowing symbol, filling in the center with its light. The alternation had changed her symbol into the one she had for Dagen. She could see him laughing at her through the golden haze of the circle. Dagen leaned forward and put his head through the shimmering center, and Kitaj leaned in to meet him with a kiss. The suspended sunstar warmed their faces through their sweet and prolonged endearment, while faint crackling sounds met their ears. As Kitaj let go of Dagen's hand, the luminous mark disappeared. They both sat back from each other, laughing and wondering in amazement at the person sitting in front of them.

As Dagen shifted his weight under him, a shard of broken pottery stuck him, causing Dagen to jump and let out a small yelp. Kitaj, already in a giddy state from their shared experience, could not help but find his unexpected discomfort comical.

"I'm in pain and you laugh. This is disturbing," Dagen teased.

"Excuse me for laughing," she apologized, matching his playful manner, "We *are* dangerous together. Best that we get these broken pieces up before someone gets seriously injured," Kitaj said half jesting, as she stood and began going about the cave, scooping up the remains of the pitcher.

Dagen found a large chunk of the base behind him and alerted Kitaj, "Here, catch."

Kitaj tried to say, "Wait, don't!" but it was too late.

Dagen threw the broken pitcher base in Kitaj's direction. Her reaction was too slow and her hands could not meet the airborne piece of heavy pottery before it met her face. CRACK! was the unwelcomed, yet extremely familiar sound that came from the bridge of Kitaj's nose.

"Ow! VEX IT! Not again!" she said as her hands flew up to her face and covered her bleeding nose.

Dagen started to laugh until he saw the blood running down her arm. The sight and realization of what had just happened made Dagen break into a cold sweat and his color went ashen.

"I am so sorry! I thought you could catch it," exclaimed Dagen.

"Obviously, your expectations are a bit higher than my abilities," said Kitaj, with a plugged nose and watering eyes.

"What can I do? What can I get you?" pleaded Dagen.

Kitaj felt the swollen bridge of her nose and stated as she breathed through her mouth, "I've had worse. You may have helped to even it out a bit. The other side usually takes the brunt. I might have matching knots on either side now," she said, trying to make humor from her untimely mishap.

Dagen took the edge of the blanket and wiped the blood off her hand and arm, but let Kitaj clean her face in fear he might make matters worse.

The sound did not escape Aergo's ears. Within moments, he stood waiting at the cave entrance.

"The nose, again?" asked Aergo in a monotone manner.

Kitaj nodded yes.

"How did it happen this time?" Aergo questioned.

Kitaj looked at Dagen. Aergo began to growl as he stepped toward him. His massive furry body filled the entire entrance, giving Dagen reason to step back.

"Calm down. It was an accident," said Kitaj holding up the broken pitcher base, "I missed the toss."

Aergo backed down and coolly stated, "She doesn't catch well, as you now see. Hand me that blanket."

Dagen obliged. Aergo shredded a corner from it with a prick of his enormous claws.

"I'll be back shortly," said Aergo as he left with the blanket scrap.

Kitaj met Dagen's confused look and replied, "He's going to get some healing herbs and soak them with the cloth in the stream for me to apply to my nose. It's almost routine for him, I'm sad to say. Don't fret, I'll be fine. Tjetajat medicinals are fast for healing, but unfortunately, they don't necessarily restore injuries back to perfect condition."

Dagen sat down near Kitaj, not sure what to say and slightly afraid to touch her. He did not want to cause any more harm.

"Don't worry about me, I'm not that fragile. I'm just clumsy. We have more important matters to occupy our concerns," said Kitaj, as she playfully nudged him with her elbow.

Dagen sat quietly next to her, not saying another word until Aergo returned with a poultice to reduce the swelling of her nose. Aergo was aware of the quiet between them and felt it best to dismiss himself again.

Kitaj applied the remedy to her nose, waiting for the swelling to subside as well as waiting for Dagen to say something— anything in reply.

Eventually, Dagen quietly asked, "Do you want to continue... after this?"

"Of course I do! How could you think otherwise? It was an accident and in no way your fault. Truthfully, I don't think I ever had much choice in the matter when it came to you," she smiled and removed the poultice from her cracked nose. "How does it look?"

"Better, the swelling is going down," said Dagen.

"See, I'll be fine. It will probably be healed by the next time we see each other."

"When do you think that will be?" asked Dagen.

"I can't say for sure. I wish I knew, but I don't," stated Kitaj.

"I have a thought. On the nights we expect to meet, if for some reason you cannot come, I'll leave the sunstar symbol for you here in the cave, so when you do, you will at least know I was here," said Dagen as he referred to the image he had drawn on the ground.

"And I'll fill in the circle, to let you know I did make it here at some point. I like it. At least we'll know the other arrived without the risk of sending so many messages back and forth with Aergo," said Kitaj.

"I am sure he'll appreciate that too," laughed Dagen as he wiped the symbol away with his hand.

"We had both better be going, it will be light soon," said Kitaj.

Aergo stood waiting at the cave entrance. His thoughts were the same; it was time to go.

"Hopefully, tomorrow night?" said Dagen.

"I'll do my best," said Kitaj.

She started to leave but turned back to embrace Dagen once more, both carefully minding Kitaj's sore nose.

"We will figure this out," he said and without reservation, she believed him.

In the following days, Dagen and Kitaj continued to meet as often as opportunity would allow. Together, they worked on exploring the connection between them and how it might help solve the Queen's dilemma. As promised, Dagen would leave behind a sunstar symbol on the nights Kitaj was unable to join him. She would find a reason the next day to go in that direction, usually under the guise of collecting herbs and berries as part of her duties. Aergo would misdirect any curiosity of her whereabouts by mimicking her voice near where she was expected to be, allowing her to proceed to the cave to fill in the sunstar symbol and return to her duties before being discovered. It gave Dagen some reassurance to know Kitaj had been there at some point. He stayed at the cave as often as possible in the hopes she would arrive, even if her stay was for only a brief time. Each brought different items to make their time together more comfortable and the cave soon had the appearance of a dwelling. When he was not at the cave, Dagen's time was spent working at the Idle Sickles. With a little persuasion on his part, Dagen negotiated a paying position from Ismadalia. She had conceded. The Wild Hunt was to start soon and she would be needing the extra help.

Aergo became more accepting of Dagen, as evidence of his commitment to Kitaj was made more obvious with each day. While Corynth, well aware of Rûni's affection for Kitaj, kept putting the two together during training and meals, as well as general duties for the grounds; making it harder for Kitaj to find any personal time without Rûni's presence.

The Council would bring Kitaj in daily and ask if there were any new developments. She shared nothing, and was so thankful she remained unreadable to them. The only news for the Council was from Tanadra and Corynth, who attested to fluctuations in the flow of energy coming from Kitaj through the void. All members of the Council agreed that the void around Kitaj was staying consistently intact.

◆

It had been three days since Kitaj had seen Dagen, for the moon was in its fullest cycle and lessons in night transcension required her participation. Kitaj did her best but could not keep her mind on her studies. She was anxious to see Dagen again. The following day, the anticipation was overwhelming and she enlisted Aergo to help her take supplies to the cave prior to meeting Dagen late that night. She wanted to surprise him on his arrival with special treats she had saved back over the last few days. She and Aergo proceeded to implement their diversion, which had been previously successful in tricking her guards. But on this occasion, her departure caught the curiosity of Rûni. He found it strange that Kitaj would be going into the forest with a full basket when she was supposed to be gathering winter blooming herbs. Rûni followed at a far distance, so not to be detectable in any way by her. He knew the area well where Kitaj usually picked herbs and headed in that direction. When he came near to the location, he heard her talking but happened to see movement in another direction and went to investigate.

He saw Kitaj crossing the stream and disappear behind a rock face. He proceeded to follow and spied her entering a cave, and waited to see her exit with an empty basket. Rûni's curiosity was piqued. Once Kitaj was out of view, Rûni entered the cave to find a cozy setting, as if someone lived there. There were blankets and lanterns, glow wine and different edibles treats arranged next to a vase of flowers in a corner of the cave. It was clear to him; Kitaj had made herself a hidden getaway, but why?

What is she up to? Rûni wondered.

◆

Night was falling as Rûni made his way back through the forest to Kitaj's secret cave. He was breaking the rules by leaving the camp without permission but he felt compelled to find out what Kitaj was doing. Rûni's intentions were to wait at the entrance, to see when Kitaj would return to the cave, but when he arrived, he saw a light coming from what he had anticipated to be a dark entrance. His first thought was possibly Kitaj had taken a shorter route to reach the cave before he had. Rûni crept to the entrance to peek inside; his curiosity overtaking his feelings of wrongly invading her privacy. He saw a silhouetted form illuminated by one of the lanterns. The form's shadow cast a familiar profile on the cave wall, familiar but completely unexpected by him. Rûni's footing slipped causing him to stumble.

"I thought you weren't going to be able to come until late tonight. I'm so glad you could make it earlier," said Dagen, turning around to see, "Rûni!"

"What are you doing here?" asked Rûni, as any composure of himself unraveled.

"I could ask you the same!" said Dagen.

"You're not supposed to be here. Why aren't you on Swedu?" demanded Rûni.

"Long story, another time— maybe," stated Dagen. "You're spying on Kitaj!"

"And you're making her break her covenant by meeting you here in secret!" Rûni fired back.

"I'm not making her do anything!" retorted Dagen.

"This is wrong, Dagen, very wrong!" Rûni argued.

"You have no idea what is happening here," Dagen stated.

"I can imagine," Rûni said snidely.

"This does not concern you, Rûni!" defended Dagen.

"Of course it does! As a fellow member of the Order, it is my responsibility to ensure…" Rûni was interrupted by a voice behind him.

"Rûni, calm down, please. I am sorry if this comes as a shock. Neither of us would have wanted that for you," said Kitaj.

Dagen walked past Rûni to stand beside Kitaj. Rûni could not help but notice how Kitaj and Dagen appeared next to each other. They stood defined and separate from one another; strangely separate for a pair.

There's something very odd between these two, he thought.

"Are you all right?" Kitaj asked Dagen. "We were on our way when I sensed Rûni was with you. We got here as fast as we could."

Rûni blurted out, "We? Who else is here?"

"Please try to calm yourself, we hope you will understand. There are some pressing issues that Kitaj and I are trying to..." Dagen said but was cut off by Rûni's impatience.

"But are you two together?" he asked.

Kitaj and Dagen looked at each other. To acknowledge themselves as a couple to someone else felt awkward and out of place to them.

"You could say that," Kitaj said slowly, feeling exposed and vulnerable in declaring her feelings toward Dagen to Rûni.

"Kitaj, you of all people, know what you are doing is wrong," insisted Rûni.

"Actually, no. I've never felt more in the right in my life! There's more at stake here than what it seems and you're just going to have to trust my judgment. In turn, I need to be able to trust you. I'll forgive you for following me, if you promise you will not pressure us for answers we cannot give you at this time," Kitaj stated to Rûni.

Rûni was taken aback, not only by Kitaj's words but by Aergo entering the cave behind her and Dagen.

"Do you need any help in here? asked Aergo.

Rûni turned pale and backed up several steps as Aergo's body filled the cave's entrance.

"No, all will be fine," Kitaj said stroking Aergo's furry arm.

"Thank you, Aergo," said Dagen with appreciation.

"Aergo? Your cat?" puzzled Rûni.

Aergo shook his head as he laughed in a low growl that made Rûni's knees weak.

Kitaj directed to Dagen, "You know what this means— we are as good as discovered, or at least we will be once Rûni returns to camp. My mother will read him before he makes it back to the sanctuary. I need to go and explain to her before that happens; it's our best course of action in dealing with the Central Council. We can have no more secrets from them."

She turned to Rûni, "I'm sure a full disclosure will be expected by you when you return. They will read you anyway, so just be honest with your feelings and intent and you'll be fine. Rûni, Dagen's and my involvement concerns business I have with the Central Council which I am not at liberty to disclose. What I can tell you is that some of my abilities were heightened because I have met Dagen and they continue to grow when I am near him. This is what the Council will be interested in knowing. I have yet to make them aware of his involvement because we were trying to sort out the cause ourselves first. That's no longer possible," Kitaj concluded.

Rûni's jaw dropped from her disclosure. He was overcome with embarrassment and felt ashamed of his actions.

"Kitaj, I'm sorry, I should not have followed you. Dagen, I don't…" said Rûni.

"You two have much to discuss. Aergo and I had best leave now; I'll need the time to compose my thoughts before I reach the Council," said Kitaj.

"You shouldn't have to do this without me. Let me come with you," Dagen pleaded.

"It will go better if I can prepare them first. Imagine how thrown they will be to discover there's yet another being close to me that they cannot read. It's as if I'm collecting," she laughed.

"I don't like this," said Dagen.

"Trust me, it's our best approach," said Kitaj.

Kitaj reached over to squeeze Dagen's hand. Rûni thought his eyes must be playing tricks on him for he thought he saw a faint glow surround their clasped hands. The look he saw in both Kitaj and Dagen's eyes however, was unmistakable. With that serving as her farewell, Kitaj and Aergo departed.

Dagen spent the better part of the night trying to explain what he could to Rûni. Rûni left Dagen just before day break feeling at a loss. He was upset with himself for forcing the situation and could imagine, from his own experience with his father, Kitaj's discomfort in having to disclose her secrets to her mother. He had pried and had put his friends in a difficult situation, but he also thought they should have come forward from the beginning instead of breaking the laws of the Tjetajat. They were bound to be caught, if not by him, by someone, and Rûni was left feeling divided in his loyalties.

ﻉﻟﻪ

Dagen was exhausted from their night's turn of events. The strain was finally catching up with him. He walked for a short distance along the stream until his legs would take him no further. Dagen stopped to rest on a large slab of rock. He was too tired to sleep, and equally, too tired to move. The rock was cool to his back as he felt warmed by the morning Sun pouring down on him. The sound of the stream was lulling. Conditions seemed to be in his favor to slip into his state of disembodied awareness, and he wondered if exhaustion was the key to his ability to reach "flight." Dagen had not attempted to travel outside himself since leaving Carcadoc and he hoped he might be able to find Kitaj and at least be beside her while she faced her mother and the Council. He remained concerned and bothered not to be there to support her. Dagen also hoped that exploring his ability to travel might give him helpful insight into his and Kitaj's predicament. Drained as he was, he knew it was worth trying and concentrated on the bright yellow glow behind his eyelids.

"You foolish, ridiculous girl!" You have no idea what is at stake. Your safety is of the utmost importance and now I find out you have been sneaking off to meet some boy!" exclaimed Corynth.

"It's not like that! You have not listened to what I just told you! And, it's time you recognized I'm a grown woman!" Kitaj said, trying to stifle her temper.

"Then conduct yourself as one! What do you know of this boy? Other than it would seem he is adrift, without prospects, knows nothing of our commitments, and disregards our rules. There is no respect in this!" said Corynth.

"And what do you know of him, Mother?" Kitaj argued.

"Only what I have heard from you and what I have read from Rûni, which is enough to see..." Corynth started but Kitaj cut her words short.

Kitaj yelled back at her, "YOU CAN'T SEE WHAT'S HAPPENING! YOU NEVER HAVE, NOT WHEN IT COMES TO ME! AND I KNOW YOU CAN'T SEE ANYTHING ABOUT DAGEN EITHER!" She tried to compose herself with her next statement, "Let me try to explain to you again. Somehow he is part of this. We don't know how or why, but meeting him is the cause for these changes in me. We have been trying to put the pieces together to understand more about how we are involved with the Queen's quest before we came forward."

"Do you have feelings for this boy?" asked Corynth.

"Why is that important for you to know, in light of what I just told you?" Kitaj retorted. "And Mother, he's not a boy!"

"It has significant importance! Do you have feelings for him?" Corynth asked her again.

"Yes I do, and it's something more profound than anything I knew existed! But why am I even trying to explain this to you? YOU WOULDN'T UNDERSTAND!" Kitaj said, throwing her arms in the air out of frustration with the energy inside her growing.

"What makes you think I wouldn't ?' Corynth said, sounding slightly wounded.

"You never share anything about my father, or what your lives were like together, what your hopes were when you were younger— or even once asked me what I might be experiencing. You're cold, shut off and unyielding!" Kitaj said, cutting through to Corynth's core.

Corynth knew Kitaj was right. She sank back. She could no longer stand and sat down. All of her walls and pretenses were failing her! The streaming power from Kitaj's eyes was seeping through and breaking down Corynth's defenses. Her truth came gushing out from her in a flood of memories and emotions.

"I wasn't always like this. I was once open to possibilities and all life had to offer. It was the happiest time in my life when I met your father. Kade Jafnan was the most captivating person I have ever met. I was so entranced by him. Kade and I met on *The Night of the Twin Stars*, and I knew in that moment, I would love no other. Soon after our meeting, we were vowed. He was to leave with Wodan's forces, and we did not want to part from each other without securing our bond. Our times together were brief since the Nine Worlds' War raged on. During his absence, I joined the Tjetajat, which had always been my path as part of the Ellor legacy. The year sequestered for my training was not an inconvenience since he was away in a rotation that was part of the occupying forces in Léohetwin. I was settled in the Order and he would return to me periodically. Those days we had together were magical... I was unable to see what was to come, so I never took a moment with him for granted."

"On your father's last true visit home, I was able to read from him what he knew concerning his next orders. Wodan's spies had discovered the Vane had combined the forces of the Léohets that had escaped the occupation with the strength of the Gicels. Together, they planned to reclaim the devastated world of Léohetwin. Wodan's army was to intercept the Vane's forces at Gicelfolde and hopefully put an end to this long-lived war. Wodan's forces were prevailing, but it was rumored that even the King could see there was little left to be gained other than the Vane conceding."

"All your father would tell me was that he promised he'd be home by the New Year... it was a promise he was able to keep; just not in the way he had intended. As you know, Kitaj, the Midangardian New Year marks when the veil between this existence and the next is the thinnest, and The Sacred Passages of Eormensyl are able to allow prior-lived souls to revisit their loved ones as it awakes for summer. This timing worked bittersweetly to your father's advantage, and allowed us a few more days together," Corynth said, wiping her eyes and composing herself to continue.

"The last battle of the war was fought on Gicelfolde during the arrival of Midangard's New Year. Wodan's forces succeeded. There were many deaths on both sides; one of those being your father. I felt him fall."

"When I found him at our front door early New Year's morning, I knew his soul was holding on without recognition of his own demise. I'm still amazed how your father's soul was able to retain his strength and conviction and almost existed in its wholeness of being. I was not ready to lose him, so I did not tell him of his true state. We barricaded ourselves in our home. I knew it was a matter of time before he would discover his truth and would have to pass onward."

"Three days after the battle, his body was returned, along with several others from Lerakrey. When his unit brought his body to me, I tried to conceal it from him, but Kade knew, and in that moment, he was gone," Corynth explained, then paused to gather her strength to continue.

"Soon after, I found I was miraculously expecting you. From the beginning, I could not read or sense anything about you. I should have known many details about you. But, you had the void encasing you even then, even inside me," Corynth added with a hint of the familiar edge in her voice Kitaj was so accustomed to hearing. "It felt like I had a gaping hole, running straight through my chest from the loss of your father and I had a complete unknown growing inside me. My heart and mind struggled to continue. I don't think I would have survived if it had not been for Tanadra and the Elders."

"It was never your fault Kitaj, but I will admit to you now; my sanity hinged on me shutting myself off to you as much as you were shut off from me. I truly believe had I not, neither of us would have lived. I could feel nothing from you, so I wanted to feel nothing for you. But, you were all I had left of Kade. I could not disregard you. The Elders convinced me you gave cause for hope, though admittedly they, as well as I, were afraid of what you might be. It is so easy to fear what you do not understand," stated Corynth.

Kitaj stood in crushing awe. Her mother had never shared any part of her past before. As painful as it was to hear and feel the emotional memories coming from Corynth, Kitaj finally understood her mother's reasons for her cold and distant nature.

༄

Dagen achieved flight again. With ease, he left his body behind and began to search for Kitaj. He had a general idea of which direction the Tjetajat camp could be found and flew over the tree tops towards it but discovered his core sense of navigation was based on his intuition. He *felt* where Kitaj would be instead of following landmarks. Dagen was anxious to be beside her. He found he could increase the speed of his travel and was marveling at his own abilities, unaware he was being tracked. Two small dark objects were gaining on him. On their approach, the ravens flanked either side of him. Dagen realized, just as with the hawk, these two were also aware of his presence. But in contrast, these birds were not friendly and seemed they were trying to herd him! Dagen abruptly stopped in mid-air, leaving the ravens to fly past him. The birds immediately turned and were coming straight for him. Dagen wondered what he could have done to cause their upset. He weaved about, and dropped lower to swerve in and out of trees to try to shake their pursuit, but could not. When the birds were close to him, they snapped and clawed at him as if trying to catch a solid object. Their attempts went through him but were not completely harmless. Each snap or grasp left Dagen with an odd and unsettling sensation of torn space within him. The ravens were becoming more hostile with each attempt to snare him. Dagen knew this could not be a random act. As his memory flashed, he recalled seeing the hawk circling above him after his flight and how it had been chased away by two black birds.

Dagen wondered, *Could these be the same two?*

He could not rid himself of them. The ravens' attack viciously amplified and Dagen had no choice but to turn back. He was not about to lead these vile creatures anywhere near Kitaj. He raced back, still trying to dodge the squawking frenzy that trailed him. There was no time for gently waking and Dagen did not know what his own response would be from his hurried re-entry. He could only hope his reflexes would be sharp enough to respond as he plunged his awareness back into his still body. Dagen threw open his eyes and saw the two birds within striking distance. He threw one arm across his face for protection while the other swatted out at the flying menace. He felt his blind aim manage to push one of the birds away, but in the process, tore open the palm of his hand on an outstretched claw.

In his moment of desperation, Dagen yelled, "STOP!"

To his surprise, everything did. Suddenly, there was no sound, no movement. He was confused by the sudden stillness and cautiously moved his arm away from his face to see what had occurred. His arm felt strangely weighted as he moved it. Dagen could see a path of warped ripples form through the air, following the movement of his arm. The air itself felt dense and almost fluid-like. Dagen was stunned to see the birds motionless and suspended slightly above him.

ﻉﻠ

"It does not excuse how I treated you. I kept you at arm's length all your life, but I hope you understand my actions better. Please know, I do have some understanding," said Corynth.

"Dagen..." said Kitaj out of context, as a sense of unease wavered her equilibrium.

"This... Dagen, you have feelings for; you believe he is integral in your new found change. You think he is instrumental, in some way, to resolving our greatest loss. If this is as you say, we must bring him before the Council and make Queen Frija aware at once! The importance of the matter far out weighs any personal..." Corynth said, but was interrupted.

"Mother... something's wrong..." said Kitaj, as she was overwhelmed by the feeling that the ground she stood on had abruptly slipped out from under her. Kitaj panicked, "Something's happened... I can't sense Dagen anymore! It's as if he no longer exists! I don't understand... I can't feel him! "I have to go!"

"How could this be?" Dagen said to himself and the frozen birds that hung above him.

He noticed a gold band around the right leg of each raven. As he looked closer, he could see an engraved mark of Aesingard— Wodan's symbol.

The realization hit him and exclaimed, "These are the King's ravens!"

Dagen cautiously reached up to touch the extended wing of one of the birds. As he touched it, the feathers smeared and elongated. Black sooty residue covered Dagen's fingertips.

His mind reeled and he tried to scramble out from under the suspended birds; only to find a gelatinous surface was now beneath him where previously there had been solid rock. His coat was adhering to the gummy surface and provided little traction under him, as his boots and elbows became caked with the slated gunk. He was slowly sinking deeper into the rock. Dagen struggled to get his arms out of his coat's sleeves to release himself and managed to slide from beneath the forms of the hovering ravens. He slipped and stumbled his way across the rocks; their surface smearing with each step.

He noticed the creek had transformed into what resemble a long and winding glass sculpture. Its cascade had been suspended in a single moment of time. Blood dripping from his cut hand disturbed the otherwise solid appearance of the stream as he crossed. Each drop caused the surface to bounce before absorbing his blood into the suspended state. Dagen had no knowing of the extent this effect had taken, and questioned if time had halted within all existence. Everything around him as far as he could see had been affected.

He began to cough and wheeze, then choke. The air's thickness was settling in his lungs and his ability to breathe was being compromised. Though time was frozen around him, his own time was running out. He knew he had to escape his altered surroundings if he was going to survive! Dagen tried to run, without any thought to which direction he should go. His breathing became increasingly labored as he stumbled up a small slope away from the stream. Dagen felt his life fading from him. His vision went black as he collapsed and tumbled into a viscous crevice within the previously rocky slope. The fall knocked from him the last bit of air he carried in his lungs. In Dagen's final conscious moment, he realized his hand lay resting on what felt to be a cold, muddy patch of ground, and he etched Kitaj's sunstar symbol into the stone's surface with his blood soaked fingers.

Kitaj ran out into the open of the camp and began yelling for Aergo and Rûni. Corynth followed behind her. Aergo was immediately at her side. He could tell from her tone, she was in extreme distress. Aergo responded by appearing to Kitaj in his horse form to provide her with his fastest transport. Rûni followed. A small crowd gathered near them, partly from the noise but mainly from the sensing of Corynth's concern.

"What's wrong? asked Rûni.

"It's Dagen, something has happened to him!" Kitaj replied.

Corynth asked, puzzled, "Where are you going?"

"Mother, if it isn't obvious… to find Dagen! Oh, sometimes I wish so badly you could read me!" Kitaj exclaimed.

"How can I help?" asked Corynth.

Even in her haste, Kitaj could not help but be taken aback by her mother's offer. She would have expected these words from Tanadra, but not Corynth. Through her fears, Kitaj's mind had full clarity of her actions and surroundings while her heart felt as if it would burst from her chest by the speed it was beating.

"Through Rûni, you can know what's happening. Keep your focus on him to know when and where we need help," Kitaj stated, as she and Rûni climbed onto Aergo and sped away.

All three scanned the forest for any sign of Dagen as Aergo hurried toward the cave. It was the last place they knew Dagen to be and it seemed the most logical place to begin searching for him. The deeper they ventured into the forest, the more Aergo felt ill-at-ease. The hairs began to stand up on his fur and a crackling sound buzzed in his ears. Kitaj was feeling the change as well. This energy was familiar to her and gave her hope they were closer to finding Dagen.

A sudden wave of stinging force lifted Kitaj from Aergo's back and sent her flying backwards. She hit the ground hard but was unharmed other than the nerves throughout her body felt numbed and singed. She focused on the sight in front of her, but could not comprehend what she was seeing. Aergo was stuck in mid jump, motionless. Rûni hung in the air slightly behind Aergo, launched from Aergo's back, and flipped upside down in mid fall, motionless. Part of Aergo's tail remained unaffected; the last few inches of its hair blew freely in the breeze within the forest. Kitaj reached out and touched his tail, it felt unchanged. She tried to move her hand to the stiffened part but found herself zapped by a sharp charge from the formed barrier that held her friends. She felt along what should have been thin air and was met with a power impermeable to her. The barrier sent out sparks and stung her skin as she touched it.

Kitaj said to herself, "I know this energy. Dagen... what have you done? And why are you intentionally keeping me out?"

She tolerated the discomfort of multiple stings as she felt along the invisible wall, while she kept a close watch on any change in Aergo's and Rûni's condition. The barrier was smooth but had an uneven surface and shape, causing Kitaj to believe its results were from a first attempt at... whatever this was. She pressed her ear against the barrier, wincing at it's touch. She could hear no sound from the other side. There was no visible movement either for as far as she could see. She paced and thought there must be some way she can release this stronghold. Kitaj felt a small shift within the barrier, which prompted her to press her ear against it again. She listened more intently and was able to hear the faint sounds of the forest coming from deep within.

ॐ

Hyge and Myne had discovered the source of what they sought, but within an instant, the person who housed the power they were chasing had vanished in front of their eyes. Hyge panicked. Suddenly her balance was lost to her and she fell awkwardly on the rocky slab beneath her. Myne flew to her side. Both were frightened and distraught at the sight of her condition. Some of the feathers on her left wing had elongated and distorted. A metallic burnt smell hung heavy in the air and added to the birds' confusion. The ravens noticed the surface of the rock they had landed on was also distorted and smeared. A grainy powder covered the strange mottled surface of the slab as well as a coat that lay left behind. Hyge squawked and flapped about, unable to regain her ability to navigate steadily. Myne flew over her and clasped her back to give support as Hyge attempted her frenzied ascension. The ravens found they could only move forward in a small area before running into an unseen charged and solid surface. The screeching pair made a hastened and cumbersome flight upwards to find open air to take them to the Ports of Eormensyl.

Guardsmen witnessed the odd scene of the ravens' approach as they flew through the Eormensyl's corridor and directly into the portal to Aesingard. By the Kings orders, the ravens were granted open access to come and go as they please, but their circumstances looked questionable. Their unusual appearance prompted the new guardsman to make an inquiry to his superior officer.

"Pardon me, sir, the King's ravens? One seemed to be injured and assisted by the other. Shouldn't we alert the King?" said Brieg.

Brieg was barely recognizable. His face was clean shaven and his hair was short enough that the bright red stayed hidden by the rim of his helmet. His unmistakable smile was also absent due to the propriety of his duties.

Guardsman Rand did not give Brieg a second look as he opened communications with the connecting Aesingard gate. A small port adjacent to the travel portal served as means to notify the Aesir guards. The guardsman at the other end said they would ensure the ravens' arrival through the portal and would send a message to his Majesty immediately.

With urgent news for their master, the ravens did not delay in finding Wodan's exact location. Instead, Myne helped Hyge fly directly to the Well of Wisdom. Its caretaker, Mim, heard the ravens' shrilled cries as they approached the well's temple. His ancient and withered body struggled to stand as he witnessed one bird carrying the other in frantic flight. Mim rubbed the scarred skin of his balding head in response to the perplexing scene. His curiosity piqued as the birds flew past him without hesitating and dove directly into the center of the well.

Mim leaned heavily on his walking staff to hurry to the well's edge. He looked down and watched as the water swirled around the ravens. The birds separated and were pulled downward into the well's depths. Spinning as they descended, the birds were drawn ever closer to Wodan's eye that rested at the very bottom. Only under extreme conditions would Wodan's loyal spies dive into the well to expedite urgent news for him. Their connection to his eye allowed the well to welcome them and protect them, while the ravens were carried deeper and deeper until they reached Wodan's sight.

ℰ

At the kestel of Wealdriht on Aesingard, in the Hall of Assembly, all the Dryhtens from the Nine Worlds had gathered to meet with the King and his advisors. Final details of the Wild Hunt were being settled and required the input of all involved delegates. Because it was the first time since the Great War's inception that all worlds were to be included in the hunt, the King ordered tensions between rival factions to be put aside, and demanded that a presentation of unity be carried through for the duration of the hunt. Wodan was voicing his final decree when the visions from Hyge and Myne reached him. He saw what the ravens had experienced through their eyes, and felt their fear and confusion about Hyge's injury and the disappearance of the person they had identified as the source of the anomaly they were following. Abruptly, Wodan stopped talking and walked out of the hall, leaving the Dryhtens unsettled. Wiljo and Wæ followed closely behind him.

A messenger approached and bowed to the King before delivering his news. Wodan briefly stopped and took the note, but did not need to open it. Both brothers reached Wodan at his pause.

"What is it, brother?" asked Wæ.

"Ready my watch! We leave at once for the Asbjorn Forest," announced King Wodan.

The Sun's placement was the only noticeable movement Kitaj could detect in her line of vision. Within the barrier, sounds of water running and leaves blowing were increasing in intensity, giving her hope that time's known flow was being restored from its center and growing outward.

She thought, *There must be some way I can help speed this process!*

Kitaj drew from what she and Dagen had learned from their focusing exercise. She thought of various things, moments and events and concentrated her energy to combine with the barrier's, but continued to be repelled.

"What was he thinking when he did this?" she said, talking to herself.

Kitaj pondered the thought. It had to be simplified, and she tried with saying the command, "Protect."

The barrier glowed at her touch and for once, did not sting her.

"All right, we're getting closer," Kitaj said, coaxing the barrier. "I need to be more direct than that, do I? How about..." she looked over at Aergo and Rûni, still frozen in a moment of time, and said, "Stop."

The invisible wall lit up around her and radiated beams to her fingertips as she pressed her hands against its surface.

Wiljo had ridden ahead to the Aesingard portal for Lerakrey to alert the guardsmen of the unscheduled passage. The heavy gates protecting the port were made ready by drawing them back for the King and his watch.

On Wodan's arrival, one of the guardsmen announced, "Arrangements are prepared, your Majesty— the closest portal to the Asbjorn Forest, as requested."

Wodan paid little attention to the pulsing lights of the Eormensyl's slumber radiating throughout the winding branch of their portal path. He was more concerned with rushing to Lerakrey through the entity's slowed winter passage. Though the Eormensyl continued its offering of condensed time within distances between worlds, traveling during its rest was much more cumbersome compared to the lightning fast expediency of its summer travel. King Wodan's drive to discover what had happened to his prey urged the hunting party forward and they did not slow their pace upon reaching their destination.

"Welcome, your Majesty," said Guardsman Rand as the King charged through the Lerakrey side of the portal.

"Happy hunting, your Majesty," Brieg called to the King.

Brieg's gesture, though welcoming, was not exactly protocol for a Portal Under-guardsman, and gave Rand cause to eye Brieg with the warning of his disapproving scowl. Even though Brieg was new to his position, he already found his duties monotonous. His father had thought the portal post would be a good introduction to following orders and being patient, but Brieg was bored beyond anything he could have imagined. The company of Rand was even less inviting. Rand was quick to point out the smallest of Brieg's transgressions and he knew he would be getting an earful once the King and his hunting party were beyond the passage entry. Brieg's curiosity was piqued by this unexpected hunt, but he had already learned Wodan's actions were anything but predictable. He welcomed the opportunity of something new to speculate while standing guard. Also, imagining what beasts the King might be hunting could help carry him through another one of Rand's rants.

Once outside the Eormensyl, Wodan signaled his watch to go at a full run. His wolves and the others charged after Wodan's lead. Wodan had to temper Slepsil's gait to ensure the others could keep close, for if Slepsil was allowed his head, he would have left the hunting party far behind. The forest edge was a short distance from the Eormensyl and the vision from his ravens lead Wodan closer to the site of Hyge and Myne's unnerving encounter.

ﻌ

Kitaj stood with her hands against the barrier, grateful that it was finally responding to her. She pressed her ear against it again and heard that sounds coming from the other side were growing louder, but still sounded far away.

At least it seems to be resolving from the inside out, but we don't have the luxury of waiting for this to clear on its own, she considered. Kitaj concentrated her thoughts on the barrier. *If "Stop" was what caused it, then something just as simple should return the space to normal.*

"Release," she said hopefully.

ﻌ

As Wodan entered the Asbjorn Forest, Slepsil came to a sudden stop, pawed nervously at the ground and shook his head in protest of proceeding further. The wolves caught up with them and stopped as well. They began to growl at an unseen enemy ahead.

"Something is upsetting them! They won't go any further. Wiljo, ride ahead and see if you can see anything out of the ordinary!" commanded Wodan.

Wiljo reluctantly urged his horse ahead. It would only go a short distance forward. Wiljo felt uneasy himself. He turned back to look at his brother. Wodan gave him a nod to proceed. Wiljo dismounted and walked ahead and came to a stop.

"What do you see?" yelled Wodan.

Wiljo did not respond. He stood perfectly still looking forward with his back to them and seemed momentarily frozen. The forest itself seemed too still.

Wiljo? What is it?" Wodan demanded.

Wiljo turned back to the King to say, "Nothing your Majesty. I see nothing unusual."

"Then let us proceed," said Wodan, frustrated by their delay.

At Wodan's command, the wolves and horses began to move onward. The animals were still on edge but did as they were directed.

اللہ

The barrier had dropped. Aergo galloped ahead a short distance as Kitaj was helpless to reach Rûni before he finished his fall. Rûni landed hard on his shoulder and arm. The cracking sound was audible and followed by Rûni's muffled yell. Aergo turned and rushed back to Kitaj and Rûni in his goblin form.

"Rûni, stay as still as you can! Let me see!" said Kitaj.

As Kitaj looked over Rûni, Aergo assessed their surroundings and noticed the Sun was in a completely different position in the sky from just a moment before.

"Is he going to be all right?" asked Aergo.

"I think so, with a little healing time and help," said Kitaj.

"What happened to us? Time has quickened around us!" said Aergo.

"You two were caught in some sort of manipulation of time and were frozen in a still state. It ejected me from it as you entered. I'm sure Dagen caused it. It took a while but I was able to figure out how to release it.

"Dagen caused it!" said Rûni, shocked as he tried to get up but let out a yelp as he moved.

"I think it was a defensive measure. But against what, I don't know. You have a broken shoulder blade and arm. I am going to make a sling for you and Aergo will take you back to camp." said Kitaj.

"But, what about Dagen?" asked Rûni.

"I'll find him, I can sense him again since the barrier released," Kitaj added.

"You know where he is?" asked Rûni.

"No, it's just the feeling, and it's faint, but I know he's alive," said Kitaj.

"That settles it, we are going with you. He'll manage," said Aergo, as Rûni winced while Kitaj fitted him with a sling she made from tearing material from the edge of her tunic.

"Aergo's right. We've already lost too much time," said Rûni.

Rûni struggled to his feet. Aergo lifted him carefully in his arms and supported Rûni's wounded shoulder against him. Kitaj climbed onto Aergo's neck and they proceeded deeper into the forest. Though not as fast as his horse form, Aergo's goblin speed was barely slowed by the weight of carrying Kitaj and Rûni.

The forest's surroundings looked unchanged, but the air felt altered and wrong. They arrived at the cave where they had seen Dagen last and found no sign of him, except for his satchel he had left behind. The three agreed he must not have gone far and decided to continue their search on foot moving further downstream. Kitaj took the satchel and drew it close to her. She held it safe to her, with the futile hope that somehow her action could help hold him safe as well.

"Dagen has to be here somewhere," Kitaj said, trying to stay calm. "Aergo, can you pick up his scent?"

"I am having difficulty distinguishing it. There is something else clouding the air. It smells burnt and of iron," he explained.

Kitaj's heart dropped, her sense of Dagen remained just as faint. The energy around her was distorted and she wondered if that was what was deterring her.

A realization came to her and she asked Aergo, "That smell... that must be the source! Can you track it?"

The three combed up and down the rocky embankments on each side of the stream for any sign of Dagen but were without luck until they spotted Dagen's coat ahead of them. It lay sprawled haphazardly across a rocky slab next to the stream and appeared to be covered in a thick chalky dust.

There was no time to reach it. The sounds of distressed horses and wolves snarling in protest alerted them to the King's rapid approach. Aergo grabbed Kitaj and Rûni, hoisted them into a treetop, and silently dropped to the ground in his cat form. Rûni fought to remain silent. The sudden jolt of being tossed into the tree caused waves of pain to radiate through his arm and back. Aergo darted to safety amongst the rocks. The three sat powerless as they watched the King's guards descend upon the spot where Dagen's coat lay crumpled.

Wodan dismounted Slepsil and reached for the coat, noticing the grainy residue that clung to it along with the smeared appearance of the rock. To his surprise, the coat could not be moved. Its material was partially encased in the rock's surface. Wodan contemplated the discovery, as waves of frustration, curiosity and excitement crossed his face. He tore what he could from the rock; handed the remnants of the coat to one of his guards, who took the pieces of fabric over to the wolves to catch a scent. The guards looked at the rocks' appearance with puzzled expressions and wrinkled up their noses at the strong metallic smell. Their questioning faces reflected their thoughts; wondering as to what dark magic could have caused this scene.

"This is the place! Search the surrounding area. We are looking for a young man; a Midangardian. If you find him or anything else that appears disturbed, I want to know immediately!" demanded Wodan.

"Brother, explain. What has happened here?" whispered Wæ.

Wodan ignored the request. His interest turned to the wolves pursuing the scent.

"Your Majesty, the smear pattern continues in this direction, and there seems to be some blood," said one of the guards.

Kitaj shuttered at the news of their findings, causing the tree branches she and Rûni stood on to shake and drawing attention in their direction. Wodan turned to look but redirected his attention to the guard's findings.

"You say that with some question," said Wodan, as he followed the smeared rocks to where the guards stood.

"Yes, your Majesty. As you can see, the blood appears to have become part of the rock."

Wodan came closer to exam the surface of the stone. It appeared the blood was not merely a stain but that it had merged into the rock's outer layer.

"I have no knowledge of this magic. This is— new!" Wodan said, as a huge smile crossed over his face and he began to laugh heartily.

Wæ gave Wiljo a slight smile as Wodan came over to them. He was still laughing as he shook his brothers by their shoulders. The guardsmen remained puzzled but knew not to ask for an explanation.

As Kitaj overheard Wodan, she was panic stricken! Rûni looked to her with mounting confusion.

Kitaj whispered, "Wodan's realized Dagen's connected to his quest— the Queen's quest!" in hopes the Tjetajat were able to read Rûni through the distorted energy in the atmosphere.

"I still don't understand," whispered Rûni.

"Dagen's in more danger than you can realize, that's all you need to know," she said urgently to him.

Kitaj was powerless to help Dagen. The wolves and guards moved up the rocky slope with the King following closely. Aergo had climbed a nearby tree to get a better view of what was transpiring. As the wolves reached the top, they began to growl and dig at a large crack in the rock. Kitaj, Rûni, and Aergo watched as two of the wolves and half of the guardsmen ran the length of the rock's crest and disappeared over its edge.

Aergo tried to work his way closer to get a better view of what the wolves had found. In doing so, Aergo also disappeared from Kitaj and Rûni's view. A heightened commotion of voices and growls ensued, but went quiet as Dagen's body was carried from behind the rock toward the bank of the stream. Kitaj held her breath. She felt Rûni tense beside her. She tried to reassure him, and herself, by whispering to Rûni that Dagen was still alive— but she knew he was just barely. The wolves and the men had not harmed him, yet. Aergo's head reappeared from behind the slope as Wodan came closer to examine Dagen. Aergo felt just as powerless. As fierce as he was in goblin form, his strength and speed would not be enough to save Dagen from the force of almost forty armed men.

Wodan knelt down beside Dagen, "What's wrong with him?" he asked himself.

By hearing their brother's question, Wiljo and Wæ felt the need to reply, "We don't know."

"Once we get him back to Aesingard, we can determine the cause of his condition," added Wiljo.

"Load him. We return NOW!" commanded Wodan.

Kitaj and Rûni sat looking on helplessly as they watched Dagen being loaded into the cage wagon. When the King and his men began to pull away, Kitaj and Rûni saw Aergo silently jump onto the wagon's sideboard, slip through the cage's bars undetected, and disappear under the straw lining.

"We have to go after them— Rûni, can you climb down?" asked Kitaj.

"Yes, but I'm no good to you with these breaks," said Rûni, already trying to work his way down the tree one handed.

"I'm sorry to leave you like this, but I have to..." stated Kitaj.

"I understand. Find him," said Rûni.

"I don't know what they could read from you through the altered energy in this area. Head back toward the camp. The Council will soon know you are returning and are injured. I'm sure my mother will meet you with help shortly! To be sure the Council knows everything; tell her what you saw and that I am going to Aesingard to get Dagen," said Kitaj.

Kitaj hurried down the tree, glancing up to make sure Rûni was managing. His descent was slow and careful. He saw her concerned expression and gave her a reassuring smile and nod ahead.

"Be careful!" he said to her.

"And you!" Kitaj replied, before racing toward the Ports of Eormensyl.

Guardsmen Brieg and Rand heard the oncoming thunder of King Wodan and his hunting party as they approached from the Eormensyl's entrance in a stampeding haste to enter the Portal to Aesingard. They came into view as they came around a large sweeping bend within the port's tunnel. The look on the King's face gave Brieg reason to believe it was wise not to add any comment to their return. The cage wagon was the next to pass by. Brieg was curious to see what prized game they had caught but was stunned to find Dagen laying unconscious in the hold of the wagon. Brieg started toward the wagon but realized any rescue attempt under the current circumstances would be short-lived and of little use to his friend.

There has to be a mistake! What could the King want with Dagen? And how is Dagen still on Midangard? Brieg thought as he questioned his own eyes to what he had just witnessed. *This can't be happening!*

Brieg's thoughts swam in his head as to how he could help his friend. *What could be the reason for taking Dagen under guard?* He hid his concern and anxiety behind a cold blank face that accompanied his uniform and turned to pose questions to his superior.

"Excuse me, sir," said Brieg to Rand, "I was wondering do you have any information about the King's capture?"

"No, other than it was an unscheduled outing. Why do you ask?" said Rand.

"Just curious, sir. They were in such a hurry. It caught my attention," said Brieg, knowing revealing his connection with Dagen to Rand would be of no service in helping him.

"You would do better not to ask questions," replied Rand.

"Understood, sir," said Brieg.

Brieg searched his mind for some solution. He wondered if his father might be able to provide information, or if by bringing it to his attention would only make matters worse. Knowing his father never cared for his choice in friends, Brieg decided he would talk to his father as a last resort and see what he could discover on his own. Brieg stood biting his lip. The thought of having to wait until he was relieved from his post that night to try to help Dagen was torturing him. Brieg racked his thoughts for an excuse to enter Aesingard! He was weighing his options, when he heard the approaching click of boots on the tunnel's hard floor. The source of the sound was hidden from view by the bend in the tunnel. The clicking stopped, but was followed by a sudden clatter.

"Go see what's making that noise," said Rand.

Brieg went to investigate. He reached the bend and was out of view from Rand when he found a barefooted young woman holding one boot in her hand while reaching to pick up the other she had dropped on the floor. She looked up at Brieg with an expression of relief and recognition.

"Excuse me. What are you doing?" said Brieg.

In a whispered voice, "I'm sorry, Brieg, I didn't know at first it would be you! My mind's too distracted at the moment to see clearly. I can't tell you how relieved I am that it is you! I was trying to be quiet..." she said, holding up her boot, "honestly, I had no idea how I was going to sneak past."

Very agitated and confused, Brieg said, "Pardon me Miss, but what in the Nine Worlds are you talking about?"

"Again, sorry. We've met. You once tried to help me out of the mud. I'm here to help Dagen," Kitaj said, still whispering.

The recognition slowly came to Brieg. He saw she had Dagen's satchel and fought to contain his surprise when he realized who she was.

Brieg tried to speak quietly to her, "The Muddy Mermaid! Did I understand you to say you were here for Dagen? What happened to him? Please explain!"

"It's a long story. My name's Kitaj. The short of it is, I'm with Dagen, he's in trouble, and I have to get him away from King Wodan. Oh, and I should add the Queen would urgently want us to save him, but she is not aware of needing to help us yet."

"All of this happened since I saw him last?" Brieg said. He took a deep breath and blew it out as his mind tried to absorb the details, "All right." He paused to question, "Wait... you said you're *with* Dagen?

Kitaj nodded.

"You can't be, he's engaged," stated Brieg.

"Trust me, I am! Now, how are we going to save him?" asked Kitaj.

"Maybe you should leave that to me," said Brieg, lacking confidence in any abilities he had seen in her for a rescue attempt.

"I'm going, whether you're with me or not," Kitaj stated, determined to follow through.

"Well... for a start, put your boots on," said Brieg.

"What's your plan?" asked Kitaj.

"There's no time. Just follow my lead," said Brieg as he began pulling a long blue-green scarf out from under his armor. "Here, take this and wrap it around you. Your clothes give you away as Tjetajat."

Kitaj looked questioning at the inordinately long scarf, "Why do you have this?"

Brieg, befuddled as to why she would think to ask, replied, "Armor chafes."

Kitaj took Brieg's scarf and draped it over her head to conceal her mass of untamed hair, and tied it around her, changing the appearance of her modest linens. She completed her transformation by turning her cloak's dark lining to the outside. She tucked the scarf closely around her throat to conceal her most telling symbol of being Tjetajat— the talisman in her skin.

"Ready?" Brieg asked warily.

Kitaj nodded. She and Brieg stepped out from the concealment of the port tunnel's bend and began walking carefully toward Aesingard's portal entrance, where Rand stood with an impatient look across his face.

༶

"He's barely breathing. He won't be much good to you to interrogate in this condition," said Wiljo.

"That much is obvious, brother!" Wodan shot back, then focused his attention on his captive. "What's this powder residue around his mouth and nose?" he asked as he examined Dagen's face more closely. "Whatever it is, I imagine his lungs are full of it and that's why his breath is shallow. We have to get it out of him if we expect him to ever talk. I need both of you to help. If we use a binding force, we might just be able to push enough of these particles from him."

Aergo sat perched in the rafters above the King's chamber, questioning when he should take action. His options were to

283

attempt to extract Dagen now while the King and his brothers were alone with only two guards posted on the outer door, or chance that the number of guards would stay few and wait to see if King Wodan's treatment would help Dagen recover. Aergo listened to the soft wheezing sound of Dagen's labored and shallow breaths and decided Dagen would be in greater danger to remove him while he narrowly clung to life. Aergo could only hope he was making the right choice.

Wiljo and Wæ took their positions with the King around the stone table where Dagen lay unconscious on his back. The brothers drew from the dark magic they had used to bind the Essence. This was a more delicate transaction than they had performed before. Wiljo and Wæ looked to each other, unsure if what they were asked to do was even possible. The brothers were wary and suspicious. Wodan had withheld his reasons for obtaining this person, yet he still expected their cooperation in this matter.

"Do proceed gently! I believe this Midangardian will be very important for our future use," added Wodan. "Let us begin."

"Who is this, Ingólf?" asked Rand.

"This young woman has urgent news for the King. It concerns his prisoner," said Brieg. "She has never traveled by the Eormensyl's passage before and is afraid to approach the King alone. She has asked for me to accompany her," said Brieg.

"That's not your place; it's against protocol. One of the Aesir guards will escort her," said Rand.

Brieg felt confident he could talk his way out of the situation and tried to sway Rand.

"What sort of guard would I be if I didn't help one of the King's subjects to the best of my ability? Duty and loyalty first, Commander. And it is in the King's best interest that this woman feels at ease so she can share her information," said Brieg.

Kitaj looked back and forth from Rand to Brieg. She read Rand did not trust Brieg and he was finding Brieg's explanation questionable. She tried to project a calm exterior as she began to move slowly out of Rand's line of sight. The two guards faced each other and gave little notice of Kitaj's repositioning.

"What is this urgent news? I will pass it on to the King. It is for him to decide if this peasant gets an audience," said Rand.

Kitaj thought, *He's determined not to let us pass. We are losing precious time!* She needed a solution.

Inside her, anxiety was growing. Fear was taking over! Her head began to throb as the pressure within her skull rose! A distant rushing noise grew louder in her ears until its roar was the only sound she could hear!

In that moment, Rand shuttered. His eyes rolled up in his head as he fell forward. Brieg inadvertently broke his fall, causing both of them to topple to the ground.

෴

The brothers reluctantly obliged, and each sliced open the palms of their hands. As their blood began to flow, the three used the binding power of their shared blood to summon magic of dark deeds for the King's selfish gain. Their blood converted to a swirling red fog that surrounded the table and lifted Dagen's body. His limp form hovered above the table's surface as the red fog formed a concentrated webbing to bind him. The scarlet strands entangled around Dagen's rib cage; and on Wodan's cue, contracted, forcing air from Dagen's lungs. A puff of powdery mist escaped from his nose and mouth while Dagen remained unconscious with no sign of change.

"Again," said Wodan.

The tangled mass strangely turned from its blood red to dark as pitch and contracted again. Dagen began to cough up large amounts of residue. The pain from constricting his chest caused Dagen to respond by flinching, but his eyes remained closed.

Wodan became impatient with their results and cast aside any conscious concerns for his captive's well being.

"Again!" demanded Wodan.

Wiljo and Wæ exchanged expressions of doubt, fear and confusion in regards to their brother's order and the odd distortions occurring in their binding web.

Wiljo expressed his and Wæ's thoughts, "Another attempt might crush him and we know that's not the end result you were wanting, and look how the binding is changing! Something is wrong!"

"YOU DARE TO QUESTION ME? I SAID AGAIN!" roared Wodan.

Wiljo and Wæ withdrew slightly to lessen the intensity of the compression as the tangles spasmed once more around Dagen's chest. Sharp pains jolted him into consciousness and intensified with each cough. A flash of light pulsed from Dagen so swiftly it was barely visible, but it was enough to caused the dark webbing that bound him to retreat into the room's shadows. Dagen fell hard onto to the table's surface and let out a yell with his impact.

"What did you do!" exclaimed Brieg as he pushed the unconscious Rand off of him.

"Your way wasn't working. Something had to be done!" Kitaj shouted over the loud ringing in her ears, "He needed to be subdued, and... I... I don't know, but somehow... the solution came through me— for lack of better words," she said as she rubbed her irritated eyes and throbbing temples.

"WHAT?" exclaimed Brieg in confusion, "You should have given me a chance! I was winning him over!" retorted Brieg.

"Trust me, you weren't!" returned Kitaj, blinking rapidly as she tried to regain clear vision in her stinging eyes, "And by the way, why is he so upset with you about his wife? I could only read part of it, but he clearly doesn't trust you."

"None of your concern!" said Brieg, as he checked Rand's breathing. "He will recover, right?" he asked.

"I believe so, I've never done anything like this before... I only wanted him out of our way. I can't say how long he'll be unconscious," stated Kitaj.

"We'll need to hide him! It will be strange enough that the portal is left unguarded, but all alarms will sound if Rand is found."

Brieg bound Rand's hands and feet with the shackles both he and his commander carried with their uniforms. He grabbed the unconscious Rand under the arms and began to drag him from the portal. Kitaj grabbed Rand's legs to try to help Brieg deposit him in a secluded pocket of the tunnel away from their post. With Rand secured, Brieg hastily ushered Kitaj through the portal to Aesingard.

≈Ɔ≈

"What just happened?" Wæ asked his brothers.

Wiljo shook his head to indicate he had no explanation, while Wodan ignored his brother's question and focused on his newly woken prey.

"Oh good, he's awake," said Wodan, with a saccharine edge to his voice. "Sit him up," he barked to Wiljo and Wæ.

The two brothers took Dagen from the table and propped him up in a chair. Dagen was too weak to resist or aid himself. He continued to cough up clumps of powder and gasp for air. Each painful breath caused him to double over in his chair.

"Hold him upright," Wodan directed to his brothers.

Wiljo and Wæ steadied Dagen as Wodan circled them, contemplating his approach.

Dagen fought to make sense of his surroundings. He tried to speak but found his throat and lungs burned with his attempt and his voice was grave and hardly audible.

"Where am I?" asked Dagen.

"You are in my care on Aesingard. I don't believe we've had the pleasure of meeting before now," the words slithered from Wodan's tongue, "It is your good fortune, we found you when we did. Otherwise, you'd probably be dead. We just saved your life."

"My life? Aesingard?" said Dagen, still confused. "I don't understand."

"You will," Wodan said flatly.

While Brieg and Kitaj moved as swiftly as they could through the portal's slumbering branch, Brieg tried to regain some semblance of structure to what he and Kitaj were undertaking. In his opinion, Kitaj was unpredictable and erratic, and could very easily endanger their attempt to save Dagen.

Brieg interjected, "No more surprises from you. We can't afford to draw attention to ourselves."

Kitaj had been assessing their situation as well and found Brieg to be overconfident, stubborn, and impulsive. She knew they needed to overcome their differences and find a way to work together for Dagen's sake.

"Why don't you say I have a message for her Highness and that you have been ordered by the Queen to accompany me?" offered Kitaj.

"That sounds plausible. Audiences with the Queen are much less regimented," Brieg concluded.

Though their passage to Aesingard gave them time to align their tactics, it was not long enough for Kitaj to prepare herself to face Wodan's guardsmen when they reached the port opening. The guardsmen were in the process of locking down the portal's gate for the Aesir night. Brieg and Kitaj managed to squeeze through before it was shut.

"State your purpose!" said one guardsman.

A second guard joined his side. Before Brieg could begin to explain their need to see the Queen, Kitaj knew she and Brieg would not be permitted beyond the gate. Her new found knowledge for rendering her opposition unconscious once again came to their aid. Brieg jumped as he saw two small crackling sparks launch from Kitaj's eyes and reach their targeted destinations—the guardsmen's foreheads. The rapid transaction gave the seasoned guards no time for defensive measures and they crumpled to the floor where they stood. Kitaj winced and covered her eyes in an attempt to soothe them.

"Thanks for the warning!" commented Brieg.

"They were ordered to let no one pass!" Kitaj replied.

"You didn't give me a chance!" retorted Brieg.

"I thought it best to act before they could remember your features. They aren't familiar with the newest recruits in the Midangard patrol yet. If we can avoid your implication in Dagen's escape, wouldn't that be to your advantage?" added Kitaj over the loud pounding in her head, while she wiped away a few tears that had inadvertently escaped her.

"I guess a thanks is in order," said Brieg, still irritated, but paused to notice how bloodshot Kitaj's eyes had become, "It hurts, doesn't it?"

Kitaj nodded to confirm as she struggled to hear Brieg over the throbbing, gushing sounds ripping through her ears. She tried her best to keep Brieg unaware of the added pain behind her noticeably inflamed eyes.

"Try not to rub; you'll only make them worse," Brieg said to offer some comfort.

Brieg looked around and found a small room next to the gate, where he and Kitaj could hide the guards' bodies.

"I have to say, your skills are *handy*. But next time, could you tap my arm or something to warn me?" asked Brieg, as they drug one of the guards into the room.

"I'll try. Maybe it's best to expect the unexpected from me," added Kitaj.

"You have that in common with our King," Brieg stated.

Kitaj shot Brieg a displeased look in return. She did not appreciate Brieg's comparison of her to the King, especially considering Dagen's current circumstances.

"I am beginning to think Rûni was right. He thought you'd bring Dagen nothing but trouble," said Brieg sharply, revealing his frustration and worry.

"You don't know half of what Rûni thinks of me," Kitaj lashed back at Brieg.

She felt she had disclosed too much. Kitaj knew that no good could come from them turning on each other in their shared anguish.

She diverted the conversation as they began working together to move the second guard, "Never mind that. You should know Rûni assisted in finding Dagen. He sustained some injuries, but should be back with the Tjetajat now and mended soon."

Brieg momentarily stopped Kitaj and asked, "Were they serious?" with genuine concern.

"Not too, an arm and shoulder blade. He managed well through it, you would've been proud of him. He was determined and brave. Rûni wanted to continue but knew his condition would slow our efforts and risk Dagen's return."

Brieg and Kitaj hurried to bind the limp guardsmen together with their own shackles. Their rushed efforts became less cumbersome as they began anticipating each other's work to secure the guards and could stay out of each other's way.

Brieg added, "It sounds like you've gotten to know both of my friends very well."

"Yes, I believe I have," Kitaj said, with a small smile.

Wodan did not want to appear unmoved by Dagen's condition and had Wiljo help Dagen drink from a cup of glow wine. The warm liquid poured down his rough and swollen throat with soothing comfort. The memory of what had happened in the forest was slowly returning to Dagen and the recognition that he had been seized by the King and his brothers had taken hold. Dagen became very aware of his present danger.

"Now that you're feeling better, can you tell us what led to your ill state? Our concern is not just for you, but for everyone. If this is an illness or a foe, we need to address it immediately," said the King.

Dagen spoke respectfully, "I wish I understood it myself, Your Majesty, but thank you for your care and kyndness in restoring me."

Wodan's patience was wearing thin again, as it was made evident in the manic edge that crept back into his voice, "Not at all, not at all. I am not sure if you are aware but my prized ravens happened to be witness to... shall we say, part of your misfortune."

Wodan's inaudible signal escaped Dagen, and Myne's cued appearance startled him when he landed on Wodan's shoulder. Myne continually squawked and appeared very agitated in Dagen's presence.

"You would usually see them as a pair, but one was slightly injured in the same incident that afflicted you. Is there anything at all you can remember that might help us?" asked Wodan, with his false veil of concern for Dagen fading.

"I honestly can't tell you, my King. I sincerely hope your raven will recover quickly and mend unscarred," said Dagen.

Dagen feared it was only a matter of moments before any information he might have would be extracted by the prompting methods of torture. Wodan turned away from Dagen and stretched out his arms and hands. Dagen braced himself for what might come and anticipated metal bands to spring from the arms, legs, and back of his chair to secure him completely. Wodan seemed poised to unleash his wrath. Aergo's anxiety grew as he watched the scene from above and prepared to intervene. Instead, Myne flew away from Wodan as he turned back to greet Dagen with a calm expression. Dagen found this new calm of Wodan's to be even more disturbing. He looked to the faces of the King's brothers for any clue as to what might happen next and saw them to be just as puzzled as he was.

Dagen concluded, *The rumors of King Wodan are true; he's a madman!*

The Aesir sky was darkening as Brieg and Kitaj followed the wooded path into Wodan's sanctum, Wealdriht. Torchlights along the pathway accentuated the intricacies of the elaborate canopy composed from Wealdriht's ancient trees. Only glimpses of the red and violet veined sky could be seen through the blanket of its intertwining branches.

As Brieg and Kitaj entered Wealdriht, they encountered more guards. Both Brieg and Kitaj stayed to their plan and used Kitaj's explanation as their purpose. The Head Guard accepted Brieg's statement without question and they were permitted to pass and headed toward the Queen's wing. The wing's location was the opposite direction of the holding rooms where Brieg suspected Dagen to be contained. Brieg and Kitaj doubled back through a connecting hallway once they were out of the Head Guard's sight.

Brieg noticed Kitaj's expression was faltering and whispered to her, "Look as if you know where you're going. Confidence is key," then saw the small dark trail of blood coming from her ear that had soaked through his scarf.

They passed the guarded corridors, without incident or question, as they traveled down the long hallway to the King's wing. Kitaj kept a vigilant eye for any sign of Dagen or Aergo.

৯৫

"What is your name?" asked King Wodan, in an unsettlingly kynd manner.

Dagen stammered. He knew if he told the King, it could endanger anyone associated with him.

"I don't remember, Your Majesty," said Dagen.

"You don't remember! My, this is a problem. And I imagine, you don't remember where you are from or anyone you know either," said King Wodan, ending with an odd smile.

"Yes, Your Majesty," said Dagen.

"Someone is bound to inquire after you. It's only a matter of time. Until then, you will be our most welcomed guest. Wiljo, Wæ! Escort our new friend to our most comfortable... room," added Wodan.

Aergo knew if he were going to help Dagen this would be his best opportunity. To Wodan and his brothers surprise, Aergo's massive dark form appeared, as if out of nowhere, between them and Dagen.

৯৫

Brieg whispered, "We're here," as they walked down the long corridor leading to Wodan's private chambers while peering in at the numerous rooms lining either side. "Wodan likes to keep his enemies close. Can't you use your special senses to narrow down which one of these he might be in?" asked Brieg under his breath.

"It doesn't work in that manner for me, unfortunately," said Kitaj quietly to Brieg while acknowledging a passing guardsman.

They walked down the long hall in silence until they heard muffled yells and crashes coming from a room near the end. Brieg and Kitaj could see the door was shut but rattling from impact.

"But— we do have help! This is it, trust me!" she said, knowing the commotion could only be Aergo.

Brieg and Kitaj started to run toward the noise and turned their heads back to see four other guards running down the hallway towards them. A few more had made it to the chamber door before she and Brieg could reach it.

Kitaj reached out to touch Brieg's arm to warn him of what she was about to do. He gave her a quick nod. She turned and tried to aim the stunning force rushing through her head while she ran, but she missed her marks in all directions. Kitaj cried out from the intense burning pain behind her eyes! She blindly grabbed for Brieg's arm and forced her eyes open to focus on her targets. The striking charges spanned the distance between her and the guards, causing them to topple and rendering them all unconscious. Kitaj threw her arm over her face, as she clenched her teeth to stifle another cry of pain. Unfortunately for Brieg, Kitaj's other hand had remained holding onto his arm. A small dose of the immobilizing power had transferred to him as well, and left Brieg rigid and quivering on the floor. Kitaj pushed aside her discomfort at the sight of Brieg.

"Oh, no, Brieg! I'm so sorry! That's not what I intended at all!" she exclaimed, as she rolled Brieg's stiffened body off of her feet.

The doors to the King's chamber tore open, as Aergo came flying through, and crashed on the floor in front of Kitaj and Brieg. The stone floor cracked loudly and gave way; leaving a deep indention where the enormous goblin had landed. Aergo sprang up and shook off dark red tangles of smoke surrounding him.

Aergo caught sight of Kitaj; he lowered his head and growled, "Stay back!" as he ran back into the King's chamber.

Kitaj could not see the turmoil within the room, but heard men yelling and more thuds and crashes. Brieg was just as stunned by Aergo's appearance, as he was Kitaj's jolt. Still unable to talk, he shot her a quick questioning look.

"That's Aergo," she said, reassuring Brieg with a nervous smile before she slid him across the polished floor and propped him against the nearest hall corner.

Kitaj had no time to explain further; her attention was diverted to the set of single hurried footsteps approaching from a connecting hallway between them and the chamber door. Kitaj sensed it was Queen Frija approaching, and stepped into view to draw her attention.

"Your Majesty!" Kitaj whispered loudly.

The Queen stopped abruptly and looked closely at her. It took Frija a moment to recognize that it was Kitaj. Her appearance had caught the Queen off guard, but Kitaj's arrival was not completely unexpected. Kitaj was able to read that the Queen had received word from the Tjetajat of Dagen's capture and of his suggested importance to her quest. Kitaj was relieved to know Rûni had been able to reach the Tjetajat and relay her information. A strange mixture of emotions flooded from the Queen that Kitaj found hard to comprehend, but clearly through them all was a sense of urgency.

"Dear girl, what is happening here?" the Queen whispered as she looked at the guards' bodies scattered about her.

Kitaj was about to try and give the Queen a brief account of their current circumstances when two more guards appeared from a corridor on the far side from the King's chamber.

As the mighty goblin crashed through the chamber doorway with Dagen's weak body draped over his shoulder, Aergo turned to face Kitaj and was unaware of the two guardsmen at his back. Arrows flew from behind them, narrowly missing Dagen; but one arrow found its way to plant deeply into Aergo's shoulder. He laid Dagen on the ground and turned to face the two guards. Kitaj spied the arrow protruding from her friend's shoulder. She did not hesitate. Kitaj launched herself forward as she cast two stunning jolts around Aergo; taking down the two guardsmen. Aergo looked at Kitaj in surprise for her new found ability and flashed her an approving devilish smile. Gritting her teeth, she forced a smile in return.

A battered Wodan appeared inside the large crumbling opening of the unhinged and splintered chamber doors. His rage engulfed him as he caught sight of his Queen. Wodan called for Myne. He spoke inaudibly to his prized raven and sent it flying high to escape from the fury that was to follow. Kitaj instinctively threw herself over Dagen's crumpled form to shield him from Wodan's certain wrath, as Aergo hovered protectively over both of them.

Dagen reached out for Kitaj and grabbed her hand. In the instant of their grasp, a sudden powerful blast burst from the two, repelling Dagen and Kitaj farther from Wodan's reach, and sending Aergo airborne! Wodan and his brothers were thrown back to the far wall of the chamber. A blinding light emanated from the pair and extended to encase the gaping hole of the demolished doorway. The boom from the surge echoed down the corridors and caused the walls to tremble and crack.

While the piercing light emanated from them, the notions that had appeared during their focusing practice returned in their minds. Unlike before, where the details had eluded them, the two images appeared in Kitaj's thoughts with pristine clarity, as simultaneously, one word rang out as a chiming affirmation over the loud low hum within Dagen's mind. From their hands entwined, the powerful surge linked them in thought to the first clues in their quest to restore the lost future of knowledge!

The surging light moved away from Kitaj and Dagen, to concentrate completely on the chamber's archway and formed a barrier. The barrier of their combined power was unlike Dagen's solo attempt in the forest. Their's was visible and stood suspended, pulsing and crackling with lethal charge. The surge had provided Dagen with renewed strength, and he was able to stand independently but remained holding tight to Kitaj's hand. The energy they had created soothed Kitaj's aching head, calmed the roaring in her ears, and her eyes no longer felt like open wounds. Queen Frija stood near the archway, untouched by its force, but was shocked and amazed by the scene before her. She looked from the doorway, to Aergo, and back to Kitaj and Dagen in complete awe. Dagen and Kitaj were equally dumbfounded by what they had created.

"How did we..?" asked Dagen.

"...I have no idea," Kitaj answered numbly.

Wodan and his brothers rushed forward. Wodan signaled his brothers to conjure their dark forces with him. Each dug into their freshly cut palms, releasing swirls of red smoke webbing. The heinously, twisted mass sped toward the archway and slammed into the resonating barrier; only to shrivel on contact and fall to the floor as embers and ash. Neither their combined dark magic nor Wodan's rage could break the electrified encasement holding them within Wodan's chamber.

More guards arrived from every hall to investigate the source of the explosion. Aergo readied himself for the King's newly arrived reinforcements. His imposing massive form caused the new guards to take an initial step back. He stood towering over all surrounding him. Aergo let out a roar that shook the hall, almost as intensely as Dagen and Kitaj's surge, and threw out his two great arms in a sweeping motion that sent the guards on either side of him bouncing off the corridor walls. Aergo started forward to eliminate the remaining opposition. With Kitaj still holding tight to Dagen's hand, she sent out a wave of stunning bursts before Aergo could reach them. The jolts rippled through the guards, causing half to fall to the ground. Aergo jumped. He let out a small yelp followed by a long growl, for Kitaj had accidentally stunned his hind quarters. She cringed at the realization of hurting her friend. The remaining guards were able to draw their bows and advance. Kitaj projected another stunning wave, taking down the last of the opposing force. Aergo yelped again, louder and snarled. He looked over his shoulder to Kitaj with a heavily furrowed brow. With her second wave, she had struck his arm.

Kitaj yelled out to Aergo, "Sorry!" before her free hand flew up to her mouth.

Aergo shook his stunned arm and opened and closed his hand while curling in his long sharp claws. He turned back to Kitaj and Dagen and used his good arm to pluck five arrows out of his chest as if they were small splinters and reached back to dislodge the one from his shoulder.

Kitaj looked to Dagen to make sure she had not caused him harm as well. Though holding her hand, he remained unaffected, other than being taken aback by Kitaj's new skill. Queen Frija remained close to the wall, not wanting to make any movement that might provoke the imposing goblin. Aergo caught sight of the Queen. Frija's expression was one he had seen many times before, and it always disturbed him to see fear in the face of someone that he did not mean to intimidate. Aergo shifted back to his cat form and darted away from her.

Wodan and his brothers stood seething and trapped behind the barrier, and could only watch as Dagen and Kitaj disappeared from view of the chamber's archway. Wodan's anger raged, as he shredded the remaining contents of the room.

As Kitaj and Dagen reached the corner, they found Aergo waiting next to Brieg's shaken form. Kitaj swept up Aergo with her free arm and held him close.

"Thank you, Aergo!" she said as she nuzzled him close.

Her attention went back to Brieg as he said, "That wasn't very nice, you're a menace!" with his jittery voice, still affected by Kitaj's stun.

"Again, sorry," said Kitaj, "Can you stand?" she added as she released Aergo to aid Dagen in helping Brieg up.

"Dagen, so glad you could join our little party," Brieg said, smiling and wincing.

Dagen started to speak, but Brieg interrupted, "Thank me when we get out of this."

Kitaj looked down at her and Dagen's clasped hands to say, "We have some time before the barrier fails, but I couldn't begin to guess how long."

Dagen assumed the same as Kitaj. Their bond was keeping the barrier intact.

Frija stood gazing at Wodan with pity and heartbreak. She gave Wodan one last look, and went in pursuit of the fleeing couple. She turned the corner and caught sight of Kitaj, Dagen, an unsteady guardsman, and the black cat trying to move stealthily down the corridor to the side hall.

"Wait! This way! " Frija called after them.

The Queen scanned the carvings on the wall of the hallway and felt along its grooves for a specific notch. Queen Frija turned her ring, baring the symbol of Aesingard, to the palm of her hand and placed it in a notch of the ornamental facade on the corridor's wall. The ring worked as a key, and as she twisted her hand, it unlocked the passage behind the wall. Kitaj and the others reached Frija as the wall slid away to reveal a dark descending tunnel.

"Follow this passage, it will take you outside the gates. No one will see you. From there you can follow the tree line straight to the Eormensyl. Once you get there, go to the outer wall of the far side of the portal. There you will see the symbols of the Nine Worlds. Kitaj, place this ring in the notch for Midangard and it will expose a separate port to get you back to Lerakrey," said the Queen as she handed Kitaj her ring.

Kitaj and Dagen made sure not to let go of their grasp, as Dagen took the ring from Kitaj and placed it on the third finger of her free hand. He turned the Aesingard symbol to face her palm, just as the Queen had done to open the secret passage.

"Thank you, your Majesty, but what about you? Aren't you coming with us?" asked Dagen.

"It's not safe for you here, my Queen," said Kitaj, as she took in the thoughts of Wodan and his brothers.

"Don't concern yourselves with me. I will follow shortly and find you secure within the Tjetajat," said Queen Frija.

Brieg was about to grab one of the lit torches from the hall when Kitaj waved him off.

"They'll notice it's gone and know which passage we've taken," Kitaj whispered.

She pressed her intertwined fingers in Dagen's hand more deeply, allowing her to produce a ball of light in the palm of her other, and setting the Queen's ring aglow on her finger.

"Thank you again, your Majesty, for helping us!" added Kitaj.

Queen Frija nodded and urged them, "Please, go now!" as Wodan's heightened roars of frustration echoed through the rafters.

Frija gave them a reassuring look, but her expression and emotions held more than Kitaj could gather. They left Kitaj with what she could only interpret as hope. The passage door slid shut behind them and they could no longer hear any noise from the other side.

"Do you think she'll be all right?" asked Dagen.

"She has lived as Queen for a long time, she knows Wodan well. I hope she's right," stated Kitaj.

"That's a helpful trick you have there," said Brieg to Kitaj. referring to the ball of light suspended in her hand.

"She's not the only one," said Dagen, as he turned to smile at Brieg and produced a second light in his own free hand.

Aergo, who was leading through the passage, turned back, flattened his ears and thought, *Now is not the time to be showing off.*

"So, I was right, much has changed since I saw you last!" concluded Brieg.

Dagen briefed Kitaj and Brieg on his experience in the forest that had lead to his arrest by King Wodan. All agreed they had never heard of anything comparable to what Dagen had created. Kitaj informed Dagen of Rûni's help and injuries. She assured both he and Brieg that Tjetajat medicine was swift and he should heal very soon. The passage was short and though there was more to tell, it would have to wait for a calmer time. They reached the end of the passage and easily opened the door concealing its secret entry. Night was starting to fall on Aesingard. Kitaj and Dagen extinguished their lights so not to draw attention to themselves and followed the tree line as the Queen had instructed. They reached the Eormensyl when the last streaks of a dying sunset faded from the sky and made their way to its back wall. Kitaj and Dagen had not let go of each other's hand. Both of their hands were throbbing and shook from the tight grip that bonded them, and they wondered when it would be safe to release their hold. Creating a dim light in her open palm, Kitaj ran her hand slightly above the line of symbols and found the notch for Midangard that Frija had described. She placed the ring in the notch and found no turn was required. Immediately, a small breach formed around the notch and began to grow. Kitaj swept up Aergo and held him tight as they all stepped through. The private royal passage accessed a different branch of the sleeping Eormensyl and they soon arrived outside, near Brieg's post at Lerakrey.

It was late afternoon on Midangard. It's longer day gave the illusion that little time had passed since Dagen's capture. Whether measured by Aesir or Midangardian time, they had lived through a day of mayhem and each knew their situation was far from over. Kitaj released Aergo from her tight hold. Her other hand continued to ache desperately from gripping to Dagen.

Brieg looked to Dagen and said, "This is where I leave you. I'm not sure what's to come, but I need to be here. I can help you more from this side."

"I know what this will mean for you, and the danger you're in because of us. I am so sorry to have put you in this position!" said Dagen.

"What position? You would have done the same for me," added Brieg.

Kitaj stated, "Your commander is not yet lucid. You could appear to have been incapacitated as well, which in fact you were. You would not be lying, and for any interrogation, that would hold true. You carry physical proof to back your story. Give us your armor, we need to make it appear that my accomplice dressed as a guard. It's your best choice to erase doubt of your involvement. If we hurry, you can stage your alibi before anyone else arrives!"

"I like the way she thinks. If there's one thing I'm good at, it's making partial stories believable," Brieg said to Dagen while flashing one of his iconic smiles at Kitaj.

Brieg rushed to remove his uniform and placed the pieces of it on Kitaj and Dagen. They situated the pieces as best they could while still maintaining the hold of each other's hand.

Kitaj stepped toward Brieg, kissed him on the cheek and whispered, "Thank you!" into his ear, causing a first for Dagen to witness; seeing Brieg blush.

"I'll find you as soon as I can. Stay safe," said Brieg.

"You as well," said Dagen.

Kitaj, Dagen, and Aergo silently worked their way along the cover of the outer wall of the Eormensyl. Dagen and Kitaj held to their grip, knowing relinquishing their hold would most certainly release Wodan from his chamber. They both look down at their clasped hands and knew they could not hold on for much longer, but they tried to give Brieg more time to appear part of his alibi.

Brieg returned to his post to find Rand as Kitaj had described. No one was in sight. The unmanned portal had gone unnoticed, much to all their good fortunes. He removed one set of shackles from Rand to secure his own wrists and sprawled out on the ground next to his commander in the passageway's secluded niche.

"Brieg is settled," Kitaj reassured Dagen.

Letting go of each other left their hands feeling weighted and phantomed. The energy created by their bond disappeared like a wisp of smoke, leaving Kitaj and Dagen drained.

Aergo shifted into his horse form to carry them. Kitaj tried to climb onto Aergo's back but found every muscle in her body was shaking from exhaustion. Dagen attempted to help lift her, but he was hampered by his extreme fatigue, bruised lungs, and ribs. Aergo lowered himself to aid both tired souls onto his back, and with his greatest speed, he ran toward the safety of the Tjetajat camp. Kitaj's tired mind kept searching behind them for any sign of Wodan, while Aergo raced in and out of the trees. She did not trust what her weary mind's sight was perceiving, for Kitaj could detect no one following.

At the moment Dagen and Kitaj released each other's hands, the chamber barrier dissolved. Wodan's excessive pacing promptly ceased, while Wiljo and Wæ ran through the doorway to assemble more guards for pursuit.

"No!" yelled Wodan to his brothers. "Let them go!"

Wiljo and Wæ turned back toward the King. His command made no sense, and each was alarmed by his reaction.

"You *want* them to escape?" asked Wæ, puzzled.

"For now. Frija recognized the Midangardian woman. Myne has been sent to follow the Queen. I believe Frija will lead us to the pair— and the truth," said Wodan.

"But if we were to detain the Queen, you could... encourage her... to give up her secrets," suggested Wæ.

"Extracting information is tenuous at best. Information can be unreliable under persuasion unless you know the right questions to ask— and have the right leverage. Frija does know more, but she was just as shocked by their combined power as we were. No, let's see where this leads us. I believe this is the link we've been waiting to discover."

"You're missing your opportunity to get to the truth by letting them go!" stated Wæ.

"You disagree— you overstep and take liberties because of your blood. Must I point out to you, not only am I your King, but YOU DARE SUGGEST HARMING MY WIFE?" Wodan roared.

Wiljo and Wæ stepped back from Wodan and lowered their eyes.

"We meant no disrespect," said Wiljo.

"We were merely providing our council," said Wæ.

"Don't think that I'm not onto the two of you and your aspirations!" said Wodan, glaring at his brothers.

"We humbly apologize to you, our beloved brother, our King. Let us assure you; we have no other cause than to serve you and the realm to the best of our abilities," said Wæ, on behalf of Wiljo and himself.

Wodan huffed and walked away from them muttering, "Vultures!" under his breath as he exited the chamber.

≈℧≈

Darkness fell earlier within the forest's winter evening. As Aergo neared the Tjetajat camp, he slowed his gait. A line of burning torches lie ahead, and he had an uneasy feeling about their welcoming party. Kitaj sensed the unrest and tension more clearly, and Dagen could tell Aergo and Kitaj were both on edge.

"Something has happened. There's been a shift. Their fear has grown, and not just of Wodan. It's not everyone, but many within the Council are afraid of us." said Kitaj. "This isn't good."

Aergo stopped in front of what appeared to be a barricade of Council members. Rûni and Corynth stood in front of them. They were pleased to see their loved ones returned, but even they appeared uneasy. Rûni so badly wanted to break protocol and go to his friends but refrained by staying his place just as the Order required of him.

Kitaj was spent and her patience was thin on ceremony. She remembered her treatment by the Council, when she first learned of her importance in the Queen's quest and vowed she would never allow anyone to treat her in that manner again. Kitaj was not sure where the words came from that were emerging inside her but she did not question it. She was grateful to have them, just as she needed them, and addressed her intentions directly to Head Council Adrex Sorrel.

"As you are now aware, there are two of us who are crucial to the Queen's quest. It is a collective misfortune that you cannot read either of us," Kitaj said knowing her words were making them anxious, and paused before continuing with added conviction, "But, I can read you. You have received no sight from the Queen since last notifying her. You have no reference that Queen Frija assisted us in escaping from King Wodan. If it had not been for her help, we would not be here," Kitaj said, holding up her hand, to show them the Queen's ring. "Her trust is in us, as ours is in her. We followed her orders to return to you, where she assured us we would be safe. She will be following soon, and I believe she expects to find us in good standing when she arrives."

"We need you to come with us," replied Head Council Adrex.

No other statement was made. The Tjetajat broke into two groups with Corynth and Head Council Adrex leading the other Central Council members, while Rûni and the remaining members followed behind Aergo, with Dagen and Kitaj still riding on his back.

Dagen found the whole scene surreal. No one spoke as they made their way through the forest. He whispered to Kitaj to ask if she too found this all strange. She nodded to indicate yes. Dagen also asked if Kitaj had sensed any sign of Wodan; to which she shook her head no.

"What are they going to do with us?" asked Dagen.

"From what I am able to tell, I believe they are going to hold a tribunal," said Kitaj warily.

Kitaj and Dagen were taken back to the location of the hidden hut where Kitaj had first met the Queen. The Tjetajat had extended the protective circle and it now encompassed several tents surrounding the large domed structure. Kitaj knew the Tjetajat had prepared to stay hidden for an extended time if necessary. Dagen and Kitaj were ushered to one of the outer lying tents, where they were to remain until they were called before the Central Council. Aergo followed, resorting to his goblin form because of the heightened tension. He remained outside the tent to intimidate anyone who might come near.

ﻉ

Dagen held back the opening for Kitaj to enter the holding tent to find Tanadra standing across the makeshift room to greet them. She was a much-welcomed face and Kitaj ran to her.

"Tanadra, I am so glad to see you!" Kitaj said as she hugged her.

Tanadra's eyes were on Dagen. She had fixated on him as he walked into the tent.

"'I'm sorry, but I don't think we can wait for whatever it is the Council has in store. Don't they understand? The King will be looking for us!" said Dagen urgently.

Tanadra stated, "Wodan is waiting on his search for you. You are safe here."

Dagen directed his question to Kitaj, "He's waiting?"

"Yes, I've received news from a source near to the King," said Tanadra. "There is much to tell you. Please forgive me, but it will need to wait."

Tanadra's words left Kitaj wondering but she had every confidence in her. She needed Dagen to feel the same.

"You can trust her," said Kitaj.

Tanadra continued to stare at Dagen. Her incessant gaze jarred something in his memory.

"Pardon me, but have we met before?" Dagen said to her, with his voice wavering and ill at ease; he had not yet recovered himself.

"You have been traveling," Tanadra said understandingly.

"Yes, I have..." Dagen said and paused as he realized Tanadra was not referring to his journey from Carcadoc.

"I saw you," Tanadra added with a small smile.

He stared, puzzled; the realization of where he had met Tanadra came to Dagen, and with much surprise.

"You were the hawk!" he said excitedly, "You flew with me! But how did you recognize me?"

Tanadra's smile grew, "I sensed you. It is the same with your recognition of meeting me before today. You are one of us."

"I don't know about that," said a very self-conscious Dagen, as an uncontrollable blush made his ears turn bright red.

"It is true, you are, and I can tell you are much like Kitaj... yet different. Though you are not readable, you do not carry the void with you as she does," she said, and stood back to look at Kitaj and Dagen standing next to each other, contemplating them. "You two... whatever brought you together, I am glad you found each other," Tanadra added.

She approached Dagen and touched his arm. Immediately his pulse slowed and he felt relaxed in her presence. Kitaj was pleased that Dagen had found Tanadra to be his flight mate and thought this revelation could only work in their favor with the Council. With Tanadra's acceptance of Dagen, Kitaj hoped the other members' opinions would soon follow, including her mother's.

Kitaj took Dagen's hand, and a small glow formed around them, outlining the pair. In that moment, the power emanating from Kitaj intensified and came beaming through the void, striking Tanadra! She was overcome as incomprehensible images flooded through her, with one exception of knowing that came through unmistakably clear.

Kitaj let go of Dagen's hand and rushed to her. Dagen joined her and helped Tanadra to sit. As the visions concluded, Tanadra caught her breath and looked back and forth from Kitaj to Dagen in a state of awe.

"Tanadra?" Kitaj asked with concern.

"Yes dear, I'm fine," said Tanadra as she looked at Kitaj and Dagen with stunned amazement, "I was able to read you, you and Dagen!" she added as she clasped their hands with her trembling fingers, "You two are of the rarest!"

"What do you mean?" Kitaj said, knowing Dagen was as confused as she.

"Dear child, it is no accident you two have found each other! Some people go through their lives with the notion of trying to find another person's soul to complement theirs; to be the mate to their own. Some even follow the misguided illusion that another soul could be responsible for completing their own; I say this to clarify. The two of you stand before me, not as soul mates but something else, something more and completely new to everything I have known! My dear ones, all I can do is tell you what I know to be true."

Kitaj and Dagen look to Tanadra with trepidation. The truth they had sought was unfolding.

"Something *new*?... This must be related to whatever this energy is you are detecting inside me... that's affecting us..." Kitaj's voice faded off as her mind struggled to connect the pieces.

Tanadra continued, "There was a soul that became too much, and somehow, it became two— twin souls. I have seen this within you. Your souls are of gelic kynd! You are of the same! You've been drawn to each other in this life and have chosen to be together."

Kitaj and Dagen's first reactions were of surprise. They looked to one another as a deeper understanding settled within both of them.

"I can see you recognize my words to be true. Though you were of the same soul, the two of you stand before me as two complete and separate souls unto yourselves." she concluded.

Kitaj turned to Dagen, "It does explain how we are. Considering everything— our meeting; our initial core recognitions, our connection that we couldn't explain until now! It does fit the abiding perception between us, acknowledging the distinction of our separate selves— this strange yet familiar wholeness within each of us as we stand together as *two*."

"You're right. It does explain us!" Dagen said in return to Kitaj.

Aergo had overheard what was transpiring. He was worried for Kitaj and Dagen and wondered what this might mean for them. He listened intently to try and understand, but in that moment— even in his imposing goblin form, he felt utterly helpless.

Dagen asked, "How did this happen to us, and why?"

Tanadra reassured them, "How remains unseen, but you already know the reason why."

Dagen replied, in a numbed, but matter of fact voice, "We *are* somehow to serve a part in this restoration of knowledge. I hadn't completely believed it all until now— that's our purpose."

"I fear you are right," Tanadra added, "I have no idea what this will mean for the two of you in the future but know this; no matter what may come, you will always have my support," said Tanadra.

"Thank you," Kitaj and Dagen said at the same time.

"There are external forces at work here, the Council has to be made to understand. I will stand for you at the tribunal."

"We appreciate all that you are doing for us," said Kitaj.

As Tanadra was departing, she took Dagen aside to tell him, "Beyond what you and Kitaj are to each other, you and I both know— Dagen, you are of our nature."

Tanadra unbuckled the clasp of her cloak, removed the heavy garment from her shoulders and placed it around Dagen's. Its weight and warmth surrounded him and provided an extra sense of her reassurance for what he and Kitaj were about to face. Dagen was visibly moved by Tanadra's kynd gesture.

"Thank you— but I truly can't see myself becoming a member of the Tjetajat Order," Dagen answered humbly and honestly.

Tanadra smiled with her conclusion, "Whether you accept it or not does not change the fact. You are one of us."

ذ‍

The two took the moment to try and regain some strength before having to face the Central Council. Each stood silently, contemplating the revelation of Tanadra's reading. Though they accepted her vision as their truth, it's full meaning was still lost to them and only brought forth more questions.

The gravity of their situation, accompanied by his physical exhaustion, caused Dagen's composure to finally break. Kitaj had little warning as a sudden burst of energy flared from him, shooting around them and causing the air to sizzle!

He erupted, not at Kitaj, but to rage at their fates, "Because we met, I THOUGHT WE HAD A CHANCE! For a moment, I thought we could choose the paths of our futures! Instead, we are just PREDESTINED PAWNS— A MEANS TO AN END! WHAT ABOUT US? We know we can't walk away from this! "

"You could still walk away," stated Kitaj solemnly.

"No— I couldn't! Not from you— or knowing what would be destroyed if I didn't follow through! You must understand— THERE'S NOWHERE ELSE I WANT TO BE THAN WITH YOU! How I feel about you, Kitaj, THAT'S ME— JUST ME! IT'S NOT AN ILLUSION— AS PART OF A DESIGN TO BE BESIDE YOU!" Dagen stormed.

Tears formed in Kitaj's eyes. She threw her arms around Dagen and held him as tight as she could to her. Energy flowed from her as she tried to soothe Dagen's frustration by wrapping them in a warming glow.

"I know, I know! I feel the same!" Kitaj exclaimed. "And we'll do what we have to do! When this is over, if there's any hope, we'll have our choices— *new* choices we could never before have dreamed of..."

Dagen pulled back to look at her. The tears in her eyes had magnified the depths of their colors. He wanted to believe her, but could not share in her optimism. The rage around him calmed as he held her close.

"I just hope we have a future," declared Dagen.

Kitaj and Dagen had little time for recovery before they were brought before the Central Council. They remained half dazed, exhausted, and reeling from their experience with Wodan, as much as the realization of their connection. Tanadra was shocked to find the Council had allowed an audience to newest members of Tjetajat. She could not fathom the Council's decision to discuss the Queen's quest openly. For her to represent Kitaj and Dagen, there was no averting the truth. Aergo became more suspicious when he was refused entry into the tribunal. The Tjetajat Council was no match against him in his goblin form, but he decided to maintain his diplomacy and agree to bow out; only to change into his cat form and slink in unnoticed amid the long cloaks of the members.

Tanadra stood before the Council on Kitaj and Dagen's behalf and presented her notions of the two. She reiterated how the scinan energy that she and Corynth had experienced emerging through the void was their first true hope of solving The Great Mystery of knowledge's lost future. She confirmed the Council's suspicion that the energy was not only to be found within Kitaj but also in Dagen. Tanadra braced herself for their reactions when she shared her astonishing revelation concerning Dagen and Kitaj's souls, and though the reason for their unusual beginnings still alluded her, she was confident it confirmed Kitaj and Dagen were meant to find each other and restore what was lost. Tension and the unease amongst the Central Council members permeated the air within the confines of the domed hut as a wave of confusion ran through those in witness. All, but Tanadra, were blocked and blinded from seeing the extraordinary circumstances of Kitaj and Dagen's souls' origin. Tanadra's words only escalated the Council's trepidation. Without sensing direction, they had no guidance, and the Tjetajat were found groping for unseen answers and on the verge of panic.

"Fate has brought these two together, we should not interfere in matters we do not understand," stated Tanadra.

"Their union seems unnatural, nothing good can come from this," stated one Council member.

"It's unheard of! What dark magic could do this?" said another.

"Tanadra, you are respected highly within the Council, but is it possible your judgment could be skewed because of your connection to Kitaj?" asked Head Council Adrex.

Corynth interjected, "You may wish to think so of Tanadra, but have you ever had reason to doubt her word? From my experience, I know to be true this energy coming from Kitaj is intended for mending. And if it is intended to mend the loss of knowledge, we should protect and aid Kitaj — and Dagen, in this quest."

"But what about their connection? It's a distortion to nature!" said the first Council member.

Tanadra retorted, "This is not blasphemy! I believe the Elders and our kynd agree that all souls are made of the same matter and their beginnings come from the same origin. Exactly where and how they enter our bodies or which body they choose, remains a mystery to us— a mystery I feel I must point out is one we freely accept. We are content in its nature being unknown to us. We embrace that we are not allowed to fully understand the powers spanning all that has been and all that will be. I ask you to draw from that thought to accept the circumstances of these two individuals, who are fated to the task of this monumental correction, for the sake of our future."

"These two have found each other again and should be celebrated. They have no crossing corporal lines and their relationship should be perfectly acceptable. They, with their souls, are two different entities. Each soul is whole and complete, unto itself. I have seen it! They are most definitely individualized with a shared origin. Can Kitaj and Dagen be faulted for that?" she added.

"Do not fear them, but embrace this unique occasion. The fact that it happened to Kitaj, who is one of us, who we have known since her birth and of her connection to the void. Do you think this could be chance? We all know she carries the signs of great sight. Wouldn't it stand to reason that her connection to this young man, Dagen, is part of it? I know for a fact that he has great gifts as well. He has traveled, without any training. I have flown with him and seen into his heart and know it to be pure. They have my blessings. I believe it would be best to entrust our faith in them, not only for the Tjetajat, or even the Nine Worlds, but for the entire universe. We need to accept them for not only what they are, but who they are. This has more meaning than we realize!" Tanadra concluded.

"Do you anticipate any others alike in their origins?" asked Head Council Adrex.

Tanadra could not speak in absolutes, her insight into Kitaj and Dagen's origin remained limited. She did not know the cause of the soul to split and could only answer, "I seriously doubt we will encounter another case such as this. I ask the Council to please take into account the extraordinary circumstances of this case before defining a conclusion for these two. But mostly, I caution you. You are dealing with forces bigger than yourselves, and I plead for your understanding and acceptance of these pure intentions and the fated design of Kitaj and Dagen."

There was a burst of chatter from the crowd and the Council Board. When Corynth raised her hands in the symbol for silence, the room grew still.

"We will adjourn, but we ask you to return for our decision," said Head Council Adrex.

The unease of the Council and members increased again. Kitaj and Dagen stayed close to Tanadra as she led them out of the crowded hut. Aergo weaved his way in and out of feet to keep up with them. They passed Rûni as they maneuvered through the agitated scene. Dagen squeezed Kitaj's hand twice to let her know he would catch up with her. He needed to speak with Rûni. Kitaj understood. She spied Aergo and scooped him up in her arms. She and Aergo continued with Tanadra back to her tent while Rûni followed Dagen to the open area between the domed hut and surrounding tents.

"Are you all right?" Dagen asked, looking at Rûni's arm.

Rûni glanced in Kitaj's direction and said, "I'll heal. You shouldn't worry about me."

"Maybe this will all be for the best— now that it is out in the open," said Dagen with an exhausted sigh.

"We can hope," said Rûni.

"I owe you a debt of thanks for helping Kitaj find me," said Dagen.

"You would have done the same for me," stated Rûni.

Just like Brieg, thought Dagen.

He wanted badly to tell Rûni of Brieg's involvement with his and Kitaj's escape but knew Rûni was too easily read by senior members of the Tjetajat.

"This is all so strange. I can't imagine what this must be like for you. Did you know you were twin souls when you met?" Rûni added.

"No, not exactly. We knew we shared a deep connection, but we've *just* discovered our origin through Tanadra. I'm still trying to understand it. It does explain so much about Kitaj and me. When this is all behind us, I'll tell you more... if you wish to know," Dagen added.

Rûni burst out, "Dagen, again, I'm sorry. I shouldn't have tried to come between you two. I was selfish. I hope someday you'll forgive me."

Dagen gave Rûni a tired smile, "It's already done. We'll talk more when this is over— promise."

Corynth stepped out of the hut. Dagen could tell from the look on her face that the Council had reached their decision. Sensing the Council reconvening, Kitaj, Tanadra, and the other members returned to the hut to hear the Council's official ruling.

Tanadra went to Dagen's side and quietly explained to him, "The Council remains divided. Their decision is inconclusive. Please know no matter their decision to support you or not, help will always be here for you both."

Unsure of the statement the Council was presenting, Kitaj reached for Dagen's hand.

Head Council Adrex spoke, "Ellor Kitaj and Dagen Ságaher, your circumstances have raised many concerns for our Council. The matters of you, Kitaj, breaking your vows as a newly inducted member of the Tjetajat seems to pale in comparison to the situation set before us all. Your membership remains in question, for we do not feel we have the proper information to make a decision at this time. We do feel compassion for your current situation and the decisions you have recently had to make. Not one of us could say what would be the correct course of action under these conditions. We maintain our trust in Tanadra, and it is fortunate that she has the ability to gather some sight from you— though this sight is not one she can share, but only relay to us. It is apparent you two are key in this quest to restore the balance of knowledge; hopefully back to a form that many of us can still remember. It is imperative that progress be reinstated. For that, we do not wish to do anything to impede your search. The unusual nature of your souls' origin and their connection to this restoration remains unknown at this time. And with the unknown, it is natural to let fear overtake our decisions. We are daunted as seers that we cannot read you. We have decided though we remain in loyal service of the Queen and her deep desire to secure the future of innovation and truth, we cannot deny we are under the rule of King Wodan. We cannot harbor a fugitive from him, yet we do not condone his actions. It is our verdict, as Tjetajat, to send you forward in your pursuit, but we cannot support what we do not understand. Until we have a clearer vision of your circumstances, the Council will not assist you. Members of our Council who are close to you must decide for themselves what is right in aiding and protecting you. It is not our place to judge your relationship as right or wrong, for what made you and brought you together is also beyond our knowing. We will not actively assist in or detain you from your departure, but we do agree you should leave by sunrise. Otherwise, we may be forced to turn you over to the King. Take what you need, but no further aid will be provided. We trust you will be leaving us before dawn's light."

ﻌﻟﻌ

Kitaj, Dagen, and the feline Aergo followed Tanadra to the supply tent. They were relieved that the Council had concluded, but were faced with the task of preparing for their immediate departure. Many questions and concerns raced through their minds. Dagen urgently wanted to know if Tanadra had sensed any movement from Wodan.

"The King does not move. It is unclear why," Tanadra replied.

Exhaustion overcame the two and Kitaj and Dagen collapsed into a hug. Tanadra watched the faint glow surrounding Kitaj and Dagen grow to fill the tent. Only Tanadra's shadow was cast against the canvas walls.

Unannounced, a hand pulled back the opening to the tent and a figure dressed all in grey entered. Aergo was startled by the unexpected guest, and arched his back and hissed. Gloved hands lower the hood of her cloak to reveal Queen Frija.

"Welcome, my Queen," said Tanadra, as she bowed her head.

As Kitaj and Dagen pulled away from each other with Tanadra's announcement of the Queen, the room dimmed slightly. They, along with Aergo, bowed to greet her formally but their faces told their state of relief and astonishment by the Queen's undetected arrival.

"Don't be alarmed, please. I had to know more before I came forward," said the Queen.

Kitaj promptly addressed Queen Frija, "We are most thankful for your aid in helping us," she stated as she removed the Queen's ring with her shaking hands.

The ring dropped from Kitaj. Dagen caught it and returned the ring to the Queen with his sincere gratitude.

Kitaj remained disoriented by the lack of detection of the Queen's presence and was compelled to ask, "Pardon me, your Majesty, but how did you slip by without being read or seen?" The bewildered Kitaj added, "We have been concerned for you since we parted, and the Council was terrified when they lost sight of you."

"I have Tanadra to thank for that. She gave me this amulet for protection," said Queen Frija, as she revealed a small slender metal vial at the end of a delicate chain she wore around her neck.

Tanadra interjected, "I suspected there would come a time when our Queen would need to hide as she sought the answers to restoring knowledge. Not only would she need to protect her information from Wodan's aspirations, but from anyone who might gain access to her thoughts; to block her from all seers.

Controlling the knowledge of the universe would be a tempting prize others might seek for their own gain. After your birth, Kitaj, I began searching for a way to protect the Queen in much the same manner as the void protects you, my dear. I had been unsuccessful in finding any known solution. The idea to devise the amulet came to me after my first exposure to the energy coming through the void around you. Yes, the idea was a *new* thought! I was sure once Queen Frija knew of your connection to her quest, very soon her own thoughts would need protection. After you were presented to the Queen, I gave her this amulet. It even blocks anyone in the Tjetajat from knowing I created it." Tanadra said with some regret and continued, "It pained me not to tell you when we spoke in your cabin, Kitaj. With all that is at stake, I had no choice but to wait."

Kitaj was shocked by Tanadra's statement and wanted her to explain further, but she waited as the Queen spoke. Kitaj's need to understand was growing exponentially.

"When I received the message from Tanadra that your and Dagen Ságaher's connection was thought to be important to the restoration of knowledge, and of Dagen's capture by Wodan, I anticipated I would need to use the amulet and shield my thoughts and myself soon. After your escape, there was no other choice. Now, much like it is for you and Dagen, I am unreadable. I also went unnoticed at the tribunal. Only you four know I am here," said Queen Frija. She looked to Tanadra and asked, "It is so; they are twin souls?"

"Yes, I have seen it, through both of them," said Tanadra. "This fact of their souls is somehow linked to your quest, is it not?"

Queen Frija earnestly said, "Yes, and I believe I can explain how this came to be. I have been searching for you all your lives," she said looking back and forth between Dagen and Kitaj with an empathetic expression radiating kyndness and hope.

"I am sorry, your Majesty, but I don't understand," said Dagen.

"Please proceed, Queen Frija," said Tanadra eagerly.

Kitaj and Dagen were overwhelmed by a night filled with revelations, and now the Queen held the promise of telling them the origin of their connection. Each reached for the other's hand for support as they anticipated Queen Frija's words.

Frija began with care, "Are you familiar with *The Night of the Twin Stars?*"

Aergo flattened his ears. He did not know where the Queen's question was leading but felt it could not be good news for Kitaj or Dagen.

Dagen added, "It was a night when a star that raced across the sky and burned so bright, it divided into two.

Frija confirmed, "That is the story."

"Some say it originated on Aesingard," continued Kitaj.

Frija nodded, "Yes, that is true."

"It was also the night my parents met," Kitaj added.

Dagen looked to Kitaj with an odd recognition, "My parents told me it was their lucky stars because it was the night of my beginning."

Frija smiled at their comments, but her smile was a mixture of sadness, longing, and confirmation.

She continued, "What is not known to anyone, beyond those who were present and those connected with Oblivion, is that was the same night all progress stopped; when new knowledge ceased to flow through the universe."

Tanadra saw the pieces coming together. Where before there had been a diversion blocking her ability to equate the two events in her mind; there was now understanding! Frija reached out and touched Tanadra's arm. Frija's emotion overcame her with the relief she could finally share her secret with someone else! Tanadra moved closer to support her.

Kitaj and Dagen's grip tightened. Sparks flew in intensity from their joined hands and a burst of energy rippled out from them with the uniting of their powers. Queen Frija, Tanadra and Aergo stood in awe as the energy swirled around them. A new link had formed between Dagen and Kitaj. They spoke to the Queen; entranced in one voice— as Amicus!

"I remember my only thought was to keep you safe," said Kitaj.

"I couldn't contain it, I tried. I flew as high as I could, then it erupted..." said Dagen.

"...and I was torn in two. There is not one who can hold all knowledge," said Kitaj.

Frija could not control the steady stream of tears that flowed from her eyes. She had found Amicus, but Kitaj's statement reaffirmed why both he and Wodan were lost to her.

"I knew you would try to find me. I wanted to leave you a sign. With my last conscious thought, I searched the knowledge within me and found a name—'Ságaher." You were known as 'Sága' on Vangard. Along with Gicelfolde word for 'here," I hoped it would be a start. I was passing beyond and clung to that name, which brought me to be as Dagen."

"When your name reached me in Tanadra's message, I dared to hope!" cried Frija.

Kitaj continued in her voice as Amicus, "I was sent in a different direction, with no self-control. As my momentum slowed, I drifted. Aware of the knowledge contained within me, I wrapped myself around it as tight as I could to protect it! I remember calling out for help to preserve what I held inside me. My own thoughts fade from that moment. How I was brought to be as Kitaj is a mystery to me—" she paused to say, "I do not know by what means or how, but it would seem the universe is trying to correct knowledge's flow through both Kitaj and Dagen."

Frija took Dagen and Kitaj's free hands in hers and said, "Amicus, I have missed you so!"

Kitaj and Dagen spoke in unison, "As I have missed you, but I am now..."

"Kitaj," "Dagen," they said simultaneously.

Frija understood, but the pain of loss tore through her. Amicus would not be returning.

Tanadra could see Kitaj and Dagen's link was fading and asked urgently, " What of knowledge's loss?"

Together, Dagen and Kitaj replied, "It is stored within me."

Queen Frija pleaded, "But, how do we restore it?"

"The universe is righting itself," said Kitaj and Dagen.

"What do we do? How can we help?" the Queen pleaded.

The link was broken. Her Amicus was gone. The weight of their reality was evident in the Queen's expression as she let go of their hands. Kitaj and Dagen turned to one another with dazed and questioning expressions.

Kitaj said to Dagen in a stunned monotone voice, "Our souls spoke to Queen Frija."

Dagen's face turned pale as he muttered, "Our souls... that used to be one soul."

Tanadra added for Kitaj and Dagen's benefit, "Your souls were once the dear friend of our beloved Queen."

"Your Majesty, please help us understand!" Kitaj begged.

With her red-rimmed eyes cast downward, Frija recounted how Wodan and his brothers had formed a triad to trap the Essence of Oblivion. She explained that the Essence was forced to relinquished the Orb and how Amicus's attempt to save them all had gone terribly wrong. She began to cry and wrapped both of her arms around herself to regain her composure.

"Each of you has unknowingly carried the lost knowledge of the universe inside you. As Amicus told us, the universe is righting itself. The answers will come forth in time. I know there is no comfort in those words for either of you," said Frija.

Tanadra also wished to reassure the two but had little to offer, "There is nothing we know to do. Those answers lie within both of you as well."

"We must hide you both and keep you safe until the answers present themselves," said the Queen.

Dagen and Kitaj, though shaken from the full recognition of their shared understanding, looked to each other with resolve. Each conceded; the crucial roles that they must play had already emerged and been set in motion. They knew the clues they held could offer some reassurance to the Queen and Tanadra.

The energy between them grew stronger and brightened as Kitaj spoke, "The answers already are! As we tried to discover what was coming from inside the void through me, we received vague glimpses, but it wasn't until..."

"...the surge when we detained King Wodan that we both received clear clues!" chimed Dagen.

"The notions were different for each of us— but related," said Kitaj. "I saw two separate shapes. I was able to identify one as a Léohet carving."

"Do you know where this carving is?" asked Frija.

"Sweduetwin. The knowledge of where rang through my mind as a distinctive tone," Dagen explained.

"And we know who has the carving— Isla Malu, or I should say, Isla Tajey, the woman to whom Dagen was betrothed," added Kitaj, remembering Isla's comb.

While Tanadra recalled Rûni's shared reading about Dagen and his decision to stay on Midangard with Kitaj, Queen Frija was unaware of Dagen's past circumstances and needed more information to understand.

"The arrangement between our families dissolved. Isla secretly married another. Her father, Kama, was kynd to me and I believe he will help us," said Dagen, then he cautioned, "We need to go to Swedu, but the King will try to find us wherever we go. We'll be putting anyone connected with us in danger."

Tanadra and Frija could not deny the threat of the King, but knew the carving must be retrieved.

"And I fear there is something more, something foreboding around Isla, I cannot see what— it is beyond us. Sunrise will be approaching soon, and we'll have to leave. I don't want to put the Malus or anyone in danger, but I don't see another way. Dagen, I think you know as well as I that it has to be us to ask for the carving." stated Kitaj.

Tanadra interjected, "I believe I can help! The amulet I made for the Queen can be duplicated and given to whomever helps you in your quest. It will keep them from being read or known!" She continued as she rummaged for the proper supplies, "I will give you several vials to create them for anyone who assists you."

Along with Tanadra, Dagen, Kitaj and the Queen gathered what might be needed for their known destination of Swedu and prepared as best they could for the probability of more clues to be followed. Aergo fidgeted as he waited to be his most useful.

Tanadra handed Dagen a box full of empty vials as she stated, "It's quite simple, thanks to Kitaj."

Kitaj was puzzled and asked as she continued to gather items, "What did I do? Why don't I know what you mean?"

"Amazing isn't it?" Tanadra said back to Kitaj, "You— who it comes from, cannot read it from me! My dear child, it's your hair! The void that surrounds you is also part of you. I put a lock of your hair in the Queen's amulet. She carries part of the void with her now. Like you, she can go unread. But, to my surprise, the thought itself carries the void's protection! The fact the Queen cannot be read is shielded from the minds of those who are near her and gives her the advantage of easily going unnoticed. I believe it is this same protection within this thought that keeps anyone from discovering that I know how to make the amulet!"

Queen Frija added, "This diversion is very similar to what I have witnessed when questioning anyone to recall when knowledge was lost."

Kitaj said, looking at a strand of her wild unruly curls "There should be enough to protect as many as is needed."

"It is those closest to you that remain here who will be at the greatest risk. If you are discovered, they will be under the eye of the King. I'll do what I can for them as well," said Tanadra, as she took a pair of trimming shears from the supplies and cut a few locks of Kitaj's hair.

They quickly began making more amulets. Tanadra put one around Dagen's neck and kissed him on the forehead.

"Though you naturally cannot be read, this may help keep you from being noticed," added Tanadra.

As Dagen thanked her, his thoughts went to Brieg, Rûni, and his family, and he worried if they could remain safe. Kitaj's thoughts darkened over the possibility of other losses.

"Can you tell me, if either of us were to die, would that part of knowledge's future die as well?" asked Kitaj.

Tanadra looked to Frija and back to Dagen and Kitaj, "Honestly we cannot say for sure, we would assume so or at the very least it would be lost to us again. If it is lost to this generation, the next will not recognize the importance of looking for it. It would become a distant fable from the time of invention. There would be a universal acceptance that all has been invented and there is nothing more to discover. Can you deny this is what you have witnessed in your lifetime? Our hopes are with you two..." said Tanadra.

Kitaj searched her thoughts for understanding. What they sought to restore partially rested dormant inside her. It was something she had never felt or recognized as a loss to her worlds. Until recently, the thought had not crossed her mind that everything around her had been invented before her lifetime and all remained the same. Existence was just a history being passed forward. As she looked deeper inside herself to try to find the makings of progression buried within her, the energy seeping through the void radiated out. Once again, Tanadra could feel it's effect as it poured over her through the windows of Kitaj's eyes.

"...or should I say... three?" added Tanadra, as she was presented with more sight into Kitaj.

"Three?" asked Queen Frija.

Kitaj and Dagen looked to each other in their confusion.

"There is a third?" asked Kitaj, but answered her own question as the symbol she had seen in the cave flashed back to her, "There is a third— Tanadra, you see it too!" Kitaj smiled.

"Yes, but I cannot see who or how, just that there will be three to complete a triad of pure intentions," stated Tanadra.

King Wodan anxiously awaited for Myne's return. He had resumed his pacing to keep his destructive tendencies in check. On Myne's arrival, the prized raven flew to its master's arm. The bird trembled as Wodan drew from the swirling well water contained in the alabaster jar. Wodan, hungry for answers and ready to view all that Myne had observed, gave little thought to his pet's behavior. As he rubbed the water over the bird's head and back, images flooded Wodan's mind of Myne's flight. There was nothing to see of the Queen. Myne had not found her! He had not gained any of the answers Wodan sought.

Wodan boiled, "HOW COULD THIS BE? HOW COULD SHE NOT BE FOUND? IT DOESN'T MAKE SENSE! I've always known where she was or who she was with, BUT NO SIGN OF HER AT ALL! THIS IS NOT POSSIBLE!"

Wiljo and Wæ appeared as if on cue. Their eagerness to please their King sickened Wodan. Their overblown bows and praise made Wodan question whether to inform them at all. Wodan concluded, in spite of his disdain for their transparent flattery, he could count on Wiljo and Wæ to carry through with whatever he might decide; if for no other reason than it might serve their own purposes.

"It would appear the Queen has aligned with the two Midangardians and that beast! Wherever she's gone; she must be with them," Wodan's mind began to spin, "Watching those two and their combined powers, they showed abilities that I can only believe are something new to what we have known. And by that... THEY MUST BE RELATED TO OUR SEARCH!" the King deduced. "I NEED TO KNOW WHY! WE MUST FIND THEM!"

The King's brothers watched as Wodan's thoughts raced to a fever pitch. They stood back at a safe distance and observed as his madness escalated.

Wodan was manic as he spoke to himself, "Somehow they are the key, I just know it! We must retrieve them and keep them close. With those two within my control, the solutions will come forth and I *will* have it! ALL KNOWLEDGE WILL FINALLY BE MINE!"

Wodan interrupted his rant and reached out to give his raven a gentle reassuring pat. With his back to his brothers, he spoke in a calm steady voice as he directed his next statement to them, "I need you to take a message to Dryhten Ingólf."

⁙

Brieg had been subjected to rigorous questioning. His alibi held; he was incapacitated, and his armor had been taken. He was found unconscious and shackled next to a disoriented Rand. But with Rand's statement, Brieg was faulted for breaking protocol and allowing a possible assassin access to the King— as they saw it. Brieg's father, Dryhten Ingólf, was furious with his son's behavior and contributed his poor decisions for his attempt to impress a woman. Brieg's reputation had worked in his favor to cover his tracks. He sat in an adjoining room to his father's office at Kestel Midlen after a harsh verbal lashing. Phrases of being an embarrassment to his position had been aired. Brieg expected no less and played his part for the safety of his friends. It would not serve him, or them to try to regain his father's graces. He sat dismissed and silent. As he sat waiting, he heard two people enter the far end of the hall. Their voices mingled with his father's in a distant room. It was beyond the mid of night and too late for this to be any sort of happy news. Brieg crept down the hall nearer to the closed door to hear the conversation.

"The King has requested your assistance in a very private matter. It is a delicate situation that will require your utmost cooperation and secrecy," said one voice.

Another chimed in, "As you are aware, the King was attacked and a prisoner in his care was taken."

Brieg heard his father say, "Yes, and I regret my own son's involvement in the matter. I do not excuse his conduct."

"The King is unconcerned with that circumstance and it in no way reflects on your loyal service to his Majesty."

"The King is most gracious," said Ingólf.

Brieg was able to peer through the keyhole and saw his father and two men— the King's brothers.

"King Wodan requires your discretion. It is our belief that this prisoner and his accomplice forced a Midangardian woman to aid them in their escape and have abducted the Queen," stated Wæ.

"The Queen, abducted!" exclaimed Ingólf.

"The King has reason to believe, from the dangerous nature of these individuals, they are holding the Queen and the Midangardian woman hostage. King Wodan wants the fugitive and his accomplice found and brought before him unharmed. The King wants to deal with these criminals personally. Only your most trusted officers are to aid in the search. Any word of a full manhunt may force the demise of the Queen," said Wiljo.

Brieg expected to hear word of the King hunting for Dagen but did not expect this turn of events. His mind raced as to how Dagen's name could ever be cleared of the King's false charge.

"I understand," said Ingólf. "Discretion is imperative."

Wæ continued, "Here are scraps of the assailant's coat. Distribute them to your officers for tracking with their hounds, and remember, the King wants him captured unharmed. No scratch is to be found on him. King Wodan is to decide his punishment."

"We realize you will be briefing your forces at the short of the morning for the launch of their exercises during the Wild Hunt. Gather your chosen officers and let them know they are searching for more than just fleógans," said Wiljo.

"Here is a general description of the fugitive and the Midangardian woman he has taken," interjected Wæ as he handed Dryhten Ingólf a small scroll.

Brieg did not wait to learn more from his father's conversation. He had to warn Dagen of the King's plot! Brieg exited Kestel Midlen unnoticed and raced through the darkness in the direction he believed to be the Tjetajat camp.

⁓

A worried look came over Tanadra as she spoke to Kitaj and Dagen, "The guard that helped you—" she stated as she glanced back to the Queen in reference to Frija's last readable thoughts, "he has entered the forest and is headed toward the campsite. It is urgent that we send someone to retrieve him!"

Kitaj looked at Aergo. It was all he needed to know for his departure.

Kitaj fidgeted and crossed her steps while they completed packing. They needed to be ready to leave once Brieg arrived.

Time seemed to slow while the sky remained pitch with no trace of the Sun. Dagen and Kitaj agreed they would have a small advantage over the King by moving before day break. It nagged at Dagen that there had been no word of Wodan's search for them and he wondered what the King's reasons could possibly be. He had no wish to encounter Wodan again, but there was no sense he could make of the King's actions. Dagen could only speculate that something bigger than he could imagine was about to happen, and Kitaj wished she possessed the sight to see it coming.

From Tanadra's bidding, Corynth arrived with Rûni. Queen Frija had turned away as they entered and stood unnoticed by them. Tanadra was ready with amulets for Corynth and Rûni, and put them around their necks. With their protection in place, the Queen was safe to reveal herself. Both Rûni and Corynth were stunned to find Queen Frija in their presence but had no moment to ask how she had appeared. Their loved ones' weighted expressions clouded the atmosphere. Dagen was transparent with his concerns as he pulled Rûni aside.

"You need to know Brieg helped us to escape from the King. I'm sorry I couldn't tell you before now," said Dagen as he looked to Rûni's amulet. "He's on his way here. Aergo has gone to him."

Rûni stood speechless.

"And, I have a favor to ask of you," stated Dagen.

"Anything," replied Rûni, in a slightly stunned voice.

"Please get word to my family that my circumstances have become... dire. For their own safety, I can't explain or let them know where I am going, or foresee when I might be able to reach them. Tell them to cooperate but not trust the King. They have to be prepared if at some point he finds them because he can't find me. I worry for their safety. Just make them understand I am trying to do what's right. I'll contact them when I'm able. Can you do that for me?" asked Dagen.

"Of course, I will, "Rûni said with a lump in his throat, for their reality had become too clear.

"I leave Sunniva in your hands. She's yours now," offered Dagen.

"Only until you return," said Rûni, but he also felt this was inevitably a permanent transaction.

Tanadra announced to them all, "They're almost here."

With the Queen's horse weighted with all the supplies they could acquire, they made their way to the rim of the protective circle. Tanadra cast another enchantment around where they stood, so they were not to be seen or heard by anyone within their surroundings; much like a bubble within a bubble. They stood at its edge, as they watched the outlines of Aergo and Brieg gallop toward them from out of the darkness.

Brieg's horse had managed to keep up with Aergo as they made their way to the concealed Tjetajat headquarters. Aergo stopped at the edge of the circle. Brieg was baffled that Aergo would deliver him to a site that appeared to be only woods. He could not see his friends looking back at him from the other side. As Tanadra released a small portion of their protective charms, Dagen, Rûni, Kitaj, and three other people became visible to him.

"Please join us," Tanadra beckoned.

Brieg entered on horseback with Aergo following. After they crossed the opening to their concealment, Tanadra sprinkled more of the spellbinding powder to close the breach. Brieg dismounted and went to Dagen, Kitaj and the bandaged Rûni. Brieg hesitated and looked to the eldest woman for permission to speak. Tanadra approached Brieg and put an amulet around his neck.

"This is for your protection, it will conceal your thoughts. You are free to talk now. We are sealed in," said Tanadra.

Brieg looked puzzled by the transaction, but thanked her and turned his attention to Dagen, Kitaj, and Rûni.

"I'm relieved to find you three in better shape than I imagined," said Brieg to his friends, then recognized he was in the presence of the Queen and bowed deeply.

"Your Majesty, I am grateful you are well. Thank you again for your help in their safe return," said Brieg. "I have news of the King's plan to regain Dagen, Kitaj and yourself. The King has sent word to my father, the Dryhten of Lerakrey, that you and Kitaj have been abducted by Dagen and an accomplice. He has requested my father assemble his most trusted officers to seek Dagen out through the guise of the Wild Hunt. They do not know Dagen's or Kitaj's identity, but have sent out a general description of both and have Dagen's scent from his coat for the hounds to follow. The King has asked your abduction be kept quiet in fear that a large show of force would cause Dagen to threaten your life," Brieg explained to the Queen, but his eyes were fixed on Dagen and his reaction to his news. "The King also demanded that Dagen should not be harmed; he wanted to hand out his punishment personally."

Dagen looked to each face, hoping to see some possible solution. There was none.

"There's no coming back from this," Dagen said as the color drained out of his face and he began to pace. "Your Majesty, can't we go to King Wodan and try to explain before this escalates?" asked Dagen.

"I wish it were that simple. What you and Kitaj carry inside you is what Wodan prizes most. I believe our best course of action is to follow your notions. They must be leading us to an answer," stated Queen Frija.

Brieg looked to Rûni, confused by the Queen's last statement. It appeared to him that he was not alone in his confusion; neither Rûni nor Corynth seemed to have a full understanding of the circumstances.

The Queen nodded with her approval for Tanadra to share with Corynth, Rûni and Brieg their confidence, for these would be the people who would be risking their lives to keep her, Kitaj and Dagen safe as they sought out the resolution.

"Trust that I will explain all to you later. Right now we have little time," Tanadra stated to their confused faces.

Little was said as they worked together in haste to distribute the supplies between the Queen's horse and Aergo.

As Dagen finished securing Aergo's load, he looked to the Queen, "Excuse me your Majesty, but we can't risk your safety."

"I have to see this through with you. I owe it to Amicus, and if you are caught, you have a better chance of being heard and not harmed if I am there with you to explain," Queen Frija assured him.

"We need to get the three of you far from Midangard," stated Brieg.

"We're going to Sweduetwin," Kitaj said with hope that her answer would help calm the worry building around them.

Dagen pleaded "Kitaj, you and the Queen need to be away from me! Have the Tjetajat hide you. I don't want you part of this. I need to know you're safe."

"You know you can't do this without me. It's going to take both of us to find whatever we'll need for the restoration. And do you really think I would be safer here, away from you? The King has seen me. We have a much better chance of surviving this if we're together," Kitaj said, trying to be rational about their circumstances.

Dagen paced back and forth, trying to grasp the details of their situation. Reality, as he knew it, was slipping away from him. A slight charge began to form within their concealment.

"You know I'm right," said Kitaj without a trace of doubt.

Dagen stopped and pressed his hands on either side of his head in a desperate attempt to contain some trace of normalcy in their extreme circumstances. Brieg and Rûni looked on with pained empathy. They did not know how to comfort their friend.

The air around Kitaj carried an audible crackle; she could no longer hold back the words inside her, "Whether our existence and meeting are all of some universal design, where you and I are just pawns— a means to an end as you said, I don't care! I just know, with all my being, that I love you, and that is stronger than any of this! I WILL be with you."

A buzzing was added to the crackling sound. The charge in the air intensified and put everyone on edge!

"All right! We'll do this together, but..." Dagen paused,

"if we are going through with this..."

"As if we had a choice..." Kitaj added.

"If we are going through with this... I want you to have my vow," Dagen said with certainty.

The crackling stopped to dead silence. The collective surprise was implied on Rûni's, Brieg's and Corynth's faces.

"Are you sure?" Kitaj asked.

Dagen came closer to Kitaj and took her hand in his. A glow formed from their linked hands and expanded around them.

Dagen continued, "There are very few things I'm sure of right now. Who knows how long we'll be running, or what will happen to us? This moment may be all we'll have. I know I love you, and in my heart, I am already yours. I have been since before I ever met you."

"As I to you," Kitaj said in return.

"I can't offer you a home, or a future. All I can offer you is me. Will you have me?" asked Dagen.

"Yes," said Kitaj, without any doubts.

Their energy grew brighter. Darting lights formed within the intense glow and ricocheted within the containment of their protective bubble. Rûni, and Corynth stood speechless.

Brieg's frustration grew as he swatted at the lights buzzing near his head and stated, "Dagen, there's no time for this!"

"We don't need much time," said Kitaj as she looked at Dagen and with a plea to Queen Frija.

Frija stepped closer to Dagen and Kitaj, put her hands around their joined hands, and proclaimed, "With your love and commitment to one another as your testimony, in front of these witnesses, and by my power as Queen of Aesingard, Sovereign of the Sacred Vows of Marriage, and Maternal Patron of the Nine Worlds, I bless the two of you and pronounce you, from this moment forward, vowed to each other."

There was no exchange of bands, nor any of the usual trappings that go with the most modest of ceremonies. Even the customary congratulations were missing, but for Kitaj and Dagen, they weren't necessary. With a simple kiss and embrace, they sealed their pledge to one another. The glow subsided.

"Dagen, we can't linger, we have to go— now!" urged Brieg.

Kitaj hugged Tanadra and Corynth.

Corynth pulled Kitaj closer to her and said, "This is not the life I would have wanted or wished for you. Stay safe! I will do what I can here to ensure that."

Kitaj could not stop the single tear that escaped her eye and her mother wiped the tear away as it rolled down her cheek.

"We will all do our best to keep you safe," Tanadra added with a sad smile. "We will make sure they are looking in the wrong places."

Rûni came over and hugged both Dagen and Kitaj. He could not find any words. He gave each of them a reassuring look and backed away.

"I'll return with news of their departure," Brieg stated, addressing Rûni, Corynth and Tanadra. "Your Majesty, Dagen, Kitaj, we must—" he ended.

Brieg assisted the Queen onto her horse, while Dagen and Kitaj settled themselves on Aergo's back. In one fluid move, Brieg was astride his horse and ready to escort them. Tanadra again created an opening to their inner bubble and allowed passage from the Tjetajat's protective barrier.

Frija gave a nod to Tanadra conveying she would get word to her as soon as possible. Kitaj and Dagen gave Rûni, Corynth and Tanadra one last look as they disappeared into the morning's darkness.

Keep reading for a preview of
SCINAN LEGACY
CHAPTER 10

CHAPTER 10
THE WILD HUNT BEGINS

Wodan's mind was wrenched with turmoil. He could not fathom how his queen, Frija, could somehow slip past him! For all the times she believed she was outwitting him, he had always been able to observe or uncover the details of her whereabouts. Now, she had disappeared and he had no idea where to begin. King Wodan had contacted his Dryhtens for the Nine Worlds the morning of the Wild Hunt's launch and made them aware of the sensitive nature of her disappearance. The truth that she was a willing participant in her departure was a fact that would not work to Wodan's benefit. Having the Dryhtens and their officers secretly searching for the Queen and her captors, under the guise of the Wild Hunt, was much more pragmatic. A heavy show of force would only endanger the Queen's return, or at least that was the rationalization Wodan and his brothers were offering.

Brieg was aware of the King's deception to frame his friend, Dagen, for the Queen's abduction. His plan was to remain within Wodan's ranks and use his unique position to his friend's advantage. Known as the philandering son of the Dryhten for Lerakrey and a lowly entry to his own father's forces, Brieg could access high-level information with little thought to his motives.

He had delivered the Queen, Dagen, Kitaj, and Aergo safely to the Ports of Eormensyl and had seen to their secure departure by means of the Queen's private passage to Sweduetwin. With the protection of Kitaj's amulets that both he and the Queen carried, traces of their departure had been erased from the possibility of prying minds or questions. For the moment, his part in their disappearance was all he could do for his friends.

On Brieg's return to the hidden site of the Tjetajat, he relayed that those dear to them had safely escaped and Tanadra was now able to explain Kitaj and Dagen's entire circumstances to him, Rûni, and Kitaj's mother, Corynth. Each could only hope the deflective powers of amulets they carried would be enough to keep their secrets safe from King Wodan. They could not have imagined their loved ones to be in this position— twin souls, each carrying part of the universe's lost knowledge inside them; hunting for clues to restore it, while being hunted by King Wodan. Kitaj and Dagen had the advantage. Wodan had not discovered their identities nor did he know they carried the prize he sought most within them.

After leaving the Tjetajat's concealed grounds, Brieg returned to Kestel Midlen. He was relieved to find his absence had gone unnoticed. Kitaj's amulet held true during the further questioning Brieg was subjected to that morning before the Wild Hunt. His own father suspected Brieg was withholding information, but that was common to the nature of their relationship. The King's investigation had led nowhere. For a man who craved to know everything, King Wodan was left with too many unanswered questions, which ate at him like acid.

To maintain the pretenses set for this Wild Hunt, Wodan returned to the hunt's traditions. He would appear at each world's dawning of the launch in his customary manner by conjuring with his brothers the spectacle of arriving through an oncoming storm. The eager participants and ravenous crowds expected nothing less and greeted their King with an eruption of cheers.

The Wild Hunt was an important part of the combined cultures of the Nine Worlds, and like the Winter's Nátt Festival, held an even higher importance for being the first time to include all the worlds since the end of the war. The hunt symbolized the people's conquering of the elements and survival against the odds of strife, no matter what prey had been decided for that season. But, unlike Winter's Nátt, the Wild Hunt fevered the competitive natures between worlds, for the first group to capture their prey would leave the game with their own pockets much heavier and extra riches to benefit the world they represented.

One band of Midangardian participants took the hunt to its most dangerous level by revving themselves into a frenzied bloodlust. It was what they lived for; no holding back, no rules, and the pure rush of the hunt. They camouflaged themselves in black and were known by many names, but on Midangard, they were the feared Bezerks.

On this early Midangardian morning, winter rolled in with Wodan at the helm, just as anticipated. Flanked by his brothers, lead by his wolves and charging in on his powerful steed, Slepsil, Wodan arrived to speak to his ranks and the willing participants.

Though his speech was familiar to those he had given over the many years, there was an urgency to his words that felt new. His appearance was noticeably altered. Much darker circles encased his tired eyes, his face was visibly inflamed, and his disposition was madder than ever. Wodan's delivery was not just an opening for sport, but a battle cry for a full assault. The Bezerks fell in step and began to shake and beat themselves in anticipation of the start. The horn blew and the fleógan chosen for Midangard darted out of its cramped cage and momentarily froze in terror before it tried to escape into the sky. One of the chains binding him had not released properly and prevented him from taking off. The poor animal flapped awkwardly and fell several times. The gold band around his throat, that identified him as prey for the game, flashed in the morning light as the animal thrashed about and spat fire at the anxious crowd. One of its keepers ran forward with a large ax and broke the chain to release the animal. Once unbound, the fleógan spouted one last defiant flame before he took to the air and soared across the horizon. The crowd cheered and poured over itself to watch the departure.

Once the fleógan could no longer be seen, the second horn sounded. The participants roared as they sprinted in the direction the animal had flown. Some went as organized groups, others as individuals. Some ran with the hunters, just to be a part of their initial trek. The Bezerks were a chaotic pounding mass, flattening anyone crossing their erratic path. Thirty plus people lay trampled and beaten at the Hunt's start. Initial casualties were expected and almost considered tradition. For the Bezerks and other blood craving participants, the more people who were injured, the more thrilling the hunt.

As members of Wodan's forces, the Hunt provided young recruits an opportunity to learn strategies from their seasoned officers. Brieg's training was the least of his concerns. There was much more at stake with this hunt, and the fleógan was not the only fugitive from an oncoming wrath. Brieg decided to stay close to his father's officers and learn of any news that could be helpful. He tried to reassure himself with the knowledge that Dagen, Kitaj and the Queen were no longer on Midangard and could only hope they would be protected on Sweduetwin.

The band of fugitives' arrival at the Eormensyl Ports on Swedu went unnoticed. Their portal deposited them at a small outlet off the edge of Swedu's main branch port in the city of Blysca. They were relieved their escape from Midangard had been successful, and the cover of the perpetual darkness of this world would only work in their favor. Kitaj and Dagen were taken aback by how rich Swedu's black sky appeared. Stars took on a shimmering glow that could never have been seen in a Midangardian night sky. They looked alive and pulsing, as if speaking to one another through a flashing code.

The province where they were to find the Malu family was located a short distance from Blysca. They would arrive soon and hoped the Malu family would accept them.

Kitaj could not distinguish if it was night or day and referenced her time tracker to see where they were within the day's setting. From her estimate, they would be arriving at what was considered early evening and would more than likely intrude as extra guests for what the Swedu referred to as "last meal."

Queen Frija smiled at the prospects. She was, in some way, with her beloved Amicus again, and she was taking measures to correct what took him from her and reset the course of knowledge. She had not been this hopeful in many Aesingardian years. She could not remember when that time would have been, except it had to have been with Baldar. Her heart fell to think about him, but she had a duty to fulfill and the outcome would make right what was needed, not only for her realm, but every being in existence and beyond. She thought Baldar, as well as her Amicus, would have wanted her to do exactly this, and that thought would carry her forward, no matter what she and her companions were to encounter.

THANK YOU

for reading the first book
in the series of

SCINAN LEGACY

I look forward to you joining me
in seeing where the following books lead us.

A special gift is waiting for you!

Please go to **scinanlegacy.com/free-prequel**
for your *free download* of
SCINAN LEGACY – THE OPENING
An exclusive prequel story to $C.1-9$

Well wishes,

Acknowledgments

I never saw myself doing this.
Me– who can't send a text without a typo...

A Special Thank You

Several family members and friends have been incredibly supportive over
the 11 years this book has been in the making. A huge thanks to those who
did me the honor of reading the first chapter, first drafts, editing my strung
together words, and letting me bother them with the struggles
of my learning curve. I appreciate and love you all very much!

Encouragers, Inspirers, and Advisors
(in chronological order of *Scinan Legacy's* development)

Kathy Hayes • Mary Donnet Johnson • Orville Blackledge • Lise Bender
Damon Pickel • Donnie Pickel • Renee' Barber • Cathy Brundage
Krista Petersen • Nancy Wells • Mary Blackledge • Peggy and Paul Pickel
Betty Sims • Marion White Linder • Dykes Hayes • Beth Schultz
Christopher Weed • Sandy and JJ Tracy • Rebecca and Stuart Henry
Gina Dwyer • Carol Strong • Alice Power • Rachel Henry Cole
Heather Beverly • Jenny Stewart • Jill and Tom Geisler • Leanne Loveday
Susanne Dawson • Tori Carraway • Dannon Schroeder
Hannah Elaine • James Fulmer • Jessica Petersen • Kat Mason
And Those Who Prefer to Remain Anonymous

Through these very strange and difficult times,
I hope we will remember to be
kynd to each other.

ACKNOWLEDGMENTS

Story, artwork, cover, and book design by Kathy Blackledge Pickel

Fonts used were as following: Body text is set in 11-point New Caledonia. Initial caps are Paliard. Chapter headers and page numbers set in Keeple. Ornamental dividers are Bodoni Ornaments.

Royalty-free textures 278, 421, 470, 470, and 539 by Sirus_sdz, used in background cover art.

Scinan Legacy logo designed by Kathy Blackledge Pickel, utilizing royalty-free font UnZailish by Manfred Klein, with the understanding that a portion of the profits of this series and related merchandise will be donated to **Doctors Without Boarders.**

Critique Partner– Beth Schultz

Developmental Editing– Rachel Henry Cole

Alpha Reader– Renee' Barber

Published by Kathy Blackledge Pickel
Oblique Creative, LLC
P.O. Box 10475
Knoxville, TN 37939

Printed and Distributed by IngramSpark
1 Ingram Blvd.
La Vergne, TN 37086

ABOUT THE AUTHOR

Kathy Blackledge Pickel lives in Knoxville, TN
with her family and several gargoyles.
Her love for fantasy and science fiction began at a very
young age and inspired her curiosity for creating.

She is the owner of Oblique Creative, LLC.
Kathy has a professional background in graphic design
and several years of experience in implementing
neurodevelopmental therapies. She is also one of many
individuals within the neurodivergent community.

Storytelling is a relatively new adventure for her.
When she isn't writing, teaching, designing, or dreaming,
she can often be found rescuing saplings, subjecting
family and friends to her experimental cooking,
and encouraging imaginings into existence.